No Turning Back

Susan Lewis is the bestselling author of twenty-six novels. She is also the author of *Just One More Day* and *One Day at a Time*, the moving memoirs of her childhood in Bristol. She lives in Gloucestershire. Her website address is www.susanlewis.com

Susan is also a supporter of the childhood bereavement charity, Winston's Wish: www.winstonswish.org.uk and of the breast cancer charity, BUST: www.bustbristol.co.uk

Praise for Susan Lewis

'One of the best around.' *Independent on Sunday*

'Utterly compelling.' *Sun*

'Deliciously dramatic and positively oozing with tension, this is another wonderfully absorbing novel from the *Sunday Times* bestseller Susan Lewis . . . Expertly written to brew an atmosphere of foreboding, this story is an irresistible blend of intrigue and passion, and the consequences of secrets and betrayal.' *Woman*

'Spellbinding! . . . you just keep turning the pages, with the atmosphere growing more and more intense as the story leads to its dramatic climax.' *Daily Mail*

'A multi-faceted tear jerker.' *heat*

'Sad, happy, sensual and intriguing.' *Woman's Own*

No Turning Back

arrow books

Published by Arrow Books 2012

2 4 6 8 10 9 7 5 3 1

First published in Great Britain in 2011 by
Arrow Books
Random House, 20 Vauxhall Bridge Road,
London SW1V 2SA

www.randomhouse.co.uk

Addresses for companies within The Random House Group Limited
can be found at: www.randomhouse.co.uk/offices.htm

The Random House Group Limited Reg. No. 954009

ISBN 9780099550723

A CIP catalogue record for this book
is available from the British Library

The Random House Group Limited supports The Forest Stewardship Council
(FSC®), the leading international forest certification organisation. Our books
carrying the FSC label are printed on FSC® certified paper. FSC is the
only forest certification scheme endorsed by the leading environmental
organisations, including Greenpeace. Our paper procurement policy can be
found at www.randomhouse.co.uk/environment

Typeset in Palatino by Palimpsest Book Production Limited,
Falkirk, Stirlingshire
Printed and bound by
CPI Group (UK) Ltd, Croydon, CR0 4YY

For my gorgeous, glamorous friends, Alex and Sonia

'Go away.'

Eva turned her face into the pillow, wincing at the pain that seared and crackled all over her, splintering her flesh, as though her entire self was trying to burn and bleed out through the wounds. There were so many of them, cruel, jagged gashes torn into the flawless fabric of her skin, grinning, grimacing, like silent, gruesome mouths. From her eye to her jaw, across her lips, slicing her ear, down into her neck and shoulders, gouging lethally into her chest and lungs. Each wound was held together by stitches now, or clamps, or grafts of gossamer-fine flesh that had been carefully harvested from tender places untouched by the maniac's blade. Somebody else's blood now ran through her veins, and perhaps it was someone else's heart beating dully in her chest, and a stranger's mind that had taken control of her senses.

Everything hurt.

There was nothing, not a single part of her that didn't ache, throb or blaze with the kind of pain that was as relentless and cruel as the memories of that terrible night. She had no idea where he'd come from, how he'd got into her flat, or why he'd chosen her. She still didn't know his name, nor did she want to. All she wanted was Nick.

Nick. Nick.

The screaming had stopped now; long shrill echoes of human torment that had filled the labour room for the past six hours, rushing out into the corridors, fleeing through open windows into the night. They stretched all the way into the past, contracting time, bringing the attack to now, taking her back to the horrific, unstoppable slashing of the blade.

She couldn't breathe. Panic was overwhelming her.

'It's all right,' someone whispered. 'Everything's fine.'

It was Patty, her sister. Patty was there, next to her, keeping her safe.

How could Patty say everything was fine when she knew that nothing ever could be again?

We have to put what happened behind us and move on.

Nick's voice. The coldness and betrayal cut through her more cruelly than the knife.

Anger, fear, desperation surged out of nowhere. He knew what had happened; he'd been there. If it weren't for him she wouldn't even be alive now; she wished she wasn't. What had been the point in saving her only to leave her like this?

'Why don't you hold him?' Patty whispered gently.

She was talking about the baby.

I can't. I can't. Take him away.

'He's so sweet,' Patty murmured softly. 'He needs you to feed him.'

Eva's breasts were full and disfigured as though someone had tried to slice them open for milk, and a careful hand had tried to stitch them together again.

The baby started to cry.

Eva turned her face more deeply into the pillow.

Patty looked at the nurse who was holding the infant, her eyes pleading and helpless. 'She needs more time,' she said, as though apologising. The nurse would understand. No one was surprised. 'Perhaps later, or tomorrow,' she added.

'No! Never!' Eva's fury was muffled by the pillow. 'Get out of here! Go away . . .'

'Ssh,' Patty tried to soothe.

'*I said go away.*'

Afraid of the mounting hysteria, knowing what it would do to her sister's wounds, as well as her mind, Patty obediently backed away.

Outside in the corridor she took the baby from the nurse and held him close to her face, inhaling the intoxicating scent of him. 'I'm sorry,' she whispered brokenly, to him, not the nurse, 'I wish there was something I could do, but there isn't.'

'It'll change,' the nurse assured her.

With all her heart Patty yearned to believe that, because she never wanted to let go of this tender little soul, not ever. He was her nephew, a living, breathing part of her, and she could already feel him burying himself deeply in her heart.

His mother would love him too, she reminded herself, given time. She hadn't meant what she'd said, that she didn't want him and never would, because Eva wasn't cold-hearted and selfish, much less cruel or vindictive. This was only a temporary change in her character, brought on by shock and post-traumatic stress. Four months wasn't nearly long enough to get over what she'd been through, so Patty must be patient and try to make the right

3

decisions for her – for them all, especially this dear little boy.

Knowing what they were facing, how could she possibly fathom what the right decisions should be?

'Patty?' a voice said behind her.

She turned to find the detective in charge of Eva's case coming towards her. He'd visited often during these past few months, had actually come to feel like a friend, even a saviour in some ways.

As he drew closer she felt embarrassment warming her cheeks. The last time she'd seen him she'd broken down, spilling out her emotions as though they had no right to exist, and he'd been so kind, so sensitive. He hadn't even backed away when she'd confessed her biggest fear.

Lowering his eyes from hers he looked at the sleeping baby, and put a finger to its cheek. 'Are you all right?' he asked quietly.

Knowing what he was referring to, what he was waiting for her to tell him, Patty tried to summon a smile of reassurance, but it wouldn't come. She should never have told him. He wasn't a relative, he shouldn't be made to feel responsible or as though he had to carry any more burdens for her family.

He looked up at her, and held on to her gaze in a way that made her almost fearful of letting go. 'Have you heard?' he asked.

She nodded, and felt herself starting to fall apart.

Waving to a nurse, he waited until she'd taken the baby, then easing an arm through Patty's he led her to a chair.

Patty didn't want to talk; she didn't have the courage to repeat what she'd been told that morning. So she simply watched the nurse walking away, listening to the soles of her shoes squealing quietly,

4

following the rhythmic sway of her hips, while trying not think of herself, or anyone else, just that dear little baby and the fear that she might not live to see him again.

Chapter One

Eva Montgomery didn't want to believe her eyes.

The sheer unexpectedness of it was making her light-headed. In the space of mere seconds she'd felt so many emotions struggling for recognition that she could hardly identify one. Then anger swooped in from the wings, clearing the muddle, with outrage barking at its heels.

Why had no one told her about this?

Going back to the beginning of the article she started to read it again, but found herself unable to focus on the words. It didn't matter, she already knew what it said – how could she not, when it was exposing practically every triumph and tragedy of her life? From the photographs laid out among the paragraphs like colourful pieces of a jigsaw, she could be in no doubt that someone had not only trawled the archives, but had been watching her for at least a month, stealing secret moments of her day, her whereabouts, even her pets, to splash across this colour supplement and help answer the headline question: *Where Are They Now?*

It wasn't as if she'd been hiding for the past sixteen years; however, since her life had been shattered in the most horrific way she'd chosen to shun the limelight, and had no wish to do otherwise. True, she'd been tracked down before, once by a producer who'd wanted her to judge a modelling talent show, and several magazines had written at one time or another to request interviews. However, on the whole, she'd been left to rebuild her world far from the flashing lights and glittering locations that had once filled every moment of her dazzling existence.

They'd called her Angelina then, or Angie.

Not even in her wildest teenage dreams had she imagined being so successful, but by the time she was twenty all the fame she could ever have wanted had been hers, and had only been set to grow. Talks had been under way to make her the next face of Dior; a perfume bearing the name 'Angelina' was in development; and a leading rock band of the time had produced a number one cover version of the Stones' classic 'Angie'. She'd even starred in the video, dancing about the set as high as the rest of them, and why not? They were young, famous and rich enough to do anything they pleased, so they would.

No one called her Angelina now – apart from here, in this article where they were retelling the story of the 'beautiful and tragic' twenty-one-year-old who'd disappeared from the catwalks and front covers after four sensational years of virtually dominating the scene. They'd given a good description of how, aged seventeen, she'd been discovered by the powerful agent, Bobbie Shilling, while shopping in Oxford Street with friends. Her first swagger down a Paris catwalk, when she'd tripped and crashed into the model in front, was given its usual airing – funny how she'd never managed to live that down. It was, she supposed, what had helped to make her a name, since the model she'd sent sprawling into the front row had already been at the very top of their profession. Amazingly, it had started one of her closest friendships of that time, and she occasionally saw Carrie-Anne now, but no one else from that world, apart from Bobbie, who'd resolutely and loyally stayed in touch, like a mother, yet not.

Unsurprisingly, the photograph that everyone said had launched her had been given an entire page to itself. Looking at it now made her heart ache with pride and sadness to remember how thrilled and excited she'd been the first time she'd seen it. Nick Jensen had taken the shot, capturing the smouldering challenge in her indigo-blue eyes and the exotic, even erotic curve of her lips. Even these many years later, the image still stirred her. The silhouette of her lithe, naked body beneath a shimmering, diaphanous wrap was a masterpiece of light and shadow, leaving nothing, yet everything to the eye of the beholder. *Your eyes, his eyes, her eyes, their eyes* . . . For her they'd been Nick's eyes, only Nick's, with whom she was already, at the tender age of eighteen, madly, recklessly in love. There was no mention of their relationship here, in this article, but there wouldn't be, because no one, apart from Bobbie, had known, and Bobbie would never tell.

There were at least a dozen more shots of her from *Vogue*, *Elle*, *Harper's*, wearing Galliano, or Lagerfeld, or McQueen. Shots from the gossip mags showed her partying on private yachts in St Tropez or Monaco; others captured thoughtful or hilarious moments, mostly unguarded, of her shopping, coming or going from her flat and occasionally with men she was rumoured to be seeing. 'No matter

9

how the camera caught her,' the article said, 'she never managed to look anything but ravishing and so infectiously happy that she brought smiles to even the grumpiest of hearts.'

She was thirty-seven now, still willowy and blonde, and with an aura of femininity that seemed to swathe her in as much sensuousness and mystique as the clinging silk in the most famous of her photographs. Her hair was thick and luxuriant and cascaded in a glossy sweep over one side of her face, almost like a curtain over one side of a stage. For a long time after the attack she'd dyed it, partly to disguise herself, partly to try to forget who she was. In recent years she'd allowed her own colour to return and had found herself feeling happier, even braver, for it. It had been like saying she was no longer a victim, or ashamed to be herself. Even so, she'd continued to style it so that it masked the disfiguring scars that had devastated the left side of her face. She was lucky not to have lost an eye, they'd told her, but not so lucky with her ear, which had been ripped in half by a single strike of the knife. The surgeons had performed miracles of course, not just on her face but her whole body, internally and externally, but there had only been so much they could do. The jagged, silvery lines that criss-crossed her tender skin like shadows of empty veins were constant reminders of how long she'd lain in a hospital bed fighting for her life.

Turning to the next page she found the famously moody shots Nick had taken of her for L'Oréal and, later, Lancôme. Even after all this time it was still hard to look at how flawless and fresh her face had been then, how guileless and radiant her eyes, and exquisite her lips. Feeling herself caught for a moment in the time when she'd known nothing of the future, only the erotic romance of the present, she could almost feel Nick beside her, the magnetic force of his body as he tilted her chin or rearranged her hair, his elegant fingers sending frissons shooting between them like live currents.

Nick, she whispered silently to herself now, as though wherever he was he might hear her.

Everything was there, written with a typical reporter's frankness, but no lack of compassion. They didn't know the entire story, thank God, but they didn't hold back on the recorded events of that terrible June night when a psychopathic maniac by the name of Micky Bradshaw had managed to get into her apartment.

Skimming past the detail, for she had no desire to relive even a single moment of the nightmare ever again, she moved on to the final paragraph that accompanied the stolen shots of where she was now: living in Dorset and happily – they should have said blissfully, she thought – married to Don Montgomery. Many readers, it said, would remember that Don Montgomery's previous life as a detective chief inspector with the Met had provided the inspiration for the highly rated cop drama *In Depth* that had kept the nation gripped, back in the days when Eva was modelling. It said that the attack was what had brought them together, and it was true, he had been involved in the investigation; however, they'd first met a year or so before that at a fund-raiser for Shelter, where he'd been a guest speaker and she was making her first appearance as the charity's new patron. In spite of mixing with all kinds of celebrities and dignitaries on a daily basis she remembered how excited and nervous she'd been

11

that night at the prospect of meeting the real-life DCI Ross, who by then was trying hard to escape the indignity of fame. He'd made her laugh so much with his drily told accounts of how DCI Ross was impinging on his world, that she couldn't remember eating a thing, or even talking much to anyone else. When asked later to comment on how she'd found the high-ranking and famously outspoken police officer she'd given a cringe-making, typically twenty-year-old response. 'He's completely fab, really cool and nowhere near as scary as I'd imagined he'd be.' When asked the same question he'd said he'd found her to be an exquisitely beautiful young lady who no doubt wished she'd rendered him foolishly tongue-tied rather than embarrassingly garrulous, as he had to confess he had been.

Remembering how she'd laughed the first time she'd read that, she gave a gentle sigh now as more waves of nostalgia swept over her, drawing her more deeply into the days when she'd revelled in her wildest dreams and loved with a young and innocent abandon. Though she'd worked gruellingly long hours in a world governed by tyrannical egos, unlike some of her contemporaries she'd loved every minute of it – perhaps because she hadn't had time to grow tired or jaded, or to fall out of favour with a fascinated press and public before it had all come to such a horrifically abrupt end.

Since she had no more power to turn back the clock than she had to erase the scars she still bore, she let her memories fade into the shadows, and reminded herself of how lucky she was to be alive – and to be where she was now. This magnificent white house on the wildly dramatic cliffs of Dorset that she'd painstakingly and lovingly restored, during the years following the attack, was her pride and joy, her haven, her passion. It was as though they'd come back to life together, and now they were as much a part of each other as the spectacular views all the way out to Lyme Bay were part of the landscape, and the waves that rolled on to the shore were a part of the sea. The house's light and spacious interior, now that its original grandeur had been restored, was her very own paradise, with as much sumptuousness in its style as there was welcome in its heart and history in its walls.

Hearing a low-level buzz coming from the wall-mounted CCTV monitor in the kitchen, she looked up from the magazine to watch the solid iron gates at the end of the drive start to glide open. Since she was expecting her sister, Patty, who had her own remote control and whom she'd called the instant she'd discovered the article, it came as a not altogether pleasant surprise to see that her seventeen-year-old stepdaughter, Jasmine, had decided to turn up. For a brief, shaming moment, she toyed with the idea of pretending she wasn't at home, but since that would mean having to lock up and alarm the place before Jasmine reached the house, not to mention hiding once the girl had managed to let herself in, she resigned herself to a difficult few minutes before Jasmine breezed on through and up to her room at the top of the house. She rarely spent much time talking to Eva, which might have been a blessing if Eva weren't still hopeful that one day they might find a way to get along.

Glancing down at the four-page spread again, she found herself wondering what Jasmine might have to say about it if she saw it. Not that Eva had any intention of showing her. They never discussed Eva's previous life, or indeed anything much about the current one either, though Jasmine was well aware of what had happened to Eva in the past. She also believed, because it was what her sadly embittered mother had told her, that Eva was responsible for the break-up of her parents' marriage. However, that wasn't the case, in spite of some press claims to support it, because Don had told his wife – Allison – long before Eva had even come into his life that sooner or later they'd have to face the fact that their marriage wasn't working. That he'd ended up moving out of the family home around the same time as Eva had finally left hospital had been nothing more than coincidence – in fact, Eva had been at Patty's, in Dorset, for more than three months before Don had even come to visit. This was when he'd surprised them all with the news that he'd resigned from the force and was in the process of setting up a security business of his own. It was also when Eva had started to hear about how often he'd visited her bedside while she'd been undergoing the frequent and painful surgical procedures to repair her wounds.

In fact, Don had become something of a rock for her whole family, she'd found out, most particularly for her father, who'd gone to pieces after the attack. Even her stepmother, whose spiritual strength could normally be relied upon during times of crisis, had found it difficult to cope, so she too had leaned on Don. Eva often wondered now if her father had ever really got over the attack, because right up to his death just over three years ago he'd never been able to discuss it, or even look at her without seeming to experience every one of the stab wounds and moments of terror himself. And perhaps it was her attacker's shockingly early release from Broadmoor that had triggered the stroke that paralysed her father. There had been no more communication between them after that, so she still had no idea if he'd been able to hear Don telling him that Micky Bradshaw had been found dead at his mother's house after taking an overdose of drugs. At the time she'd hoped, prayed that the news would unlock something inside her father to help bring him back to them, but it never did.

Closing the magazine, Eva slid from the barstool she was perched on and went to open one of the sliding doors that formed an entire wall of the kitchen and allowed easy access on to the sweeping half-moon terrace outside. The kitchen, with its impressive bank of appliances along the back wall and stylish crescent-shaped bar that housed the double sinks, a five-ring hob and numerous under-counter cupboards, was one of her favourite places in the house. Since it faced fully south it was almost always flooded with light, even on a dull day, and because it was so welcoming it was where everyone seemed to congregate when they came.

Moments after the sound of Jasmine's car door slamming carried through from the carport the CCTV monitor buzzed again, this time signalling Patty's arrival – Eva hoped. Indeed, it was her sister's familiar white Audi with its roof down for the first time in more than a week after a virtual non-stop deluge of rain. Eva had been more than glad of it. Loving her garden as she did, she'd almost felt it sigh with relief when the violent downpours began. This summer had been persistently hot and humid, a boon for local businesses and tourists who flocked to the coast, but a great hardship for lush green lawns, thirsty beds, and a pond whose level had started to alarm its resident ducks. Even Eva's precious wild-flower meadow and orchard that sloped gently towards the cliff path had started to wilt. Happily all heads were up on stalks now, faces turned gladly to the sun as new energy made them sparkle and shine in the late season's cascading bands of light.

Watching Jasmine stalking in through the conservatory, Eva summoned a smile as she said, 'Hi, I wasn't expecting you.'

Jasmine's regal attitude was, apparently, her mother all over, as was her diminutive frame, the cornflower-blue eyes and honey-gold hair. The winning smile was a gift from her father and the troubled complexion was, Eva thought, nature's reminder to teenagers that they weren't quite as perfect as they might like to think.

Not bothering with a greeting, Jasmine kept her focus on her mobile as she said, 'Where's Dad?'

Starting to wipe down the counter tops, Eva said, 'I'm not sure. Probably at the office.'

Still texting, Jasmine said, 'It's Saturday. Anyway, I called and they said he's not there.'

'Then I imagine he's playing golf.'

Jasmine's eyebrows rose, though her eyes remained down. 'Aren't you interested to find out? He's your husband, after all. Most wives would care.'

Wondering why she was even getting into this, Eva said, 'I do care, but I'm familiar with his habits, and if I need to get hold of him I only have to call his mobile.'

'But he's not answering it, is he?'

Deciding to cut out of the pointless exchange, Eva gestured to the fridge. 'Would you like a drink?'

'No thanks. I'm going out again in a minute. So how come you're not at the shop today?' The shop was Perdita's – a small boutique in Bridport that Eva owned.

Since Jasmine knew that Eva's Saturdays were always devoted to her charitable works, both local and national – international too, though she rarely did more than send cheques for them – Eva simply said, 'I might pop down there later to make sure everything's OK.'

'Oh, you mean Olivia might not be able to manage,' Jasmine retorted with a sarcasm that Eva knew was spawned from a jealousy she'd rather die than admit to.

'I'm sure she can,' Eva responded mildly, knowing full well that her twenty-one-year-old niece and their part-time assistant Zoe were more than capable of running the place without her, particularly with business being so slow.

'So Olivia still doesn't have a proper job?' Jasmine commented archly, showing no reaction to the sound of another car pulling up outside. Eva suspected she thought it was her father, so she probably wasn't going to be best pleased to discover it was no less than Olivia's mother.

'She does if you count working for me,' Eva replied, starting to sift through a pile of mail she'd left on the table.

Jasmine snorted.

Eva cast her a glance.

'I don't mean to be rude, or anything,' Jasmine lied, 'but surely she could find something better to do with her degree than running a crummy little boutique in Bridport?'

Eva's eyebrows rose.

Jasmine had the grace to blush. 'You know what I mean. You'd think that someone who's got a first in fashion and textiles from St Martin's would be able to do a bit better for themselves than hanging about around here.'

'Dorset is Livvy's home,' Eva reminded her, 'and the kind of jobs she's going for are extremely hard to get these days.'

'But with all your contacts I'd have thought . . .'

'That was a long time ago,' Eva interrupted, trying to ignore the face Patty was pulling behind Jasmine's back. 'Anyway, fortunately for you, you're not following Livvy's footsteps into fashion and textiles, but if you're still set on reading business studies, I'm sure I can find a job for you too.'

Jasmine's lip curled. 'In your dreams,' she retorted, and without even glancing over her shoulder to answer Patty's friendly hello, she stalked on across the kitchen to disappear into the hall beyond.

'I see she's being her usual charming self,' Patty remarked as she came to kiss Eva on the cheek. 'I've no idea why you put up with her.'

'I've told you often enough, because underneath it all you can tell she's lonely and insecure and . . .'

'You're too forgiving, that's your trouble.'

'I just don't want to make things any more difficult for Don than they already are where she's concerned. It's only been two years since her mother allowed her to start visiting . . .'

'So you'd think she'd be trying a bit harder to fit in by now.'

'She's made quite a few friends round here.'

'I meant with us. It's not as if we haven't tried to make her welcome, and frankly . . .'

'Patty, let's drop it, please. I'm as frustrated as

you are by the way she is, but we can't blame her for the way her mother's poisoned her against me. Now, what's really bugging you, because something obviously is and I'm willing to bet it's not Jasmine.'

Patty sighed irritably. 'Everything's fine, unless you count the twit of an entertainment manager who's just gone and thumped one of the magicians, and the fact that the regular cleaning company has apparently gone bust. Oh God, who's this?' she groaned as her mobile started to ring. 'Great,' and clicking on she promptly launched into a stinging tirade that left Eva in little doubt that the entertainment manager with flying fists was at the other end of the line.

Used to these frequent and often lengthy breaks in their conversations, Eva carried on clearing up the kitchen while Patty stomped on to the terrace to add some verve to her reprimand by pacing up and down. Though she was as tall and slender as Eva she was a full eight years older, and her hair, which had once been as blonde, was now a chaotic shock of short caramel tufts that framed her lovely face like a rakish sort of hat. She'd been wearing it that way since chemotherapy had robbed her of her crowning glory, and time and nature apparently hadn't felt the urge to restore it to the lustrous mane it had once been. However, she was still a remarkably striking woman with their father's shrewd but gentle grey eyes, and the kind of smile that could easily light up a room. No sign of a smile right now though, as she dealt with the issue at the caravan park she'd managed for the past twenty years along with half a dozen or more holiday cottages. (No dazzling career for her thanks to playing parent to Eva and running the household for her father.)

Anyway, when the demands of her job were put together with the stress of her divorce and the challenge of supporting two children who still hadn't quite flown the nest, she had enough going on in her life, she often remarked, to keep the lines on her face from the danger of extinction.

'So, is this it?' she demanded, reaching for the magazine with the offending article as she came back indoors. 'What page?'

Before Eva could answer Patty's mobile rang again, and seeing who it was Patty groaned with frustration. 'Sorry, I'll have to take it,' she sighed. 'It's Coral.'

Eva looked at her askance, but made no comment as Patty clicked on and turned her back. 'Hey, Coral,' she said quietly, 'how's it going? Where are you?'

As she wandered into the conservatory Eva tried to bite back her irritation, or was it resentment at the way Coral Best and her wretched affair were forever claiming Patty's attention these days? It wasn't that Eva felt that *she* always had to come first with her sister; on the contrary, that place definitely belonged to Patty's children. Anyway, it wasn't a contest; it was simply that to Eva's mind Coral was taking advantage of Patty's good nature by embroiling her in a web of lies and deceit that was highly likely to end up backfiring on Patty in a way that she really wouldn't deserve.

Deciding to abandon the idea of making tea and pouring two large glasses of ginger beer instead, Eva carried them out on to the terrace where the abundantly colourful hanging baskets and overflowing pots of petunias, fuchsias and trailing begonias were still, in spite of it being mid-September, in exuberant bloom. Noticing that the birdfeeders were in need of refilling, she put the drinks down and went to scoop some seeds out of the storage container beside the rainwater barrel. Hearing a grunting behind her she turned around and laughed to see Elvis, her adorably mischievous Kune Kune pig, trotting off across the lawn with a tennis ball in his mouth that belonged to Rosie, the golden retriever. With his comically smiley pink snout, black and ginger hide and cute little piggy eyes Elvis was a real Babe, Don often remarked (enjoying the pun), and he was so much a part of the family it was hard to remember a time when his hilarious antics and perky personality hadn't entertained them.

Since Rosie was nowhere in sight Eva guessed that Jack, the gardener, had stopped for elevenses, and Elvis was now on a mission to distract Rosie from pole position in order to get to the food first. What a pair of characters they were, the pig and the dog, providing hours of amusement for the family and never ceasing to surprise with their devotion to each other. Both had been rescued from a farm in Devon, around four years ago, while the two Shetlands and four geldings, who now blissfully grazed the buttercup field that flowed away from the garden walls on the opposite side to the wild-flower meadow, had come to Eva via an animal refuge just outside Poole.

By the time she'd dealt with the feeders and wandered on to the oriental footbridge to throw handfuls of bread to her greedy collection of Aylesbury and Cayuga ducks, who came paddling at full speed from under the weeping willow, Patty still hadn't finished her call. Resisting the urge to go and stand in front of the conservatory with her hands on her hips, Eva sank down in a chair and picked up her drink. How on earth Patty could summon any sympathy, never mind patience, for Coral Best and her adulterous affair after what she'd been through herself when she'd found out that her husband, Reece, was involved with someone else, Eva simply didn't know. Surely to God cheating women were the last members of their sex Patty would want to deal with, especially when Patty – and Eva – was so fond of Will, Coral's slightly dull but unfailingly sweet-natured husband.

Still, Eva decided she should hardly be surprised by Patty's concern, when she of all people knew how impossible Patty found it to turn her back on someone in need. Ever since Eva could remember Patty had been there for her, taking care of everything from what time she went to bed, to sorting out Eva's petty squabbles at school, to helping her get ready for her first date when the time came. In fact, since their mother's untimely death in a car crash when Eva was only four Patty had all but taken charge of Eva's world. There were even times when Eva actually felt like Patty's eldest child, though she'd never voiced that thought to her sister, partly because she didn't think Patty would like it, but mainly because she didn't want to make Patty feel even more responsible for her than she already did.

'Why doesn't Mummy come back?' she used to ask Patty during the months after the crash.

'Because she can't,' Patty would say.

'Doesn't she love us any more?'

'I don't know if it's possible for dead people to love, but she definitely loved us when she was here.'

'Did we do something wrong?'

'No, you know what Daddy said, it's not our fault.

22

It just happened. She was driving too fast and lost control of the car.'

'Does he know where she is?'

'Nobody knows where dead people go, and you mustn't ask him, because it'll upset him.'

Hating the very idea of her adorable, indulgent father being upset about anything, Eva would usually drop the subject then, at least for a few weeks, or maybe even months until she needed to bring it up again.

'When is Mummy's birthday?' she asked Patty on the day she was six.

'I can't remember,' Patty answered.

'Shall we ask Daddy so we can send her a card?'

'We don't have anywhere to send it,' Patty cried angrily, 'now stop keeping on.'

Eva tried to stop, but she never could.

'I want Mummy to come to my birthday,' she sobbed the year she was seven. 'It's not fair that everyone else has a mummy who makes them cakes, and puts a bouncy castle in the garden and tucks them up at night and we don't.'

'You've got a bouncy castle, and Daddy always tucks you up – and he bakes cakes every now and again.'

'I know, but it's not the same.'

'Oh, Evie, please don't let Daddy hear you say that. He tries very hard to make us happy and we are, really, aren't we?'

Eva nodded because she was supposed to, and actually she wasn't unhappy with her father and Patty – and Granny B when she came to help take care of them – she just wanted the mummy who used to swing her round when she was little and make her laugh; who told her stories about fairies and sang her songs; who lay on the bed with her when she was afraid the monsters would get her; who loved to dance and made everything smell so nice.

'I know what happened to her now,' she confided to her best friend when she was twelve. Though the suspicion was choking her, making her want to scream out with all sorts of emotions she'd never felt before, she had to tell someone and she was afraid of what Patty would say if she told her. 'She ran off with another man.'

Her friend's eyes had almost burst from her head.

'I reckon that's what happened,' Eva continued knowledgeably, 'and no one wants to tell me.'

'But it would be really mean to say she's dead if she isn't,' her friend pointed out.

'They only tell me that to stop me going to look for her.'

'So is that what you're going to do?'

'I don't know. I mean, I think I should, but I don't really know where to start.'

Her friend gave it some thought, apparently wanting to be helpful. In the end she'd said, 'Why don't you ask Patty where the grave is? If there isn't one, then it could be that you're right, she isn't dead.'

So Eva had asked and Patty had told her that their mother had been cremated and her ashes were scattered in a wood where she used to go with Daddy.

Eva hadn't really known whether or not to believe that, but she did know that it was around about then that she'd stopped asking about her mother, and tried to stop thinking about her too. She wouldn't even let herself cry in secret any more, because she obviously wasn't coming back and anyway she didn't want her to, because if she had

24

gone off with another man and broken Daddy's heart then they definitely didn't want her.

It was only when her fame had started to grow that Eva had allowed herself to wonder about her mother again, and how proud she might be of the young model who was taking the fashion world by storm. She'd only changed her name to Angelina because her father had insisted. 'One day you might want to go back to your studies and start living a normal life again,' he'd said. 'You'll find that easier if you can separate the real you from who you're about to become.'

Though she'd argued at first, she'd soon let it drop, afraid that her father might put his foot down and veto her fast-developing career altogether if she didn't agree – or at least until she'd acquired three decent A levels, and probably a university degree. He had tried very hard to talk her into putting her education first, which, being a teacher himself, was hardly surprising, but with Patty and Elaine, his oldest friend and by then soon to be second wife, fighting her corner he'd reluctantly accepted that he was never going to win.

'Oh, there you are,' Jasmine accused from inside the kitchen. 'Does this belong to anyone?'

Eva turned and found to her dismay that Jasmine was holding up the *Saturday Siesta*. 'Actually, I was keeping it for Patty,' she replied.

Jasmine looked around. 'So where is she?'

Eva glanced over to the conservatory and to her surprise saw that it was empty. 'She must have gone out to the car,' she answered. 'So what are your plans for the rest of the day?' *Please don't let her be intending to hang around here*, she was praying inwardly. She wanted to speak to Patty alone, and

25

Jasmine's uncanny knack of sensing when she wasn't wanted almost always resulted in a decision *not* to make herself scarce.

'Actually, I'm going over to Weymouth with some of my friends,' Jasmine told her. 'There's a concert on the beach so we're taking a picnic. Is there anything in the fridge?'

'I haven't done a shop yet,' Eva replied, 'but help yourself to whatever you can find.'

Starting to rummage, Jasmine said, 'Have you spoken to Dad yet?'

'I don't have a reason to,' Eva answered, 'but you can always call him yourself, if you need to speak to him. I'm sure his mobile will be on again by now.'

Jasmine shrugged. 'It doesn't particularly bother me where he might be. I just thought you might be, you know, worried?'

Already guessing where this was going, Eva could only wonder why she even bothered to say, 'Why would I be worried?'

Jasmine broke a couple of yoghurts from a six-pack. 'Because,' she replied.

Eva waited.

'It's just that personally speaking,' Jasmine went on, 'if I were you, I'd be worried but hey, what do I know?'

Deciding not to allow this to go any further, Eva walked round the bar and offered to help cut some sandwiches.

'It's OK, I'll get a baguette on the way,' Jasmine informed her. Then, after a beat, 'So you reckon Dad's playing golf?'

'Jasmine, either come to the point, or change the subject.'

Flushing at the rebuke, Jasmine said, 'You know

what they say about men who dump their wives, if they've done it once they'll do it again, so if I were you I'd watch out.'

Eva could almost hear Allison's voice blending with Jasmine's, and had to wonder if there would ever be a time when the woman would let go of the bitterness that must be eating her up like a cancer by now. Not that she minded for herself, as far as she was concerned the woman could fester all she liked, it still wouldn't make Eva responsible for the break-up of her marriage. However, using Jasmine to try and cause trouble for her father did bother Eva, since, to her mind, it was an unforgivable way to treat her own daughter.

Resisting the temptation to ask how Allison was, thereby letting Jasmine know that she wasn't fooled, Eva turned with a smile to watch Elvis and Rosie lolloping across the grass towards her. By the time they arrived, all snorting enthusiasm and tail-wagging joy, Patty was coming back through the conservatory.

'I'm sorry about that,' she said, stooping to join Eva's fussing of the imperfect pair – or the odd couple, as they most often referred to them. 'I didn't think it would take so long and now I'm afraid . . .'

'Do you have something I can put this in?' Jasmine interrupted.

'There's a picnic basket, top shelf in the hall cupboard,' Eva told her. 'What are you doing about drinks?'

'We'll buy something there. I don't suppose you can lend me ten quid, can you? I haven't had my allowance from Dad yet this month.'

Knowing that wasn't true, but not prepared to argue, Eva cocked an eyebrow at Patty before going to take her purse from her bag. 'Here,' she said, handing over a ten-pound note, 'you can pay me back when your allowance comes through.'

'Don't worry, I will,' Jasmine said sweetly, and grabbing up the assortment of goodies she'd laid claim to, she flounced off to the hall.

'I'm sure she knew her father wouldn't be here this morning,' Eva murmured as the door closed behind her. 'So I can only assume she gets a kick out of trying to wind me up.'

'Or out of telling her mother about it later,' Patty commented. 'Actually, probably both. Anyway, please don't hate me, but I'm afraid I have to love you and leave you. Oh, no, Evie, don't look like that. You knew I was short of time when you rang.'

'Are you trying to avoid me?' Eva challenged. 'You've never got any time lately . . .'

'Don't be ridiculous,' Patty interrupted. 'I happen to be busy, that's all.'

'But never too busy for Coral, it would seem.'

Patty flushed guiltily. 'All right, what do you want to talk about?' she said. 'The article, of course . . .'

'Not just that. There are other things going on in my life that I want to tell you about . . .' She broke off as Patty put her keys and phone on the table and pulled out a chair to sit down.

'OK, I'm listening,' Patty said.

Annoyed at being made to feel childish, Eva said, 'Now is obviously not the time.'

'I said I'm listening. Tell me what's bothering you, up here in this perfect world of yours.'

Eva's eyes flashed. 'It might seem that way to you, and OK, I know I'm luckier than most, but it's not my fault your marriage fell apart . . .'

Patty put up a hand. 'If this is going to be about Reece . . .'

'It's about me,' Eva shouted, 'and the great big empty space in my life that belongs to my son.'

Patty's face fell as a wave of unease coasted across her heart. 'Oh, Evie, Evie,' she murmured, coming to embrace her. 'You found out twelve years ago that adoptions can't be reversed, so what do you want me to say? If I could change what happened I swear I would, but you know I can't.'

Maybe not, but you could at least let me talk about him sometimes, Eva wanted to cry. *Letting him go was the biggest mistake of my life and I can't get over it just because you don't want to discuss it.* What she said was, 'I'm sorry.'

'You know you don't have to be, I understand how difficult it is for you.'

'Do you?'

Patty seemed surprised. 'Do you doubt it?'

With a sigh, Eva shook her head. 'Of course not.'

Tilting Eva's face up, Patty said, 'At least you have the letter-box contact that allows you to send him cards and presents on his birthday . . .'

'But never to know anything about him,' Eva cried helplessly, 'not even his name. I don't even know if the things I send actually reach him . . .' She broke off, afraid if she went any further she'd end up blurting out the fact that she'd recently reapplied to the court for more information, even if it was simply to be told how he was getting on at school now he was so close to sixteen. She hadn't told Patty – or Don – because they'd only have tried to talk her out of it. They were always so protective of her – to a point that sometimes felt stifling – and they wouldn't have forgotten how traumatised she'd been after her first application for information had failed.

'I can see that this article's unsettled you badly,' Patty said softly. 'So where is it? Let me have a look.'

After a quick search Eva realised Jasmine must have taken it with her. 'What a fool to tell her I was keeping it for you,' she muttered. 'But you'll be able to pick one up at any newsagent's.'

Gazing tenderly into her eyes, Patty said, 'I really do have to leave now, so are you going to be OK?'

'Of course,' Eva sighed. 'We can talk again after you've read it.'

'Has Don seen it yet?'

'I don't think so. He won't be pleased.'

'Probably not, but at least we don't have to worry about Micky Bradshaw picking it up and deciding to come and find you.'

Eva shuddered at the mere thought. She wouldn't mention anything about her fear of copy-cat maniacs, because voicing it might make it worse, so she simply pulled a face and said, 'Jasmine had another go just now at trying to insinuate her father's having an affair.' Then, with no little irony, 'I wonder where – or perhaps I should say *who* – on earth that could have come from.'

Patty's face was tightening with annoyance. 'Her mother, obviously,' she retorted, 'but you shouldn't take any notice, because you know he's devoted to you.'

Eva smiled fondly. 'You'd better run,' she said. 'Where are you going, by the way?'

Patty rolled her eyes and reached for her keys and phone. 'Would you believe, I've allowed myself to be roped into running Marianne's jewellery stall from twelve till three? Without pay, I hasten to add.

And I have to stop by her house on the way to pick up her mobile which she managed to leave behind this morning, as only Marianne can.' Cupping a hand round Eva's cheek, she said, 'We'll talk tomorrow, OK? I should be free in the afternoon. Or hang on, I promised Jake I'd go and watch him play cricket. We'll sort something out, anyway.'

'Of course,' Eva said. 'Give my love to Marianne, and tell her we sold three of her necklaces this week, including the snowflake obsidian.'

Patty looked impressed. 'She'll be thrilled. Now, promise me you won't worry, but if you do I'll be at the end of the phone.'

A few minutes later Eva was gazing up at the security monitor watching Patty driving out through the gates, and feeling so absurdly abandoned that she almost wanted to run after her. Fortunately, she'd had enough counselling after the attack to recognise why she found it so hard to let go of her sister at times – it was all to do with the loss of their mother, of course, and seeing Patty as her security now – and since she'd learned to take deep breaths while waiting for the moments of panic to pass, she began to do just that.

Once the gates had closed and Patty's car had disappeared from the screen, Eva picked up the remote control and began to flick to each of the other cameras dotted around the property. Everything was as it should be, including the garden, which had been landscaped by a very talented local designer, and fortified magnificently by a builder who, to his own surprise, had discovered a flair for making what were effectively prison walls blend magically into a spectacular view. Don, who owned and ran the security company that protected the house, had even trained a camera on the field where the horses were currently trundling towards the stables. Another flick of the remote showed Sasha, one of the local girls who mucked them out, fed them and rode them, getting out of her car.

Eva's world as it existed now was right there on a CCTV screen. She could even, if she went to the computer, check what was going on at the shop. Deciding she would, she carried her ginger beer off to the study, and after a few strategic clicks a grainy black and white image flickered to life. A moment later, her niece's lovely elfin face loomed grotesquely towards the lens.

Laughing, Eva closed the image down, and wandered back into the circular entrance hall where a travertine staircase swept in a dramatic funnel shape to the upper landing, and a huge domed glass ceiling allowed copious rays of sunlight to stream like misty rain into the house.

She was safe and happy, Don had made sure of that, and with her family around her, Patty at the cosy little barn that she'd renovated near Burton Bradstock, and Elaine, her stepmother, running the spiritual retreat between Waytown and Salway Ash, she had no reason to feel lonely or afraid. Her niece and nephew were close by too, and all the friends she'd made during the years she'd been here. This was home now, and she couldn't imagine ever wanting to be anywhere else. Only her parents were missing . . .

And her son.

Her son.

Where was he? What had happened to him? How on earth could she have done what she had? She'd never held him, hadn't even allowed herself to look at him. What kind of person did that make her? What kind of mother could turn her back on her own child? Better that she had died, leaving the same kind of void her own mother had left in her life, than to have abandoned, rejected, him the way she had. She didn't deserve any forgiveness for that, and she wasn't asking for it, she only wanted to be sure that he was safe and loved and perhaps to know his name. Was that really too much to ask? The courts had thought so when she'd tried to find out about him before, so she knew there was a danger she was going to end up being bitterly disappointed by the action she'd recently taken. However, the alternative of trying to carry on as though he didn't exist had, some time ago, ceased to be an option.

Chapter Two

Don Montgomery's presence was always felt the instant he walked into a room. He was a tall, powerfully built man who, though close to fifty, remained remarkably good-looking with strong, though misaligned features, thinning silver hair and a healthily tanned complexion, thanks to the sailing and golf he somehow managed to cram into his hectic life. Though not in any way a chauvinist, his years on the police force had honed his self-confidence to a point that could easily be confused with arrogance. And it was true, he didn't suffer fools in any shape or form, nor did he have much tolerance for those who broke the law, whatever the excuse. However, he was one of the kindest, most sensitive men Eva had ever known, with the sort of integrity that made her proud to be his wife, and an unshakeable commitment to making her feel loved and safe.

Right now, he was heading from the spacious study he occupied next to Eva's, while finishing a phone call to the security chief at the caravan park Patty managed. He was dressed in a tailor-made dinner suit with the bow tie hanging loosely down the front of his pin-pleated shirt and his cummerbund stuffed into a trouser pocket. 'OK, we'll get the engineers on it first thing tomorrow,' he was saying, 'so keep an operative on the spot for tonight. Great. Good man. Call if there are any problems, I'll have the phone with me.' Without waiting for a response, he clicked off the line and shouted up the stairs, 'Are you ready? Taxi'll be here any minute.'

'Were you calling me?' Eva said teasingly, as she appeared at the top of the stairs.

As he turned to look up his deep-set brown eyes darkened with feeling. She was exquisite in a gold floor-length silk dress that clung to her slender curves like a wish, and showed off one angular shoulder to heart-stopping perfection. The other was covered by a single wide strap that rose from the bodice of her gown at the front and descended at the back to mask her scars, while a matching pair of full-length gloves provided a suggestive sort of modesty for her arms. 'You look sensational,' he told her as she began her descent.

Tilting her head to one side, she treated him to a coquettish smile that trembled slightly as the intensity of his eyes seemed to reach into places he kissed and stroked during their intimate moments. Her hair was swept high and held by a diamanté clip, while a loose cascade of tendrils provided a corkscrew veil for the damaged side of her face. 'Thank you,' she said, taking his hand as she reached the bottom. 'You're looking fairly dashing yourself. Or perhaps I mean rakish.'

With an arched eyebrow he turned to the mirror, and realising he wasn't quite ready himself he began to knot his bow tie as Eva drew the cummerbund from his pocket and found his eyes in the mirror as she fastened it around him. It was a while, she was thinking, since they'd flirted like this, and it felt so good that she was starting to wish they didn't have to leave right away.

'If it were any other event,' he murmured, as her thoughts passed through her hands to the place she was touching.

Smiling, she let him go, but paused as she turned away. 'Do you love me?' she asked, over her shoulder.

He looked surprised, and taking her arm turned her back to him. 'What kind of question is that?' he whispered. 'Why would you even need to ask?'

Almost laughing she said, 'I just like to hear it,' but as he started to tell her she put a finger over his lips. 'Let's save it for later,' she said. 'Or tell me on the dance floor and let me feel how much you mean it.'

'If that happens, we'll definitely be leaving early,' he warned darkly.

As it turned out, it was almost two o'clock by the time a taxi finally delivered them back from the Dorset Police Charity Ball, and while Don, exhausted by his role of life and soul of the party, snored gently in the back seat, Eva rested her head on his shoulder, struggling to keep her own eyes open.

'Are you OK?' he asked sleepily when they eventually tumbled into their enormous bed with its waterfalls of black and amethyst voile and, in daylight, breathtaking views of the bay.

'I think so,' she answered with a yawn. 'Are you?'

'Mm, shattered.'

A few moments ticked by as they lay, side by side, relishing the sensation of sleep as it started to enclose them, and the thought of how they would wake one another in the morning. Then he surprised her as he said, 'I saw the article. When were you going to mention it?'

In spite of the jolt in her heart she kept her eyes closed as she replied, 'I've been trying not to think about it.'

There was a moment before he said, 'Do you want me to find out who's behind it?' The tension in his voice reminded her of how deeply he resented any invasion of their privacy. Perhaps even more than she did.

'I'm not sure,' she replied. 'Maybe it's best ignored.'

He turned his head to look at her. 'Damn press think they have a right to do just as they like . . .'

'Sssh,' she soothed, reaching for his hand. 'They didn't say anything disparaging or libellous and it doesn't change anything, so there's no point talking about it now.'

She could see his eyes watching her in the darkness, and leaning forward she touched her mouth to his. 'Don't be angry,' she whispered. 'I'm fine, so stop worrying.'

With a sigh he put an arm behind his head and stared at the ceiling again. It was hurting and frustrating him, she realised, to know that she'd been forced to look at photographs of how she used to be, but there was nothing either of them could do to change it now, so there really was no point in dwelling on it.

A few more minutes ticked quietly by until, realising he'd managed the manly act of sinking like a stone from a problem, straight to the heart of oblivion, she smiled and brought his hand to her lips.

'Goodnight,' she murmured, but instead of snuggling into him, she pushed back the duvet and after making sure she hadn't woken him, she tiptoed across the room to let herself quietly out on to the landing. This sudden wakefulness at the point she thought she was about to fall asleep wasn't unusual and generally, though not always, she went down to her study to spend a quiet hour or two on the Internet, putting herself through a search that she knew even before it began would prove as fruitless as all the others she'd tried over the years.

Deciding to spare herself the torment tonight she started down the stairs anyway, already feeling buoyed as she imagined Elvis's and Rosie's delight when she took a cup of tea into their den. She'd sit with them for a while, snug in their little world, watching the moon fan-dancing over the sea before making its slow dawn escape from the sun. She'd probably even fall asleep in there and not wake up before Don came to find her in the morning.

She'd almost reached the kitchen when she noticed that a light was on inside and immediately tensed. She could hear voices carrying softly through to the hall, and realising it was Jasmine returned with some friends, she breathed easily again. Wondering how long they'd been there, if they'd heard her and Don come in and hadn't bothered to let them know they were already home, she went to find out if the friends intended to stay the night.

'They might,' Jasmine answered shortly when Eva asked. She didn't bother to turn round, simply kept her focus on the other two girls who were seated at the table with her, their backs to the window. Between them stood a half-full bottle of red wine with three smeary glasses and the debris of a Chinese takeaway.

Eva glanced at the other girls, whom she vaguely recognised and who also appeared to be a long way from sober. 'You're very welcome to,' she told them. 'It's too late to ring for a taxi.'

'If they want to go home I'll drive them,' Jasmine informed her with an impatient sigh.

Eva didn't respond, nor did anyone else.

'So what we were saying?' Jasmine demanded.

'Where are your car keys?' Eva asked.

Jasmine paused, then carried on as though Eva hadn't spoken.

Knowing she couldn't let this go, Eva said, 'I want your promise that you won't make any attempt to get into your car tonight.'

'I'm not going to, all right?' Jasmine snapped. 'For God's sake, can't anyone have a joke around here?'

Failing to register where there had been one, Eva watched Jasmine refilling the glasses and would have liked to tell her she'd had enough, but not relishing the prospect of a full-blown scene, particularly with an audience, she decided to go and put the kettle on.

As the muttering and whispering started up again, punctuated with gasps and sniggers, Eva stood with her back turned, resenting being made to feel awkward in her own home, and debating whether or not to tell them it was time they went up to bed. She could always go and take the bottle away; however, not even wanting to think about the kind of eruption that would cause, she remained where she was, willing the kettle to get on with its job.

'So,' Jasmine slurred, hooking an elbow over the back of her chair, 'where have you been tonight?'

Already knowing this wasn't likely to end well, Eva said, 'To the Dorset Police Ball.'

Jasmine's eyebrows arched.

'My mum and dad were there,' Sophie – Eva remembered her name now – offered.

'Yes, I saw them,' Eva told her.

'My mum was wearing one of your dreshses,' Sophie chattered on. 'It's amazing. You should shee it,' she told the others. 'She loves your shop,' she added to Eva.

Jasmine treated Sophie to a withering look, as though reminding her where her loyalties lay. Then to Eva she said, 'You have all the luck, don't you?'

Eva tensed.

'What I mean is,' Jasmine explained, 'you get to go out to all these fancy dos and restaurants, whereas my mum never gets to go anywhere. And do you know why she doesn't?'

'Jasmine,' Eva said softly.

'My mum doesn't go out,' Jasmine informed her friends, 'because she's got no one to take her.'

'Jasmine, I think you've had enough of that wine now,' Eva told her. 'It's late . . .'

'You don't get to tell me what to do,' Jasmine cut in nastily. 'Just because you're married to my dad doesn't give you any rights over me.'

'You're in my house,' Eva reminded her, 'and you're very close to becoming offensive.'

Snatching up the bottle, Jasmine rose to her feet.

'Jas, leave it,' one of her friends advised.

Jasmine's eyes were blazing as she glared at Eva. 'How's this for offensive?' she challenged, and letting the bottle slip through her fingers she kept her eyes on Eva's as it smashed on the floor.

White with fury, Eva said, 'That'll stay there until you clean it up, and if the stain won't come out I'll make sure your father deducts the cost of the new stones from your allowance.'

'Go fuck yourself,' Jasmine shouted, as Eva started to walk away.

Why don't you? Eva wanted to shout back.

'My mother told me . . .'

Spinning round, Eva said, 'You're brave now, Jasmine, while you've had a lot to drink and your friends are here, but you're impressing no one and as we both know this isn't the real you, why don't you just damned well *stop*.'

Jasmine's face was ashen.

Already regretting her outburst Eva said, less forcefully, 'Will you now please go up to bed.'

As she turned away Jasmine said, 'We saw the article about you today, you *has-been*. You think just because you were famous once, and someone stalked you, that the world owes you . . .'

Eva was taking no more. 'You're supposed to be an adult,' she broke in furiously, 'but you act like a child.'

'And you don't? Always having to be taken care of like you're some princess in an ivory tower? For your information you're not any better than the rest of us . . .'

'I'm not having this ridiculous conversation now, or at any other time. Just clear up that mess and go to your room – and I'll thank you for not speaking to me again until you're ready to apologise.'

'In your dreams,' Jasmine muttered as Eva slammed the door behind her. 'And if you can't see that my dad's sick to death of you,' she shouted, 'then you're thick, because the rest of us can.'

Shaking with anger, Eva walked towards the stairs, took a deep breath and started to climb. She wasn't going to allow the girl to get under her skin, because that would be playing straight into her mother's hands, a trap Eva had carefully learned to avoid over the years. However, it was never easy trying to shrug off all that hostility, or to rise above the attempts to sabotage her marriage, particularly when she'd like nothing more than to send Jasmine home with a message that would knock Allison right into the middle of next week. She'd never do it, satisfying as it might be – and more than deserved – because she simply didn't have it in her to use Jasmine that way. Any fool, if they bothered to look, could see what turmoil the girl was in, though she had to confess Jasmine was pretty good at hiding it under all that teenage attitude and bristling contempt. Nevertheless, Eva was totally convinced that at heart Jasmine was as lost and bewildered as any young girl might be when she had no clear idea of who she was or where she really belonged. The problem in trying to reach out to her was that it always seemed to set her defences higher, and even Patty's attempts to be friends had met with suspicion, even scorn.

'It's like trying to cuddle a porcupine,' Patty had once commented, and Eva couldn't disagree. Yet as difficult, impossible, as Jasmine could be, Eva wasn't going to allow herself to give up on her, especially when she knew how much it would mean to Don if they could somehow make her feel a part of their family.

Finding him still fast asleep with one arm flung across her side of the bed and a pillow half over his face, Eva smiled down at him, losing herself for a moment in the pleasure of loving him so much. She was glad the raised voices hadn't woken him; he had a difficult enough conscience over Jasmine as it was, and any sort of confrontation between her and Eva upset him like few other things could.

She wouldn't mention it in the morning either, there would be no need to if Jasmine pulled herself together and cleared up the mess she'd made.

Pigs might fly, she could hear a voice mocking inside her as she crossed quietly over to her dressing room. And well they might, she decided, as she sank into an armchair and closed her eyes. A moment later a wry smile began to play on her lips as she recalled the comment about a princess in an ivory tower. If that hadn't come from Allison, then she, Eva, would go down there now and clean up the mess Jasmine had made herself.

With a turbulent sigh, she lifted a hand to her face and unconsciously traced the scar that snaked in a jagged half-moon from the corner of her eye, across her cheek and back to her ear. This was something she did when feeling tired or fretful, as though reminding herself of how much worse things could be. Not that she ever allowed herself to relive the attack, only madness lay down that route, but the article that morning had drawn her former life so sharply back into focus that she was finding it impossible to escape for long. If it were only the good times she was having to deal with then maybe it would be fine to take a few more trips than usual down memory lane, but unfortunately there was never any way for her to go into the past without recalling the horror of what she'd done to punish Nick for the crime of not wanting her any more.

Merely to think of it now made her want to cower from the shame and run to him to beg his forgiveness. Did he know that she'd rejected their baby son in order to hurt him? Had anyone ever told him that? She didn't know because she'd never had the courage to ask.

We have to put what happened behind us and move on, he'd said when she'd called from the hospital the day they'd finally taken her off life-support to find out why he hadn't come to see her. It wasn't that she'd forgotten he'd ended their relationship; it was simply that she couldn't believe he'd still mean it after everything that had happened.

But it had turned out that he did, and not even the fact that she was pregnant was going to change his mind.

Of course, he'd had no idea a madman was watching her apartment the night he'd come to tell her it was over between them. Much less had he expected, when he'd returned with Bobbie, her agent, to find himself caught up in a deadly struggle to save her life. His intention then had merely been to leave Bobbie with her to make sure she didn't do anything stupid, while he returned to his wife.

It was what he had done in the end, perhaps that very night, though Eva guessed he must have spent many hours, if not days, talking to the police. She had only scant detail of that time, but she was in no doubt that if Nick hadn't returned with Bobbie and managed to knock Bradshaw unconscious then the maniac might never have been caught, and she almost certainly would have died.

She had no idea where Nick was now; they'd never attempted to contact one another after that one brief, devastating phone call. She only knew that that her insane attempt to punish him had ended up causing her more heartache and anguish than she could ever have imagined possible. The longing for the child that was hers but that she could never know, or hold, was far worse than what she'd suffered from the attack, because it was endless and would never, ever heal. Adoption was as irreversible, as incontrovertible as time.

If only she could have seen things clearly back then, but the last four months of her pregnancy had been spent mostly in a semi-conscious state, or in the kind of pain that wouldn't allow any clarity of mind. She couldn't even recall the birth. However, she did remember the squall of a tiny creature as the midwife had swept it up into her arms, saying, 'It's a little boy and he's beautiful.'

And she remembered how Patty had always been there, keeping vigil at her bedside, in spite of having a husband and two small children at home who needed her, and having to deal with the horror of knowing that the lump she'd recently found in her breast was malignant. Of course she hadn't mentioned it to Eva then, it wasn't until the treatment had begun that she'd finally broken the news, and probably only then because she had to explain why she wouldn't be able to visit so often.

Dear Patty. Dear, wonderful Patty, the best sister anyone could ever wish for. Even now to think of what she'd been through, of how terrified she must have been and of how little help she, Eva, had been to her, was enough to break her heart. It was why, of course, Patty hadn't tried to change her mind about having the baby adopted, because she was afraid she might not be around to help bring him up.

Eva moved restlessly, as though to escape the memories that were flooding in too fast and too painfully, but she knew already that there was no escape, and nor did she deserve one. She had rejected her own child and no matter how many excuses she concocted to try and salve the guilt, or how much understanding she was offered from others, nothing – simply nothing – would ever make it all right.

He was going to be sixteen next month. *Sixteen.* She'd missed so much of his life already, and for all she knew she might never know him at all. She often thought about women whose children had been snatched and wanted desperately to reach out to them, as though by somehow sharing their pain she could help to soothe it. Though their torment would naturally be considered far worse than hers, in many ways it was the same, because she had no idea where her child was either, or if the people who'd adopted him were treating him well. Whenever stories of abuse came on the news or appeared in the papers she'd start tormenting herself with the fear that the victim might be her little boy. How would she know? If the age was right, and the colour of his skin, then it could be him. Don tried to be patient during those times, but she knew he found it difficult, mainly because he hated being so powerless to help.

It was just after she and Don had married, at which time her son would have been almost four, that Eva had decided she couldn't go on the way she was. She'd been spending more and more time trapped in the madness of watching small boys playing football in the park, or trailing round supermarkets with their mothers. She'd watch them performing wheelies on their bicycles, building sandcastles on the beach, digging worms out of dirt, falling asleep in their daddy's arms, and wonder constantly what her son might be doing now, or if the child she was looking at might even be him.

Though she'd known for some time about the 'letter-box scheme' that would allow her to send him cards and presents without knowing his name, or where he was, she'd been afraid of using it in case it made the longing worse. Patty had agreed that it probably would, and so had Don, but in the end, realising that nothing could be worse than what she was already going through, she'd braced herself and got in touch with social services.

'You understand, don't you,' the social worker had said, 'that it will be up to his adoptive parents whether or not they pass on your gifts and letters. If they decide to, they can hold on to them until he's older.'

'Yes, I understand that,' Eva had assured her, so eager to start writing that she was already getting to her feet.

'And they're under no obligation to tell you anything about him other than what they choose to.'

'I'm sure they'll let me know his name though, won't they?' she'd said, desperately. 'And how he's doing at school?'

The social worker had smiled kindly. 'Since they've agreed to the contact I'm sure they will,' was the reply.

But they hadn't. In fact, in spite of saying they would, his adoptive parents never wrote to her at all. At first she'd felt sure it could only be a matter of time before they got round to it, so she'd continued to buy toys and books, clothes and videos – taking guidance from her nephew's preferences, even though he was three years older. By the time a year had passed and there was still no word she found herself storming into the social services administrator's office one wet April afternoon, demanding to know whether or not her packages were getting through.

'Is someone stealing them? Is that what's happening?' she'd accused. 'Are you keeping the money for yourselves?'

After sitting her down with a cup of tea and a biscuit, a harassed but kindly man had assured her that no one was stealing her son's gifts or money, it was simply that the adoptive parents were exercising their right to withhold information until such time as they deemed it in their son's best interests for the situation to change.

'*Their son*'. He was theirs, not hers, and she, as his real mother, apparently had no rights whatever. It was unbearable, almost worse than when there had been no contact at all. What sort of people were they that they could do this to her? They must be cold and callous, so what were they doing to her little boy? Was he lonely and frightened? Did they keep him locked up in a cupboard, or chained to a table? Was he roaming the streets, or was he safe at school? What sort of food did they give him? How was his health? The fear, the panic began to drive her so crazy that in the end Don had talked her into getting some counselling. She'd agreed, and she had to admit it had helped. Nevertheless, even calmer and in a more rational state of mind, she'd remained determined to find out why the adoptive parents, caring and loving though they might be, were so unwilling to let her have any information at all about her son. And whatever the law might say, he was still her son, and nothing could ever change that.

From the start Shelley Rolfe, the lawyer Bobbie had found for her, had made it clear how unlikely it was that they'd ever achieve the kind of outcome Eva was after. Eva had assured her she understood that, but since all she wanted to know was her son's first name, she couldn't believe a judge would consider that too much to ask.

'Probably not,' Shelley had concurred, 'but judges are funny people, there's never any knowing how they might react, even when a situation seems perfectly straightforward and fair to the rest of us.'

The ruling had gone against her, and no explanation was offered as to why the adoptive parents weren't willing to provide information about their son – *their son* – they simply didn't want to. Nor had the judge been prepared to issue an order for them to comply with the terms they'd agreed to at the time the letter-box scheme had been set up. Whoever they were, these strangers who were so intransigent, so heartless, had had the final say, and Eva wasn't even allowed to know their name.

At the end of it all she'd been so traumatised and drained that Don and Patty, worried out of their minds, had told her she must never put herself through it again. Because she loved them, and didn't want to cause them any more distress, she'd allowed more than eleven years to go by before she'd finally managed to summon the courage to break her promise and steel her nerves to get in touch with Shelley for the second time. 'Anything could have happened by now,' she'd insisted when she'd spoken to Shelley just over a month ago. 'The parents might have softened, maybe they're not even together any more and if they aren't, surely the judge will look more kindly on me.'

'It's possible,' Shelley had conceded, 'but remember

you only have two years to wait before he can access the register to find out about you.'

'But what if they haven't told him about me? He might not even know he's adopted, and if he doesn't the register means nothing. Can we ask the judge to make them tell him they're his adoptive parents?'

'You know we can't,' Shelley had replied gently.

'Then can they at least be made to swear that they're passing on all the gifts and money I send? Surely it must mean something that I've never missed a single birthday or Christmas.'

'The problem is, the regularity of your contact could make you seem obsessive which I'm afraid won't work in your favour.'

'But he's my son! What am I supposed to do? Ignore the fact that he exists?'

'That's not what I'm saying. I'm just trying to prepare you for another disappointment, in case it happens. But it might not, and I don't see any reason why the judge shouldn't understand that all you're asking for is some sort of confirmation that your son is being well taken care of.'

'And that he's still in the country? Can we ask that too?'

'OK.'

'Do you think we can request a photograph? I've read on the Internet that it can happen, so why not for me?'

After agreeing to add a photograph to the list of requests Shelley had taken the new application to court.

A decision still hadn't come back, and Eva had no idea whether that was good or bad. All Shelley could tell her was that as soon as she had some news she'd be in touch right away. So Eva was left waiting – and hoping with all her heart that one day, quite soon now, she would, at the very least, be able to look at a photograph of her son.

Chapter Three

Bringing her Suzuki jeep to a standstill outside the carport at Eva and Don's house, Olivia was about to turn off the engine when she spotted the dreaded Jasmine's car parked next to Eva's. Given it was Sunday she hadn't been expecting to find her aunt alone, but Don never minded when she rocked up to drag Eva off for a 'girlie chat'. Jasmine, on the other hand, rarely failed to make some sort of comment about knowing where she wasn't wanted before stalking off to her room in a strop, or just hanging around being exactly where she wasn't wanted. Honestly, talk about having a chip on her shoulder – as Olivia's boyfriend, Dave, had once remarked, if she turned her head too fast she'd knock herself out.

Killing the engine, Olivia reached into the back seat for her bag. She had important matters to discuss with Eva this morning, so whether Jasmine liked it or not she was going to claim her aunt all to herself.

Giving a jaunty salute to a camera perched in a beech tree, just in case anyone was watching, Olivia started towards the conservatory with a brisk, salty breeze rippling the waves of her long dark hair, while a dozen or more seagulls swooped and screeched through the warm air above. At five foot nine she was an inch shorter than her mother – two below Eva – and her sunny smile and slender physique were more gifts from that side of her family. However, her large, brilliant eyes, olive complexion and slightly aquiline nose were all her father's.

Finding the conservatory door unlocked, she'd barely made it through the tropical oasis before the odd couple came bundling across the kitchen to greet her. 'You two make me feel like the most special person alive,' she laughed, as their race to get to her rendered them jammed in the doorway.

Rolling her eyes, Eva watched her beloved animals squirming in their girth as Olivia dished out hearty hugs, before scooting them ahead of her into the kitchen.

'This is a nice surprise,' Eva told her, abandoning the raspberries she was washing to take two mugs from a cupboard. 'I wasn't expecting to see you today. Are you doing espresso or cappuccino this morning?'

'How about a skinny latte?' Olivia replied, perching on one of the barstools. 'I swear I've put on five pounds in the last two days. Please tell me how that happens.'

Treating her to a sceptical once-over, Eva said, 'You're slimmer than I was in my heyday, so quit whingeing. Have you had breakfast? I've just picked the last of the raspberries, so you can have them with muesli, if you like. Or on their own.'

'On their own would be fab. Dave only went out to get fresh croissants this morning. How mean is that when I'm supposed to be dieting? Anyway, where is everyone?' Dropping her voice to a whisper,

'I saw the J person's car outside. Which stone is she hiding under?'

Eva slanted her a meaningful look. 'Don's taken her and her friends to the Hive Cafe for breakfast,' she replied. After planting a bowl of fresh raspberries on the bar she added, 'It might, in part, have been to get her away from me, because I'm afraid I had a bit of a scene with her last night.'

Groaning in sympathy, Olivia helped herself to a raspberry as she said, 'So what was it about this time?'

Eva shrugged and brought two coffees to the bar. 'The usual nonsense. She ended up smashing a bottle of wine on the floor, but it seems either she, or her friends, cleaned it up before they went to bed because there was no sign of it when I came down this morning. Anyway, how was everything at the shop yesterday? I meant to call before we went out last night, but time ran away with me.'

Olivia fanned her hands proudly. 'Everything's so cool that you're going to start wondering any day now how you ever managed without me.' Then, with a gloomier expression, 'However, I'm afraid to say we didn't get that many people through the door, so the takings aren't terribly high. Oh, and wait for this, Zoe's given in her notice.'

Eva looked surprised and concerned. 'Has she got a better job? I thought she liked working with us – or with you, given that she only does Saturdays.'

'Apparently her mother's saying she has to focus more on her A-level coursework, because she didn't have such great results when the last ones came through in August. Anyway, miss her as I will, I'm not sure it's a bad thing, because at least we won't have to pay her.'

Eva's expression was pained. 'That's true, but honestly, Liv, things aren't that bad yet and you need someone to help you on a Saturday, so we'll put a notice in the window tomorrow.'

'OK, and we'll have to hope that our neighbourhood shoplifters don't apply. They were hanging around again yesterday, eyeing up the jewellery, but don't worry, they didn't manage to get away with anything.'

'The same girls who came in before?'

'One of them was.'

With a sigh Eva said, 'Don't forget we have a hotline straight through to the police station, so if they do cause any trouble . . .'

'Don't worry, I'll use it. Anyway, listen, I saw the *Saturday Siesta* last night. Mum showed me when I popped over there. She said you didn't have any idea they were going to run that piece. How can they do that without your permission?'

Eva's eyebrows rose. 'I believe I'm considered public property,' she replied, 'or fair game, or whatever they want to call it. Amazing they think anyone would be interested after all this time.'

Unable to imagine anyone *not* being interested in her gorgeous aunt, Olivia said, 'You know, what gets me, is that they obviously didn't spare a thought for what it might stir up for you. I mean, they know what happened, they've even written about it, for God's sake, so how could they have just gone ahead with it? If I were you, I'd sue. Do you think you can?'

Smiling, Eva said, 'I've no idea, but I wouldn't anyway. It'd only invite more publicity and that's definitely not what I want.'

Olivia's eyes shone with affection and

understanding as she said, 'We're never going to let anything bad happen to you again, you know that, don't you?'

Reaching for her hand, Eva squeezed it warmly. 'Yes, I do,' she replied.

Olivia slipped off the stool and drew her into a crushing embrace. 'At least they spelled your name right – both names, in fact – and they picked some gorgeous shots of you,' she declared as she sat down again. 'I swear I could look at those photos all day, and I'd still want more. I guess that's what made you famous. It's so damned impossible to stop looking at you.'

'Was,' Eva corrected, putting it into the past tense. 'And you're biased.'

Olivia shrugged. 'Maybe, but it's still true.' She watched Eva moving back to the sink to wash raspberry juice from her fingers, and felt so much love for her that she almost got up to hug her again. Though she was too young to have any clear memory of her aunt's amazing career, or of what had happened to bring it to an end, Olivia did remember her coming to live with them when she, Olivia, was no more than five, and staying until this house was ready for her to move into. It was when the real bond between them had begun, and over the years it had become every bit as vital as the one she shared with her mother.

Catching Eva's eye, she smiled.

'What are you thinking about?' Eva prompted suspiciously.

Realising she wasn't exactly withdrawing, Olivia dared to say, 'Mum told me about Nick Jensen, the photographer? He's the one who saved you that night, isn't he?'

Eva's eyes went down, and so many seconds ticked by that Olivia was afraid she'd gone too far.

'I'm sorry,' she whispered. 'I shouldn't have asked that.'

'It's OK,' Eva told her, bringing her head up. 'Yes, Nick was the one who saved me.'

Though Olivia knew from her mother that Eva had been very deeply in love with Nick Jensen she'd never been entirely clear about whether Nick had felt the same way. Nor had her mother ever elaborated on why Eva and Nick had parted, other than saying that it had happened around the time of the attack. That was Eva's story to tell, her mother insisted, if and when she ever wanted to.

Was this the time, Olivia was asking herself. Probably not, with Don and Jasmine due back any minute. Nevertheless she heard herself saying, 'What happened to Nick after, um, you know? I mean, I've read about how he turned up with Bobbie, your agent, and that he was the one who fought off Micky Bradshaw, but after that . . .'

'The night of the attack,' Eva said finally, 'Nick was there before it happened because he'd come to tell me it was over between us. I was devastated, utterly beside myself . . . We had a terrible fight, and in the end he walked out. I didn't know then that he'd gone to fetch Bobbie. She lived in the next block, and I suppose he thought she'd be able to calm me down . . . What they came back to . . . Well, I guess we should say thank God they did come, or we wouldn't be sitting here talking about it now.'

Not even wanting to contemplate that, Olivia said, 'So what happened to him? I mean, are you still in touch?'

'No.'

In spite of knowing that the shortness of the reply should stop her, Olivia said, 'Did he come to see you in hospital? I guess he must have.'

Though Eva was starting to seem tense, her voice was steady as she said, 'No, he didn't. He was married, you see, so our affair was secret, and somehow, in spite of all the publicity, he managed to keep it that way.'

Olivia's heart skipped a beat. This was the first she'd heard about Nick Jensen being married. It explained the secrecy, obviously, but what else? she wondered. How would she know unless she asked, but did she dare to?

Eva's smile was distant as unprompted she said, 'I'm glad now that Nick stayed with his wife, because he clearly loved her. Someone like me, who'd never spared a thought for the woman she was deceiving, only for herself and the man she loved and how much she wanted him, really didn't deserve him.'

Caught in a rush of naivety, Olivia cried, 'No, you deserve a lot better. Who wants someone who cheats and lies and can't even be bothered to find out how you are when you're in hospital? I know I wouldn't.'

Eva swallowed hard and brought her eyes briefly to Olivia's. 'It was all a very long time ago,' she reminded her.

For Olivia, who'd rarely dared to ask questions before, these revelations had the immediacy of the present, so not allowing herself to stop she said, 'Do you know where he is now?'

Eva seemed surprised, then almost uninterested as she said, 'The last I heard he'd moved his family to Italy and I think he opened a restaurant there, or perhaps it was a hotel.'

'Family? So he had children?'

Eva frowned. 'A little girl,' she answered quietly. 'He's probably got more children by now. Who knows?'

Feeling desperately that Eva had missed out on having children of her own when she'd have made such a wonderful mum, Olivia resisted the temptation to ask if it was the attack that had ended her chances, since her mother had always made it very clear that this was another subject not to be discussed unless Eva chose to bring it up herself. As Eva never had, Olivia didn't have the courage to go there now, so instead she said, 'That sounds like he doesn't work as a photographer any more.'

Eva shook her head. 'Maybe he doesn't,' she replied. 'I think Bobbie's still in touch with him, but I don't ask and she doesn't tell. It's best that way. It's all in the past now . . .' She trailed off for a moment, seeming caught in a deep inner world, until looking at Olivia again she said, 'There's no point to us being in touch. Apart from anything else I don't think Don would like it too much.' Her eyes were twinkling mischievously now, which made Olivia smile.

'I guess they must have known one another though,' Olivia ventured.

'They certainly met,' Eva confirmed. 'With Don being the officer in charge of the case, that was inevitable, but as for saying they *knew* one another . . . After Micky Bradshaw pleaded guilty and was sent to Broadmoor, that was the end of the case, so there was no reason for Don and Nick to meet again. Between us though, I think Don took rather a dim view of Nick, but I guess that's part jealousy, because he knows how much he meant to me, and part disapproval of the way Nick cheated on his wife.'

Olivia grinned. 'He's quite old-fashioned in his way, Don, isn't he?' she remarked fondly.

Eva smiled. 'He'd be more likely to say that he believes in all the traditional values,' she replied softly. She shook her head disbelievingly. 'Looking back on those times now it's amazing to think we all survived them, with his marriage breaking up, me trying to take care of your mum, her trying to take care of me and two small children . . . Your father couldn't handle it all, I'm afraid, nor could Grandpa, and once Don realised there was no man in charge he stepped right in, in his usual masterly fashion, giving us all orders, ferrying us around, making our decisions . . . Well, you know how he is.'

Olivia did indeed, which was why she was mad about him too. 'Did you fall in love with him straight away?' she asked, in spite of knowing the answer. It was always lovely to hear Eva talk about Don.

'I wish I could answer yes to that, but I can tell you this, I love him now in a way that's far, far healthier than the way I ever loved Nick.'

Delighted with the answer, Olivia felt brave enough to go further as she said, 'If Nick wanted to see you now, would you agree to it?'

The light in Eva's eyes dimmed as she said, 'There's only one set of circumstances that would make me want to see him, but as they're not likely to come about, I think we should talk about something else now. In fact, I need to go and dig up some vegetables for lunch, so would you like to come and help me? You're welcome to stay if you don't already have plans.'

Disappointed, but accepting she'd already gone further than she might have, Olivia said, 'Love to, but before we go outside there's something I need to ask you.'

Eva did a fake double take. 'More?' she teased.

Blushing, Olivia said, 'Yeah, but about something else completely. Actually, it's the reason I came over.'

Eva was all interest.

Olivia pulled a face. 'I want you to promise to answer me honestly,' she challenged.

Eva blinked with surprise. 'If I can, of course I will. What is it?'

Starting to brace herself for news that wouldn't be at all welcome if her suspicions were correct, Olivia said, 'I need to know if Mum's seeing Dad again. OK, I'm sure she's sworn you to secrecy if she is,' she added hastily, 'but this is something Jake and I need to find out, especially Jake, because you know what Dad's like with him.'

Eva could hardly have looked more stunned. 'What on earth makes you think that?' she asked.

Taking heart from the reaction, Olivia said, 'You mean she hasn't confided in you?'

Eva shook her head. 'I'm sure you've got it wrong, Livvy. It ended so badly between them . . .'

'I know, I know . . .'

'. . . and he's married to the dental nurse now.'

'Yeah, but I don't think it's going too well and I'm worried that he's trying to sneak his way back in with Mum and if he does, he'll only end up hurting her all over again.'

Eva was still looking reassuringly doubtful.

'He rang three times on Friday,' Olivia told her, 'and each time she took the phone outside so I couldn't hear what she was saying.'

'Are you sure it was Dad?'

Olivia threw out her hands. 'I think I know my

own father,' she answered. 'I answered the phone myself . . .'

Eva signalled for her to stop. 'He still supplies the meat for her caravan park, remember, so that must be what he was calling about.'

'Then why take the phone outside? OK, we all know he got it seriously wrong when he gave up one of the most wonderful women on the planet for that little toothpick, but if he's regretting it now . . . Oh my God, Mum surely can't have forgiven him, not after everything he did.'

Clearly finding it equally hard to believe, Eva said, 'If something was going on she's sure to have told me.'

'Unless she's embarrassed and afraid of what we might say.'

'Have you asked her outright?'

'Yes, as a matter of fact, and do you know what she did? She laughed. I think it might have been a touch hysterical, I'm not sure, but I ask you, what kind of an answer is that?'

'But did she deny it?'

'Not really. She just kind of fudged around it, so you see, I can't help being suspicious. Jake's beside himself. He'll leave home if she takes him back. You know how vile Dad's been to him ever since he came out, saying he's no son of his, and accusing Mum of turning him "queer", as he so grossly puts it.'

'Which is one good reason why they wouldn't be seeing one another again. Your mother's not even close to forgiving any of that.'

'That's what I keep telling myself, but Jake's worried sick and the way she's behaving every time Dad rings . . .'

'So why not ask Dad what's going on?'

'I've been thinking about that. Do you reckon I should?'

Coming down from the high of certainty, Eva started to frown. 'On the one hand they're grown-ups, so can do as they please,' she said, 'but on the other . . .'

'Mum's a lot lonelier than she wants to admit, and we all know how easy it is to make mistakes when we're vulnerable.'

'Where is she now?'

'No idea. I've tried calling but she's not answering her mobile, and Jake says she's not at home.'

'I'll bet she's at Coral's,' Eva muttered, picking up the phone. As she speed-dialled Patty's number her eyes went to Livvy's, but finding herself diverted to voicemail she hung up and was about to try Patty's barn when her own phone started to ring.

'Hi, Patty?' she said.

'No, it's me,' Don told her. 'Everything OK?'

'Fine. Livvy's here, we're just having a chat. Where are you?'

'On my way to Horizon View. Apparently a couple of caravans were broken into last night, so I'm going over to find out what's what.'

Since Horizon View was the site Patty ran, Eva said, 'Does Patty know?'

'Yep, she's the one who called me so I'm meeting her there. Are we out for lunch today?'

'No, but Elaine's coming over for drinks at six. If you speak to Patty before I do, ask her to call me when she gets a chance.'

'Will do.'

'Hang on, before you go, what about Jasmine? Are you taking her with you?'

'No, I'm dropping her at the gates on my way past so she can come in and pick up her stuff. She told me about last night, by the way, but we'll have to talk about that later. Say hi to Livvy. Love you,' and a moment later he was gone.

After ringing off and telling Livvy about the break-in, Eva said, 'So at least we know where Mum is now – and Jasmine's on her way back. I'm afraid to say I've had enough of her for this weekend, so shall we take Rosie and Elvis for a walk?'

'Great idea,' Olivia cried, leaping down from the stool.

However, by the time leads were found and titbits packed, the gates at the end of the drive were starting to swing open and as Eva watched Jasmine coming through on the CCTV she realised she didn't quite have the heart to rush off without seeing her, especially when Jasmine would probably guess that she'd deliberately avoided her.

'Tell you what, why don't you deal with her?' she suggested to Livvy.

'Me?' Livvy protested.

'You've always got along better with her than I have.'

'Since when? She hates me.'

'Not as much as she hates me.'

'Uh uh,' Livvy said, shaking her head. 'We're in this together or not at all.'

A few minutes later, Eva and Olivia had the Sunday papers spread out over the bar and affected looks of pleasant surprise as Jasmine came in through the conservatory.

'Hey,' she cried cheerily, making them both blink. 'Thought you were here, Livvy, saw your car. Sorry can't stop, have to get home before the traffic builds up. Great top, by the way. Did you design it yourself?'

Livvy was so dumbfounded that she only just managed to say, 'No, it's from the market.'

Instead of scowling, or adding some nasty little rider, Jasmine threw Eva a sweet smile and breezed on through.

'I think I prefer it when she's acting up,' Eva murmured when she was sure Jasmine was out of earshot. 'At least I've got some idea where I am with her then.'

'I know what you mean,' Livvy mumbled. 'She's up to something, isn't she? I can feel it in my bones.'

'She's cooked up some trouble for me with her father,' Eva decided. 'That'll be what it is.'

'I don't know what gets into you at times,' Don shouted from the bathroom. 'How the hell do you think calling her mother sad and bitter is going to help things between you?'

Zipping her jeans and snatching a smoky blue vest from a drawer, Eva shouted back, 'You can't seriously believe I said that?'

Appearing in the doorway, his face half covered with shaving foam, he said, 'Maybe not, but you think it.'

'As do you, my darling, and apparently Jasmine does too, or why would she say it?'

Stepping back to the mirror he carried on shaving.

Tugging the vest over her head, she went to the bathroom door. 'Are you angry with me?' she asked curiously.

He seemed surprised. 'No, why?'

'I don't know, you just seem a bit edgy I guess. Is everything OK?'

'As far as I know, it is. How about with you?'

'I'm fine, except I'm missing you. I hardly saw you at all yesterday . . .'

'I was sorting the problem at Horizon View, and I was back way before your stepmother arrived.'

'Twenty minutes before, which you spent in the bathroom with the door closed. And what was that about? You never close the bathroom door.'

His razor stopped mid-air. 'I don't?' he said, frowning.

'Never.'

He turned to look at her. 'I didn't know that.'

A teasing light shot to her eyes. 'So what were you trying to hide?' she challenged playfully.

He looked down at himself. Apart from a fleck of foam that had dropped on to his chest he was completely naked. 'Whatever it was, I think it must have gone now,' he retorted drily.

Laughing as she turned back into the bedroom, she said, 'We're getting off the point. It's not good that Jasmine lies to you about the things I say. Her mother's having a really negative influence on her . . .'

'OK, we both know my ex is not the most stable of women, so let's leave it there.'

Under her breath Eva said, 'You have a gift for understatement.' Then more loudly, 'Whether you want to hear this or not, Jasmine is being used by her mother in the most reprehensible way . . . If you'd insisted on her spending more time with us when we first got married she might be a very different person now.'

'You know very well I tried.'

'Then maybe we should have tried harder.'

'Why, because you're the perfect mother, I suppose?'

Eva's face instantly paled, and realising what he'd said Don threw down his razor as he all but ran into the bedroom. 'I'm sorry, I wasn't thinking . . .'

'Go away,' she said, as he tried to embrace her.

'Eva, you know I didn't mean it.'

'It doesn't matter,' she mumbled, starting through to the dressing room.

Following her, he said, 'Yes it does, and you're right, if Jasmine could have been part of our family she'd be a different girl now, because actually you'd have made a wonderful mother.'

'Just stop,' she snapped.

Seeming lost for what to say next, he waited in the vain hope that she might find a way to forgive his appalling gaffe, but to his dismay she said nothing. 'Maybe if we'd had children of our own,' he ventured tentatively.

She turned away. 'If my son ever does come to find me,' she said, wishing she could believe it would happen, 'I don't want him thinking I got on with my life as though he never mattered. And you didn't want them anyway, because you've always felt the same about Jasmine.'

'It's true,' he agreed, 'and I'm not saying . . .'

'Actually, shall we change the subject?' she cut in.

Looking miserably helpless and contrite he watched her twisting her hair into a rhinestone clip, before arranging the long side sweep to help hide her scars. 'I'm sorry,' he said again.

'I know you are. So am I.'

'Eva . . .'

'I really don't want to discuss it any more. Every time we talk about Jasmine we end up like this, and frankly it's not the way I want to start the day. Now, where are you going to be later? Is there any chance we can have lunch?'

'I'll have to check my diary, but I think it's OK. Unless Vic Andrews at Dobbs Security gets in touch, and I'm hoping he will, because he should have got back to me by now.'

After pulling on a neutral linen jacket and pressing her feet into a pair of silver pumps she turned to look at him. His deep brown eyes were so full of regret and hope of forgiveness that she couldn't help but soften. 'How's that going?' she asked, knowing how much this new deal meant to him. 'Do you think he is ready to sell?'

Clearly relieved to be back on safer ground, he returned to the bathroom. 'Word has it his wife's keen for him to retire,' he answered, retrieving his razor from the sink. 'It'll make us the biggest outfit in the county if I can buy him out, if not the entire south-west.'

'What happened to Eden's offer? Is it still on the table?'

'Not sure. That could be what's holding things up. If that devious bastard's outbid me and Vic's already gone ahead and done a deal, I'm telling you, I will not be happy.'

'And we can't have that, can we?' she teased, swinging round the doorway to slap him playfully on the bum.

'Absolutely not,' he agreed, 'and if you do that again you won't be leaving this room for at least the next half an hour.'

Her eyebrows rose, and as a sharp bite of desire caught her unawares, she heard herself saying, 'Well, I could always call Olivia and ask her to open the shop.'

His eyes came to hers in the mirror. 'Do it,' he challenged softly.

Turning back to the bed she picked up the phone.

By the time she'd finished the call he was standing behind her, his hands covering her small breasts and his mouth pressing a trail around her long, slender neck.

Twenty minutes later, as he rolled on to his side of the bed, panting and sweating, he groaned irritably as the phone started to ring.

'Do you think we can leave it?' she said, still caught in the electrifying throes of an explosive climax.

'Not really,' he muttered, 'it might be important,' and reaching for the receiver he passed it to her.

'Thanks,' she said drily. Then, 'Hello?'

'Evie, it's me,' Patty told her. 'Are you OK? Livvy just told me you asked her to open the shop.'

'I'm fine,' Eva answered with an exasperated smile. News moved at lightning speed in their family. 'Just running a bit late. How about you? Elaine was sorry not to see you last night.'

'I know, I spoke to her when I got back from Jake's cricket which I thought was never going to end. Anyway, now I'm on the line, is Don still there? I tried his mobile, but I can't get an answer and the police have changed the time they want to meet us this morning.'

'I'll pass you over. Call me later and we'll catch up, OK?'

After handing the phone back to Don she got up from the bed, feeling thankful that he was distracted by the call as she walked to the bathroom, since she was still, even after all this time and the boundless intimacies they'd shared, self-conscious about the brutal scars that carved their grisly reminders across her back and buttocks.

Stepping into the shower, she quickly hosed herself down and was just reaching for a towel when she heard Don saying, 'All right, all right, calm down. I told you, I'm on my way. Yes, I'm leaving now, OK? I swear,' and with a long-suffering sigh he planted the phone back on its base.

Concerned, Eva came to dry herself in the doorway. 'What was she so worked up about?' she asked.

Starting, as though he'd forgotten she was there, he shook his head in bemusement. 'I don't know,' he replied. 'It's just a meeting with the local chaps. Anyone would think it was a matter of life and death the way she's carrying on.'

Puzzled, and worried, since Patty was usually able to deal well with stress, Eva said, 'Livvy told me yesterday that she thinks Patty's seeing Reece again. I wonder if that's what's getting to her.'

Don blinked with amazement. 'You've got to be kidding,' he retorted. 'No way would she have anything to do with that toerag again.'

'They've been on the phone to one another quite a lot lately, apparently. And she's out all the time.'

Going past her into the shower, Don said, 'I'll try to have a chat with her after we've seen the cops, find out what's eating her, because obviously something is – and if she is seeing that waste of space again I'm afraid I shall be telling her exactly what I think.'

Fifteen minutes later Eva was driving out of the gates ahead of Don, with so much going round in her mind that she almost forgot to wave as he turned in the opposite direction. She was worrying about Patty to an extent that she knew was probably irrational, but now the fear that Patty's cancer might have staged a return had suddenly presented itself, there was no way she could ignore it. If she was right, and Patty was keeping it to herself . . . Oh dear God, Eva hardly knew what she'd do, but one thing was for certain, she couldn't allow another minute to go by without speaking to her sister to find out if her worst nightmare was turning into a reality.

So, pulling over to the side of the road, she opened up her phone and clicked through to Patty's number.

'What do you mean am I all right?' Patty cried with an irritable laugh. 'Of course I am. What makes you think I might not be?'

Finding herself able to breathe again, Eva said, 'I just got it into my head . . . No, it doesn't matter. I thought, when you were uptight with Don . . . Is something stressing you? Something you're not telling me about?'

'You mean apart from this break-in, trying to be in five places at once, fire an abusive entertainment manager, persuade my darling daughter that no, I am not getting back together with her father . . .'

'So she asked you about that?'

'Yes, she did, *again* last night, and I told her that she's right, I have been talking to Reece more often than I'd like lately, because, bigoted prick that he is, he's trying to get me to talk Jake into seeking counselling for his – I quote – unnatural ways. Can you believe that man? I might understand it better if he was from Malawi or the bloody Vatican, but . . . oh, hang on, looks like the police have just turned up. I'll have to get back to you.'

After clicking off, Eva tossed her phone on to the passenger seat and closed her eyes with relief. Nothing was wrong with Patty, or nothing she couldn't handle, and as long as that was the case, there was nothing wrong with the world. Or nothing that she was willing to discuss with any member of her family when she knew how much it would worry them. Only Bobbie knew about her new attempt to get information about her son, and Shelley of course, and since Bobbie was holidaying in Hawaii, and Shelley had promised to call as soon as there was some news, she must do her best now to put it out of her mind.

Chapter Four

Eva loved everything about the quaint little market town of Bridport, from its proud red-brick town hall with jaunty clock tower and bandstand belfry, to the elegant colonnaded home of the arts centre with its creamy facade and big red doors, to the whole wonderful mishmash of old-fashioned cottages, colourful shopfronts and surrounding green hills. Vibrant strings of bunting zigzagged in merry triangles across the high street, while abundant towers of flowering tubs spilled like waterfalls into each other, and large black sandwich boards boasted a host of mouth-watering delights from nearby delis. Each Wednesday and Saturday the place turned into a bustling open-air market selling everything from T-shirts to tea towels, beach toys to garden tools, cabbages, caulis, artichokes, apples, pears, eggs, and every imaginable style of handcrafted jewellery, second-hand furniture and gloriously gaudy amateur art.

Most of all though, Eva loved the friendliness of the place, especially around Bucky Doo Square where old people often whiled away their time on benches under the huge, leafy trees, while local farmers hawked their produce from white-tented stalls, and buskers enlivened proceedings with anything from bluegrass banjo, to classical clarinet, to good old-fashioned rock and roll. This morning a juggler was entertaining anyone who cared to stop and watch, while in the middle of the square a red-coated military band was setting out chairs ready for an audience that was, as yet, very thin on the ground.

Perdita's, Eva's exclusive design shop, was in one of the narrow lanes leading off the square, nestled in between the cobwebby den of a bric-a-brac gallery and a smart new health-food store, with a card shop opposite, and a rambling old antiques emporium at the far end. Since the money she'd earned while modelling had enabled her to buy both her home and the entire three storeys of this building, she'd turned the first floor into a workroom where she and Livvy did most of their designing, and the second floor was a spacious studio apartment currently occupied by Livvy and her boyfriend Dave. To say Perdita's meant everything to Eva would be going too far, but it certainly came a close second to her family. She was immensely proud of what she'd achieved with the shop, having turned it into an outlet for her own creations and those of other local artisans and designers. Each handbag, belt, piece of jewellery and item of clothing that occupied the inner room of the shop had been individually made and was displayed as an example of what a client could order in any colour, size or even alternative shape that she – or he – might choose. And should they wish to add a little personal flourish, Eva would work on it with them until they arrived at exactly the style that suited them best. There was also an eclectic collection of fashions that she bought in from Italy and Germany. This took

74

up the first third of the shop, making the space easily accessible for passing browsers and providing something a little different for those on a less generous budget than that required for the exclusive designs.

Eva was just turning into Perdita's lane, as she called it, when she spotted her nephew, Jake, ambling towards her from the opposite end. Her heart instantly melted, the way it always did when she saw him. Not that she favoured him over Livvy, far from it, she adored them both, but there was no getting away from the fact that Jake, mainly because he was a boy, had the power to evoke emotions in her that were sometimes hard to bear.

On reaching the shop she waited for him to join her, loving the way he moved with an athlete's confidence and a dancer's grace. And with his tousled mop of inky-black hair, lazy cobalt-blue eyes and perfectly chiselled features, he was as handsome as any of the men she'd ever modelled with.

'Hey,' he said cheerily as he kissed her on both cheeks, 'fancy seeing you here.'

'Funny, I was just thinking the same about you,' she quipped, pushing open the door for him to go in ahead of her. 'Don't tell me, you've come to start a new line in menswear. The job's yours, terms and conditions the same as Livvy's.'

Grinning, he said, 'Count me in, just don't ask me to sew.' Then, 'Wow, it smells good in here.'

'Mm,' Eva agreed, inhaling the pleasingly delicate aroma of something that seemed to combine jasmine, rose and a hint of musk.

Coming through from the back, and brandishing the Dyson, Livvy said, 'It's a new room fragrance brought in by . . . Actually, I forget her name, but I've got it written down. She dropped by about ten minutes ago with some samples and I said we'd give them a go.'

'Great idea,' Eva replied approvingly. 'Having a place that smells good is the first step towards making people want to be here. This one's heavenly, though I'm hoping by the time I go through to the back I'll be assailed by something of the fair-trade variety, preferably dark roast, but mild will do.'

'Don't worry, coffee's on,' Livvy assured her, her eyes following her brother as he sank into one of the cream leather sofas beside the counter, where clients were invited to browse the design portfolios while sipping coffee or white wine. 'Huh! Will you just look at him,' she snorted in disgust. 'What are you doing here?' she demanded. 'And take your feet off the table.'

'That's nice,' he retorted, keeping his feet where they were and putting his hands behind his head. 'I thought you'd be pleased to see me.'

'Delusional. I thought you were going with Mum this morning.'

'I was, but then she said she could manage without me, so I thought I'd come and see if I could be of any use here. I'm free until eleven, which is when I start my shift at Waitrose. I don't mind telling you, Eva,' he called after her as she disappeared into her office, 'it's absolutely doing my head in stacking those shelves, so I'm hoping Bobbie's going to be in touch with you today.'

'Apparently she was due back from holiday this weekend,' Eva told him, 'so if she hasn't rung by the end of the day I'll try her again.'

'She's seen my portfolio, right?' he asked.

Eva hid a smile as she came back into the shop, since his portfolio, as he liked to call it, consisted of no more than half a dozen amateurish shots of him, taken by a budding young photographer mate, and styled – rather well, it had to be said – by Livvy. 'As far as I know,' she told him, 'but if she hasn't I know she'll make a point of digging it out, because she said herself, the last time she saw you, that you could have a great future in modelling, if it was what you wanted.'

'Not a chance,' he replied, stifling a yawn. 'No offence, and all that, it's just that I'm dead set on the law, but I need to earn some cash to pay for my South America trip, and if I rely on what I'm getting at Waitrose I won't be going this January, that's for sure. Can I have one of those?' he enquired, pointing to a dish of individually wrapped truffles on the coffee table.

'Help yourself,' she said, going to pick up the mail that was stacked next to the till.

'Mainly bills,' Livvy told her. 'And I've been trying to draft an ad to put in the window.'

'What for?' Jake asked.

'Zoe's leaving,' Livvy explained, 'and finding someone to replace her who's bright, willing and knows the meaning of customer service isn't going to be easy, as we know, thanks to the two nightmares we had before her.'

'Is that it now?' Eva asked Livvy. 'She can't even do this coming Saturday?'

'Maybe her mother can be persuaded if it's only one more week,' Livvy replied. 'At least that'll buy us some time.' As she finished speaking she was casting another rather dubious look at her brother. 'Of course, there's always you,' she muttered in a tone that seemed to doubt her own sanity.

His eyes widened with shock. 'Thanks for the

vote of confidence,' he drawled, 'but I'm definitely not aiming to be a camp little sweetie poncing about in ladies' frocks for the edification of Dorset's crème de la crème. I have a reputation to think of, you know.'

Laughing, Eva said, 'We're not asking you to model them, just to help with the sales, but one day a week isn't going to be enough for you, is it? It'd never satisfy your cash requirements, even if you topped it up from Waitrose. Besides, we're staying optimistic about Bobbie, but remember, if she does come up with something it's obviously going to be modelling.'

'Yeah, but that's kind of a different league – and it'll be men's stuff, not girls'.'

Eva grinned mischievously.

'You are so winding me up,' he protested, tossing a cushion at her.

'I thought gays liked wearing women's gear,' Livvy commented, starting to flick the clothes rails with a feather duster.

Jake gave her a pitying look. 'You are so not funny,' he informed her.

Livvy's smile was winning. 'Why don't you finish vacuuming while I set up the till?' she suggested. Then, as the phone started to ring, 'Do you want me to get that, Eva, or will you?'

'It's OK, I will,' Eva replied, still leafing through the mail as she walked into her office. 'Hello, Perdita's. Eva speaking,' she said as she sank down in her chair.

'Hey, it's me,' Don announced. 'I just put in a call . . . Oh hell, what's going on . . .? Sorry, hon. I'll ring back in a few minutes.'

Used to his abrupt ring-offs, Eva put the phone

down and after sorting the mail into various action piles, she turned on the computer to check the diary. A second fitting for a mother-of-the-bride dress at ten thirty; a visit to Charmouth to discuss projected workload with one of their best seamstresses (a meeting she wasn't looking forward to, since orders were definitely on the decline, and Eva already knew how upset the poor woman was going to be when she admitted she didn't actually have anything for her). After that she was due to drive up to Evershot to sort out menus for the fashion lunch she was hosting at the Summer House Country Lodge at the end of next month. A note next to this entry reminded her to get in touch with the local charities – one animal, one cancer – to which she was donating the show's proceeds.

So, a busy day ahead that couldn't be allowed to run into tomorrow, since she was off to London first thing to meet up with the agent of one of her Italian designers who wanted to discuss a new, 'price-friendly' range they were about to put in production. She hadn't yet made up her mind whether to stay the night. If there was a chance of seeing Shelley she wouldn't even hesitate, but maybe it would be a good opportunity to catch up with Bobbie – if Bobbie had the time, which she almost never did.

Deciding to give her a quick call if only to be sure she was back, she quickly dialled the number and went straight through to Naomi, Bobbie's long-time PA.

'Yeah, she's here,' Naomi informed her, 'and I know she wants to talk to you so I'll go and put a note in front of her. She's on the line to some twit from a Spanish ad agency at the moment, and you know what her Spanish is like.'

Laughing, Eva said, 'Is she gorgeously tanned and relaxed after three weeks in Hawaii?'

Naomi gave one of her famous scoffs. 'That woman doesn't do relaxed and with half of just about everyone she knows staying at the same hotel, they were nursing hangovers from dawn to dusk so couldn't bear even a peep of the sun. She seems on good form though, considering, and you won't be surprised to hear that this place already looks like El Niño passed through in a particularly nasty mood, and she only turned up half an hour ago. Are we going to see you soon? It seems ages since you were last in London.'

'That's kind of why I'm calling,' Eva told her. 'Is Bobbie around all week?'

'Yep, till Friday when she's off to Sicily for six days. Actually, I think that's what she wants to talk to you about, but I'll let her tell you, because, contrary to what she thinks, I haven't managed to hardwire into her chaotic circus of a weirdy head yet. Anyway, can she get you on your mobile, or at the shop?'

'Either,' Eva replied, looking up as Jake wandered in carrying a tall, perfectly formed caffè latte in one hand and a feather duster in the other.

'For my favourite aunt,' he told her, setting the coffee down on the desk as she hung up the phone. 'OK, you're my only aunt, but I swear you'd still be my favourite if I had ten thousand of them.'

Her eyes were dancing as she picked up the mug. 'I've just put in a call to Bobbie,' she said. 'I'm pretty sure she'll ring back before the end of the day.'

'Cool,' he declared excitedly, and tossing the feather duster into a corner he collapsed into her visitor's chair and treated her to one of his best smouldering looks. 'Time for a chat?' he asked, hooking a leg comfortably over one arm of the chair.

'Not really,' she replied, opening up her emails, 'but don't let that stop you. Oh God, look at this,' she murmured, as a dozen or more names from the past started dropping into her inbox.

'What is it?' he asked, coming to look over her shoulder.

'I guess you could call it fallout from Saturday's article,' she replied. After scanning them quickly she closed the screen down. 'Doesn't matter, I can deal with them later. You were saying?'

Going back to his chair, he said, 'OK, I've been thinking. Well, actually, it just occurred to me when Livvy said you'd lost your Saturday girl.'

Eva's eyebrows rose.

'This is probably going to sound a bit off the wall,' he warned, 'well, right off the wall I expect, but I was wondering . . . Well, why don't you offer the job to Jasmine?'

Eva allowed her jaw to drop.

'She's the right age,' he continued unabashedly, 'she's dead bright, when she's not being a pain in the proverbial that is, and I reckon she'd love to do it.'

Eva's eyes went to Livvy as she came to stand in the doorway. 'Did you just hear that?' she asked her incredulously.

Livvy nodded. 'He's on another planet, I know, but actually, having had a few minutes to think about it . . . Well, it might not be one of his worst ideas.'

Eva looked at Jake again, not quite sure what to say.

'I know you're worried she'll be rude to the

customers,' he said, 'but if you think about it, it's only you and Liv she's vile to . . .'

'And it's only us who work here. You know, I still can't quite believe you're saying this. You're not serious, are you?'

'I swear I am,' Jake insisted. 'She really isn't all bad . . . OK, I know it looks that way sometimes, but I reckon once you get past all the crap you'll find that all she really wants is to be accepted by you two. You especially.'

Eva blinked. 'The one she's most horrible to?'

He nodded. 'OK, it's wacky, but ask yourself this, if she really didn't want anything to do with you, why does she bother to come?'

'To see her father?'

'Yeah, but she could ask him to meet her halfway, or take her off to London or somewhere for weekends, but she keeps turning up here, trying to make trouble, I grant you – or the other way of looking at it could be that she's trying to get noticed.'

Since his quirky analysis was chiming, more or less, with her own way of thinking, Eva found herself starting to smile. This was part of what she loved most about her niece and nephew, how willing they were to see good in someone even when that person had rarely shown them affection or interest. 'Let me get this right,' she said, looking from one to the other, 'you think Jasmine, my stepdaughter Jasmine, secretly wants to be friends with me?'

Livvy nodded. 'In fact, probably more than just friends,' she ventured, 'because I reckon what's really going on with her is that she's looking for a mum.'

Eva immediately stiffened, but her only outward movement was to pick up her coffee as she tried to think. Though the job offer was a good idea, on the face of it, at least she thought it was, could she really imagine Jasmine wanting to work in 'a crummy little boutique in Bridport'?

'I bet,' Livvy said, 'Mum would agree with what we're saying, if we asked her.'

Being in little doubt of it, since Patty had suggested something similar not too long ago, Eva found herself recalling the words. 'I know you do your best to make her feel welcome and to try and be friends with her,' Patty had said, 'but if you ask me I think she senses that you don't want her to get too close, and that's why she's always difficult with you, and resentful. She's hurt. She feels rejected.'

Patty's observation had upset Eva at the time, and it was unsettling her again now, mainly because she knew there had to be some truth to it. She couldn't bear the idea of someone trying to fill the space that belonged to her son, so it was highly likely that without fully realising it she'd always kept Jasmine at arm's length, without ever really considering how hurtful or damaging her distance might be to the girl.

In the end, prompted by her conscience, as much as Livvy and Jake's eagerness, she came to a decision. 'Tell you what, I'll try the idea out on Don first. If he thinks it's a good one then we'll ask her. And if by some miracle she says yes, then on your head be it,' she warned Livvy teasingly, 'because you're the one who'll have to work with her.'

Livvy pressed a finger to the top of her brother's head. 'This is where the blame will sit if it all goes wrong,' she insisted, 'because he's the one who came up with the idea.'

'I can handle it,' he responded, squaring up his shoulders.

Reaching for the ringing phone, Eva said, 'Perdita's, Eva speaking.'

'Darling girl, it's me!' Bobbie gushed down the line. 'How are you? Tell me you're wonderful and happy and that you're coming to stay with me while you're in London.'

Laughing, Eva's eyes went to Jake as she said, 'Hi Bobbie, how are you?'

'Oh, you know me, rushed off my feet as ever. You should see the avalanche I've come back to. If you can't find me when you come to the office, please start digging. I take it you are coming – and sweetie, bring that godlike creature of a nephew with you. I need him. Send him today. Is he still available? We've got a shoot in Sicily starting this weekend. Not much pay, but hey, it'll be better than he's getting at Tesco's.'

'Waitrose. Does he get to keep his clothes on?'

'I don't mind if I don't,' Jake called out.

Bobbie chuckled. 'He's with you. Marvellous. I'll have a chat with him as soon as I've finished with you. Nao tells me you're going to be in London tomorrow. I want to see you. It's time we had a proper catch-up.'

'Are you sure you can fit me in? You're sounding pretty hectic.'

'When am I not? But we'll work something out. Who else are you seeing while you're here?'

'Only a rep from Milan. And I thought I might call Shelley.'

There was a moment's silence. 'Mm. I take it there's no news on that front, or you'd have told me?'

'No,' Eva replied, wishing she hadn't brought the subject up in front of her niece and nephew. 'Why don't I pass you over to Jake? I'll see you tomorrow night, if you can make it. Thanks for the offer of somewhere to stay.'

'My home is yours, you know that. Where's Carrie-Anne these days?'

'Rio, launching her new swimwear. She's got some great stuff. I'm taking quite a bit of it myself for next year.'

'I've seen it. She's got style. You both have. OK, put me on to the family god and I'll see you tomorrow.'

After handing the phone over, Eva left Jake to it and followed Livvy out to the shop. 'Do we really think this'll work with Jasmine?' she said.

Livvy shrugged. 'I guess we won't know unless we give it a try. To be honest, I reckon she'll turn it down flat at first, but after she's had some time to think about it, you never know, she might recognise it as the olive branch it's supposed to be.'

Eva nodded thoughtfully, then winced as Jake gave a whoop of excitement.

A beat later he bounced back into the shop. 'Sorry, got to go, off to Sicily,' he informed them, sailing straight on to the door.

'Hey, what about Waitrose?' Eva called after him. 'You can't just abandon them.'

'It's OK, I'm doing my shift today then I'll catch a train to London tonight. Must call Mum and get her to help me pack. This is so awesome. Evie, did I ever tell you I love you?'

Laughing as he returned to sweep her into a bruising hug, Eva said, 'I kind of get the picture. How long will you be gone?'

'About a week, Bobbie reckons, and she might have something else for me by the time I come back. Yay! I'm going to be rich and famous. Bring it on.'

As the door clattered shut behind him Livvy muttered, 'Bet he won't be telling Dad about his new job.'

'Probably best if he doesn't,' Eva commented. Then, 'Right, I've got about twenty minutes before Kathy Emmins turns up for her fitting, so I'm going upstairs to get things ready. Are you OK here?'

'Perfect. I've set myself the glorious task of stuffing envelopes with invitations for the fashion lunch this morning, but I suppose I ought to check through the emails first.'

'Actually, don't worry about that,' Eva told her, stepping back down from the stairs. 'I'll do it myself,' and returning to the office she resisted the urge to delete all the messages from old friends and colleagues rather than find that one was from Nick.

In the end, it turned out that none were, and she couldn't really be sure whether she was more relieved about that, or disappointed.

Much later in the day Eva was driving across country from Charmouth to Evershot, when Don finally got round to ringing back. 'At last,' she cried when she clicked on her earpiece. 'I was beginning to wonder what had happened to you.'

'Believe me, I'm beginning to wonder the same thing,' he grumbled. 'This merger business is getting more complicated by the minute, and now I've got to start interviews for three new guards. Let's just hope they don't send the same sort of blockheads that turned up the last time. Anyway, how are things with you?'

'OK-ish. Actually, I've just left Camilla's place,

you know, our lovely seamstress, and I'm feeling pretty bad about not being able to put as much work her way for the next few months. She's become quite dependent on it since her husband lost his job.'

'Mm,' he responded thoughtfully. 'What's he like? Would it be worth interviewing him for one of the guards' jobs?'

Loving the way he always tried to step in to the rescue, she said, 'I'm afraid he's partially handicapped, so I don't think he'd be quite right for it. If something comes up in the office though, maybe you could give him a chance there.'

'Consider it done. So, where are you now?'

'On my way to Summer Lodge. I'll probably be there for a while, if you feel like joining me for a cocktail later.'

Sighing, he said, 'It's doubtful I'll get away much before eight. What are you doing tomorrow? I thought we might try to have lunch with . . . Oh, hang on. I'm on the phone,' he shouted to someone at his end. 'Tell him I'll be there in two minutes.' Then, coming back on the line, 'Where were we?'

'Lunch tomorrow, which would be lovely if I wasn't going to London.'

'Of course, sorry, it slipped my mind. Are you staying overnight?'

'Yep, with Bobbie. She's just signed Jake up for a modelling job, by the way.'

'So I hear. I was with Patty at Horizon View when he rang to tell her. What was your inbox like this morning? Pretty full, is my guess, because I know mine was.'

'Anyone interesting?'

'Not really. How about you?'

'The same.'

'Have you answered any of them yet?'

'A few, I'm not sure I'll bother with them all.'

'You're sounding a bit fed up.'

'I'm fine. I just wish . . .'

'Sweetheart, I'm sorry,' he cut in, 'I have to go or someone round here's going to have a mental breakdown, and I fear it might be me.'

It wasn't until after she'd rung off that Eva remembered she wanted to talk to him about Jasmine, but since there was no particular urgency, and he was clearly up to his eyes, she didn't bother calling back.

Instead, she pulled over to the side of the road and pressed in Patty's number. 'Hi, it's me,' she said when Patty answered. 'Fancy meeting me at Summer Lodge for a drink later?'

'What heaven,' Patty murmured. 'I can't think of anything I'd like more, but thanks to you, my darling, I've been roped in for washing, ironing and packing half my son's wardrobe before taking him to the station.'

'Of course.' Eva smiled. 'I'd forgotten. He should have a great time and we know Bobbie'll look out for him. So how about later? Do you fancy coming over for dinner? It's just me and Don tonight and he'll probably end up locked in his study most of the evening, with all that's going on for him.'

'Oh, Evie, I'm sorry. I've just promised Coral I'd go over there.'

Unable to stop herself, Eva said, 'Isn't she seeing her *boyfriend* tonight?'

With a sigh Patty said, 'Please don't be like that. It's not as though you're going to be on your own, is it?'

'No,' Eva admitted grudgingly. 'I just thought . . . Well, I've hardly seen you lately, and we haven't even had a chance to talk about the article at the weekend.'

'I know, I'm sorry, but we will, I promise. How are you feeling about it now?'

'OK, I guess. It's just made me a bit reflective.'

'Which is only to be expected. Has anyone interesting been in touch as a result of it?'

You mean like Nick, Eva wanted to retort, but all she said was, 'Not really. Anyway, good news about Jake, yes?'

'He's thrilled to bits. I've already texted Bobbie to thank her. She only texted back with an offer to put him up while he's in London, but I couldn't possibly inflict him on her for that long. He's staying with an old schoolfriend until they go to Sicily at the weekend.'

'He'll have the time of his life,' Eva said, laughing. 'So, I'm not sure when we're going to get together, because I'm off to London tomorrow until Wednesday, maybe Thursday. If anything changes with Coral tonight, give me a call.'

After ringing off, instead of driving on, she called up her stepmother's number. 'Elaine, hi, it's me,' she said into the voicemail. 'I should be going home your way later and I thought I might drop in. Let me know if it's convenient.'

Twenty minutes later she was parked outside Summer Lodge, still on the phone and unable to register anything of her beautiful surroundings, as she waited to be connected to Shelley. She knew it was crazy to put herself through this when she had no doubt at all that Shelley would be in touch the instant there was any news, but she couldn't help it. Besides, hearing from her might prompt Shelley into trying to speed things along.

'Eva, I'm really sorry,' the secretary said, coming back on the line, 'she's still on the same call and it doesn't sound as though it's going to end any time soon. Why don't I get her to ring back?'

'OK,' Eva replied, somehow stifling her frustration. 'What I really want to know is if she'll have time to see me while I'm in London this week.'

'Mm, that could be difficult. She's pretty chocka. Let me talk to her and see if we can move something around.'

'Yes, please do that. I'm completely free, apart from a meeting late morning tomorrow, and I don't mind staying in town on the off chance she might have a last-minute cancellation. Could you tell . . . Could you tell her I'd like to bring something with me?'

'Yes, of course,' the secretary said kindly, and though Eva tried to pretend that it was the kindness that brought a lump to her throat, she knew very well that it was much more than that.

By eight o'clock that evening Eva was back at the house, buoyed by an encouraging meeting with the event organisers at Summer Lodge, but at the same time flat because she was alone. Not even Elaine had been able to see her this evening – unsurprisingly, since she was on her way to Cornwall to take part in a conference on spiritual awakening.

Realising Elvis was gazing up at her, his dear, snouty face seeming curious to know what was bothering her, while Rosie leaned against him, as though egging him to go first, she melted into a smile and went to give them both a hug. On returning home she'd taken them across the field to the cliff path where they'd met several of their chums – Barnie the three-legged Yorkshire terrier; Coco and Lulu the fiery little concoctions of white fluff known as Cotons de Tuléar; Randy the black Lab whose passion for Elvis was not returned. Watching them having such a good time never failed to raise her spirits, and they were comforting her again now.

Wondering what her son might think of them were he ever to meet them, Eva went back to her cooking with the same feeling of emptiness around her that she always experienced when thinking about him. However, when the CCTV monitor buzzed and she looked up to see the electronic image of Don's car coming in through the gates, she felt much of her tension starting to ebb. Knowing he'd had a long and stressful day made her glad to think it would be just the two of them tonight. They could talk, if he wanted to, or not if he didn't. Maybe they'd snuggle up in front of the TV, or work on their computers, or even go to bed early. It hardly mattered. Being together, and safe, was enough.

'Hey,' he said gruffly as he came in the door. 'Something smells good.'

'You mean apart from me?' she teased, going to put her arms around him.

'You're always good enough to eat,' he told her, and was about to kiss her when he was treated to an indelicate nudge from behind. 'And so are *you*,' he informed Elvis, turning on him with a menacing glare.

'No, no, don't say the b-word,' Eva warned. 'You know it upsets him.'

'Bacon!' Don growled, and they started to laugh as Elvis did a quick about-turn and trotted off to his bed. 'Hello, Rosie, my girl,' Don crooned as the retriever nuzzled affectionately against him. 'I guess you guys have already been out for a walk tonight?'

'We have,' Eva assured him, returning to the hob where she had dinner under way. 'There are half a dozen messages for you on the machine and Mrs H left one of her shorter notes thanking you for the extra tenner, but it really wasn't necessary, because it's her job to do your ironing and keep everything nice and clean. She can more easily afford a birthday present for her grandson now though, so she hopes you won't mind that she took the cash. Oh, and PS she's happy to come and cook an evening meal for you while I'm in London. And PPS her brother will be back from sick leave by Wednesday at the latest. He's had terrible flu so she made him stay at home because she didn't want you, or anyone else to catch it.'

With a laugh of fond exasperation he came to taste the sauce she was making. 'Mm, that's good,' he murmured approvingly. 'What time are we eating?'

'In about ten minutes. Do you want to set the table?'

'Will do.' Then, groaning as his mobile started to ring, he took it out of his pocket and groaned again. 'Keep your fingers crossed I don't have to go back out,' he told her. Then, clicking on, 'Johnny, what can I do for you?' As he listened he was taking cutlery from a drawer. 'Of course I'm at home,' he barked. 'Where the heck else do you expect . . . All right, all right. I'm going to my computer, I can pick it up from there.'

As he disappeared off to his study, taking the knives and forks with him, Eva dug out some more and went to set the table herself. The fact that he was helping to protect a good proportion of the county, and knowing how capable he was of doing it, rarely failed to give her a thrill of pride.

'OK, Johnny's motoring, and I'm dry,' Don announced, coming back into the kitchen a few minutes later. 'Do we have any wine open? Actually, I'd kill for a beer.'

'In the usual place,' she told him, happy that Mrs H was so devoted to her master that his needs were taken care of first. A couple of beers were always in the fridge door, easily accessible and perfectly chilled.

'Can we turn off mobiles?' he asked, taking the top off a Peroni. 'If anything's urgent there's always the landline, and I for one am done with today.'

Picking up her own mobile which had lain silent since she'd come in the door, Eva promptly switched it off. This was a gesture she felt to be more for Jasmine than for Don, or herself, since she really wanted to talk about his daughter without interruptions.

In the end, they didn't get around to it until after finishing their main course, mainly because Eva felt they needed time to relax away from the pressures of their day before tackling an issue that might take some time to resolve.

It turned out she was right in her assumption, because Don's first response was a pensive silence that became more perplexing the longer it went on.

'Well, are you going to say something?' she prompted in the end. 'I'm willing to offer Jasmine a Saturday job if you think . . .'

'I heard,' he interrupted, and getting up from his chair he went to fetch the bottle of red wine he'd left on the bar. 'I guess it's a good idea,' he said, coming back to the table, 'I'm just . . . I . . . Where do you think you're going with it?'

Puzzled by the question, she said, 'I wasn't thinking about *going* anywhere except trying to make her feel valued and part of our family. Is that too much?' She didn't mean to sound sarcastic, it just came out that way, and the sharpness in his eyes showed he didn't much appreciate it.

'No, of course it's not too much,' he retorted. 'It's just I wasn't expecting it, and I guess I'm wondering why now?'

Starting to feel annoyed, Eva said, 'I just told you, Zoe's leaving so I need a replacement and I thought – actually, Livvy and Jake thought – that it might be something Jasmine would like to do.'

He fell silent again and stared fixedly out at the darkness.

Baffled by what was going on, Eva said, 'Apparently you have a problem with it, so maybe you'd like to tell me what it is?'

His eyes came briefly to hers.

'You're worried about what her mother will say?' she asked.

'She won't be for it, I can tell you that much.'

'But Jasmine can make up her own mind.'

'True, but have you thought about how you're going to react if she turns you down?'

Eva threw out her hands. 'What am I supposed to say to that? If she does, then we find someone else. I don't understand why you're being like this. I thought you'd welcome the idea.'

He took a sip of wine. 'What does Patty think?'

Eva's eyes widened in angry surprise. 'I don't know, I haven't asked her, but I imagine she'll be all for it. Anyway, what's it got to do with her? I can take decisions without her, you know.'

His eyes immediately softened. 'I didn't mean to imply that you couldn't,' he said, reaching for her hand. 'It's just that she's pretty wise and has an opinion on most things.' Then, shaking his head as though still not entirely sure what he was thinking, he said, 'I don't want you to be hurt.'

Bringing her other hand to close it around his, she said, 'I think I can handle Jasmine by now.'

His smile was weak. 'Just give it some more thought before you commit, is all I ask. And maybe talk it over with your sister.'

Minutes after he'd disappeared into his study Eva picked up the phone to call Patty, not to take his advice, but to discuss the strangeness of his response. Then remembering Patty was nursemaiding Coral this evening, she hung up before the connection was made. Damn Coral! Why couldn't the flaming woman find someone else to lean on? Better still, why didn't she stop cheating on her husband and get on with her life so that Patty could get on with hers?

'If she could, she would,' Patty said when they finally spoke just after ten, 'but I'm afraid it's not easy when you're as besotted as she is.'

'It's Will I feel sorry for,' Eva retorted, referring to Coral's husband.

'As well you might, but believe me, it's no fun feeling helpless and consumed and unable to think about anything else. You remember what it was like with you and Nick. You were so crazy in love with him . . .'

'That was a long time ago,' Eva interrupted sharply. 'And I don't understand why you'd bring

95

that up now. I'm married to Don, in case you'd forgotten.'

'Of course I haven't, I'm just saying that Nick meant everything to you and I don't think you ever spared a thought for his wife, did you?'

Stung by the truth of that, Eva's eyes went down. She really wasn't proud of the fact that she'd had an affair with a married man, and even got pregnant by him without ever really considering anyone but herself. True, her life had fallen apart after so she'd paid for her selfishness, and now she could only hope that Nick's wife had never found out and that he'd ended up holding his marriage together. 'Is Coral thinking about the wife she's hurting?' she asked.

'Actually, yes, she is, all the time. She hates herself for what she's doing, she just can't seem to make herself stop.'

'And what about him? You said earlier that she thought he was going to break it off.'

'He hasn't yet, but she's still afraid that he might. It might be best all round if he did.'

'I'm sure it would.'

'Yes, well you would think that.'

Eva blinked, as though she'd been slapped.

'I just wonder where you get off moralising,' Patty ran on, 'when you're as guilty as anyone of cheating . . .'

'For God's sake, why are you having a go at me? I'm not the one having an affair, and the one I did have was *sixteen years ago*.'

There was a long silence before, sighing heavily, Patty said, 'I'm sorry, it's been a difficult day, and Jake's gone now, so the house is empty . . . No excuse, I know, but I'm obviously feeling more uptight than I realised. Maybe we should change the subject. You said you rang about Jasmine. Jake's already told me about the job. I think it's a good idea, but why don't we discuss it when you get back from London? Do you know when that's going to be?'

'Not yet. I'll call while I'm there to let you know.'

'Eva?' Patty said, before she could ring off.

'Yes?'

'I'm sorry I brought up about Nick.'

'It's OK,' Eva assured her, still thrown by the bewildering exchange. 'Like I said, it was a long time ago.'

Chapter Five

Patty was sitting behind the wheel of her car, staring out across the stony sand of Hive Beach to the churning grey mass of the sea. The sky seemed angry and desolate, with mountainous purple clouds gathering ominously over the wide sweep of bay, and distant rays of sunlight fanning out like hope over a far horizon. There weren't many people around, just a handful of hardy hikers working their way down from the cliffs that ran between Burton Bradstock and West Bay. It was a path she knew well, having walked it many times over the years. The large cafe beside the car park was another place she knew well; it was where she occasionally met Eva for breakfast, or held business meetings when it felt more politic to be out of the office. Her home – the small barn that she and Reece had lovingly renovated during the early years of their marriage – was about two miles inland from here, snug in its half-acre of land with a rambling wood behind it and a small lake close by. Livvy and Jake had grown up there, attended primary school in the local village, learned to sail in nearby Weymouth, built sandcastles on most of the beaches, starred in pantomimes over in Bridport, led groups of trick or treaters around the caravan park, joined in with Christmas carols at church each year.

Patty was surrounded by friends and family and so much familiarity that, like Eva, she'd come to feel as though she'd been born here. It was virtually impossible for her to go anywhere without running into someone she knew, and her social calendar was as hectic as the constant demands of her professional day. Even the break-up of her marriage hadn't left her isolated or forgotten, because her friends had rallied with the same unswerving support as they had when cancer had struck sixteen years ago. How thankful she'd been for them then, particularly when Reece decided to bury himself in denial. He was so used to her being strong and capable, the one who took charge in a crisis knowing exactly what to do, that discovering she was as human and vulnerable as anyone else had been too much for him. He'd never discussed it, not even when the vomiting began and her hair fell out. The only time she realised he cared was when she found him crying in the woods behind the house, and then he'd turned to her for comfort as though she had it in her power to make it all go away. She'd often wondered since if it was during this time that the end had begun for them, because he hadn't only allowed her to struggle on alone with her treatment, he'd barely done anything to help when it came time to start rehabilitating her sister.

And where had her father been throughout it all? The answer was, in an even greater state of fear and denial than Reece, since he'd been facing the unthinkable horror of having both his daughters taken from him at once. What on earth would they have done without Don and his quiet and constant support? Would they ever have got through it?

Even now, to think of how close they'd come to losing Eva could start a wave of panic coasting across her heart. What her sister had suffered, the terror, the devastation of her body, her life, her dreams, had been so brutal and so wholly undeserved that for a long time Patty herself had been plagued with nightmares. She kept waking up in a cold, trembling sweat, tormented by images of the knife plunging into Eva's beautiful face, slashing her tender skin, causing near-fatal damage to her perfect lungs and heart. She used to wish it had happened to her – if it had to happen at all, but why had it? What kind of god or fate would bring such a cruel and needless end to a young girl's blameless career? Why even give it to her in the first place if the intention was to snatch it away with such malice? How proud Patty had been of her sister's success – and how shamefully she had ended up letting her down. Had it not been for the cancer, Patty knew she'd never have allowed Eva to do what she had to punish Nick for abandoning her, but having no idea whether her illness was going to prove terminal or not, or how psychologically damaged Eva might turn out to be after the attack, she simply hadn't had a proper grasp on the decision they were taking.

And now it was too late. There was no going back, not for Eva, not for any of them. Yet, since reading the article last Saturday, she'd felt strangely as though the past was calling out to them, urging them to look again at the mistakes they'd made and perhaps not give up hope that something might be done to repair them. On the face of it there was no chance of that, and never had been, and though she longed to be wrong about that, she couldn't help wondering if she was only trying to persuade herself that an answer could be found in order to absolve her guilt over everything else.

Eva would have a child now if she, Patty, hadn't been diagnosed with cancer.

But that wasn't the end of it, it was only the beginning.

So many secrets, lies and burdens of shame.

As a car pulled up next to her own Patty kept her eyes trained on the sea, and tried to drown her thoughts in the ceaseless motion of the waves. It was no good, because the truth was like the tide: no matter how far it might ebb, it would always make a return.

She still didn't look round when her passenger door opened and Don slipped in beside her, bringing a cold, damp waft of salty air.

'Are you OK?' he asked.

She nodded, even though she wasn't. 'Did she get the train on time?'

'Yes, she did.'

They continued to sit side by side, silently watching the raindrops that had started to roll down the windscreen. There was so much to say, too much, yet sometimes, like now, it was probably best not to speak at all.

The nervousness Eva experienced during the build-up to seeing, or even speaking, to Shelley Rolfe was always difficult to handle. Today, with a ruling on her application due at any time, it was reaching a whole new level. She'd received a call from Shelley's secretary while she was on the train to London, letting her know that Shelley could see her briefly

101

at noon. And now, having somehow got through her meeting with the Italian agent, she was here, being shown into Shelley's office which was on Gray's Inn Road, opposite a pub that she, Eva, had once gone to with Nick.

'I can't thank you enough for seeing me,' she said as Shelley stood up to greet her. 'I know how busy you are, and that I'm probably being a pain with my impatience . . .'

'You've had a long wait,' Shelley interrupted with a smile. She was a large, motherly-looking woman in her late forties, with the arresting dark eyes of her Indian father and an air of compassion that Eva had always found reassuring. 'Sit down,' she said. 'Molly will bring us some coffee.'

Taking the chair she was indicating, Eva perched on the edge of it and opened her bag. 'I've brought a card,' she said. Shelley was always busy so she didn't want to waste her time. 'He's going to be sixteen next month.'

Shelley waited for her to look up, and when their eyes met Eva felt her heart stand still.

'I have some news,' Shelley told her. 'It came through this morning.'

Eva couldn't breathe. *Please God, please, please, please let it be good.*

'I'm sorry,' Shelley said gently, 'it hasn't gone in your favour.'

Eva continued to look at her. She knew if she tried to speak, or move, she'd fall apart.

'I'm so sorry,' Shelley whispered.

'Nothing – nothing at all?' Eva finally managed. 'Not even his name?'

Shelley shook her head.

'Or a photograph?'

Again Shelley shook her head. 'I've made a copy of the ruling,' she said. 'You're welcome to read it here in case there's anything you'd like to ask.'

Eva's eyes were still fixed on Shelley's, wide with shock and disbelief. How could the judge have been so unfeeling? Was he or she a parent? Didn't they understand? She looked down at the envelope in her hand and felt as though it belonged to another world.

Shelley came round the desk and perched on the edge of it.

'I didn't seal it,' Eva told her, still looking at the card. 'I know you're not supposed to.'

After turning to put the envelope on her blotter, Shelley said, 'For what it's worth, I think the judge could have been more lenient.'

Caught in a sudden wave of desperation, Eva said, 'Do you know how he is? Is there anything at all you can tell me?'

Shelley's soothing eyes filled with more regret. 'I don't know any more than you do,' she reminded her.

Eva looked away, not sure if she believed her, but even if she didn't what difference would it make? The judge had ruled against her.

'How are things at home?' Shelley asked, as though trying to steer her thoughts to a happier place.

Eva said, 'Fine. Good. Don's a little stressed over a business deal and things are quite slow at the shop, but hopefully it'll turn around again soon.'

'Have you told Don – or Patty – about the application yet?'

Eva swallowed drily. 'No. They'd only worry.'

Shelley nodded, and reaching behind her she picked up a slim buff file.

Realising it must contain the ruling, Eva felt herself shrinking inside.

'It's not particularly easy reading,' Shelley warned, 'in either sense of the meaning.'

Taking it, Eva kept her eyes down, not quite knowing what to do next.

'I've highlighted the most relevant parts,' Shelley told her. 'Would you like me to leave you alone while you read it?'

Eva shook her head, then nodded. 'OK, thank you,' she said.

The document was nine pages long, the section marked by Shelley was towards the end. ' . . . *therefore, I have found no reason to grant the application. On the contrary I find myself to be in accord with the social workers' and adoptive parents' concerns that if the birth mother were to be given the information she has requested, or granted access to photographs, then she will be likely to use all means of new media at her disposal to try and trace him.*

The natural mother, as a matter of law, is no longer the parent and should therefore not consider herself to be so. An adopted person is to be treated in law as not being the child of any person other than the adopters. The arrangements for contact should not be imposed *upon the adoptive parents but should be left to their good sense to do what they believe to be in the best interests of their son.* (Their son!) *Concern has been expressed by the social workers about the unpredictable behaviour of the natural mother . . .'*

Eva stopped reading. It was too hard, too cruel of the social worker to pay her back like this for the hysterical outburst when she'd accused the woman of poisoning the adoptive parents against her.

Or maybe she wasn't fit to be a mother. Maybe her son was with the right people and she shouldn't be trying to interfere in his life like this.

Getting to her feet as Shelley came back into the room, she said, 'Tell me the truth, do you think I have everything out of perspective? Do I want him as much as I do because I'm confusing him with myself and how desperately I used to hope that my mother would come back, even though I knew she was dead? I mean, I'm not dead, so I could be there for him. It is possible. Except he probably doesn't even know I exist, so he wouldn't be creating fantasies the way I did.'

Shelley said, 'We don't know what his adoptive parents have told him, and we won't until such time as he's able to tell us himself.'

Eva's eyes went down as her throat tightened with too much emotion. 'If that time ever comes,' she managed to whisper. She was still holding the file and wasn't sure that she wanted to take it with her. In the end, she put it on Shelley's desk and said, 'I know it's not the outcome I was hoping for, but thank you for trying.'

Looking crushed herself, Shelley said, 'Your name is on the adoption contact register, remember, and two years isn't so long to wait now.'

'No, it isn't,' Eva agreed, though she knew very well that she could be waiting for the rest of her life and still know nothing about her son.

'Sorry, I can't talk now,' Patty was saying into her mobile. 'I'll call you back in about an hour. Are you at the shop?'

'Of course,' Livvy replied. 'Where are you?'

'Just going into one of the Seatown cottages. The

new cleaners are due at three and it's already five to. Is everything OK? Do you need some help?'

'No, I'm cool. I was just calling for a chat. Any chance we can get together later?'

Using her foot to kick the car door shut, Patty said, 'I'm not sure. Depends how things go here. Call me if you need to,' and letting her mobile slide on to the top of one of the boxes she was carrying, she struggled along the path to the front door.

After letting herself into the picture-book dwelling with its rose-covered porch and quaintly crooked rooms, she dropped the boxes in the kitchen and went on through a narrow archway into the sitting room. Finding the door to the wood-burner open reminded her that the last tenant had warned her there might be a bird's nest in the chimney, so she quickly put in a call to the sweep telling him he must please come before the next family arrived at the end of the week.

This was probably the most popular of the rental cottages she managed, thanks to its panoramic sea views and isolated setting. She'd always had a special fondness for it herself, since it was where she and Reece had stayed during their first trip to Dorset, though that once-romantic fact hardly endeared it to her now. What continued to appeal was the way it seemed so gently alive with its own character. Though she knew much of its history, she occasionally found herself wondering about the many stories the cottage could tell of the occupants it had seen come and go. How much love and anger it must have witnessed during its two hundred years; what passion, hope, grief, anxiety. The names of most who'd spent time here in the past twenty years were to be found in the visitors' book that was kept on the hall table, but only the cottage itself knew what had really transpired within its walls.

It wasn't that Patty wished to know the details of other people's lives, far from it, she'd never been the nosy or gossipy type. It was simply that she took some small comfort from the fact that what she herself had allowed to happen here was perhaps not so terrible when compared to the indiscretions or misdemeanours of others.

Sinking down on the sofa, she put her head in her hands, and might have allowed herself the luxury of tears had her mobile not started to ring. Expecting it to be the cleaners letting her know that they'd been held up or were lost, she went to fish the phone out of the box where she'd dropped it, and was about to click on when she saw it was Coral. Feeling unable to cope with her friend right now, she let the call go through to messages, and started to unpack the things she'd brought in with her. Disinfectant. Loo rolls. Washing-up liquid. Kitchen towels. Brillo pads.

Ordinarily she didn't get involved in shopping for the household products, but her assistant, Greg, was off this week, so she'd added his list to her own when she'd gone to the supermarket to purchase the welcome pack of white wine, milk, tea, coffee, sugar, eggs, a loaf of bread, a small pack of half-fat butter and assorted marmalades and jams.

Realising her mistake, she let out a groan of dismay. The next guests weren't due to arrive until Saturday, and today was only Tuesday. How could she have been so stupid? Where was her head? This was a complete waste of time, never mind milk, bread and butter, and exactly when had the owners started providing such an expensive bottle of wine for their guests? Since it was one of her brother-in-law's favourites, maybe she should give it to him, except she couldn't because she'd have to give a reason for the gift, and as that would mean admitting she'd made a mistake she'd better just take it home and hide it.

Or maybe she'd sit here and drink it.

Not an option with the cleaners on their way and her mobile ringing again.

Taking a deep breath, she reminded herself firmly that she could do this. She could speak to anyone and everything would be all right. Everyone knew Patty could cope, and the reason they knew that was because it was true. The instant she saw who was calling, her resolve fell apart. The very last thing she needed right now was Reece preaching at her like some evangelical lunatic, so he could go through to messages too.

No sooner had the ringing stopped than it started again.

'Hey, Mum, you're not going to believe this . . .' Jake began when she answered. A few minutes later, realising she'd registered almost nothing at all of what he'd told her, she said, 'That's fantastic. Great news, but I'm afraid I can't stay on now, my darling. Ring any time, though. Love to everyone,' and ringing off, she put the phone down on the table to start . . . To start what? She couldn't remember what she was supposed to be doing.

Experiencing a moment of panic, she looked around the kitchen, and realising where she was she felt herself starting to steady . . . Wayfarers Cottage at Seatown. Cleaners on their way. Changeover happening this week. A fortnight's rental and then the decorators were coming in to freshen the place up. If she focused on the small things then maybe the rest wouldn't seem to matter so much.

Her phone rang again. It was like that all the time. It almost never stopped.

Seeing who it was, she was tempted to let it go to messages again, but since Don was just about the only person she felt able to speak to, she allowed herself to click on.

'Hi,' he said, 'are you OK? I got your message.'

Message? She couldn't recall leaving one. What had she said? 'I'm fine,' she answered, summoning a smile to try and calm herself. 'Well, actually, a bit wound up,' she confessed, 'but nothing new there.' She laughed, and found herself wondering when she'd last really laughed.

There was an unsettling concern in his voice as he said, 'Where are you? Do you want me to come?'

'No! No,' she answered quickly. 'I mean, thanks, but I'm fine, honestly. Have you . . . Have you spoken to Eva since this morning?'

'About ten minutes ago. She was on her way to Bobbie's.'

On her way to Bobbie's. That meant she was still in London. 'Did she say when she's coming home?'

'Some time tomorrow, she'll let me know what time to pick her up.'

Patty's head fell back in an effort to sink the rising tears.

'Where are you?' he said more firmly this time. 'I'm coming to get you.'

'No,' she protested. 'There's no need, honestly.'

Unbearable seconds ticked by before he asked, 'Has she told you about offering Jasmine a job?'

Patty swallowed. 'Yes, she mentioned it, but we haven't really discussed it yet.'

'So what do you think?'

What did she think? Did he really want to hear what she thought? She was sick to death of hiding things from her sister – that was what she was thinking. All the secrets and lies, the efforts to protect her from any more pain, were starting to wear her down, and sometimes there were days when she didn't know how much more she could take. She didn't say any of that, though – instead, before she answered, she forced herself back from the brink so he wouldn't think she was losing her mind. Finally she said, 'She means well. Her motives are good.'

'I don't doubt that,' he replied. 'I'm just wondering about what'll happen if . . .'

'. . . things go wrong? Yes, I'm worried about that too, but if she's determined to give it a go I don't see how we can stop her.'

There was another long silence during which she realised that he had no more idea what to say than she did, so what else was there for her to do but hang up?

'Olivia!'

Livvy looked up from her sketchbook, and seeing her mother's best friend, all bubbly auburn hair and lively blue eyes, coming in through the open door, she broke into a smile of welcome. 'Coral, hi,' she said, putting her pad aside to go and greet her. 'To what do I owe the pleasure?'

With one of her typically flamboyant hand gestures Coral said, 'You know me, I like to keep up to speed with all the new stuff you've got in. Plus, I'm interested to see the latest designs. Will's firm is having a big do in Exeter again this Christmas, and much as I love what Eva created for me last

110

year, I can't be seen wearing it for a second time, now can I?'

Unable to disagree, Livvy steered her towards the portfolios stacked on the coffee table and took off to the kitchenette to pour a glass of wine. Knowing Coral as well as she did, she didn't have to ask what she'd like to drink after the clock struck five. Livvy was also au fait with the kind of style Coral preferred when it came to couture, which some might say was a tad young for a woman in her mid-forties, but since she had the figure for tight fits, low cuts and slashed seams, and actually wore ruffles and bling pretty well, Livvy saw no reason to try and coax her towards less extravagant designs.

'No Eva today?' Coral called out.

'She's in London,' Livvy replied, coming through with a generous glass of Pinot Grigio. 'Back tomorrow, I think.'

Giving a sigh of pleasure as she took the drink, and following it with another straight after the first sip, Coral smiled playfully. 'Perfect,' she declared. 'Won't you join me?'

'I'm still working,' Livvy reminded her. 'Actually, now you're here you can take your invite to the autumn show. We've already got you down for it, obviously, but you can save us the cost of a stamp if you take it with you.'

Laughing as though Livvy had made a very funny joke, Coral slipped the envelope into her bag, saying, 'I take it Mum's going?'

Livvy looked incredulous. 'Like ye-es,' she answered. 'In fact, Eva's hoping to persuade her to model some of the stuff for "the older woman", same as last time.'

Coral raised an eyebrow. 'Mm, I'm sure she'll be

delighted, provided you don't mention the older bit.'

Livvy chuckled. 'She's got a grip on it, and like I keep telling her, she's really great for her age.'

'More advice,' Coral cautioned, 'cut the last three words. Anyway, I was hoping I might find her here. I've been trying her all day, but I can't seem to get through. Do you know where she is?'

Livvy went to fetch herself a coffee. Returning with it, she said, 'The last time we spoke she was over in Seatown sorting out one of the cottages. I think she's got a pretty full schedule this week.'

Coral rolled her eyes. 'When hasn't she? In fact, I'm starting to become a little concerned about her.'

Instantly worried that she might have missed something, Livvy said, 'That's weird, because she'd been giving me the impression she was worried about you.'

Coral's eyes narrowed curiously. 'Why, what did she say?'

Livvy shrugged. 'Nothing specific, just that you were having a bit of a stressful time with one thing and another, which was why she was seeing so much of you, to offer some moral support.'

Coral nodded slowly, and her eyes went down as she took another sip of her drink. 'Well, we all know how marvellous she is at that,' she murmured, 'and I must admit, I'm very grateful for it. Now, let's have a look through these books, shall we? I'm in the mood for something pink this time, and I'm keen to see what you've been coming up with, young lady, because I think it's high time I commissioned something from you.'

* * *

Eva was on the roof terrace of Bobbie's penthouse apartment topping up the birdfeeders and pulling parched plants from dry pots, while Bobbie lay stretched out in the midday sun barking instructions down the phone at her long-suffering assistant. She was a large, vibrant soul on the home stretch to sixty, with a cloud of fiery red hair and a lusciously creamy complexion that was the envy of many women half her age. Her laugh was famously raucous and her eyes as shrewd as they were merry, while her copious kaftans were as much a part of her colourful image as her vast collection of Indian jewellery.

'OK, all yours again – at least for five minutes,' she said, yawning as she clicked off the line. 'And will you please stop fussing with all that? Come and sit down. Is it time for a cocktail? Hell, what time is it? This jet lag has really got me pooped. Whenever have you known me to peg out over dinner the way I did last night? Never been heard of. Was it last night, or the night before?' Her eyes softened as Eva came to sit on the lounger next to hers. 'Look at you,' she said, reaching for Eva's hand, 'you can still make this old heart melt, do you know that?'

Eva smiled as she watched a chaffinch hop along the railings towards the feeder.

'Do you mind that I've got your photo back in pride of place downstairs?' Bobbie asked gently.

'No, of course not,' Eva assured her, though it had taken her aback when she'd arrived the previous evening to see it hanging in its old place. It was the one that had launched her, blown up to at least ten feet by eight, so that it virtually dominated the sitting-room wall. There were dozens of others filling up the rest of the space, many of models she used to know well, but plenty more of those who'd come along since. She'd wondered why Bobbie had chosen to rehang hers now, when there had been no sign of it for years. Could it be because Nick had come to visit? she'd wondered. The thought of it had caused a ripple of unease to coast across her heart. She hadn't asked, and nor would she.

'Did we talk about that last night?' Bobbie said, screwing up her nose.

Eva nodded and smiled. 'A couple of times, but don't worry, we're not going to have you committed yet.'

Losing another yawn to a chuckle, Bobbie said, 'Just shoot me, it's quicker and more humane. Anyway, I'm glad you could stay on today, because I've missed you, sweetie, and I definitely wasn't much company last night. Did we go to Launceston Place? Of course we did, it's where I always go. What did we talk about? Just so's I don't go repeating myself again.'

Since Eva hadn't mentioned anything about her visit to Shelley's office the day before, she only had to remind Bobbie of the trip they'd made down memory lane, to the time they'd visited Hawaii together on a shoot for a suntan-lotion commercial that had ended up running all over the world. From there they'd moved on to other trips – Barbados, Tahiti, Moscow, Cape Town, Canberra – so many locations as well as people and products to promote that they'd lost track of them all now. It was while they were trying to remember the name of a Swedish stylist who'd been arrested for indecency during a photo shoot in Berlin that Bobbie's head had started to droop. After that, Eva had brought her home and helped Manuela, Bobbie's eccentric and devoted housekeeper of thirty years, to put her to bed.

'So did we remember the scoundrel's name in the end?' Bobbie asked, massaging an arthritic ache in her hand.

'Jannik,' Eva supplied, 'but please don't ask me his surname because that would be too much.'

'Oh hell,' Bobbie groaned as the phone started to ring again. She stared at it balefully. 'Shall I answer it? Nah! They can always call back. Now tell me about you, and spare me the platitudes and pretend stuff, I want to know everything you've been up to. How's my dear friend Don? Still taking good care of you, I hope?'

Eva's eyes sparkled. 'Of course,' she answered. 'He's as wonderful as ever and he sends his love.'

'Good. Don't forget to send him mine. Oh, heavens, what am I thinking, my head's all over the place here. I heard about the "Where are they now?" piece. Naomi emailed it to me last Saturday. I'd have rung as soon as I read it if it hadn't been the middle of the night with you. Are you OK with it? They called me, you know, to ask for an interview, but I turned them down flat. I told them not to bother getting in touch with you either, because you wouldn't be interested. Naive of me to think that would make them go away. Did it upset you?' she asked.

Eva thought about it. 'Yes, I guess it did in a way,' she confessed, 'not because of anything they said, because they didn't make anything up or try to put a new slant on what they knew, but because it's brought everything back and I've found it hard to stop thinking about it since.'

Bobbie's expression was sympathetic. 'Well, that's only to be expected,' she said. 'What does Don say about it?'

'Actually, not much, but there again, what is there to say?'

Bobbie shook her head as though accepting that there probably wasn't much. Then, picking up a little crystal bell, she said, 'Time for cocktails. I'm in the mood for a margarita, how about you?'

Though she seldom drank in the middle of the day Eva could see no reason not to on this occasion, so swallowing her disappointment at the change of subject, even though she hadn't really wanted it to go any further, she gave an eager nod of her head.

Clearly delighted, Bobbie eased herself round as the diminutive Manuela came out through the conservatory, all neatly starched uniform and haughty disapproval. 'I'm guessing mai tais,' she said in her typically exhausted way.

'Wrong,' Bobbie told her gleefully. 'Margaritas with salt – and bring us some of those ghastly pretzel things you keep making.'

'You ate them all last night,' Manuela declared. 'Lucky for you I baked some more this morning. I've also ordered you a new treadmill. She broke the last one,' she informed Eva.

Eva burst out laughing as Bobbie treated Manuela's retreating back to a menacing stare.

'Dreadful creature,' Bobbie muttered. 'Time she retired.'

Since she'd been saying that the entire time Eva had known her, and since everyone knew that Bobbie and Manuela were as impossible to separate as glamour and fashion, Eva was taking no notice of the threat. They'd first met, according to Bobbie, when she'd rescued fourteen-year-old Manuela from a life of debauchery on the streets of Manila. Manuela's version had Bobbie kidnapping her from the family home and trying to sell her into slavery before deciding to keep her for herself. 'That was because I couldn't get enough for her,' Bobbie was often heard to remark.

By the time Manuela returned with the drinks Bobbie was on the phone again, but the instant she laid eyes on the mouth-watering treats Manuela set down she said, 'Smilley, sorry, something's just come up. I'll get back to you,' and clicking off the line she picked up a crab vol-au-vent and stuffed it in her mouth, while scowling horribly at Manuela.

'I'll add a rowing machine to that order,' Manuela told her, and after handing Eva a lace-edged napkin she started back inside.

'I'm taking her skiing this winter,' Bobbie commented, blowing flakes of pastry in her haste to get the threat out before Manuela disappeared.

Eva gave a choke of laughter as Manuela stiffened, allowed the nonsense to slide off her back, then continued on her way. Their last venture up the Alps, some twenty years ago, had resulted in a broken leg, wrist and collarbone for Manuela and some very hefty medical bills for Bobbie, not to mention almost a year of role reversal as she'd bullied the patient along the road to recovery.

'I'm going to guess,' Bobbie said after she and Eva had raised their glasses to each other, 'that you didn't get to see Shelley yesterday, or you'd have told me.'

Eva's eyes went down as her heart turned over. 'Actually, I did see her,' she said quietly, 'and the ruling's gone against me.'

'Oh no,' Bobbie groaned. 'Dear, dear, Evie, that's so unfair. You weren't asking for much, and this has been so hard for you.'

Eva's breath shuddered as she tried to catch it. 'Yes, but it's time . . . I have to let it go now . . .'

'Oh, I don't know, sweetie. He's your son, so it's only . . .'

'No, he's not mine,' Eva came in brokenly. 'He's theirs. It says so in the ruling and it's high time I made myself accept that.'

'That may be true, but you'll always be his real mother, and no judge with his rulings can ever change that.'

Eva swallowed hard, too close to the edge to be able to say any more.

'It's his birthday next month,' Bobbie murmured, almost to herself.

'He'll be sixteen,' Eva said. 'I gave Shelley a card to pass on. I probably ought to make that the last.'

Eva's sadness was almost too much for Bobbie. 'I so want you to be happy,' she said, lifting a hand to stroke Eva's hair.

'I am. I have so much,' Eva reminded her.

'It's true, you do, but if you'd allow yourself to have another baby – and please don't tell me Don doesn't want another, because we both know you could talk him round if you tried. It's crazy, the way you're depriving yourself of being a mother when everyone knows how wonderful you'd be. Your niece and nephew adore you, all the kids in the places you sponsor think you're God in female form . . . Which reminds me, I'll write a cheque before you go. Do I have a list of your latest worthy causes? I know it'll be the same as last time, but you're sure to have added some by now.'

'Thanks,' Eva said with a smile. 'I admit I have prepared a list. I was going to email it over to Naomi.'

'You do that. You know you can count on me. I thought adding the Smile Train last time was particularly poignant. Those poor kids with cleft palates – it's marvellous what that charity's doing to help.' After a moment's reflection she took a sip of her drink and put a hand to her head. 'You know, I've lost my thread,' she admitted. 'That keeps happening to me lately . . . Oh for heaven's sake,' she groaned as the phone rang again, and switching it off, she stuffed it under the lounger.

'Evie, I know this isn't going to be what you want to hear,' she said after a while, 'but actually I think you're right, you should try to let it go now, because we've got no idea if he will ever try to make contact, and you can't go on putting your life on hold . . .'

'Let's talk about something else,' Eva suggested, more upset than she wanted to show.

Bobbie gazed at her bleakly. 'If that's what you want,' she said, 'but please give some thought to what I said about Don. You still have time to make a family with him, and I'm sure if he thought it was what you wanted, then he would too.'

But that really would be giving up, Eva wanted to cry, and though she knew in her heart it was what she should do, she doubted she ever could.

It was past six o'clock by the time Eva finally stepped off the train at Dorchester station to find Don waiting on the platform, his handsome, worried face breaking into a smile as he spotted her.

'I'm sorry,' she groaned as she walked into his arms. 'I hope the delay hasn't messed up your day.'

'Everything's fine,' he assured her. 'I was able to rejig a few things and I even went in for a spot of delegation.'

'Never,' she cried incredulously.

Laughing, he took her bag and wrapped an arm round her shoulders as they started towards the exit. 'So how was everything?' he asked. 'Bobbie on form?'

'Still a bit jet-lagged, but, happily, as fabulous as ever. She sends her love.'

'And I hope you remembered to send mine.'

'Of course,' and going ahead of him into the car park she deliberately avoided the curious eyes that followed her. While on the train it was easier not to be noticed, simply by keeping her head down and allowing her hair to fall forward. With the wind blowing and her head up she couldn't help attracting attention, first with her height and what was left of her beauty – then with the travesty down one side of her face. This was when those who thought they recognised her realised that they did. She was even, occasionally, asked for an autograph, or offered sympathy from someone who felt for her tragedy. She was always polite, even friendly, but never engaged in anything more than the briefest exchange if she could help it.

'Oh my goodness,' she laughed as they reached the car and Don opened the door for her to get in. On the back seat was an enormous bunch of her favourite wild flowers, hand-tied with a very fancy bow. 'What have I done to deserve this?' she demanded, turning to look at him.

'I missed you,' he told her, 'and I thought you deserved a treat.'

Melting against him, she put her arms round his neck and kissed him deeply. 'I love you,' she murmured softly.

The way his eyes looked into hers left her in no

doubt that he felt the same way, but clearly afraid they were making a spectacle of themselves, he gently eased her into the passenger seat and went round to the driver's side. 'And another thing,' he added, as he started the engine, 'I thought I'd take you for an early dinner at the Riverside.'

Her eyes lit up with surprise. 'I'm starting to think I should go away more often,' she teased. 'What about Rosie and Elvis? We'll need to walk them. And the flowers have to go in water.'

'All taken care of. The flowers are in a water balloon, Livvy and Dave are on their way to the house as we speak to take care of the odds, I popped in earlier to feed the ducks and we know we can rely on Sasha to sort out the horses. So this means that all you have to do, my darling, is sit back and allow yourself to be spoiled.'

Eva laughed delightedly. How much easier and enjoyable life always seemed when she was with him, especially after how awful the ruling had left her feeling, as though she was a nobody who had no right even to want contact with her son, never mind actually to have it. 'Have you booked a table?' she asked, slipping a hand into his. 'You know how full it always gets.'

'I have and Arthur's looking forward to seeing you. He's also put some champagne on ice.'

Eva turned to look at him. Then the penny dropped. 'Oh my God, the deal's gone through,' she declared excitedly.

Rolling his eyes, he said, 'I wish. No, I'm afraid there's still a way to go. I thought we'd have champagne just because we can. So now, tell me how the meeting went with the chap from Madrid.'

'Milan, and it was a woman,' she corrected, used

to him getting these things mixed up, and settling back in her seat she began recounting as much detail as she knew he could handle of her only business appointment, while taking care to avoid her emotions as the horrible words of the ruling kept trying to break into her thoughts.

By the time they arrived at West Bay, where one of their favourite fish restaurants was nestled in sublime simplicity on the river's edge, it had started to rain. So parking as close as they could get to the small footbridge that crossed to the restaurant they ran across to find Arthur, the long-time owner, waiting to welcome them. Having been quite the dashing young man in his day, he still cut a handsome figure whose presence alone lent an air of sophistication to one of the region's most successful eateries. And the food was in a class of its own.

After showing Eva to the corner window table that she and Don generally requested, while Don stayed near the bar taking a call, Arthur instructed a waiter to bring the menus and left Eva to answer her own phone.

'Hi,' she said to Patty. 'How are things?'

'Fine,' Patty replied, sounding faintly harassed. 'Are you back now? Livvy said your train was delayed.'

'By almost two hours would you believe, but I've just sat down at the Riverside, so yes, back in one piece.'

'You're at the Riverside?' Patty repeated. 'Lovely.' Then, after a beat, 'So how did it go in London?'

As the truth contracted Eva's heart, she said, 'Great. Fine. Actually, nothing out of the ordinary. I spent last night at Bobbie's.'

'I know, I got your text. Is she OK?'

'As gorgeous as ever. Where are you?'

'Still at the office. Is Don there, by any chance? I need to speak to him.'

'Actually, he's on another call, but can't it wait? We're about to have dinner.'

'Of course. Sorry . . . I'm so up to my eyes here . . .'

'You always are. What do you need to talk to him about anyway? Has there been another break-in?'

'No, no sign of anything since the weekend. Just tell him . . . Tell him I got his email about the new alarm system, but I can't open the attachment. Actually, forget it, I'll speak to him tomorrow. Enjoy your meal and say hi to Arthur.'

As she rang off Eva was already regretting the way she'd snapped at her sister and would have called back had Don not been heading her way.

'What's up?' he asked, tucking his phone into an inside pocket as he sat down.

Eva pulled a face. 'I just got annoyed with Patty when I shouldn't have.'

His eyes narrowed.

'Please don't look at me like that,' she protested.

'So what was it about?' he asked, nodding to the waiter to open the champagne.

'She wanted to talk to you about some email attachment she can't open and I told her we were about to have dinner – so she's going to call tomorrow.'

Don was watching the glasses filling with champagne. 'Well, that doesn't sound such a big deal,' he commented.

'No, I don't suppose it was, so why don't we forget it,' and picking up her glass she waited until they were alone before saying, 'Here's to us.'

'To you,' he said with a smile.

Her eyes went down as she took a sip, and a shudder of nerves coasted through her as she considered the advice Bobbie had given her.

'You never know,' Bobbie had said before she left, 'it could work out the way it does for people who think they can't have children. Once they stop obsessing over it, it just happens. In other words, once you start focusing on another baby you could very well find your son knocking at the door.'

Eva had been mulling that over for hours now, and though it was probably an absurd way to think, she couldn't help feeling that it had a certain sort of sense. The question was, how would Don take it if she suddenly announced that she wanted to have a baby? In fact, she wasn't at all sure that she did, but maybe it was something they could at least start to consider before it really was too late.

'Something's going on in that head of yours,' he remarked teasingly, 'so come on, out with it.'

Smiling, she rested her chin on one hand as she said, quite casually, 'Bobbie and I were talking earlier and do you know what she thinks?'

'Enlighten me.'

'Wait for it – she thinks we should start a family.'

After a moment of astonishment, he frowned disapprovingly. 'Well, I guess Bobbie's entitled to her opinion,' he said, 'but it hardly has any bearing on what we've decided between us.'

'That's true,' she conceded, 'but have we decided? I mean, yes, I know we have, but I was thinking, Jasmine's seventeen now, and my son, if he ever does come to find me, will be all grown up by then, so maybe it wouldn't be so difficult for them if we had other children.'

His eyes darkened with confusion as he said, 'This

has come right out of left field. I always thought you were dead set against it.'

'I was, but things, people, change.'

He was watching her closely, apparently still trying to assimilate the shock. 'Is it what you want?' he asked directly.

Her heart skipped a beat as she wondered what he'd say if she answered yes. 'I'm not sure,' she answered truthfully. 'I guess Bobbie just got me thinking and . . .' She shrugged. 'I've been thinking, that's all.'

Sitting back in his chair, almost as though he'd been winded, he said, 'I can't help feeling there's more to this.'

Her eyes went to his. 'Why should there be? It's perfectly normal for people to start families . . .'

'But you've never wanted to before, and you know that I don't . . .'

'Because of Jasmine, but . . .'

'It's not only because of her. I have other reasons . . .' He broke off as he dashed a hand through his hair.

'Such as?' Eva prompted, not much liking the sound of that.

He shrugged awkwardly. 'I guess I just don't think now is the right time,' he responded vaguely.

She almost laughed. 'So when exactly would be a better time?'

'I don't know. Listen, you've just thrown this at me, so why don't we leave it for now and talk about something else? We don't want to spoil this evening by arguing, and this is something we should really be discussing at home.'

'Provided you're willing to discuss it.'

'Did I say I wasn't? I'm just not prepared to get

into it now, so shall we decide what we're going to eat?'

Picking up the menu Eva stared at it blankly, wondering what was really going through his mind. It had never occurred to her before that he might have 'other reasons' for not wanting children, and what he had said had thrown her completely. However, he was right, this was something they should talk about at home, and realising she was in danger of spoiling the evening unnecessarily, she reached for his hand as she said, 'I'm sorry. I didn't mean to upset you, especially when you've gone to all this trouble to make me feel so glad to be home, and special and loved.'

Never entirely comfortable with public displays of affection, his colour deepened slightly as he leaned over to kiss her on the mouth. 'Which is exactly what you are,' he told her softly.

She smiled into his eyes. 'Am I allowed to have lobster?' she asked playfully.

'You can have whatever you like. In fact, I think I'll join you, with Lyme Bay scallops as a first course.'

'And I'll have Thai-style gambas.'

Turning to summon a waitress, he winced as his phone started to ring. 'Great timing,' he muttered, fishing it out. And checking who it was, he said, 'Sorry, I'll have to take this. Hey Johnny, what's up?'

Deciding to text Livvy while she was waiting, to make sure all was well with Elvis and Rosie, Eva reached into her bag and was about to open her phone when to her surprise she noticed Johnny Frome, Don's operations manager, at one of the fish and chip stalls out on the harbour with his girlfriend – and he wasn't on the phone. Confused, she glanced at Don, then back at Johnny, and when she looked at Don again she realised from his expression that he'd spotted Johnny too.

Sitting back in her chair, she watched him start to laugh as he brought the call to an end. 'That was Johnny Silverton, head of security at a storage depot in Charmouth,' he told her. 'Apparently their alarms are going off and they can't find anyone suspicious on the premises, so I told him to call the office and get them to send someone out there.'

Surprised, she said, 'You're not going yourself?'

'Absolutely not, we're having dinner, and besides, I'm getting into delegation, remember?'

Amused and impressed, she raised her glass to him again, and after the waitress came to take their order he said, 'So where were we?'

Having no idea, Eva shrugged and said, 'Why don't I tell you what I've decided about Jasmine and the job?'

Looking instantly cautious, he said, 'Go on.'

'I'm definitely going to offer it to her,' she informed him. 'I know she'll probably turn me down, but even if she does at least she'll know I considered her.'

He wasn't looking thrilled. 'So you're OK about her being with us every weekend?'

'She practically is already.'

'And what if she does accept and it doesn't work out?'

'Well, I guess I'll have to deal with that if it happens, but let's try to think about this positively, shall we?'

'OK,' he agreed, drawing the word out slowly. 'So do you want me to talk to her first?'

'No, I just want to know that you support my decision.'

He cocked an eyebrow, and with the kind of sigh that told her quite plainly that he still wasn't sure about this, he said, 'I will if I have to, but frankly, I wish you wouldn't do it.'

'Well, frankly, I'm going to, especially as you can't give me a good enough reason why I shouldn't,' and after treating him to one of her sweetest smiles she changed the subject again.

Chapter Six

Eva was hurrying from the car park into South Street, passing the Electric Palace where she, Livvy and Dave had gone the night before to watch a couple of local dignitaries romping around in *The Mikado*, crossing the street to the ironmongers to add her name to a petition to block any more estate agents opening up in the town centre. Enough is enough! was their slogan – not very imaginative, but she supposed it got the point across.

After grabbing a couple of deliciously crumbling croissants from the baker's, she started back across the square waving a cheery hello to the eccentric milliner from West Street who, for reasons best known to himself, made the town hall clock chime thirteen at midnight on New Year's Eve. He'd also recently launched an international festival of hats in the town, which had been, to quote the local paper, a 'topping success'. Were she not already late she'd have stopped for a quick chat, but Livvy was at the dentist's this morning so it was her turn to open the shop.

Finding the mail and half a dozen trade magazines scattered over the front mat as usual, she scooped it all up and had a quick glance through as she wandered into the office. Though she could guess what most of it was, one white envelope surprised her, since it was franked with the *Saturday Siesta* logo – the magazine that had run the recent article. While intrigued to know what they had to say, she needed to get everything straight in the shop first, so moving the envelope to the top of the pile she left it next to her computer and went to put on the coffee.

By the time she'd finished vacuuming, dusting and straightening the jewellery displays, Livvy was coming through the door with a swollen cheek.

'Back already!' Eva exclaimed. 'I wasn't expecting you till gone ten. What did you have done?'

'A flaming filling,' Livvy slurred, looking mightily fed up. 'They called me at eight to say they'd had a cancellation so could I come right away? If I didn't live round the corner they couldn't have done that. Still, at least it's over for another six months.' She cast a knowing look around. 'Late in by any chance?'

'Only slightly. Coffee's on and there's a croissant for you, if you can manage it. What time are we expecting Coral?'

'Eleven, I think. It's in the diary. Actually, I'm feeling quietly confident that she's going to like what I've come up with. Well, I hope she is, anyway.'

'It'll blow her away,' Eva assured her. 'The touch of flamenco's totally her, and the colour blends are fantastic. Not everyone would have the courage, or flair, to put orange, pink and fuschia together, so bravo you.'

Perking up at the praise, Livvy said, 'And not everyone can wear it, but I think she can. Anyway, we'll see. Any sign of Mum yet? When we spoke first thing she said she might drop in.'

'I haven't seen her. Did she say how the meeting with the owners of the caravan park went?'

'No, she didn't mention it, but I bet she's glad to be home. You know what she's like, she hates being away unless we're all somewhere together, of course,' and wandering on through to the back she dumped her bag and coat in the office before going to pour them both a coffee.

'*Et voilà!*' Eva announced, turning over the sign on the door to declare the shop open. 'Good job I rang someone from crowd control or I don't know how we'd manage the rush.'

With a laugh, Livvy put the coffees on the counter and perched on the high stool to start activating the till. 'Oh, by the way,' she said, 'I had a text from Zoe saying she can definitely come in tomorrow, so we don't have to worry about getting cover. Any news on whether Jasmine's gracing us with her presence this weekend?'

Eva grimaced. 'She rarely lets us know in advance, and if I invite her the odds are she'll stay away just to be awkward.'

Livvy frowned.

'What?' Eva prompted.

'I'm just wondering if we're absolutely sure about offering her the job.'

'Oh, don't you start getting cold feet on me. It was your idea in the first place.'

'Correction, it was Jake's, and where will he be if the proverbial hits the fan? Swanning about sunny Sicily, or whatever tropical clime he manages to wangle himself along to next. Typical!'

'Well, you helped talk me into it,' Eva reminded her, 'and now I've committed I'm going to see it through. Have you looked at the emails this morning? No, of course not, you've only just arrived. I'll go and do that if you can make sure all the racks are in order. I noticed last night that we've only got a size eight left in the flapper dresses, so we ought to put out something else to fill in for the ten to sixteen.'

'I thought the oriental evening dresses would do it,' Livvy responded. 'I brought them down on my way out this morning. They're hanging on one of the rails in the office,' and lifting the credit-card machine from under the counter she began activating that too.

A few minutes later Eva was back from the office, looking utterly nonplussed as she stared down at the letter she was holding.

'Hi, Mum,' Livvy said as the door opened.

'Hello, darling,' Patty smiled, pushing a hand through her hair as she stamped her feet on the mat.

Eva looked up, but though she was relieved to see Patty after their terse exchange a couple of nights ago, she was too stunned by what she'd just read to pay anything else much heed right now. 'You're not going to believe this,' she announced, holding up the letter. 'They're only apologising.'

'No way!' Livvy exclaimed, all amazement. Then, 'Who? And for what exactly?'

'The article,' Eva explained. 'It's from the magazine. They've written to say they're sorry for any distress they might have caused.'

Appearing incredulous, Patty came to take the letter and held it so that she and Livvy could read it together.

Dear Mrs Montgomery,
    In deciding to feature you in our current series of articles entitled 'Where Are They Now?' I regret to say that proper consideration was not given to

132

you and your family before going ahead with publi-
cation. Now that the 'insensitivity' and 'recklessness'
of our actions has been pointed out to us, I would
like to offer my sincere apology for any unnecessary
distress you may have been caused. I hope it will go
some way towards demonstrating the earnestness of
this apology to tell you that the editor responsible
for the feature has now been removed from her
position.

Please be assured, Mrs Montgomery, that there
was no malice aforethought in our actions, and that
everyone at this magazine holds you and your safety
in the highest regard.

Yours most sincerely
Peter G. Giffins
Editor-in-Chief

Hardly able to believe it, Patty looked at Eva.

Eva said, 'I'm getting the impression it wasn't you who wrote to them?'

Patty shook her head. 'No, but it probably should have been.'

'I bet it was Don,' Livvy declared.

Reaching for the phone, Eva pressed in his number. 'Did you write to the magazine about the article?' she asked when he answered.

Sounding distracted, he said, 'What are you talking about?'

After reading the letter to him she said, 'So, was it you who contacted them?'

'Not me,' he replied. 'It'll have been Patty.'

'She's right here, and it's as big a surprise to her as it is to me.'

'Then Bobbie,' he suggested. 'It's the kind of thing she'd do.'

'If it was Bobbie I'm sure she'd have told me while I was there,' Eva said to Patty after ringing off.

'It could have been an outraged fan expressing their views,' Livvy suggested.

Patty looked at the letter again. 'I wonder why they sent it here and not to the house?' she said.

Eva shrugged. 'Does it matter?'

Shaking her head, Patty continued to read as she said, 'He's obviously quoting from the complaint, given the quote marks around "insensitivity" and "recklessness", and with language like "malice aforethought" I reckon he's taken advice from a lawyer.'

Eva nodded thoughtfully. 'Do you think that means whoever it was threatened to sue? But why would they, without at least speaking to me first?'

'No idea,' Patty replied, 'but for the magazine to have admitted they made a mistake, and in writing . . . Someone's obviously come on pretty strong.'

'I definitely reckon it was a fan,' Livvy declared, 'who's probably a lawyer,' and scooping a stack of sealed envelopes from under the counter, she said, 'If you'll excuse me, ladies, I need to take the last of these invitations to the post office so I can be back before Coral gets here.'

After she'd gone Eva turned to Patty and reached for her hand. 'I'm sorry I was so short with you the other night,' she said softly. 'Can I take it we're friends again now?'

Patty's tired eyes showed her affection. 'Of course we are, and it's me who should be sorry. I hope I didn't ruin your evening.'

'Of course you didn't. Everything was fine – though we went through a couple of sticky patches, one of

134

which was when we started talking about Jasmine. I'm definitely going to offer her the job, by the way.'

Sighing, Patty went to fetch herself a coffee.

'Was that supposed to mean anything in particular?' Eva asked when she came back.

'No,' Patty replied. 'You must do what you feel to be right.'

'Even though you obviously don't think it is.'

'It's not about what I think. It's about you and Jasmine. Now for heaven's sake, don't let's fall out again.'

Realising they were heading that way, Eva cast about in her mind to try and find a safer place and remembering the invitations, she said, 'Have you made a decision about modelling for the show again this year? You were fantastic the last time, so I'm really hoping I can count on you again.'

Patty glanced at the phone as it started to ring. 'Hadn't you better get that?' she suggested.

Keeping her eyes suspiciously on her sister, Eva lifted the receiver. 'Hello, Perdita's. Eva speaking.'

'Eva, darling, it's Coral. I'm running a little late this morning, I'm afraid, but I'll definitely be there. Probably closer to twelve than eleven, if that's OK?'

'It's fine,' Eva assured her. 'We don't have any other appointments today, so just get here when you can.'

After putting the phone down, Eva said, 'Coral's been held up.'

Patty shrugged. 'Sounds like Coral.'

Eva was still watching her closely. 'So can I presume she's seeing her lover?' she asked bluntly.

Patty's eyes closed. 'I've no idea, I haven't seen her since Monday.'

'So who is he?' Eva asked curiously.

Patty sighed and shook her head. 'I can't tell you that.'

'Why? Is it someone I know?'

'Eva . . .'

'It's OK, you don't have to tell me his name, only if it's someone . . .'

'You are impossible,' Patty chided. 'Just leave it alone, will you?'

Eva pouted. 'You know, it really bugs me the way you can keep secrets. I always think one of the best things about having them is being able to share them.'

Patty gave a cry of amazement. 'That is absolutely not true,' she protested, 'because you're far worse than I am. Anyway, enough . . . We were talking about the fashion show which, actually, is kind of why I came over, apart from to make sure we're friends, so please don't go falling out with me again now.'

'Oh no,' Eva groaned, 'I can't believe you're going to turn me down.'

'I'm sorry,' Patty grimaced. 'I felt such a fool last time. It's really not my thing.'

'But you looked fantastic, and everything you've tried on so far for this year looks so perfect on you. Oh Patty, you know I've been counting on you as my "older woman".'

Clearly feeling as bad as she was meant to, Patty said, 'Why don't you do it yourself? You've had all the experience, and everyone would love to see you take to the floor again.'

Eva was shaking her head. 'It's not going to happen. You know those days are behind me.'

'Then why not get on to Bobbie? I bet she'd have half a dozen girls down here in a heartbeat if you asked.'

'I'm sure she would, but it's not what I'm about with this shop, and you know it.'

'But you keep saying business is slow, so think of the publicity it would generate to have professional models showing your collection.'

'I stuck my head above the parapet once before,' Eva snapped angrily, 'and look where it got me, so why are you asking me to do it again?'

Realising her mistake, Patty groaned in dismay. 'I'm sorry, I wasn't thinking,' she said, putting her coffee down and trying to pull Eva into an embrace.

'Don't,' Eva said, turning away.

'I was only trying to suggest a way to help you.'

Eva's tone was still clipped as she said, 'It's fine, I'll work something out. Now, I expect you've got plenty to be getting on with, and I know I have . . .'

'I'm not leaving here like this.'

'Do as you please.'

'Eva . . .'

'What do you want me to say?' Eva demanded. 'That it's all right to turn me down and try to make me do something you know is out of the question?'

Patty was looking both contrite and baffled. 'I don't understand why you're making such a big deal of it,' she said gently. 'It's not like you to be so defensive.'

'And it's not like me to try and hide what I'm really thinking either,' Eva cried, 'especially not from you, but it's obvious you don't want to talk about it, so let's pretend it's not happening, shall we? I'm not a mother, you're not an aunt and there's no teenage boy out there that should be with me, but isn't.'

Patty inhaled sharply.

'Oh sorry, did you find that difficult?'

Looking slightly dazed, Patty said, 'Why now? Oh God, it's his birthday soon, isn't it? I'm sorry, I've been so preoccupied . . . Did you see Shelley while you were in London? That's what's happened, isn't it? You took a card for him.'

'As a matter of fact, I did. Do I need to apologise for that?'

'No, of course not.'

'Actually, that's not all that happened. I found out while I was there that my recent application to have some knowledge of him, maybe even a photograph, has been turned down. In fact, the judge made it clear that I shouldn't think of myself as a parent and as I'm sure you're quite happy to go along with that, that's what we'll do.'

Patty looked stunned. 'You didn't tell me about this.'

'Because I can't!' Eva shouted. 'You don't want to hear it, you know you don't, but I'm afraid it doesn't just go away because some judge says it has to . . .'

'Evie . . .'

'Stop! No! You have no idea what it's like because you have your children. You see them all the time, you know everything about them . . .'

'Please . . .'

'I love Jake with all my heart, but do you have any idea what it does to me when I see how close you two are? All these years, as I've watched him grow up, I've kept wondering what *my* son is like, if someone loves him as much as I would, if he's happy and healthy and how it would be if I could laugh with him, the way you do with Jake. I want to take care of him if he's sick, be proud when he

138

passes his exams, pack his clothes when he goes away.' She turned away as sobs tore her anger apart.

Going to hold her, Patty said, 'Evie, you know I'd do *anything* to have him with us, but it's not in my power and it isn't in yours either, so why did you . . . ?'

'Because I had to,' Eva seethed furiously. 'If you were in my position you'd understand that.'

'But I do understand . . .'

'No, you really don't, because if this had happened to you, if you'd made the worst mistake of your life and it was my nephew out there somewhere, I'd be sending him letters too, because you're allowed to, you know, as his aunt. I'd be letting him know how welcome he'd be in our family if he ever wanted to come, but you've never written to my son once. Not once.'

Patty's face was ashen. 'You don't know if his par— adoptive parents would allow it,' she said.

'Do you care?' Eva cried.

'Of course I care. I wish you'd told me about this application . . .'

Clasping her hands to her head, Eva said, 'I can't discuss this any more. Please, just go.'

Looking as torn as she did stricken, it was a while before Patty finally picked up her bag and started for the door. Turning back, she said, 'You're not the only one who carries guilt and pain in her heart, Eva, try to remember that sometimes,' and a moment later she'd gone.

By the time Livvy returned from the post office Eva had managed to make herself presentable, but Patty's parting words were still haunting her conscience like a restless ghost. It wasn't only what

139

Patty had said, it was how sad and defeated she'd looked as she'd said it. What could she be feeling pain and guilt about? Could she, Eva, have struck a chord when she'd tried to make her feel guilty for not writing to her nephew? Eva was already sorry for that, but she still wondered why Patty had never even asked to be in touch with him, when she normally had such a generous and tender heart. Perhaps she'd hardened herself in order to try and coax her sister back from the brink of despair, not wanting to encourage this impossible and futile search for her child.

'Are you OK?' Livvy asked, coming back from hanging up her coat. 'You seem very quiet.'

Eva feigned surprise at the question. 'Of course, I'm great,' she smiled. 'How are you? The swelling seems to have gone down.'

Livvy prodded her cheek. 'Mm,' she grunted dubiously. 'At least you noticed, which is more than I can say for my mother. Anyway, I'm going up to the workroom to get ready for Coral.'

'Actually, she won't be here till twelve, so would you mind if I left you in charge for a while?'

Livvy groaned in protest. 'I want everything to be set out properly.'

'I'll be back in plenty of time.'

'OK, just don't be late or I'll fire you.'

'Promise,' Eva smiled, getting to her feet. Then, realising she wasn't sure where Patty had gone, she sat down again and picked up the phone.

Finding herself directed to voicemail, she knew instinctively it was a punishment, and felt every second of it as she waited for the announcement to end. 'Patty, I'm really sorry. I shouldn't have sounded off like that. I want to come and see you.

140

Please call me back or text to tell me where you are.'

When there was still no response ten minutes later she rang Don.

'I'm sorry, he's just gone out,' the receptionist told her. 'You can probably get him in the car.'

Eva tried, but again found herself diverted to voicemail. 'I've had a big falling-out with Patty,' she told him. 'Call me back when you can.'

'What was it about?' Livvy asked from the doorway.

Feeling a jolt in her heart, Eva sighed as she said, 'I got angry because she doesn't want to model for the show. So it was all my fault and I think I've really upset her.'

Livvy looked doubtful. 'Oh you know Mum, she doesn't take these things to heart. She'll probably have forgotten it by now.'

Eva forced a smile. 'Even so, I ought to apologise, and I will as soon as I can find out where she is.'

Patty's head was resting on Don's shoulder. They were in his car, parked at the edge of a campsite close to Chesil Beach where almost no one was around, and the swell of the distant sea was like the silent turbulence in her heart.

'I almost told her,' she whispered hoarsely, still not quite able to believe how close she'd come. 'It was right there on the tip of my tongue.'

'But you didn't,' he said, tightening the arm that was holding her, 'which is all that matters.'

Was it all that mattered? She supposed so. Yes, it was, but that still didn't get her away from the fact that something in her had wanted to hurt Eva during those moments. It was still scaring her now. 'Imagine

141

what would have happened if I had blurted it out,' she said.

'You never would,' he assured her. 'It isn't in you to do something like that.'

'But at the time I did have it in me to hurt her . . .'

'And she felt it too, which is why she lashed out at you. That's what happens when sisters fight. You know that better than I do.'

'But knowing what I do, what I'm . . .'

'Stop,' he cut in gently. 'It's over. You'll make up the way you always do, and by tomorrow it'll all be forgotten.'

Because she knew it was what he needed to believe, she didn't ask what would happen after tomorrow, she only turned her head away so that he wouldn't see the tears that were filling her eyes. 'So you didn't know about the application either?' she said after a while.

'No,' he replied.

'Why didn't she tell us?'

'Because she knew we'd try to talk her out of it, and we would have.'

Patty nodded abstractedly. 'I should call her,' she said.

Putting his hand over her phone as she picked it up, he said, 'I'm still prepared to leave here and never come back. I only have to sign . . .'

'Stop, please,' she begged. 'I can't . . . It's not . . .' Unable to go any further with that, she said, 'I should go back to the shop to see her.'

'We both love her,' he whispered.

'Don't you think I know that?'

His head fell back as he closed his eyes.

In the end she pulled down the visor to check her

appearance. 'I don't think I should let Livvy see me like this.'

'You look fine.'

A hint of irony showed in her eyes as she turned to him. 'Spoken like a true man,' she said. Then, reaching for his hand, she held it with both of hers as she said, 'Thank you for coming.'

'I'm glad you rang,' he told her, and putting a hand to her face he brushed a thumb tenderly over her lips as he gazed into her eyes.

'No, no,' Eva insisted, tears blurring her eyes as she and Patty hugged. 'I'm the one who should be sorry.'

'Not true,' Patty protested. 'I should have been more sensitive . . .'

'Will you just stop!' Livvy cried. 'You're like a pair of teenagers going on and on. Or idiots, more like.'

'What I'm curious to know is what they fell out about,' Coral commented smoothly.

Eva looked at Patty as Patty said, 'It was my fault for not realising certain things . . .'

'It wasn't your fault,' Eva told her, trying to communicate even more with her eyes. 'I've been uptight since that article was published last Saturday, and as usual I ended up taking my frustrations out on my sister.'

'I see,' Coral responded, in a tone that was blatantly sceptical. To Livvy she said, 'That still doesn't tell us anything, but I guess it's good that it's all repaired now.'

'Absolutely,' Patty agreed, still looking at Eva. 'We need to talk some more about . . . Shelley,' she said quietly.

'There's no more to be said,' Eva replied.

Because this wasn't the time, Patty didn't press it. 'I ought to be going,' she said, glancing at the time. 'I'm supposed to be in Weymouth by midday.'

'You'll never make it now,' Livvy told her, starting back up to the workroom.

Giving Eva another hug, Patty said, 'Why don't you come for dinner tonight? I know it's short notice, but if you're not doing anything else . . .'

'We'd love to,' Eva assured her, promptly abandoning her plan to have a quiet evening at home with Don.

In the background Coral was making a pretence of idly browsing, while watching them closely.

'Are you coming?' Livvy asked her. 'We still haven't finished measuring up.'

'I'll be right there,' Coral responded, her eyes following Patty as she started to leave. 'I'm just going to have a quick word with your mum.'

Outside in the lane, with the door closed so they couldn't be heard, Coral looked Patty in the eye as she said, 'You didn't tell her, did you?'

Patty flushed with annoyance. 'Of course not,' she retorted. 'Do you think we'd be standing here now if I had?'

Coral's eyes stayed narrowed. 'No, I guess not,' she conceded. 'So what was it about?'

With a sigh, Patty said, 'I don't have time to go into it now . . .'

'Hey, Patty! You'll never guess,' a voice interrupted from the end of the lane.

They both turned and Patty broke into a smile of relief as Dave, Livvy's boyfriend, came romping towards them.

'I've only got a second interview with the Cherries,'

he cried with a triumphant grin. 'How amazing is that?'

'The who?' Coral wanted to know, treating him to her usual appreciative once-over.

'Bournemouth FC,' he laughed. 'I just got a text asking me to go in again the week after next. Where's Livvy? Please tell me she's inside.'

'I think you'll find her in the workroom,' Patty told him as he pushed open the door. 'And congratulations on getting this far. It's excellent news.'

'I didn't know he played football,' Coral remarked, as she watched him loping across to the stairs.

'He's a sports physio,' Patty informed her, 'and as far as I'm concerned the best part of his news is that Bournemouth is commutable, so he and Livvy might not be leaving Dorset any time soon.'

Coral's eyes went to hers, but before she could comment, Patty said, 'I have to go,' and after pressing a kiss to Coral's cheek she hurried off down the lane, feeling as relieved to get away from Coral as she was to have made up with Eva. The fact that it was all temporary wasn't something she was even going to try and deal with now.

Chapter Seven

Eva was running from the bridge, shouting for Elvis and Rosie to follow, but they'd disappeared from sight. She called again and again, but there was no sign of them and the intruder was coming closer. She raced into the house, slammed a hand against the emergency button and every window and door started to lock – except the one in front of her! It wouldn't close. *The window wouldn't close.*

'Don!' she yelled.

The stranger was in the garden. She tried to move but her feet were like lead.

'Don!' she screamed again, but no sound came out.

Sweat was burning like ice on her skin. His glassy eyes were staring straight at her. Terror tore a piercing shriek from her throat.

'Wake up, wake up,' Don was urging. 'It's all right. It's just a dream.'

'Oh my God, oh my God,' she gasped, still trying to fight. 'No, no, no!'

'Eva, it's a dream.'

She could hear Don's voice. He was nearby. She turned her head and there he was, looking worried, but calm, and then she began to register what he'd said. 'It's just a dream.'

She was safe. No one else was here. She was with Don and the house was all locked up.

'Oh my God,' she murmured as he drew her into his arms. Her heart was thundering in her ears and the nightmare still felt so real that she couldn't stop shaking. 'Rosie and Elvis wouldn't come,' she mumbled. 'And then the window wouldn't shut.'

'Sssh, ssh,' he soothed, stroking her hair. 'They're fine and so are you.'

It was several minutes before the powerful force of tension began to ease its grip, allowing her to breathe more evenly. 'It was horrible,' she said. 'I could see him. It was like he was right there.'

'But he's not. No one is.'

She nodded and kept on nodding, as though trying to persuade herself it was true. Eventually the cloying fear started to fade, and as she drew back to look at Don, still pale-faced and trembling, she attempted a smile. 'I'm sorry, I woke you,' she whispered.

'It's OK,' he replied, pulling her to him again. 'Would you like a hot drink?'

She wasn't sure. She didn't want to stay here alone. 'I'll come down with you,' she said.

Though she knew she'd find Rosie and Elvis snuggled up in their den, it was still a relief to see them when she got there – and their pleasure at this unscheduled visit was so boisterous and touching that it helped her to laugh.

'Silly me,' she murmured as she fussed them. 'Of course you're all right.'

As though agreeing, Rosie nuzzled her fondly, while Elvis about-turned and started to nudge his bowl towards her.

'You're such a pig,' she told him, and after treating

them both to a midnight snack she went back into the kitchen to find Don standing over the hob, staring blankly into space as he waited for the milk to warm.

'What are you thinking?' she asked, coming to circle her arms round his waist.

His eyes remained on the distant glow of moonlight as he said, 'That it's been a year or more since your last nightmare, so I'm wondering what might have happened to provoke one now.'

With her cheek resting against his back, she said, 'It's the article bringing everything back the way it did. It's been on my mind a lot since, so the only surprise really is that it hasn't happened before.'

Removing the pan from the heat, he turned to take her gently by the shoulders and gazed into her eyes. 'Patty told me about the ruling,' he said tenderly.

Eva swallowed and turned her head aside. 'I don't think it has anything to do with the nightmare,' she responded.

Not arguing with that, he said, 'Why didn't you tell me?'

'You know why.'

He nodded. 'I'm guessing this is why you're suddenly thinking about having another baby.'

'Maybe,' she admitted. 'Yes, I suppose it is.'

'Do you really believe that's the answer?'

She shook her head. 'Not the answer, no, because it wouldn't be him, but . . .' She took a breath. 'I'm not really sure what I want, unless you say you'd like to start trying.' Her eyes came to his. 'Would you?' she asked.

His expression was inscrutable as he held her gaze, then pulling her to him, he said, 'I don't know.

There's so much . . . I'll have to think about it some more.'

'We both should,' she agreed, and looking up at him she put her hands either side of his face as she kissed him. 'I'm sorry I didn't tell you,' she whispered.

'Like you said, I know why you didn't. I just wish you'd had a different outcome.'

Feeling the harshness of the judge's words devastating her all over again, she said, 'Me too. It didn't seem so much to ask, just his name and a photo, but it's turned out that they think I'll use it to try to find him through the Internet.'

Sighing wearily, he stroked the hair from her face as he said, 'It's been a tough week for you, what with that and the article last Saturday.'

'I've survived worse,' she reminded him wryly.

His smile was flat. 'Did you find out any more about that apology letter?' he asked, turning to replace the pan on the heat.

She shook her head. 'I haven't even tried,' she confessed.

'I'm with Livvy that it was an outraged fan,' he declared, starting to spoon cocoa powder into the milk.

'Who's a lawyer,' she added. 'You're probably right,' and going to fetch two mugs from a cupboard she said, 'Are you hungry?'

He almost laughed. 'After the enormous meal Patty served up tonight? I don't think so.'

'It was delicious, wasn't it? She's such a great cook.'

'Indeed she is. And it's good that you two have made up.'

'She still doesn't want to do the fashion show,'

Eva grumbled. 'Incidentally, I meant to ask on the way home, but it went out of my mind – what were you two arguing about earlier?'

Turning off the heat, he began to pour the cocoa into the mugs.

'Hello?' she said, leaning in to try and catch his eye.

'Were we arguing?' he asked, appearing confused.

'Well it certainly seemed that way when I found you in the study. You could have cut the atmosphere with a knife.'

His eyebrows rose. 'A bit of an exaggeration,' he said drily. 'I remember now. She was insisting that I invoice her for the time I've spent at Horizon View since the break-in, and I was saying that she only needs to be billed for the original call-out.'

'Because she's family? Or because that's how it works for everyone?'

'The former. I was trying to point out that it's the same as you giving her a discount at the shop, and as she doesn't seem to have a problem with that I can't understand why she has one with me.'

Eva smiled fondly. 'She has too much pride, my sister.'

He smiled too. Then handing her a mug, he went to turn out the lights. 'Do you think you'll be able to sleep again tonight?' he asked, as they started up the stairs.

'I'm sure I will,' she replied confidently.

But she didn't, because there was so much going round in her mind: her son, Patty, Don, Jasmine, and always back to her son. She didn't want to revisit how shattered she'd been by the ruling, but it was hard not to when she couldn't stop thinking about how different both their lives might have been if they were together now. She would no longer suffer the ache of emptiness that never went away, and he would have his real mother. What would she tell him about his father if he asked? Her heart churned with unease at the thought.

The natural mother, as a matter of law, is no longer the parent and should therefore not consider herself to be so.

'You're not asleep are you?' Don said quietly.

'No,' she replied, wondering, pointlessly, she knew, if she could ever hire someone to find him.

'Come here,' Don said, pulling her to him. 'It'll pass soon, the way it always does.'

Except it doesn't, she was thinking, or never to the extent Don liked to think.

By lunchtime the next day Eva had finished most of her charity paperwork and was getting ready to go to the shop to say goodbye to Zoe, with a thank-you bonus for how loyal and helpful she'd been. Don had taken off about half an hour ago to meet some clients at the golf club, though not before convincing himself that she was OK about being left at home alone after her troubled night. Even if she hadn't been she'd have told him she was, since she hated being a nuisance with her nightmares and paranoia and all the other issues she seemed to land on him all the time. However, she'd spoken the truth when she'd assured him she was fine this morning, because she had been – until a moment ago when she'd happened to look up at the CCTV monitor to find a car stopped outside at the gates.

She had no idea how long it had been there, or what the driver might be waiting for, because no one had rung the bell, nor were there any signs of someone getting out of the car. The image was too grainy for her to make out a number plate, she couldn't even be sure of the make, though it didn't appear particularly new, or large. For one heart-stopping moment she wondered if it was the stranger she'd seen in the garden last night, until she reminded herself that he was a dream. This, on the other hand, was unquestionably reality, and she must try to keep it in perspective, because people often pulled into the layby in front of their gates either to consult a map or turn round, or wait for someone to catch up. Almost certainly that was happening now; even so, unease was starting to gather in her chest as the car remained where it was and no one got in or out.

When a few more minutes ticked by and there was still no sign of movement, the only reason she didn't call Don was because he'd have started his game by now, and it wouldn't be fair to bring him back over something that was almost certainly nothing. He had people on twenty-four-hour duty at the office, so she could always ask one of them to come over. She would if whoever it was didn't leave in the next sixty seconds. Unless the vehicle had been abandoned, of course.

She thought about Dave then, Livvy's boyfriend, who'd come to the rescue a few months ago when a car had rolled into the layby with a flat tyre. She'd been able to see the driver doing his best to change it, but, worried that it might be a ruse to make her come out, with Don away at a conference, she'd rung Dave to ask him to pop up and check it out.

Maybe this person also had a flat and had called for roadside assistance rather than attempting to deal with it on their own. In fact, she was sure it must be some sort of issue like that. Or perhaps they'd pulled in to use the phone and it was turning into a particularly long call. There was absolutely nothing to get worked up over when it was the middle of the day, the car was in full view of the passing traffic and surely the driver had spotted the surveillance cameras training down on the gates by now. However, she wasn't going to leave the house until she was certain they'd gone, and then she'd be sure to keep an eye on her rear-view mirror to check no one was following her.

Suddenly her blood turned cold. The gates were starting to swing open. Only close family and Don's most trusted staff members had a remote control. She was already starting to dial Don's number when she noticed that the car was pulling away, and a moment later Jasmine's Mini turned into the drive.

Though her breath expelled in a rush of relief, Eva still didn't take her eyes from the monitor, needing to be sure that no one attempted to slip in behind the Mini, and that they really did leave. When they did, and the gates were fully closed again, she heaved another sigh of relief and put the phone down.

A few minutes later she was watching Rosie and Elvis barrelling off to the conservatory to greet whoever was coming in, and in their usual comic way they ended up jammed in the doorway.

'Hello, you fools,' Jasmine laughed as they popped out at her like a couple of corks, and dropping to her knees she began fussing them affectionately – not that she was ever unkind to the odds, on the contrary, she seemed genuinely to love them. However, she'd be fully aware that being mean to them was a sure-fire way of hurting her stepmother, so there was always the possibility she might turn on them, particularly if she knew Eva was watching.

'No, Elvis, my bag is not a sandwich,' she cried, swinging it out of the way, 'so please stop trying to eat it. Rosie, you're going to knock me over in a minute . . . OK, OK, I'll shake hands if I must.'

Apparently realising there really was no food on offer, Elvis about-turned and began one of his haughtier trots back into the kitchen, while Rosie decided to present her soft golden belly for a luxury rub. It was only when she stood up and caught Eva's eye that Jasmine shut down her smile.

'Where's Dad?' she demanded, hauling her heavy bag in through the door.

'Playing golf,' Eva replied, starting to unload the dishwasher. 'He should be back around five, he said.'

Jasmine sniffed, and heaving the bag on to one shoulder she started towards the hall.

'If you're not in a hurry I was hoping to have a chat,' Eva told her, keeping her tone neutral and her eyes on what she was doing.

With a long-suffering sigh Jasmine turned around. 'I'm meeting my friends at one,' she said tartly.

Eva glanced at the clock – it was just past noon. 'Then I'm sure we have time,' she said briskly, and picking up a towel to dry her hands she gave Jasmine a friendly smile.

Jasmine's eyes immediately narrowed. 'Oh God, you're about to start in with one of your dumb lectures about trying harder for Dad's sake . . .'

'Actually,' Eva cut in, already irritated, 'I'd like to offer you a job.'

Jasmine blinked, stupefied. A beat later her scowl was darkening with suspicion. 'Yeah, like, really,' she retorted rudely. 'In case you hadn't noticed I don't do horses, and I already do my share of walking the pig and the dog.'

Unable to remember the last time Jasmine had taken Rosie and Elvis any further than the end of the garden, Eva let it go. 'I need a new Saturday girl at the shop,' she explained, 'so I was wondering if you might be interested in taking it on.'

Another stunned silence lasted for several seconds before Jasmine's upper lip started to curl. 'Is this some kind of a joke?' she sneered. 'Because if it is, it's not funny.'

'It's not a joke,' Eva informed her.

Jasmine's expression was still sour. 'Why?' she demanded. 'What's in it for you?'

Eva's eyebrows rose in surprise. 'I get a Saturday girl,' she pointed out, trying not to hope she was about to be turned down.

'Yeah, but why are you asking me? Oh, I get it, Dad told you to. Well, sorry and all that, but I really don't want to work in some rubbishy little shop stuck in the middle of nowhere . . .'

'Actually, Dad isn't entirely supportive of the idea,' Eva interrupted. 'He's afraid it'll lead to more difficulties between us, and I guess it might, but Livvy happens to think you'd be great for the job and I agree. You like clothes, you get along well with people – apart from me, of course – but I'm not there much on Saturdays, so we don't need to worry too much about that.'

Though Jasmine's hostility didn't appear to be cracking, the fact that she hadn't yet flounced off with an even more stinging put-down than those she'd already managed suggested that she might not be dismissing the offer out of hand.

Eva smiled encouragingly. 'The wages are quite

good,' she continued, 'and you'd get a staff discount. OK, you get the discount anyway, and I know not much of our stock is to your taste . . .'

'You get a couple of cool things in sometimes,' Jasmine told her grudgingly. 'And Livvy always looks kind of, you know . . .' She shrugged, apparently unwilling to expand on the compliment. In the end she said, 'So do you actually really mean it?'

Eva started to feel worried. Jasmine surely couldn't be about to accept the offer. She must be planning some nasty little trick to make the rejection as spiteful as possible. 'I really mean it,' she said, bracing herself.

Jasmine was scowling again. 'What about Mum?' she said. 'We won't be able to tell her, she'll go mental if she thinks I'm working for you.'

Feeling sure she must be dreaming, Eva said, 'It's up to you what you tell her, but obviously it'll mean coming here every weekend.'

Jasmine shrugged. 'Brighton isn't that far away, and I come most weekends anyway.'

Eva said, 'What about your friends? Are you going to mind seeing less of them?'

Another shrug. 'They'll be cool about it. A couple of them have got part-time jobs now anyway, and there's always Saturday nights and Sundays.'

Realising she was starting to try and put her off, Eva said, 'So shall we give it a go?'

'Why not?' Jasmine said, as though she was the one doing the favour. 'Yeah, cool, let's do it.'

Eva only just managed to turn a jaw-drop into a smile.

For several seconds neither of them said anything as they tried to make themselves believe what had just happened. Then, clearly deeply embarrassed by seeming pleased, Jasmine said, 'This is like, totally amazing.'

Eva was thinking much the same thing.

'When do you want me to start?'

Eva threw out her hands as she laughed. 'It's Zoe's last day today, so if you have time maybe we can go and have a chat with her now. She can show you the ropes and let you know what it's really like working for me.'

Apparently not knowing what to say to that, Jasmine looked at Rosie and Elvis. 'They're so daft,' she said shakily. 'You've just got to love them, haven't you?'

Realising this could well be her way of saying thank you, Eva replied, 'I'm glad you think that, because they're pretty mad about you.'

Jasmine flushed again, then, not quite able to meet Eva's eyes, she said, almost defensively, 'I won't let you down, if that's what you're thinking.'

'I wasn't,' Eva assured her, since it was true at that moment. 'Actually, I can see you being a great asset to the place.'

Jasmine glanced at her awkwardly.

Too much too soon, Eva was thinking.

'I'll take my stuff upstairs,' Jasmine said. 'What time do you want to go? I mean, I can always call my friends and say I'll meet them later.'

'In that case,' Eva responded, 'we'll set off as soon as you're ready.'

'You're kidding me,' Patty murmured, when Eva rang to break the news. 'She went for it just like that?'

'More or less,' Eva confirmed, 'which just goes to show how brilliant your children are, because they had a lot more confidence in the idea than I did.'

'Where is she now?' Patty asked, watching Coral go to the window to find out who'd just pulled up outside the barn.

'Upstairs putting her things away, so I can't stay. I just wanted to let you know her initial reaction.'

'I'm stunned,' Patty admitted. 'Have you told Don yet?'

'No, his mobile's off, or he's out of range, but I'm sure he'll be as pleased as I am.'

'I'm sure he will.' Her eyes were still on Coral. 'Who is it?' she asked.

Coral turned round and mouthed a name that made Patty's heart sink with dismay.

'Is someone with you?' Eva asked.

'Only Coral. She came over for a coffee. So, I guess we wait to see what happens with Miss Jasmine. At least she's willing to give it a go.'

'It certainly seems so. Anyway, I'd better go before she comes down. Thanks for a fab dinner last night, by the way. Say hi to Coral for me,' and a moment later she was gone.

'What do you want me to do?' Coral asked, as Patty rang off.

'Tell him I'm not here,' Patty answered.

'He'll have seen both our cars.'

With a sigh of impatience Patty turned to the door as it opened. 'Reece,' she said, with a less than welcoming smile as her ex-husband stalked into the kitchen. 'To what do we owe this pleasure?'

'Don't be cute,' he told her. 'Hi, Coral. I'm glad you're here, because if I can't talk any sense into her, maybe you can.'

'You've got no right . . .' Patty began.

'Nor have you,' he growled savagely.

'I should go,' Coral said.

'No, stay,' Patty insisted. 'He's the one who should leave.'

'Not until you've heard what I have to say.'

'You've told me a thousand times how you feel about Jake . . .'

'This isn't about Jake,' he cut in furiously, 'and you damned well know it. Now, sit down and listen good and hard, because what's going on around here cannot be allowed to continue.'

Livvy and Jasmine were alone in the shop while Eva popped out to Waitrose and Zoe tinkered around up in the workroom. Jasmine had been up there with her until a few minutes ago, apparently eager to learn everything Zoe had to teach, until Zoe's boyfriend had rung on the mobile, when she'd come discreetly back downstairs.

'Sounds like they're having a row,' she confided to Livvy.

'It happens,' Livvy responded, admiring the bow she'd just tied at the top of a small Perdita's bag.

Jasmine looked around. 'It's not very busy, is it?' she commented.

'Not at the moment, but we had a bit of a rush earlier, though I have to admit half the people coming through the door at the moment are only here hoping to get a look at Eva.'

'What, you mean after the article in last Saturday's paper?'

Livvy nodded. 'We've had quite a few gawkers in this week, which is fine if they end up buying something, a bit irritating though if they just lurk around whispering and pretending they're inter-ested in the clothes when they're not.' Returning to the bag in front of her, she said, 'Even if someone only buys a room freshener, or a bracelet, it looks as though they're going away with something special if they have one of these,' and unfastening the bow she passed the bag over for Jasmine to try her hand.

Jasmine managed a smaller, less perfect bow, but for a first attempt Livvy decided it wasn't at all bad.

'Try again,' Livvy said, glancing up as someone came into the shop.

Jasmine looked round. 'Shall I go and ask if I can help?' she suggested.

'Not yet, we don't want to seem too pushy, and anyway, they might only be more gawkers. They're in for a disappointment if they are.'

Going back to the bag, Jasmine started tying the ribbon again, 'So, is it allowed to have phone calls while we're working?' she asked, as the sound of Zoe laughing carried down the stairs.

Livvy tried not to smile. 'Of course,' she replied, keeping an eye on the two ladies who were sifting through the rails at the front, 'provided you're not nattering away to someone while you're supposed to be serving.' Smiling as one of the women caught her eye, she said, 'Is there anything I can help you with?'

'Actually,' the woman said, taking a bright yellow top from one of the rails, 'I saw this in the window last week, and I'd really love it if it was in red, or blue.'

Livvy grimaced. 'I'm sorry, it only comes in that colour.'

'But I heard that you can make anything in any colour,' the woman protested.

'That's only in our exclusive range,' Livvy explained. 'The samples for that are on these racks

160

here. Or you can take a look through the catalogues on the table. Anything that catches your eye can be modified in whichever way you like, long sleeves, short; full-length, knee; drop-waist, Empire, and of course any colour or fabric is an option.'

The woman glanced nervously at the catalogues, muttered something to her friend, and affected a tragic smile. 'I don't think my budget would run to something like that,' she confessed, 'but maybe this top will work. I've just never worn yellow before.'

'It'd look great with black trousers,' her friend suggested.

The woman nodded agreement. 'Do you have any?' she asked Livvy. 'I mean, I've got a pair at home, who hasn't, but if I could try the top on with some it would give me a better idea of how it works.'

'We've got some really funky navy satin jeans,' Livvy told her, going to fetch them from a rail behind her prospective customer. 'They were in the window with that top last week, which is why we've only got a couple of sizes left. What are you, a twelve?'

'I wish.' The woman laughed regretfully. 'I might just squeeze into a fourteen if I'm lucky.'

Looking politely incredulous, Livvy whisked the jeans from the end of the rail. Not mentioning that they were actually a sixteen, she led the way to a changing room.

Minutes later the woman stepped out from behind the curtain, clearly thrilled with the way she looked. 'I reckon this colour's more me than I thought, don't you?' she asked her friend, turning from side to side in front of a full-length mirror.

'Your hair and skin tone are definitely dark enough to carry it,' Livvy told her, glancing round as the doorbell tinkled and two girls came into the

161

shop. Recognising them, she immediately moved in closer to Jasmine and muttered, 'Keep an eye on them, especially round the jewellery. Not to be trusted.'

Starting as she caught the meaning, Jasmine was instantly alert, and after a moment or two began a nonchalant stroll towards the display carousels. 'Can I help you with anything?' Livvy heard her ask as the girls turned their backs on her.

'Oh no, it's fine, we're just looking,' one of them answered, colouring to the roots of her scruffy blonde hair.

Jasmine continued to watch them as Livvy got down on her knees to pin the hem of the satin jeans her customer was wearing, while the second woman brought over a pair of spindly-heeled black metallic shoes. 'Aren't these just fab?' she gushed, holding them up.

'Oh my God, they're to die for,' the first woman groaned. 'Do you have them in a six?' she asked Livvy.

'We should, because we haven't sold any yet,' Livvy replied. 'I'll just pop through to the back to get them,' and after reassuring herself that Jasmine still had the possible shoplifters in her sights, she disappeared into the office. As she came back with the shoes in a box, she heard Jasmine saying, 'If you want to try anything just let me know.'

Satisfied with that, Livvy handed over the shoes. 'Here we are,' she said with a smile. 'They're a hundred and ninety-nine pounds.'

The woman's eyes nearly popped out of her head. 'You're kidding me,' she exclaimed, aghast. 'There's no way I can afford that.'

Livvy looked at her apologetically, though she

still had half an eye on Jasmine who was saying something else to the girls now, but Livvy wasn't close enough to make out what.

'I'm sorry, sweetie, I don't even want to try them on if they're that much,' the woman was telling her. 'I'll only fall in love with them and if I ended up taking them home my husband would have a fit. I really like the jeans, though. How much are they?'

'Eighty-five,' Livvy replied, starting to feel uneasy about whatever was going on over at the jewellery display.

'Gosh, that's a lot.'

'Yeah, but they're a bit different,' her friend told her, 'and they're really slimming. In fact, I wouldn't mind trying a pair myself. Do you have them in a ten?' she asked Livvy.

'I'm afraid not,' Livvy told her.

The woman looked deflated. 'I reckon you should get both,' she told her friend. 'The jeans and the top.'

'But not the shoes?'

'If they were even half that price they'd be too dear for us, and you've got those lovely sparkly ones we found in M&S, remember? I bet you haven't even worn them yet.'

Livvy barely heard the response as she watched one of the girls turning horribly pale, and the next moment she and her friend were rushing out of the shop.

It was several minutes before she could find out what had happened, since she had to wrap the woman's purchases in black Perdita's tissue, slip them into a bag and tie the bow, before taking a credit card for payment.

'So what happened?' she finally asked Jasmine as she returned from seeing her customers to the door.

Jasmine was trying to look superior, but was managing something closer to anxious as she attempted a shrug. 'I just told them that we know what their game is, so they might as well go and try their luck somewhere else.'

'Oh,' Livvy murmured, not wanting to think about how well that might have gone down. 'Did they say anything back?'

Jasmine's colour was deepening. 'Not really,' she replied, 'except one of them looked daggers at me, like she wanted to slap me if she only had the nerve.'

'Oh Jasmine,' Livvy muttered. 'You can't accuse people of doing something unless you're certain they have.'

'But you were the one who said they weren't to be trusted, so I assumed they'd been in here before, having a go.'

'They have, but as far as I'm aware they've never managed to take anything yet.'

Jasmine was biting her lip. 'Do you think they'll come after me?' she said worriedly.

Livvy shook her head. 'I don't know. No, I shouldn't think so, but you must be careful about what you're saying and who you're saying it to.'

Though Jasmine looked as if she wanted to bristle defensively, she wasn't quite pulling it off. 'Are you going to tell Eva?' she asked in the end.

Livvy had been intending to, but seeing the look in Jasmine's eyes she gave a sigh of exasperation as she said, 'Not if you don't want me to, but please make sure you don't do anything like it again.'

'I swear I won't,' Jasmine promised, crossing her hands over her heart. 'I thought I was doing the right thing, but I can see now that I was probably a bit over the top.'

Just a bit, Livvy managed not to say.

'Maybe I ought to mention it to Dad,' Jasmine said. 'You know, in case they do come after me.'

'Then he'll tell Eva. No, I'm sure you'll be fine.'

Jasmine was still looking worried. 'I'm sorry. I didn't mean . . . I've really screwed up, haven't I?'

'No, not really,' Livvy said comfortingly.

Still downcast, Jasmine told her, 'I know you probably won't believe this, but I actually really want this job.'

Touched by how much the admission had probably cost her, Livvy replied, 'I'm glad, because I think it'll suit you, but I must admit, you surprise me when you've never shown any interest in working here before.'

'That's because no one's ever asked me before. It's like you're all really close and you don't want outsiders barging in . . .'

'You're not an outsider,' Livvy told her. 'And I'm sorry if that's the way we've made you feel. It's just that you always go off with your friends when you're here . . .'

'Because I think you don't want me around.'

'Well, you know now that we do.'

It was too difficult for Jasmine to smile.

'I guess it's not been all that easy for you, with your mum feeling the way she does about Eva,' Livvy ventured.

For a moment Jasmine looked as though she might respond to that, but whatever she'd been about to say she ended up keeping to herself. 'I suppose I ought to go and see if Zoe's finished on the phone,' she said, looking towards the stairs.

Letting her go, Livvy returned to the counter and was about to enter the latest transaction in their hand-written sales book when Jasmine said over the banister, 'Thanks for giving me a second chance already.'

Astonished, Livvy looked up, but Jasmine had already disappeared around the bend in the stairs.

'It's like really weird watching her be nice,' Livvy was telling her mother that evening. 'I mean, it's cool, but I've never seen her like it before.'

'Well, I don't imagine you want her to be rude,' Patty retorted, going to take a tray of hot oil from the oven.

'No, of course not. I'm just saying, that's all. Anyway, what's got under your skin? You're all snappy and like everything's getting on your nerves today, so if you'd rather I left . . .'

'I'm fine,' Patty told her irritably. 'What time's Dave joining us?'

'He should be here any minute, but I can always tell him not to bother.'

'Livvy, you're not being helpful.'

'Oh, how sorry am I? Well, is it just the three of us?'

'Why? Do you want to invite someone else?'

'No-o, I was just wondering how many places to set, if that's all right, and I thought Don and Eva might be coming round.'

'They were here last night. Ow! Christ, that's hot.'

'Mum, for God's sake,' Livvy cried, grabbing Patty's wrist and dragging her to the sink.

'I'm all right,' Patty insisted, trying to snatch her hand away.

'No you're not. Look at you. *Mum*, put your hand under the tap.'

Doing as she was told, Patty allowed Livvy to cool the burn, keeping her head averted and almost relishing the pain as tears smarted in her eyes.

'OK,' Livvy said, pushing a towel at her mother, 'now what the hell is it with you?'

Patty started to answer, but lost it to a sob.

'Oh Mum,' Livvy wailed, tears rushing to her own eyes. 'You have to tell me . . .'

'Just leave it, please,' Patty implored, trying to turn away.

'I can't,' Livvy cried, pulling her back, 'and you wouldn't either if you were me. So come on, we don't normally have secrets from each other . . .'

'Oh Livvy,' Patty choked. 'This isn't something . . . You're so close to Eva, and I . . .'

'Mum, please. If it's about Eva you know you can tell me. Have you fallen out again, is that what's happened?'

'Ssh,' Patty said shakily. 'That sounds like Dave's motorbike outside and I don't want him to see me like this.'

Livvy was staring hard into her eyes. 'OK, but we're going to talk about this, because there's no way in the world you're carrying on the way you are without letting me do at least something to help.'

Wrapping her tightly in her arms, Patty said, 'I love you so much, my darling, I really do, but there's nothing anyone can do now. Nothing at all.'

Chapter Eight

'Hi, Elaine, it's me, Eva.'

'Hello dear,' her stepmother replied heartily. 'This is a nice surprise. How are you?'

'I'm fine,' Eva assured her. 'Are you back now?'

'No. As a matter of fact I was going to call later to let you know that I've decided to stay on in Cornwall for an extra week.'

Careful not to let her disappointment sound, Eva said, 'Then you must be having a good time.'

'It certainly is very uplifting here,' Elaine confirmed. 'Is everything all right with you? Patty told me about the letter of apology you received from the magazine. Most surprising, but certainly deserved. Have you managed to find out yet who wrote to tick them off?'

'No, because I haven't actually tried, but it's partly what I want to talk to you about. Don't worry, though, it can wait till you're home.'

Elaine fell quiet, and Eva could easily picture her soft brown eyes and endearingly wispy hair as she tried to weigh up what to do for the best. 'You know, I can always come back earlier if you need . . .'

'No, no, please don't do that,' Eva broke in hastily. 'Honestly, it really can wait.'

'You'd like me to find out for you, is that it?'

'No, because they'll know you're related to me. I've got a slightly more radical idea than that . . . Actually, it's probably completely off the wall, which is mainly why I wanted to run it past you first.'

Sounding cautious, Elaine said, 'What does Patty think of it?'

Wishing Patty's opinion didn't always count for everything, Eva said, 'I haven't told her because I know she'll think I've lost it.'

'I see.' Elaine's tone was wary. 'Can't you tell me on the phone what it is?'

Eva grimaced. 'If you don't mind, I'll probably find it easier if we're together, so why don't we forget it for now? Tell me about the conference. Did it go well?'

Reluctantly allowing the subject to change, Elaine said, 'It was marvellous, thank you. And I've made some lovely new friends, a couple from Newcastle in particular who've already booked into the retreat for a week in November. I'm afraid to say he has a tumour in a very delicate place, so I've been working with him on some inner healing and relaxation techniques. He's such a dear soul. I've already become quite fond of him.'

Unable to imagine Elaine being anything but fond of anyone, Eva smiled as she said, 'I'm glad for him that he's found you, I'm sure it's helping him immensely.'

'Well, I don't know about that, but I'm certainly doing my best.'

Being in no doubt of it, Eva said, 'I guess I should probably let you go. I send you lots of love.'

There was an ocean of affection in Elaine's voice as she said, 'God bless you, my angel. I shall look forward to seeing you as soon as I'm back.'

After replacing the receiver Eva continued to stand at her study window, staring out at the garden, where Jasmine was throwing bread to the ducks and Don was digging up a selection of vegetables for lunch while trying to fight off Elvis's enthusiastic assistance. Finding herself moved by the way Jasmine laughed at something her father said, she felt a pang of guilt for not having reached out to the girl sooner, since it was clearly, at least if the past twenty-four hours was anything to go by, all that had been needed.

Determined to carry on making an effort with her stepdaughter, she returned to her computer and the email that had prompted her call to Elaine. It was from the private investigator she'd contacted just over a week ago, saying he could see her next Friday at eleven. She knew very well if she told Patty – or Don – that she was planning to employ someone unconnected to the family to find out who'd complained about the article, they'd both see through such a pretext straight away. Elaine probably would too, but at least Elaine would be less judgemental and might even, because she was so soft-hearted, agree that using a private detective to make sure her, Eva's, son was in a loving family was a good idea. It was just a pity she wouldn't be able to talk to Elaine before next Friday. However, since she could see no harm in going to talk things through with the investigator anyway, she sent a quick message back to confirm that the date and time worked for her.

A few minutes later, she was upstairs in the bedroom going through the secret cache of three photos that she rarely looked at these days, when a knock on the door almost made her drop them.

'Eva? Are you in there?' Jasmine called out.

'Yes, yes, right with you,' Eva replied, quickly closing the precious album and tucking it into a drawer.

'I've brought you some coffee,' Jasmine told her. 'Shall I leave it on the table out here?'

'No, come in,' Eva insisted, unclipping her hair so it would fall across the unmade-up, damaged side of her face. 'I'm decent.'

As the door opened, Eva was trying to remember if Jasmine had ever been into this room before, and felt sure she hadn't. Nor, come to think of it, had Jasmine ever made her a coffee before.

'White, no sugar,' Jasmine announced, looking around for somewhere to put the mug. 'God, it's awesome in here,' she gasped in amazement. 'The colours are quality and it's so huge.'

With a smile of what felt like genuine fondness, Eva said, 'I'm glad you like it. Here, I'll take the mug. Are you having one too?'

Jasmine coloured slightly as she glanced back towards the door. 'Mine's downstairs.'

Eva only hesitated for a moment. 'Why don't you bring it up? We could sit and have a chat about how things went yesterday at the shop.'

Jasmine shrugged. 'I have to get going, actually. I promised Mum I'd be back by one today.'

Accepting that the invitation might have been too much too soon, Eva said, 'OK, but just tell me, do you think you'll like the job?'

Jasmine's response was immediate. 'Oh yeah, definitely,' she stated, her eyes burning with feeling. 'It was really cool and I think . . . Well, I hope Livvy said I was OK.'

'Actually, she said you were fantastic.'

171

The way Jasmine beamed through her spots reached straight into Eva's heart.

'So can we take it you're hired?' Eva asked, taking a sip of her coffee.

'Absolutely deffo, I mean, if you're sure.'

'I am, so's Livvy, so let's raise our mugs to Perdita's new Saturday girl – well, mug anyway. If you could stay longer we'd have a glass of champagne before lunch. Incidentally, has Dad mentioned anything to you about the job?'

'No, not really. He just asked how it went yesterday and if I'm sure it's what I want to do. You know what he's like, if it makes me happy he'll generally go for it. Excuse me, I'd better see who this is,' and taking out her mobile she checked the screen and coloured again. 'It's Mum,' she grimaced. 'I'll ring her back. Anyway, I just wanted to say thanks. I really appreciate it. Oh, and I thought I'd come on Friday night next week, if that's all right, so I'll be here in time to help Livvy open in the morning.'

Impressed and moved by her enthusiasm, Eva said, 'That's absolutely fine with me. I don't think Dad and I have anything planned for the evening, so maybe the three of us can go out for dinner.'

Jasmine's answering shrug didn't give much away, and as she turned to the door Eva was left feeling unsure whether they had a date for next Friday or not. It didn't matter, she could always get Don to check later in the week.

'Oh, just one thing,' Jasmine said, turning back. 'I kept meaning to ask Livvy yesterday. I was wondering why you called the shop Perdita's. Doesn't it mean little lost one, or something like that?'

Managing to keep her smile, Eva said, 'Yes, it does. I guess I just thought it was a pretty name.'

Jasmine nodded. 'Cool,' she muttered, and glancing at the house phone as it started to ring, she gave yet another shrug and left.

Scooping up the receiver, Eva wandered over to the window as she said, 'Hello? The Montgomery household.'

'Hey, it's me,' Livvy replied. 'Not interrupting anything, I hope.'

'Not at all. In fact your ears must have been burning, because it seems you made quite an impression on our new Saturday girl.'

'Well, if I did the feeling's mutual,' Livvy responded. 'Like I told you last night, she was dead keen to learn, and great with just about everyone who came in. Actually, there was a bit of a blip at one point, but I'm confident it won't happen again.'

'Tell me.'

'Honestly, it's not worth going into. So I take it she's now officially on board?'

'She is, starting next Saturday. I have to confess I'm pretty blown away by how much she's changed towards me in the last day. She even brought me a cup of coffee just now.'

'Mm. I don't mean to be negative or anything, but does this sudden transformation make you uneasy?'

Eva frowned. 'I'm not sure. Not while I'm talking to her, she always seems genuine enough then, but after, like now, I guess yes, it does make me wonder if it's too good to be true.'

'And you know what they say – if it seems too good to be true then it probably is. However, I'm definitely still up for giving her a chance.'

'Me too. So, is that why you called?'

'No, actually. I'm ringing to find out what you're doing this afternoon.'

'We don't have any particular plans. Why?'

'I'd kind of like to have a chat about something, so I thought if the weather keeps up we could take the odd couple for a walk on the beach.'

Liking the idea, and almost laughing at the way Don was trying to haul Elvis off the footbridge, Eva said, 'You're on. Why don't you come over around four?'

As usual, Elvis was attracting more than his fair share of attention as he strutted his stuff along the shale-strewn shoreline, where intrepid fossil hunters and a few hardy picnickers appeared delighted by his perky parade. In order to keep him from bestowing his presence on his unwary fans, Eva had him firmly attached to a lead, while Livvy repeatedly hurled a soggy tennis ball for the indefatigable Rosie to retrieve from the waves. For the beginning of October it was a surprisingly warm day, in spite of the purplish-grey clouds looming like scoundrels on a far horizon and a lively breeze blowing in from the sea. To prevent her hair from flying about Eva had pulled a black woollen hat down over her ears, and wrapped herself in a vivid red fleece with black leggings and black Nike trainers, while Livvy was all kitted out in a sublime mix of purple flouncy lace and bouclé wool, with a wide studded belt drooped round her hips and pink Doc Martens weighing down her feet.

'So I left Dave prepping for his interview,' Livvy was saying as she hurled the ball for the umpteenth time. 'He's getting really uptight about it already . . .'

'Eva! Eva, is that you?' someone called out.

Trying to hold Elvis back as she squinted into the sun, Eva's heart sank as she recognised the heavy bulk of everyone's least favourite town councillor lumbering towards her. 'Howard, how are you?' she said through an empty smile.

'Aha, it is you!' he declared jovially. 'You might try to disguise yourself under that hat and behind those dark glasses, but I'd recognise those legs anywhere.'

Not particularly enjoying the compliment, Eva said, 'Making the most of the fine weather, I see.'

'Couldn't stay indoors on a day like this, could I?' he chortled, rubbing his hands together. 'It'd be a crime even to think it. I see you've got the farmyard with you.'

His weirdly staccato laugh prickled the hairs on the back of Eva's neck.

'No Don?' he pressed on chattily. 'Don't tell me, he's on the golf course.'

'Not today,' she replied, seeing no reason to add that her husband was at home relaxing after an insanely busy week.

The councillor's beady eyes darted to Livvy and back again. 'Well, I guess he'll have plenty of time to spend there now he's sold out to Dobbs,' he commented heartily.

Stifling an irritated sigh, Eva said, 'Actually, it's the other way round. Dobbs are selling out to him and nothing's been signed yet.'

Pass drew back his head in protest. 'I think you'll find . . .'

'Howie, do you always have to charge on ahead?' his pudding of a wife gasped as she staggered through the sand to join him. 'He's always in such a hurry,' she complained to Eva and Livvy. Then breaking into a smile, 'How are you, my dears? Jolly nice to see you out taking the sun. And you too, you little rascals,' she added, glancing fondly at Rosie and Elvis, who were both impatient to move on.

'Nice to see you too,' Eva replied, wishing she could remember the woman's name. 'Anyway, you mustn't let us interrupt your walk . . .'

'Oh, no worries there,' Mrs Pass assured her. 'How's your mother?' she asked Livvy.

'She's good, thanks,' Livvy replied, hurling Rosie's ball back to the surf.

'I was just congratulating Eva on Don's deal with Dobbs,' Pass informed his wife.

'As I said,' Eva came in before Mrs Pass could respond, 'you haven't got the detail quite right, and nothing's been signed yet.'

'Then I shall be checking my sources,' Pass snorted, famously intolerant of being wrong about anything, 'because I'm positive . . .'

'Elvis!' Eva cried, as he began barrelling off along the sand, dragging his lead behind him. 'I'm so sorry,' she said to the Passes, 'he pulled it straight out of my hand. I'd better catch him. Lovely to see you,' and allowing no opportunity for protest she took off after the pig's determined little trot towards a bell-shaped niche in the cliffs. Since it was where they frequently paused to shelter from the wind while he noshed on an apple or a Mars bar and Rosie got stuck into her doggie choc drops, she had no doubt it was where he'd stop.

'Please don't let them come after us,' Eva muttered as she dived into the shallow cave and swung her backpack to the floor to unroll a blanket.

Bundling in behind her, Livvy peeped out again, trying not to be seen as she checked the Passes' progress. 'It's OK, they're moving on,' she declared with relief. 'What a couple of twitheads – or he is anyway, the way he always gets stuff wrong then turns all stroppy when you point it out.'

'I should have known better than to bother,' Eva replied with a sigh. 'All right, all right,' she laughed, as Elvis started digging his snout into her bag. 'Just let me get the wrappers off, will you?'

However, Elvis required no such niceties and had already wolfed down an entire chocolate bar, complete with paper, by the time Livvy had managed to ferret out Rosie's buttons.

'You're such a greedy pig!' Eva scolded, as he attempted to snatch Rosie's treats. 'If I didn't love you so much I'd grill you with tomatoes and eat you for breakfast.'

'Oh, don't listen to her!' Livvy cried, quickly covering Elvis's ears.

Her reward for such loyalty was a hearty burp, followed by one of Elvis's cheesiest grins.

'I swear he's half-human,' Livvy chuckled, as Eva handed both animals the kind of chew that would keep them occupied for at least ten minutes (in Rosie's case a big fat rawhide cigar, and in Elvis's a bag of Granny Smiths).

'So,' Eva said, pulling off her hat, 'you said you wanted to talk.'

'I do, about Mum – again.'

Experiencing a beat of concern, Eva said, 'Do you still think she's got something going with Dad?'

Livvy shook her head and sighed as she gazed out to where the tide was soughing back and forth from the shore. 'No, not really,' she replied, 'but something's definitely going on with her, and I was wondering . . .' Her eyes were heavy with worry as she turned to Eva. 'You'd tell me, wouldn't you, if there was anything wrong with her? I know she's bound to have sworn you to secrecy . . .'

Understanding what she was trying to say, Eva said, 'Livvy, if you're thinking she's sick, then you should know that I asked her straight out not more than a week ago and she swore there was nothing wrong. OK, I know that doesn't mean we should believe her, but if you've got any reason to suspect she's covering something up, I need you to tell me what it is.'

Putting her hands over her face, Livvy inhaled deeply as she shook her head. 'I don't know what she's trying to hide,' she said raggedly, 'but last night, it was so weird . . . It was like she was all over the place and then . . .' She swallowed hard and bunched her hands to her mouth. 'She only started to *cry* and you know Mum, she never cries.'

Feeling her own concern starting to build, Eva said, 'But what was she crying about?'

'That's just it, I don't know. We were a bit snappy with each other, mainly because she was so strung out, and then she started saying things like, "You're so close to Eva." I thought at first you'd had another row, but then . . .' Her voice was mangled by a sob, 'Then it occurred to me that she was thinking you'd be there for me if something happened to her.'

Oh my God, Eva was thinking. Patty surely hadn't lied to her about the cancer, she wouldn't, couldn't, she'd never get away with it, or not for long, so what would be the point? 'And I would be there for you,' she told Livvy, squeezing her hands, 'you know that, but I'm sure that's not it. Honestly, I'm convinced it's not,' she added, when Livvy kept her head down. 'But we have to talk to her,' she said decisively. 'We'll drop Rosie and Elvis at the house and go over there now.'

'There's no point. She's gone to some county show over in Devon with Coral and Will, and they're staying at some friend's place overnight.'

Well at least Will's there too, Eva was thinking tartly, unless it was a lie and Patty had gone as cover for Coral and her boyfriend. Hating the idea that her sister might have allowed herself to be used that way, Eva said, 'When's she back?'

'Tomorrow, I think, but I can always text to find out.'

'Do that. And I'll have a chat with Coral. Does your mobile work here?'

Livvy checked and shook her head.

'Nor mine. Come on, let's start walking back. The sooner we get on to this the better.'

'Ah, there you are,' Don murmured sleepily as Eva pushed open the door to the TV room to find him snoozing in front of the cricket. 'What time is it?'

'Almost five,' she replied, going to kiss him on the forehead. 'Have you been asleep long?'

'No idea.' He yawned loudly and gave a luxurious stretch. Then, reaching for her hand, he pulled her down next to him. 'Nice walk?' he asked, wrapping her in his arms and inhaling the salty scent in her hair.

'Mm, lovely,' she murmured, wondering whether or not to divulge her concerns about Patty. 'Rosie and Elvis were on form, as usual. They're drying off in their den now.' Maybe she'd wait until she'd spoken to Coral, or to Patty herself. 'Fancy a cup of tea?'

When he didn't answer she realised he'd half drifted off again, so easing herself gently back to her feet, she started to tiptoe out of the room.

'Where are you going?'

'To make a phone call.'

He opened one eye.

'By the way, I ran into the ghastly Howard Pass on the beach,' she said, 'who tried to tell me that you'd just sold out to Dobbs.'

At that his other eye opened. Groaning wearily, he said, 'That bloke never gets anything right. God knows how he ended up on the flaming council.'

'A question no one seems able to answer.'

After closing the door behind her, she returned to the kitchen, and taking the phone into the conservatory where she knew she wouldn't be overheard, she connected to Coral's mobile.

'Hi, it's Eva,' she said, when Coral answered. 'I'd like to talk to you. Is Patty in earshot?'

'Uh, no, not exactly,' Coral answered cagily. 'Is everything OK?'

'I'm not sure,' Eva replied, running a finger along the prickly fronds of an aloe vera. 'I need to know if Patty's confided something in you that . . . Well, that Livvy and I ought to know.'

There was a moment of nothing more than background noise before Coral said, 'That you and *Livvy* ought to know? Like what, exactly?'

Bracing herself, Eva said, 'Coral, if there's something wrong with her . . . If she's trying to protect us by not telling us that she's discovered another lump or something . . . You have to agree that trying to keep something like that to herself is crazy, so will you please . . .'

'Hang on, hang on,' Coral interrupted. 'I swear,

as far as I'm aware there's nothing wrong with her. Except she works too hard and doesn't get out nearly enough.'

In spite of it being exactly what she wanted to hear, Eva was still tense. 'Then if we're agreed she isn't sick,' she said, 'I think we also have to agree that she's stressed about something, and frankly, Coral, I can't help wondering if the strain of trying to support you through your *relationship* is starting to get to her.'

There was a horrible, loaded pause, before Coral said, 'I'm really sorry, Eva, you're probably right, I haven't given it enough thought, but I promise I will from now on.'

Feeling awful now, since she'd known Coral long enough to be aware that beneath the vampy veneer beat a very kind heart, Eva said, 'Thank you. I hope you don't think I've spoken out of turn . . .'

'No, no, not at all.'

'. . . and actually you're right, my sister doesn't get out enough, so we probably ought to try and do something about that. Anyway, I'll leave you to get on with your weekend now. Please don't tell her I rang.'

'No, course not.'

A few minutes later, after relating most of her conversation with Coral to Livvy, she said, 'So I really don't think it is the worst-case scenario, which is what matters the most.'

The relief was audible in Livvy's voice as she replied, 'Thank God for that, but I still say we should speak to her.'

'Absolutely. Have you managed to find out when she's planning to come back?'

'Tomorrow lunchtime, apparently, but she's going

181

straight to Horizon View, she said, and should be there all afternoon. So I've told her she has to be at home tomorrow evening because we're coming over and that's that.'

Easily able to imagine Patty's reaction to being bossed around by her daughter, Eva smiled wryly to herself as she said, 'I guess you didn't tell her why?'

'All I said was that it's been ages since the three of us got together properly, so we're bringing take-aways and a bottle of wine so she doesn't have to cook, or shop, or do anything except kick back, get wicked and enjoy herself.'

'Well done,' Eva laughed. 'We can pick something up from the Olive Tree or Waitrose and go straight there from the shop.'

'That's what I thought. So I'll see you in the morning?'

'First thing. We're expecting a delivery from Rowland's, don't forget,' and after ringing off she took herself back to the kitchen to make a steaming pot of Darjeeling for Don.

'Here we are,' she said, pushing open the door with her foot as she came in with the tray.

Clicking off his mobile, he sat up to clear a space on the table and used the remote to reduce the sound on the TV. 'Perfect,' he declared, as she started to pour.

'Who was that on the phone?' she asked as he helped himself to a digestive.

'Oh, just one of the guys. So, did you make your call?'

'I did, and happily everything seems to be more or less fine.'

'And you thought it wouldn't be because?' he prompted, taking the cup she was passing him.

'Oh, because I probably worry too much, especially where my family's concerned.'

Taking a sip, he nodded agreement. 'And which of us fortunate few were you checking up on today?'

She grimaced. 'As a matter of fact it was Patty, but I think it was just a case of making mountains out of molehills. Anyway, Livvy and I are going to see her tomorrow evening to make sure everything really *is* all right with her.'

He seemed perplexed. 'And why do you think it wouldn't be?'

Sitting cross-legged in front of him she said, 'She's seemed quite stressed lately, and apparently she got upset with Livvy last night in a way that isn't very like her.'

She took a sip of tea. 'But actually, do you know what I really think the problem might be?'

'Tell me.'

To her surprise, a sudden rush of tears sprang to her eyes. 'Oh God, I hate the thought of this,' she said, trying to fan them away, 'but I think she could be lonely.'

'Oh, Eva,' he murmured with a laugh, 'how can she ever be that when she's got someone who loves her as much as you do?'

'I don't mean lonely for a sister, or a daughter, or a son. I mean lonely for someone to share her life with.'

When he didn't answer she lifted her eyes to his.

He gave a lame sort of smile. 'I guess you know best about these things,' he said, 'but she always strikes me as someone who copes very well on her own.'

'I'm afraid you would think that because you're a man, but if you know someone . . . I mean someone single and suitable. We could throw a small cocktail party, or a dinner . . .'

'Evie, it might not be a good idea to interfere.'

'She's my sister. I have to do something.'

He still wasn't looking convinced.

'I want her to be happy,' she said, 'and I know you do too.'

With a sigh, he leaned forward to put his cup back on the tray. 'OK, I'll give it some thought,' he promised, 'and now, if you don't mind, I'd like to watch the rest of this match.'

'Oh, for heaven's sake, you two,' Patty laughed as she refilled their glasses with wine the following evening. 'The way you get yourselves all worked up over nothing shows I've failed completely when it comes to getting you to see sense. So I had a little cry on Saturday night. Big deal. Are you telling me it's not allowed?'

'No, of course not,' Livvy assured her. 'It's just really rare for you to get down and . . .'

'. . . and so it happened for five minutes and you start thinking it's time to get on the phone to the undertaker.'

'All right, maybe I overreacted,' Livvy conceded, 'but Eva was worried too, weren't you?'

'Absolutely,' Eva confirmed, swallowing her wine. 'Even Coral said she thinks you've been overdoing things.'

Turning to put the wine back in the fridge, Patty muttered, 'Coral's a one to talk. Now, would someone care to pop the samosas in the oven while I go to fetch some more wood for the fire?'

'There's loads right there,' Livvy declared, pointing to the huge stone hearth, where an enormous basketful of logs was practically spilling its contents on to the floor. 'Oh God,' she groaned ecstatically, 'I so love it in this kitchen when the fire's lit and something's baking and rain's running down the windows. It reminds me of when I was little and I used to snuggle up in someone's lap and fall fast asleep feeling like a princess safe from all the bad things going on outside.'

'And boy, were you a princess,' her mother responded drily. 'Almost as bad as this one,' she added, prodding Eva. 'In fact, there's a good chance you might have been worse.'

'Not possible,' Livvy protested.

'I know for a fact that you were,' Eva told her.

'And you are sure of that because you have cleverly blocked out how precious you were in your early years,' Patty remarked, returning to the fridge for more wine.

'Hang on, we're both driving,' Livvy reminded her, when she made to top up the glasses again.

'Mm, shame,' Patty retorted, 'but I'm not, so cheers, girls. Great to see you both. Oh, and Jake sends his love. We had a long chat just before you got here. He's loving Sicily and is now thinking he might give up the law after all to become a full-time model. I told him if he does he can be the one to break it to his father.'

Though Eva and Livvy laughed, Livvy sounded concerned as she said, 'He wasn't serious, was he?'

'Oh, for heaven's sake, what on earth has got into you two tonight?' Patty cried. 'You know how he likes to say these things to wind us up, and it's usually me who falls for it, not you.'

'It's great that he's having a good time,' Eva said quickly. 'I knew he would, especially with Bobbie around. Did you speak to her too?'

'As a matter of fact, no, but she did shout hi from a barstool, apparently, with an invitation to go and join her any time' – she took a quick gulp of wine – 'and frankly I felt quite tempted – except Jake tells me I wouldn't be able to handle so many fit young studs under all that sun . . . Actually, we probably ought not to go into what he really said, because I, for one, was shocked and *extremely* thankful he wasn't speaking to his father.'

After exchanging a glance with Eva, Livvy said, 'Actually, Mum, about Dad. I know you keep saying you're not seeing him . . .'

'Livvy, I see that man all the time and wish I didn't. I'm sorry to say that to you, but honestly, he's been driving me crazy. Never in my life have I been treated to so many lectures, or so much . . . stupidity. Is what I do any of his business? No! Do I want to listen? No! Does he care? Absolutely not, because he just keeps on and on ringing me up, dropping in, texting or emailing his irritating instructions on how I should run my life. His latest little nugget . . . Wait for this . . . He thinks I should join an Internet dating site.'

Stunned, but nonetheless impressed that Reece had come up with the same good idea that they had, Eva and Livvy avoided each other's eyes as Eva said, casually, 'You know, I don't think you should dismiss it just like that. I mean, it's pretty hard to meet men these days, especially the type who'd be good enough for you.'

Patty was staring at her in amazement. 'Frankly, Eva, I don't care what you, or Reece, or anyone else might think,' she retorted angrily, 'it isn't going to happen.'

'OK, there's no need to bite my head off,' Eva cried.

'But, Mum, everyone does it now,' Livvy told her. 'It's nothing to be embarrassed about, and we'd go online with you to help vet them. If nothing else, it could be a bit of a laugh.'

Patty was clearly far from amused. 'For you, maybe,' she said shortly, 'for me it would be a complete waste of time – of which I have precious little as it is. So, now, shall we change the subject?'

Livvy turned to Eva.

'Actually, no,' Eva stated. 'We agree with Reece's suggestion because we love you and we're worried that a) you're working too hard; and b) you're lonely – and don't start trying to tell me that's rubbish, because I know you are and *you don't have to be.* You're a beautiful woman, Patty . . .'

'All right, that's enough,' Patty growled. 'You've had your say, I've already given my answer, so moving on . . .'

'Mum, if you don't start doing something now, before we know it life will have passed you by and you'll be wondering why you're growing old all on your own.'

'Oh, for heaven's sake, you talk such nonsense sometimes,' Patty snapped, reaching for her glass.

'It's not nonsense,' Livvy insisted. 'It's a fact that could come true.'

Patty threw her a scathing look. 'If this is all you two want to talk about then I suggest you carry on without me,' she said, and snatching up the bottle she started to sweep out of the room.

'What the hell's the matter with you?' Eva shouted, going after her and grabbing the bottle back. 'Anyone would think we're trying to get you to do something life-threatening or insane. It's just dating, Patty. Everyone does it . . .'

'I don't want to date anyone, OK?' Patty raged. 'They're cheating bastards, the lot of them . . .'

'Don't talk rubbish. I know you've been hurt, but there are plenty of decent men out there . . .'

Patty's scoff was derisory. 'That's what you think.'

'Why wouldn't I when I'm married to one? So, if we could find you someone like Don . . .'

Patty's glass smashed against the wall. 'Just *leave it*,' she seethed.

Eva and Livvy stared at her in shock.

Seconds ticked by before Livvy said, 'Mum, come and sit down.'

'This is a total overreaction,' Eva told her, 'so now we want to know what's really going on.'

Patty's eyes closed as she growled in frustration. 'OK, if the only way to get you off my case is to go on the bloody computer to find me a man, then let's do it!'

Livvy glanced uneasily at Eva.

Eva's eyes were harsh as she stared at her sister.

'Mum, you've got to want to do it,' Livvy said lamely.

As Livvy's statement registered Eva wasn't entirely sure who started to break up first, her or Patty, she only knew the relief of falling into her sister's arms as they began to laugh, almost hysterically.

'But you have,' Livvy protested, not quite understanding what was so funny.

'You're absolutely right, my darling,' her mother told her, dabbing tears from her eyes, 'and I'm being a total pain in the neck about it, aren't I? So as soon as we've eaten we'll go online to start tracking down the fool who's dying to sweep an impossible forty-five-year-old wreck of the *Hesperus* off her size seven feet.'

Livvy looked at Eva. 'I don't think she should write her own profile, do you?'

'Absolutely not,' Eva agreed. 'You must leave that entirely to us,' she informed Patty.

'What's amusing you?' Don asked, glancing up from his book as Eva slipped into bed beside him. 'You're grinning like the proverbial, so I take it you girls had a good evening.'

'We did – in the end,' Eva sighed, sinking back against the pillows. 'It started off a bit tricky . . . You know how prickly Patty can be at times, but once we got her to relax . . .' She yawned loudly and thought about reaching for a magazine.

'So what did you talk about?' he asked, going back to his book.

Should she tell him about their hilarious trawl through the dating websites? Eva wondered. Since Patty almost certainly wouldn't want anyone to know, she decided she probably ought not – and besides, from a security standpoint she wasn't entirely sure he'd approve. 'Oh, you know, this and that,' she said airily. 'The fashion show, mostly. Patty's considering changing her mind about modelling, which is fantastic.'

After a moment he said, 'Mm,' showing that he was no longer paying close attention.

Remembering that her phone had beeped with a text during the drive home, Eva went to fetch it from her bag, and clicking through to messages she felt her heart turn over when she saw who the text was from.

Just to confirm that card has gone to letter box. Sorry should have contacted earlier, up to my eyes. Will be in touch if any more news. Shelley.

Going back to bed, Eva held the phone in her hand as she tried to imagine the journey her card would take now. Presumably his parents would be the first to receive it, but only after it had been vetted by a social worker, of course. The big question was always the same: would it get to him, or simply be thrown away – or held back until he got around to asking about her if indeed he'd even been told he was adopted? It was like reaching into the darkness from the edge of a precipice, or trying to make sense of a dream. She recalled the text Jake had sent Patty earlier saying he needed a new charger for his phone, and thought maybe she'd go over to Lyme Regis or Weymouth to get it for him, somewhere she wasn't known that would allow her to pretend in the shop that she was buying it for her son.

'He's such a scatterbrain, he loses everything,' she'd say. She might even add, 'His father despairs of him.'

Her eyes closed as she thought of how pathetic she was, stealing a few moments of fulfilment from a total sham. What would Don say if he knew? Would it make him any keener to discuss the possibility of starting a family?

Turning to look at him, she felt herself melting inside as she thought of how wonderful he'd be with a baby, perhaps awkward at first, but always loving and caring, protective and ridiculously proud. Yes, it was time, she was thinking as she rolled towards him, and she was sure he wouldn't take much talking round once he realised how much it would mean to her.

'Do you have something on your mind?' he murmured drily as she ran a hand over his chest.

Moving in even closer, she was about to take away

his book when her mobile bleeped with another text. Groaning irritably, while half afraid it might be a follow-up message from Shelley, she rolled on to her back and fished around for the phone.

'So?' he prompted when she started to frown.

'It's from Patty,' she said, 'telling me to answer my phone, but she hasn't rung. I take it the landlines are OK?'

'As far as I know,' and after reaching over to check he said, 'Yep, everything's fine.'

'I'd better give her a quick call,' and scrolling to Patty's number she clicked on. 'Hi, it's me,' she said when Patty answered. 'Is everything all right?'

There was an odd moment before Patty said, 'Yes, fine. Why shouldn't it be?'

'I just got your text telling me to answer my phone.'

'My text . . . ? You mean I sent it to you? Sorry, it should have gone to Jake. He left a message about ten minutes ago asking me to call him, and now he's not answering his phone.'

Relaxing, Eva said, 'Maybe he can't, if he needs a new charger.'

Sighing as she remembered, Patty said, 'He must have used someone else's phone to call me, and then forgot to give me the number.'

'You might have it stored if he rang your mobile.'

'Of course. This is so typical of him, ringing in the middle of the night after he gets back from a party wanting to tell me all about it. Sorry if I woke you.'

'It's OK, you didn't. Give him my love if you manage to get hold of him,' and clicking off the line she dropped the phone on to the floor beside her and turned back to Don.

'Is she all right?' he asked, raising an arm as she wriggled towards him.

'Mm, she meant to text Jake and sent it to me instead,' and, glad she hadn't bothered with a nightie, she slipped a leg over his.

'Oh, hell,' he groaned as she started to climb on to him, 'I opened one of the study windows earlier, and I'm not sure I closed it again.'

Used to how scrupulous he was about security, she let him go and rolled on to her back. 'Don't be long,' she instructed, while admiring his hard masculinity as he went to put on his robe.

However, he'd barely left the room before her thoughts were on their way back to Shelley's text.

Downstairs in his study Don used his mobile to call Patty. 'I take it the text was meant for me,' he said when she answered.

'I'm sorry. It was a silly mistake. I should have . . .'

'It's OK. Is everything all right?'

'No, yes . . . I mean . . .'

As she started to break down he said, 'I'm on my way.'

'No! You can't.'

'I'm on my way,' he repeated, and closing his phone he went back upstairs to let Eva know that he'd been called out on an emergency.

Chapter Nine

'Oh my God, they're totally awesome,' Livvy murmured, as she gazed down at the photographs in Eva's secret album.

Eva's heart flooded with love. Why had she never shown her niece these photographs before? she wondered. Possibly because for a very long time she'd actually forgotten she had them and, indeed, had only come across them last week, while looking for the adoption papers she'd signed almost sixteen years ago.

'Has Mum seen them?' Livvy asked.

'I'm sure she must have, at some point,' Eva replied, 'but I've no idea if she remembers them. I first found them years ago, when I was about seven or eight, hidden away at the bottom of Grandad's wardrobe.'

Still entranced, Livvy closed the album, smoothing her fingers over the cellophane-protected wild flowers on the cover – daisies, clover, faded little scarlet pimpernels – and said, 'I bet you picked and pressed these yourself.'

Eva gave a laugh at how well her niece knew her. 'The photos were in a scruffy brown envelope when I found them,' she said, 'and I thought they deserved better. So, I used my pocket money to buy the album, and over time I collected the flowers to make it as pretty as I could. I used to pretend I was doing it for my mother, so I'd have something to show her when she came back.'

'Oh, Eva,' Livvy murmured, putting a hand to her heart. 'That's so sad and sweet. How old were you when you finally accepted she was dead?'

Knowing that a small, hidden part of her still didn't want to accept it, Eva said, 'I guess I was in my teens. Or maybe it was before that, I just didn't want to come out and admit it. If I did it would make it real. So I used to pretend to myself that she'd run off with someone else, or that Grandad and Patty were lying to me, or that the world was lying to them. That way, there was always a chance she might come back.'

Clearly deeply moved, Livvy opened the album and gazed down at her grandmother's face again. 'I wish I'd known her,' she said. 'No one ever really talks about her. I mean, these aren't the first photos I've seen, obviously, but they're definitely the loveliest. Are you going to show them to Mum?'

Feeling a twist of unease that was part guilt and part nerves, Eva replied, 'I don't know if you can understand this, it's probably quite childish, but Mum knew her for so much longer than I did. She has lots more memories and she shared so much more with her than I ever did. These photos . . . Well, I guess they feel like mine, some small thing that I have all to myself.'

Still gazing down at the album, Livvy swallowed hard as she said, 'You must have really missed her, both of you.'

'Yes we did, but we never really talked about it much. I think Patty found it too difficult . . . I know Grandad did. After Mummy died he kind of disappeared inside himself, and for a long time I'm pretty sure his own mother was the only one who could really get through to him.'

'I always loved him to bits, but he was a bit like a child in some ways, wasn't he?'

Eva smiled as she thought of her father, and the truth of Livvy's words. 'It's what made everything so difficult for Patty,' she confided, 'even when Granny B was alive he still relied on Patty for almost everything. In some ways it was as though she'd taken Mummy's place. I remember her making sure his shirts were clean and ironed; preparing his meals; reminding him when he needed to go to the dentist, or chiropodist, or to see the bank manager. She even bought herself a birthday card once for him to write and give to her.'

'Oh my God, that is so sad,' Livvy cried, clasping a hand to her mouth.

Eva couldn't disagree. 'But we did have fun with him, too,' she insisted, 'especially when he took us on nature rambles naming just about every flower and tree we passed, pointing out birds' nests and badger tracks, inventing quizzes and games for us to play. But then we'd go home and he'd disappear into his study to mark homework or lose himself in some new research or other . . .'

As Eva's voice trailed off, Livvy said, 'It's amazing really, that you and Mum have turned out the way you have – you know, confident and normal, when Grandad was so withdrawn and shy and Granny was . . . Well, we don't really know what she was like, do we?'

Eva shook her head sadly. 'Mum knows more than I do, obviously, but as she doesn't like talking about her, and I never like to press it . . .'

Looking at the photograph of her grandmother again, Livvy said, 'You know, this could almost be you. Or Mum. You're so like her, both of you, in your own way. And she looks so . . . I don't know, thrilled I guess, like she's having a really fabulous time.'

Eva's heart tripped with pride. 'I'd love to know who was taking the picture, what they'd said, or done, to make her laugh like that.'

'You don't think it was Grandad?'

'Actually, I'm pretty sure it was, but I never dared to ask in case he took the pictures back again.'

Livvy turned to the next page and practically melted all over again to see her grandmother sitting on a swing with a bubbly-haired little girl on her lap, and an older girl standing beside her, with her arms wrapped around her neck.

'How old would Mum have been there?' Livvy asked.

'About ten, I should think.'

Livvy's hopelessly soft heart glowed in her eyes as she looked at Eva. 'I can't imagine what it must be like to grow up without a mother.'

'Luckily you haven't had to,' Eva said tenderly, 'and Patty and I had each other, remember?' She leaned across to turn to the last shot.

Captivated all over again by the picture of her grandparents together, Livvy said, 'Grandad looks so young there, doesn't he? And happy. You can see that he really loved her.'

'I think it's my favourite photo,' Eva confessed. 'When I was young, and didn't know any better, I used to think, with a child's logic, that she'd died because she didn't love us. After I found these photos I knew that wasn't true.'

Glancing up as someone opened the shop door, then closed it again, apparently deciding not to come in, Livvy said, 'Have you ever shown them to anyone else?'

Eva smiled as she shook her head. 'You're the first,' she told her, and felt a beat of pleasure to see how touched Livvy clearly felt by that. She couldn't help thinking of how wonderful it would be if one day she could show the album to her son, but knowing better than to allow herself to continue down that route, she uncrossed her legs and got to her feet. 'I promised to call Don by eleven to make sure he's up before Mrs H gets there,' she said, going to the phone.

Livvy looked startled. 'Is he unwell?' she asked.

'No, he had a call-out last night and didn't get back until gone four, so I left him to lie in this morning.' After making the connection to his mobile, she said, 'Hi, are you awake?'

'I am now,' he replied drowsily. 'What time is it?'

'Almost eleven. Your biggest fan will be turning up any minute, so I thought you'd want to make yourself decent – unless you have designs on her feather duster, of course.'

Livvy gave a choke of laughter.

'Yeah, very funny,' Don commented. 'Where are you?'

'At the shop, where else? We've had one customer through the door all morning, who bought a spectrolite pendant in the hope of raising her consciousness and blending with universal energies.'

'Mm, I detect an Elaine connection there,' he responded.

'How did you guess? It was one of her spiritual group who'd been sent by the sister of the woman who made the necklace, who, of course, is also part of the group. Anyway, I should let you get up now. Will you be home for dinner tonight?'

'I'll check my diary and call you later.'

As she rang off Livvy said, 'Seems late starts are catching this morning, because Mum was still in bed when I rang at half eight, and you know what an early bird she always is.'

Stretching luxuriously, Eva asked, 'Do you know if she's got any hot dates lined up yet?'

'She didn't say, but I think she's going to need a bit more encouragement before we can really get her to commit.'

'I'm sure you're right about that,' Eva agreed, and taking the album back she went to store it safely in the office.

'OK, you two, you're in charge,' Don informed Rosie and Elvis as he pocketed his wallet and scooped up his keys. 'Don't let that Mrs H eat too much or it'll spoil her girlish figure.'

'Oh, listen to you,' the portly old housekeeper chuckled delightedly. 'Now, I should have all your ironing done by the time you get back, just in case you're going somewhere special tonight, and unless you'd rather I didn't I'm going to give your study a good going-over today.'

'Go right ahead,' he told her, his eyes narrowing as his attention was caught by the security monitor showing a car at the gates. 'Is that someone waiting to come in?' he asked. 'Has anyone rung the bell?'

Following his eyes to the screen, Mrs H replied, 'Not that I heard, and I've been here ever since I arrived.'

As he registered what she'd said he smothered a

smile, and after telling her to keep any secrets she might find in his study he grabbed his mobile phone and left through the conservatory.

A few minutes later, as he approached the end of the drive in his Mercedes he saw, to his surprise, that the car was still there. With the benefit of real, as opposed to electronic vision, he was able to determine the colour was blue, the make a Fiesta and judging by the number plate it was about ten years old.

Driving over the sensors in the tarmac he waited for the gates to glide open, readying himself to offer assistance to someone who'd broken down, or at least to find out why they were there. However, having noticed the gates opening, the Fiesta's driver, who appeared to be a young girl of about Jasmine's age, quickly started her engine and pulled away. Presuming it was a friend of his daughter's who'd been establishing via mobile phone that Jasmine wasn't inside, he thought no more of it and let his own car roll forward to the edge of the road.

Once the traffic had cleared he was about to turn in the direction of Bridport when he noticed Patty's Audi parked in a layby across the road.

His insides tightened in a way that made him feel nauseous, and immediately stopping the Mercedes he ran across to find out what was going on.

'Patty?' he said, pulling open the passenger door.

Her hands were clenched on the wheel; her face was pinched with exhaustion and despair.

'Oh my God,' he murmured, and sliding in next to her he drew her straight into his arms.

'I can't go on like this,' she sobbed. 'I feel as though I'm losing my mind.'

'Ssh,' he whispered, feeling his own mind starting to unhinge as he held her close. 'It'll be all right.'

Pulling back to look at him, she said, 'No, Don, that's something it'll never be.'

His eyes remained on hers as the simplicity of her words tore its terrible truth through his heart. It would never be all right, because it couldn't be, and as the reality of it closed in around him as though to crush him with its might, he pulled her to him again. 'I'll sort it out,' he promised, his voice cracked with emotion.

'How? What can you do? We've tried to stop and . . .'

Taking her face between his hands, he gazed harshly into her eyes as he said again, 'I'll sort it,' and knowing that this time he'd have to, he sent a silent prayer to a god he didn't believe in for the help he knew he'd never receive.

Johnny Johnson's investigation agency was located on the third floor of a smart, Georgian townhouse, close to Exeter Cathedral. Eva had chosen to drive into the next county in the hope of avoiding anyone she knew; her visit to such an organisation would be bound to evoke curiosity and gossip if anyone saw her. As it turned out, she needn't have worried, since there was nothing on the doorbell outside, or anywhere else she could see as she walked up the stairs, advertising Mr Johnson's chosen profession. It was only when he showed her into his office, which appeared to be a room set aside in a spacious flat, that a clue was offered by a slew of crime-prevention leaflets and surveillance technology brochures pinned on his noticeboard along with a couple of 'missing' posters. One was a small boy – Terry, aged four; and the other a teenage girl – Kylie – with bunches and tattoos.

'Were they ever found?' she asked, as Johnson – a slightly overweight man in his mid- to late fifties, with intense grey eyes and a grizzled beard – showed her to a chair.

'Happily, yes,' he replied. 'But they're old cases from when I was on the force. I keep them there to remind me that not all missing kids end up lost for good. In fact, I'm glad to say, most don't.'

Unless you give them up for adoption, she couldn't stop herself thinking.

'These days,' he went on chattily, 'I tend to deal more in debt collections, pre-nup investigations, that sort of thing, and occasionally a cheating spouse. Which isn't to say that missing persons don't ever come my way, there are just fewer of them. Can I get you a coffee or tea?'

'Coffee would be nice,' she replied, feeling even more nervous than she'd expected. 'White, no sugar. Were you in CID?'

'I was indeed. Detective constable with Avon and Somerset for almost twenty years; Devon and Cornwall for the last five until I retired in 2009. Right, I'll just pop along to the kitchen to do the honours. Feel free to browse the magazines, or to use the facilities, they're just across the hall. My good wife keeps everything spotlessly clean, you'll be happy to hear.'

Liking him in much the same way she did most policemen, since one way or another they all seemed to remind her of Don, she opened her bag to take out the letter of apology she'd received from the magazine. She was wondering what Don would say if he knew she was here. He'd say she was being extreme, of course, that there was absolutely no need to go to such lengths to find out who'd written the letter of complaint when they could simply call up

201

the editor themselves. And no sooner would the words be out of his mouth than he'd realise that it was a ruse, a way of getting to know the investigator before entrusting him with the real reason she was there.

This was why she hadn't confided in Don, because she knew he'd do everything he could to talk her out of it.

'So, you've received a letter that's created a bit of a mystery,' Johnny Johnson said, bringing in the coffee and a small plate of shortbread displayed on a doily.

Eva cleared her throat. 'That's right,' she confirmed, watching him sit down. 'As I said in my email, I'd rather not contact the magazine myself, because I don't want to open up any kind of contact with them.'

'That's perfectly understandable,' he told her affably. 'Do you have the letter with you, by any chance?'

'Yes, of course.' She took it out of its envelope and handed it over.

As he read through the spectacles perched on his nose he sipped his coffee, and broke off a small piece of biscuit. 'I must admit, I saw the article,' he told her, showing no surprise at who she was, though of course he'd have realised as soon as she came in the door. 'Do you have any theories on who might have written the letter?'

'Not really,' she admitted. 'I've asked everyone I thought it might be, but it's none of them, so I'm afraid I've drawn a blank.'

His eyes came up to hers. 'Am I allowed to ask why it's important to know?'

Feeling her cheeks burn, Eva said, 'It's just curiosity really, and, well . . .'

When she didn't continue he simply smiled and said, 'Do you mind if I take a copy?'

'No, no, please do.'

After he'd run it through his printer he handed the original back and sat down again.

Realising she either had to leave now, or come to the real point of why she was there, Eva braced herself as she prepared to continue. 'There is one other thing,' she began awkwardly.

Appearing unsurprised, Johnson merely smiled encouragement.

'It's not related to this, exactly,' she informed him, 'or not at all, in fact. You see, I have a son who I gave up for adoption. He'll be sixteen soon. I know I'm probably not allowed to ask this . . .' She stopped as his hand went up.

'I'm sorry,' he said gently, 'I think I know where you're going with this, and I'm afraid it's a search we really can't undertake.'

Feeling every bit as crushed as she had by the judge's ruling, Eva forced herself to her feet. 'I understand,' she said shakily. 'I'm sorry for asking.'

'Please don't be.'

Wanting to get out of there before she disgraced herself any further by breaking down, she hooked her bag over her shoulder and turned to the door.

'I'll be in touch as soon as I have news about the letter,' he told her.

'Thank you,' she mumbled, and furious with herself for what she'd done, when she'd never really been in any doubt about what the outcome would be, she hurried down to the street as though trying to escape the frustration and despair that was building inside her.

* * *

Livvy was standing at the counter pretending to be on the phone when the shop door opened and her mother came in.

'Oh my God, it's you,' Livvy gasped, clasping a hand to her heart.

Startled, Patty glanced over her shoulder. 'Were you expecting someone else?' she asked.

Livvy put the phone down. 'No, not really,' she replied. 'It's just a couple of girls who came in here last Saturday were looking in the window just now.'

Blinking, Patty said, 'I don't think I'm following this.'

'It's OK, they've gone now,' Livvy told her. Then, registering how pale and dishevelled her mother looked, her tone immediately changed. 'What's wrong?' she demanded. 'Do you feel ill?'

'No, no, I'm fine,' Patty assured her. 'Just a bit of a headache. I've popped in to find out what you're doing tonight. Actually, whatever it is, can you cancel and come over to the house?'

Panic sprang to Livvy's heart. 'Oh, my God, Mum, you're . . .'

'It's not what you're thinking,' Patty cut in quickly, 'I swear, but we do need to talk.'

Livvy wasn't liking this one bit. 'What about?' she demanded. 'Is it Jake? Oh my God, something's happened to him.'

'He's fine, everyone is – actually, he texted earlier to say he'll be staying in London for a while when he gets back.'

'I know, I got it too. Mum, what's going on? You look totally terrible.'

'Thank you.'

'There's a mirror, see for yourself.'

Patty didn't move.

'For God's sake, will you please tell me . . .?'

'I will, darling, tonight. Can you come without Dave? Actually, maybe he could join us later. I'll organise some food.'

'I can do that. What I . . .'

'Please don't press it now,' Patty implored. 'I have something to tell you that is *not* related to my health, but it is important. Now, I'm due in Beaminster at five, so I have to go. Come when you've finished here. I should be home before you get there.'

For several minutes after the door closed Livvy stood staring at it, all concerns about the stalking shoplifters completely forgotten as she tried to imagine what was stressing her mother. She hadn't seen her like that since her marriage had broken up. Grabbing the phone, she quickly dialled Patty's mobile. 'Dad's dumped you again, hasn't he?' she cried.

'Don't be ridiculous,' Patty snapped. 'Now, please try to behave like the grown-up you are and wait until this evening.'

By the time Eva came through the door, half an hour later, there were two people in the shop and one in the changing room, so it was a while before Livvy could tell her about Patty's visit. 'Mum was here just now,' she finally managed. 'She wants to talk to me about something this evening, but she wouldn't say what it was. I don't suppose you have any ideas?'

Eva looked up from the invoices she was sorting.

'She swears it's not about the big C,' Livvy ran on quickly, 'but you should have seen her – she looked dead strung out again, and I definitely got the impression it's something serious.'

Feeling as unnerved as Livvy looked, Eva tried

to imagine what could be on Patty's mind, but after asking the same questions Livvy had about Jake and Reece, she ran out of suggestions.

'I don't know why, but I'm actually feeling scared,' Livvy admitted.

Eva was too, but trying to play it down for both their sakes she said, 'I'm sure it's something very simple, and she didn't realise what vibes she was giving off. She's like that sometimes when she's stressed or in a hurry.'

'That's true,' Livvy conceded, grasping the straw.

'But when you do find out,' Eva said, 'don't forget to call and let me know.'

Chapter Ten

It was gone seven o'clock and pitch dark by the time Eva turned her Smart car into the layby outside the gates, where she gave a wave to the surveillance camera just in case Don was watching. She knew he was already at home because he'd rung while she was in Waitrose wanting to know what time to expect her. As it turned out she was a little later than she'd guessed at, having detoured to the farm shop on the way back to collect some food for Rosie and order fresh supplies for Elvis, whose fodder had to be delivered, since it wouldn't fit in her car. Unless she took the Range Rover, of course, but after driving it to Exeter that morning, she'd swapped it for the Smart on her return home.

So, her darling husband would no doubt be pretty hungry by now, she was thinking to herself as she started up the drive, and was no doubt snacking on salami slices or cheese to keep himself going until the evening meal was ready. She hated to nag about his weight, particularly when he was in far better shape than many men his age, but now he was approaching fifty she couldn't help worrying about his diet. Only last month they'd attended the funeral of a friend who'd had a heart attack on the tennis court, and he'd been two years younger than Don.

So it just went to show that no matter how active someone might be – and with all his sailing, golf and running around for the business Don was certainly that – it was always important to eat healthily.

Inhaling the wonderful scent of woodsmoke that was drifting across the fields as she got out of the car, she went to take her shopping from the boot, loving the cold nip in the air that was making the prospect of a cosy evening at home doubly enticing.

'Goodnight,' a voice called out from round by the sheds.

Looking up, she saw the gardener kicking off his wellies before climbing into his truck.

'Goodnight Jack,' she called back. 'Has Don paid you yet?'

'Just,' he confirmed. 'I told him the bonfire's out, so no need to worry. She's just going to smoulder a bit for a while.'

'OK, thanks. Say hi to Jeanie for me.'

'Will do.'

As she headed for the house, loving the sense of nostalgia that came with chill autumn nights, she found herself wondering what everyone else was doing tonight, especially her son, wherever he might be, out there in the black beyond. Was he happy? Was he looking forward to his birthday? Livvy must be at Patty's by now, so she wondered how their chat was going, and what it might be about, then she was thinking of Jake and the fabulous time he was having on the shoot. It wouldn't surprise her if he did decide to take up modelling full-time, but she hoped he wouldn't. Far better that he continue with his plans to become a lawyer. Did her son's ambitions lie in the same direction? Or was his heart set on becoming a vet, or a banker, perhaps a musician?

Would she ever know?

'Hey, there you are,' she laughed, as Rosie and Elvis rushed to wedge themselves in the conservatory doorway. 'Yes, yes, your dinner's here, but I think you've probably eaten by now.'

'They have,' Don told her, coming to take the groceries and swinging them over the odd couple to carry them to the counter next to the fridge.

After fussing her beloved beasts, Eva edged them into the kitchen, while starting to unbutton her coat. 'Mm, it's lovely and warm in here,' she murmured approvingly. 'Did you light the fire in the den?'

'No, not yet,' he replied, and pulling the cork from a bottle of wine he filled two glasses, while she went to hang her coat in the utility room next to Elvis and Rosie's pad.

'Don't tell me, you've been on the phone ever since you got in,' she smiled, coming to give him a kiss. 'I know you have, or the snack cupboard would have been raided by now.'

With the ghost of a smile he handed her a glass as he said, 'You know me too well.'

'Mm, I've been looking forward to this,' she admitted, after savouring the delicious dark berry and wood flavours, and sipping again, she said, 'OK, I guess I'd better start unloading these bags.'

'Don't worry about them for the moment. I . . . I want you to come and sit down.'

Surprised, she said, 'But I should at least put the seafood away.'

'There's something I have to tell you,' he said, 'and . . . Well, I think it would be better if you were sitting down.'

Feeling an unsteadying unease starting to creep over her, she said, 'Has something happened? What . . . ?'

'Everyone's fine,' he assured her quickly, and taking her hand he led her to the table and gently eased her into a chair.

Her eyes were wide, almost like a child's, as she watched him sit down too. 'Is it the deal?' she asked, when he seemed unsure how to begin. 'Has something gone wrong?'

'No, no, it's not about that.' His eyes came to hers and her heart turned over to see how anguished he was. 'There's no easy way of saying this,' he told her.

She waited, searching his face, her breath so shallow that it was hardly there. Something serious had happened, or was about to, and she wasn't sure she wanted to know what it was.

'Eva, I . . .' He swallowed hard. 'I'm leaving you,' he said softly.

Though his words hit her heart like a blow, she knew she must have misunderstood, so she simply continued to stare at him.

'I'm sorry,' he said roughly. 'I'm . . . I – I don't know what else to say . . .'

'Do you mean you're going away?' she broke in. 'Is that what you're saying? It is, isn't it?'

His eyes went down as he said, 'I think you know what I'm saying.'

She sat back in her chair, a horrible tightness clenching her chest as she started to shake. She was in a nightmare, she had to be, because this was Don who she loved and who loved her. He would never leave her . . .

'I know this is hard . . .'

'I don't understand,' she whispered. 'I thought we were happy. Are you saying you're not?'

He looked away again, and as her world began to shatter into a thousand pieces she felt a horrible panic starting to rise up inside her. 'Don, what's happening?' she cried. 'I don't understand. I thought you loved me.'

'I do,' he insisted, 'it's just . . . Oh God, Eva, I'm sorry . . .'

'You have to explain. Why are you doing this?'

'Sweetheart, please don't make me hurt you any more than I already am.'

Her face was stricken with shock. Her head was reeling. 'This isn't making any sense,' she told him. 'If you love me . . . This isn't really happening, is it?'

He tried to speak, but no words would come.

'What have I done?' she urged. 'Please tell me what . . .'

'You haven't done anything,' he told her, his voice thick with pain. 'It's me and what I've done.'

'But . . . Oh my God, are you in trouble? Have you . . .?'

He was shaking his head.

Though understanding was trying to dawn, she couldn't let it. She had to be wrong, she just had to be, because Don would never cheat on her, or lie, or do anything to hurt her, and not only because he loved her – he'd just said he loved her and he wouldn't lie, he never lied – but because it wasn't in him to be that kind of man. So it had to be something else.

In the end, she said, 'I need you to tell me that what I'm thinking isn't what you're saying. Please, Don, *please*,' she begged when he turned his head away. 'This isn't you speaking. Something's happened . . . I don't know what it is, but this isn't you.'

'Eva, I'm sorry, but what you're thinking is what . . .'

Her eyes were desperate as she said, 'Actually, I'm not thinking anything, so why don't we just have dinner now and be as we always are. Shall we do that? Please can we do that?'

'Oh, Eva,' he said brokenly.

'No!' she cried, reaching for him. 'No, no. There isn't anyone else, is there? Please tell me I've got it wrong.'

His head stayed down as he looked at their hands.

'Oh my God,' she murmured, pulling away. 'Who is she? Is it someone I know?' When he didn't answer she could feel herself falling apart as she made herself ask, 'Do you love her? Is that what you're saying?'

His eyes came back to hers, and seeing so much guilt and unhappiness she leapt to her feet. 'No!' she shouted. 'You might think you do, but it's just a phase, an infatuation. It happens to men sometimes when they reach your age.'

His voice was shredded with emotion as he said, 'It's not a phase.'

His certainty was like a vice crushing her heart. She turned away, then back, her eyes glittering with confusion and pain. 'It has to be,' she told him.

Unable to look at her, he said, 'I never wanted this to happen . . . I . . . I'm so sorry. I wish I could change things, but I love her and I can't go on doing this to you, or to her.'

Devastated by his concern for someone else, someone who mattered as much – *more* – than she did, she felt herself starting to recoil and scream inside. Whoever she was, he cared for her so much that he was prepared to walk away from his marriage, turn his back on everything they'd shared and built together, like none of it mattered any more. 'Tell me who she is,' she said hoarsely. 'Please, I have to know.'

He nodded. 'Yes, you do.' But it was a long time before his eyes returned to hers, and when he said the name she reeled so hard that it was as though the world had crashed to a terrible halt and the ground was falling away. She reached out a hand to steady herself. She felt nauseous and panicked and so afraid she didn't know what to do. But it must be a different Patty, it had to be, because her sister, the only person in the world whom she loved and trusted more than Don, would never do this to her.

'We've fought it,' he said brokenly. 'Even when we knew we couldn't give each other up, we still tried . . .'

'Stop, stop,' she cried, putting her hands out as though to block the words. 'You have to stop. Patty's my sister. She'd never . . . She couldn't . . . Oh God, please, Don, tell me it isn't true. This is a nightmare. I have to wake up now. You have to make me wake up.'

'Eva . . .'

'No! Don't!' she shouted, unable to bear the sorrow in his voice. 'I can't listen to any more. If you mean this, if it's true . . . Oh God! No, no, no. Please don't let it be.'

As she dropped to her knees he came to gather her in his arms, and sitting her down again he took her hands in his. 'Eva, listen to me,' he said softly.

'I love you, Don,' she sobbed desperately. 'We

have so much together, our home, our lives, our marriage . . . You can't just throw it all away.'

Looking down at their joined hands, the diamond solitaire he'd bought her, the wedding ring, he tightened his grip as he started to speak, but she suddenly jerked herself away.

'How long?' she demanded shrilly. 'I want to know how long it's been going on, and please don't lie.' Realising what she was saying, she broke down again. 'Oh God, you're a liar, a hypocrite. You've been cheating on me while I've trusted you . . . Jesus Christ, you even let me talk about having a baby. How could you have done that?'

There was nothing he could say in his defence.

Slamming her fists into him, she cried, 'Tell me how long.'

Pushing a shaky hand through his hair he said, 'It's hard to say when it really started . . . I mean, I've always had a rapport with her, you know that . . .'

Her face slackened with shock. 'Are you saying it's been going on the entire time we've been married? Please don't . . .'

'No, of course not,' he interrupted. 'I'd never have married you if I'd felt the way I do now. It was you I loved then, and I still do, but what we have . . .'

'What we have means the whole world to me,' she told him, as though being reminded of it would make a difference to him.

'I know,' he said gently, 'and it always did to me, but with Patty it's . . . different.'

'Different how? What does she give you that I don't?' Her hands went to her head. *Patty, her Patty. How could this be happening?*

'Eva, I can see what this is doing to you, so please don't make me say any more.'

'No!' she cried shrilly. 'I want to hear how she makes you feel. I need to know what I've done wrong, why you love her more than me.'

'You haven't done anything wrong. I swear, you're not to blame.'

'Is it my scars? Do they repulse you? Is that . . .?'

'Oh God, you know that's not true. They never have, they never will.'

'Then tell me what I did wrong,' she yelled, her head thudding with confusion and fear.

'Oh Eva,' he groaned, his eyes closing in despair.

'If you tell me then maybe I can put it right.'

'Oh Jesus Christ,' he choked, covering his face with his hands.

As his pain intensified her own she stood staring at him, too distraught to know what to say or do next. In the end she said, 'You still haven't told me when it started.'

He took a breath that shook and broke as he tried to speak. He wiped a hand across his face and tried to make himself look at her. 'I guess four or five years ago,' he finally managed.

Her heart contracted with so much shock that she clasped her hands to it. 'You mean . . . You've been sleeping together . . .?'

'No, no, no,' he cut in quickly. 'That was when I realised, or I guess accepted, that my feelings for her were . . . what they are. But I never did anything about it. I couldn't, *wouldn't*. She's your sister, and nothing in the world would have made me want to leave you then. I told myself the feelings would pass, that they were an aberration, a phase as you said . . .'

Horrified to think of all that he'd managed to hide from her, and for so long, she said, 'So you stayed with me out of pity? Maybe you even married me out of pity.'

'No! It wasn't like that, I swear.'

'Did Patty know how you felt?'

'Not then, no.'

So he'd suffered in silence, wanting her sister while pretending to want her. How could she have not known? 'When did you decide to tell her?' she asked wretchedly. 'I suppose when you *fucked* her.'

Flinching, he said, 'Nothing like that happened until after her marriage broke up.'

So they *had* slept together. Why had she even doubted it? The mere thought of it was worse than the knife that had once torn into her flesh. It made her want to run and scream, do anything to try and block it from her mind. 'So until then you what? Just talked about it?'

'Sometimes, but not often.'

'And during those times, did you kiss?' Why was she asking this? Did she really need to know?

'Eva . . .'

'Did Reece know? Is that the real reason he left?'

'No, but he knows now.'

'How? Who told him?'

'He saw us together a few weeks ago. Since then he's been trying to make Patty break it off, or tell you, or leave Dorset . . .'

Reece, her champion? It hardly made sense. Nothing did. 'But she can't do either because she can't leave you?' she stated accusingly.

His head went down again and realising what agonies they'd been through, loving her and knowing they were hurting her, made her wish she was dead. 'So let me get this right,' she said breathlessly, 'you didn't sleep together until after *her* marriage broke up, so it was all right to cheat on me, but not on Reece?'

His face turned paler than ever. 'It was never all right, not ever,' he told her fiercely. 'Eva, I swear I didn't set out to hurt you . . .'

'Of course you didn't, you're the one who despises men who cheat on their wives, so I expect you despise yourself now.'

'Of course I do.'

'But not enough to make yourself stop?'

His eyes were racked with guilt as he looked at her. 'I've tried, believe me, and so has she . . .'

She turned away, unable to look at him any more. 'Who started it?' she demanded, the words seeming to strangle her. 'Who made the first move?'

Taking a breath, he let it go slowly. 'I was with her one day,' he said, 'about three months after Reece had gone. You know how hard the break-up hit her . . .'

'Yes, but I don't understand why any more, because she had you.'

'No, she didn't have me. I was – am – married to you, and how she felt about me didn't make losing her marriage any easier for her, in some ways it made it even harder.'

Unable to deal with Patty's feelings, she pushed them from her mind as she said, 'So you were with her one day . . .'

His eyes went down. 'She'd got herself into a terrible state about Reece and how she felt about me . . . I didn't know until I turned up at the cottage where I was supposed to be checking the alarm . . . She was there, and she just couldn't hold it together. I tried to comfort her and . . .'

'Oh God,' Eva groaned.

He allowed a few moments to pass. 'It wasn't planned,' he told her, 'neither of us meant it to happen, but . . .'

She wanted to shout, but her voice was like a distant lonely echo inside her head as she said, 'So the lies, the pretence, your *affair* has been going on for almost three years?'

His wretchedness was crushingly evident as he said, 'Yes and no. Most of the time we've avoided being alone together, and it was a long time, perhaps as long as a year, before anything physical like that happened again and . . . Oh God, Eva, I'm sorry,' he cried as she started to break down again.

'No, don't,' she sobbed, as he came to take her in his arms. 'To think of you . . . All this time . . . I trusted you, Don, and loved you. And all the time you've been making love to me, telling me you love me . . . It was all a sham . . .'

'It wasn't,' he told her earnestly. 'Being with you, loving you, sharing our lives, has been one of the best things that's ever happened to me.'

'But it's not enough, or it's not what you want any more. So I have to try to forget that I love you, and that my *sister has betrayed me* . . . Oh God, oh God,' she choked into her hands. 'I can't bear this. I don't want to be without you. You mean everything to me, both of you . . .'

'And you do to us, which is why this is so hard.'

As the 'us' resonated its awfulness through her, she fell against him, sobbing more desperately than ever. 'I've been such a fool.' She wept. 'Why didn't I see what was happening?' Lifting her head she looked helplessly into his eyes as she said, 'I trusted you, that's why I didn't see it.'

Knowing it was true, he tried to pull her head back to his shoulder, but she pushed him away.

'The other night, when she texted me,' she said, 'I suppose it was meant for you?'

Unable to deny it, he merely looked at her.

Her eyes closed as yet more agonies of betrayal swept through her. 'So you went out and stayed with her practically the whole night, while I thought you . . . Did you make love to her that night?'

'Eva, it won't . . .'

'*Did you make love to her that night?*'

'Yes, I did.'

As her breath caught on the admission, the image of them together cut so harshly through her that she started to slap and punch him with all her might. 'That's why you went to the guest room when you came back?' she accused hysterically. 'Not so's you wouldn't disturb me, but because your conscience wouldn't allow you to get back into our bed. I'm right, aren't I? Tell me I'm right.'

'It was both,' he confessed, touching a hand to his bloodied nose.

'And all the times I've wanted to see her and she's said she can't because she's with Coral, she was with *you*?'

'I don't know. Probably, sometimes.'

'Because it's not Coral who's been having an affair, it's *her* with *you*.'

As she smashed her fists into him again he grabbed her hands. 'Eva . . .'

'*Let go of me!*' she shrieked, trying to wrench herself free. 'Everybody knows, they've all been lying, feeling sorry for me . . .'

'Only Coral knew . . .'

'And Reece.'

'Please come and sit down,' he implored. 'Let me pour you some more wine.'

'I don't want any fucking wine,' she seethed, sending her glass smashing against the window.

As he continued to stare at her she felt something move against her, and finding Rosie and Elvis looking up at her with worried bewilderment her heart started to break all over again. He was going to leave them too, because they didn't mean enough to him either to make him stay. Dropping to her knees, she put her arms around them and wept into their adorable heads as he went to clear up the glass.

'Are you going to her now?' she asked when he came back to the table. 'Is she waiting for you?' Then, as another realisation dawned, more shock exploded in her heart. 'Oh God, this is why she wanted to talk to Livvy, isn't it? She's telling her, while you tell me.'

He didn't deny it.

Her eyes closed as she thought of Livvy and how hard she would find this. She wished she could go to her, but right now she wasn't able to go anywhere. 'So Patty didn't have the courage to come and face me herself,' she said dully.

'She'll come, if you want her to, but we – I thought I should talk to you first.'

As his words fell around her like dust, she turned to look through her reflection into the night. 'I think you should go,' she said after a while.

Stunned, he said, 'We need to talk . . .'

'What about? Haven't you said it all?'

'I don't want to leave you like this.'

'I don't care what you want,' she cried. 'It's about what I want now, and I want you to get out of my house, because this is *my* house and you don't belong here any more. No, don't touch me,' she seethed as he came towards her. 'It's all a lie, an act you're putting on, but you don't have to bother now. You've told me you're leaving, that you're in love with my sister, so go to her. Go now *and don't ever come back*.'

As she slammed out of the kitchen she was shaking so hard that she fell against the wall, banging her hands against it and willing him with all her heart to come after her – but the door didn't open and she couldn't make herself go back. Then the nightmare got worse as she heard him speaking, and certain he'd called Patty, she flung the door open ready to tear the phone from his hand. He looked up from Rosie and Elvis, and seeing the tears on his cheeks she lost control again.

'Don't speak to my animals,' she screamed. 'Don't even touch them. They're mine, do you hear, and you have no business even being near them.'

'I'm sorry,' he said, backing away.

Going to stand in front of them, she glared at him across the room. 'Why aren't you leaving?' she shouted. 'Why are you still here?'

Putting his face in his hands, he shook his head. 'Do you really, honestly want me to go right now?' he asked helplessly.

No, she didn't, she never wanted him to go, but what she said was, 'I'll send your things over to the barn, so you won't have any need to come back *ever*, and you can tell Patty that I don't ever want to see her again either,' and snatching up his car keys she threw them into his face before going to wrench open the conservatory door to make sure he left.

Livvy was staring at her mother in horrified disbelief. The room seemed to be closing in around her as the rain outside beat the windows, and the heat from the fire scorched the air. The words her mother had just spoken couldn't be true, yet the terrible angst on Patty's face told her they were. 'So now I know what's been wrong with you,' she said, sounding as dazed as she felt, 'and frankly, I wish I didn't.'

'Livvy, I'm sorry,' Patty responded shakily. 'I didn't mean it to happen, neither of us did . . .'

Livvy's eyes flashed. 'Then why the hell did you let it?'

Patty flinched. 'I know you're angry . . .'

'Angry?' Livvy spat incredulously. 'Angry doesn't even begin to do it. I'm disgusted, *ashamed* that you could do something like this to your *own sister* . . . This is going to totally devastate her, I hope you realise that.'

'Of course I do, and believe me, if I could change it . . .'

'You can, and you will,' Livvy told her, her voice shaking with rage, 'because if you don't you'll be losing me too.'

'Livvy . . .'

'No! I am not going to stand by and let you think this is all right, because it fucking well isn't.'

Wincing, Patty raised her hands and let them drop again. She didn't know what to do or say, how to explain herself, or to comfort her daughter. All she knew was that nothing Livvy said tonight could make her feel any worse than she already did.

'You have to end it,' Livvy insisted fiercely.

Patty nodded, then shook her head. 'Darling, we've tried . . .'

'*Then you have to try again*. And next time make it happen.'

'Listen, you know yourself that we don't choose who we fall in love with. It just happens and the harder you try to make it stop . . .' Why was she saying this? Why was she trying to justify it when it was completely unjustifiable?

'Whatever you say, it has to stop before Eva finds out,' Livvy told her forcefully. 'She can't know about this . . .' She fell silent as her mother's stricken eyes came to hers. 'Oh my God! Oh my God, please tell me you haven't . . .'

'Don's talking to her tonight,' Patty whispered.

'Then you have to stop him! You can't let him do it, Mum. He's not yours, he's hers . . .'

'Oh enough, Livvy, please,' Patty implored, putting a hand to her head. 'I know he's not mine, but it doesn't change the way I feel . . .'

'And what you feel matters more than what you're doing to Eva?'

'No of course it doesn't matter more, but to go on lying to her . . .'

'You wouldn't have to if you stopped seeing him.'

'I told you, darling, I've tried, but every time we tell one another it's over, all that happens is that our feelings seem to grow and the betrayal, the deception just gets worse. I can't go on like that and nor can he.'

'So why not let Eva's life be destroyed instead?' Livvy spat scathingly. '*You* are not my mother.'

'Livvy, wait,' Patty cried as Livvy started to walk out. 'I'm not asking you to try to understand, or to forgive, all I ask is that you listen – or at least that you don't go like this.'

Livvy kept her back turned.

'Dave'll be here any minute,' Patty reminded her. 'I'd like the three of us to sit down and work out how we go forward from here.'

Livvy spun round in disbelief. 'How *we* go forward?' she repeated contemptuously. 'There's no *we* here, or not that includes me, and besides, I think you've already taken that decision, haven't you?'

Almost buckling under her daughter's contempt, Patty said, 'OK, in a way, yes we have, but it's going to affect you, and . . .' She broke off as the phone rang, but Livvy was her focus now so she didn't attempt to pick it up.

They both stared at the machine as Patty's voice told the caller to leave a message, then Patty's head started to spin as Eva shrieked, 'How could you? He's *my* husband. What gives you the right . . . ?' Her voice was choked off by anger. 'I know you're there, you're hiding, you coward!'

'Speak to her,' Livvy shouted.

Patty fumbled for the phone. 'Eva . . .'

'Don't ever come near me again,' Eva yelled at her. 'Do you hear me? I never, *ever* want to see you again.'

'Oh God,' Patty sobbed as the line went dead.

'Well, what did you expect?' Livvy cried, snatching the receiver from her and banging it down. 'You had to know you were breaking her heart . . . Oh Mum, don't cry like that, just *don't*.'

'I – I'm sorry,' Patty gasped, trying to pull herself together, but the guilt and pain were too much and as she turned to press her face to the wall, sobbing and wailing in despair, Livvy came to hold her.

'It's OK,' Livvy soothed, choking on tears of her own. 'No it's not, but I don't know what else to say. Mum, it can't be good if this is how it's making you feel.'

'No, you're right,' Patty agreed, 'but I don't know what else to do. I've thought about selling up and

224

moving away, but this is where you grew up and where would I go? My whole life is here, so is everyone I love.'

'Then he should go away, at least then he wouldn't come between you and Eva.'

'Believe me, he's considered that. He's right on the brink of selling his company, but how is that going to help Eva? She won't want to leave this area any more than I do, and if Don goes without her . . .' It was all too much, she didn't have the answers and she doubted she ever would.

Livvy looked round as a set of headlights swept their beam across the curtains, and a moment later they heard the sound of a car door slamming.

'It'll be Dave,' Patty said, reaching to tear off some kitchen roll. 'Can you talk to him first while I go and try to sort myself out?'

'It's not Dave,' Livvy told her. 'I've got the car, so he'll be coming on his bike.'

Their eyes went to the door as footsteps approached. Even before it opened, Patty knew who was going to come through.

Don's face was so haggard and ashen that Patty's heart turned inside out.

'You've got a nerve coming here,' Livvy snarled.

'Livvy,' Patty said softly.

Though he flinched, Don's eyes stayed on Patty.

'So you've told her and now left her on her own,' Livvy cried in disgust. 'What the hell's the matter with you? Have you two completely lost your minds?' and grabbing her bag she slammed furiously out of the house.

Moments later, as her car tore across the gravel, Don said, 'Do you want me to go after her?'

'It wouldn't do any good,' Patty answered. Then,

putting a hand to her head, 'This is turning out to be even worse than I feared.'

Going to put his arms around her, he held her tight.

'I'm sorry. I feel I pushed you into it,' she said.

'Don't say that,' he protested, cupping her face in his hands. 'I was the one who made the decision to tell her now, and it was the right one because we couldn't go on the way we were.'

Not knowing any more if that was true, she said, 'Livvy asked how it could be right if it makes us feel like this.'

He continued to gaze into her eyes. 'I can't answer that,' he told her gruffly, 'I only know that it is.'

As his mouth came to hers she was flooded with so much love and desire, pain, guilt, shame and despair that she started to break down again. 'Oh God, what are we going to do?' she sobbed against him. 'Eva rang . . . She's beside herself. I feel I should go to her, but how can I when I'm the one who's devastating her life?'

'You should talk to her,' he said shakily, 'but not tonight. We'll see how she is in the morning.'

Patty nodded and tried to take a breath. 'I – I don't want you to go, but maybe you shouldn't stay here tonight.'

'No, I guess not,' he agreed. 'I just had to see you, make sure you're all right.'

Feeling as though she never would be again, she said, 'Where will you go?'

'I don't know. I haven't thought . . . Down to the boat, I guess.'

'Where is it?'

'Right now in West Bay, so not far.'

Putting a hand to his face, she said, 'Will you be all right?'

226

He nodded as he turned to kiss her palm. 'I'm worried about you, though. Can you call Coral? I don't want to think of you here alone.'

'I'll try her when you've gone, but you'll call me, won't you, if it all starts to feel too much?'

'Of course,' he promised, 'and likewise, you must call me.'

He kissed her again, tenderly, then deeply and passionately, holding her to him so that the entire length of her body was pressed to his. She wanted him to go on holding her and kissing her, making her feel as though their love was all that mattered, but it wasn't and they knew it and nor would it ever be, but that still didn't mean they could deny it.

In the end he pulled gently away and looked searchingly into her eyes. 'I love you,' he whispered with so much feeling that she could almost touch it.

'I love you too,' she breathed. 'I just wish it didn't have to be like this.'

'We'll get through it.'

'Will we?'

Keeping his eyes on hers he said, 'Yes, we will,' and after kissing her again he let himself out of the door.

As she heard him drive away her heart was tearing in two. She wanted desperately to go with him, to lie with him in the small cabin of his boat and try to forget why they shouldn't be together, in spite of knowing they never could. She wanted to turn back the clock so that tonight had never happened, or so that they'd never fallen in love, but that wasn't possible either. It was all too late, there was no going back now that Eva had been told, and she was so afraid of going forward that she could barely even make herself move.

Sinking down at the table, she buried her face in her hands and asked herself if anything, anyone, could be worth what this was doing to them all. How could love be so cruel, not to her, but to Eva who'd already suffered so much? Why had it felt the need to sweep through their family in such a ruthless twist of fate? She hated the fact that she couldn't control the way she felt, yet at the same time she knew in her heart that even if she was offered a way to stop loving Don she wouldn't accept it. He meant everything to her now, everything and more. It was as though she belonged to him, that all parts of her were parts of him too. She only had to think of his face, his wonderful eyes, his hands, his strong, capable body to know that without him she wouldn't want to go on.

And knowing that was how Eva would be feeling right now was almost killing her.

She was afraid of sitting here alone, but she wouldn't call Coral because she didn't deserve the luxury of comfort, were comfort even possible, and she knew it wasn't. She only deserved the hell she was going through, and would continue to go through for months, even years to come. Maybe for the rest of her life. Would it even be a life without Eva?

Starting as the telephone rang, she picked it up and said a quiet hello.

'Don just called,' Coral told her. 'I'll be there in ten minutes.'

As she hung up Patty broke down uncontrollably. Perhaps in times of need everyone should have someone, whether they deserved it or not.

Eva was standing in the kitchen, staring through the wall of sliding windows out to the stars. It would be a lovely day tomorrow, she was thinking. Cold, crisp, but sunny. In the distance the moon, looking proud and secretive in its impenetrable backdrop of night, was throwing its showy reflection over the sea, while closer to home, just beyond the patio, her little paddling of ducks was waddling off to bed for the night. She wondered what would happen to them when she'd gone, who'd take care of them and Rosie and Elvis, who'd been shooed into their den a while ago. Then there were the horses she'd rescued, her beautiful home, her shop, her charities – who would see to them all? She didn't want to leave, but if Don was serious about what he'd told her – and she knew he'd never put her through this if he weren't – how could she stay? She wouldn't be able to stand being so close to him and Patty, no longer a part of their lives yet knowing they were there, just down the road, sometimes running into them, missing them, hating them and still loving them so much that every time she saw them it would tear her apart. She wondered where they were now, if they were together, talking about her and trying to decide what to do next. Maybe they already knew; maybe they had it all worked out and it would be they who ended up leaving Dorset, not her.

Finding that prospect almost as hard as the thought of her own departure, she tried to push it from her mind. She'd find out in the fullness of time, and knowing she was going to be as helpless to stop them then, as she was now, almost brought her to her knees in heartbroken despair.

Before – and since – her eruption on the phone to Patty she'd drunk several glasses of wine, but to no avail, because nothing was blotting out her dread of what tomorrow might bring. It was looming there so large and terrifying that she could already feel it crushing her. How was she going to find the courage to deal with this, the strength to hold herself together when she wasn't even sure how she was going to make it through the night? She wanted Don back so badly, so desperately that her whole body was shaking with the power of it. She needed his arms, his comfort, his love in a way that seemed to fill her up and weigh her down and turn her inside out. But she had to deal with this alone, because he was no longer here for her to lean on, and Patty, her rock, her sister, her best friend, her mother . . . Patty meant everything to her, the whole world, so how was she going to cope without her?

'Eva? Are you all right?'

Starting, Eva turned around and felt a bolt of confusion mix with her surprise. 'Jasmine,' she said, using her fingers to dry her cheeks. 'I didn't hear you coming in.' It was Friday night. She'd forgotten Jasmine was coming. 'I'm sorry, I . . .' She didn't know what to say. How could she explain her tears? What should she tell her? She was Don's daughter, not hers, so wasn't it for him to do the explaining? Except Jasmine was here and looking worried, and Eva could already feel herself clinging to the connection to Don.

'I'm fine,' Eva managed, as she came to the table, but she wasn't because she was already falling apart again.

'What is it?' Jasmine cried, her face turning white. 'Oh my God, it's Dad, isn't it? Something's happened to him.'

'No, no, he's fine,' Eva said, realising Jasmine

needed that reassurance. What else was she supposed to say? Was he expecting her to pretend for his daughter who'd detested her until last week, who was probably plotting something terrible for her shop, who'd no doubt gloat when she found out the truth?

Looking Jasmine in the eye she said, defiantly, 'You'll probably be happy to hear that he's left me.'

Jasmine flinched as her mouth fell open.

'It seems you were right,' Eva told her, 'he was – is – having an affair and I, in my ivory tower, was too blind, too focused on myself, to notice.'

Jasmine went on staring, looking horrified and even, oddly, afraid.

'Well, don't you feel happy?' Eva challenged, snatching up an empty glass and trying to drink. 'It's what you always wanted, isn't it, to prove your mother right, that he wasn't to be trusted. Well, apparently he's not.'

To her amazement, and shame, Jasmine started to cry.

'It's not what I wanted,' Jasmine sobbed. 'I'm sorry I ever said that.' Then, 'I should go, sorry,' and turning around she started for the conservatory, but her way was blocked by Livvy coming in.

Clearly surprised to see Jasmine, Livvy moved on past her and went straight to wrap Eva in her arms. 'I don't know what to say,' she sobbed as Eva sobbed too. 'It's horrible. I just can't believe it.'

'Nor can I,' Eva told her, 'but it's happening and I don't know what to do.'

'We'll sort it out,' Livvy promised rashly. 'I don't know how yet, but we will.'

As they continued to hold one another, united in their grief, Jasmine stood awkwardly by, unsure how to help, until her eyes alighted on Eva's glass and going to fetch more wine from the fridge, and another glass, she poured them both a drink. 'I'm sorry,' she said as Livvy turned round. 'Have I done the wrong thing?'

'No, no, it's what we need,' Livvy told her, and picking up the glasses she passed one to Eva, while Jasmine watched and seemed at a loss for what else to do.

'I'm sorry,' she repeated in the end, 'I feel as though it's my fault.'

'How can it be your fault?' Livvy demanded, sounding sharper than she'd intended.

Jasmine looked at her helplessly. 'I don't know, I guess because he's my dad.'

'Did you really know he was having an affair?' Eva asked her. 'Is that why you kept saying it, because you already knew?'

'I wasn't definite,' Jasmine admitted, her face turning hot, 'but I thought – I thought something might be going on.'

'Why?' Livvy prompted. 'How come you saw it when the rest of us didn't?'

'I didn't see anything,' Jasmine explained, 'but a few times I heard him talking to someone on his mobile phone, and the way he kept his voice low, or rang off quickly when he realised I was there . . .' She looked suddenly anxious, almost afraid, as if she really did think they were going to blame her. 'I didn't want it to be true, I swear, I didn't, and I still don't know who it is . . .'

'It's my mother,' Livvy broke in shrilly.

As Eva's eyes closed, Jasmine's jaw went slack.

'Are you sure?' Jasmine mumbled, looking at Eva.

'Yes, we're sure,' Livvy stated. 'It's where he is now. I just left him there.'

Eva turned away, and realising her mistake Livvy quickly wrapped her in her arms again. 'I'm sorry,' she said, squeezing hard. 'I shouldn't have said that. I wasn't thinking.'

'It's all right,' Eva told her. 'Where else would you expect him to be?' She looked at Jasmine, and seeing how confused and upset she was, she said, 'Why don't you have some wine too?'

Going to fetch another glass, Livvy filled it and passed it to Jasmine.

'If you think there's anything I can do?' Jasmine offered. 'I mean, I can talk to him if you like . . .'

Pulling out a chair Eva sat down at the table, feeling another wave of shock and pain as she remembered it was where she'd been sitting when Don had told her he was leaving. Had that really happened, and only an hour ago? It seemed like a lifetime, another world, a dream.

Livvy and Jasmine sat down too, and for a while nobody spoke, afraid of saying the wrong thing and somehow making matters worse, if that were in any way possible.

Finally Livvy said, 'Where are Rosie and Elvis?'

'In their den,' Eva answered. 'You can let them out if you like.'

Going through the small passage that led to the odd couple's inner sanctum, Livvy pushed open the door and was almost bowled over as they rushed to get to Eva.

'Hello,' Eva smiled, tears welling in her eyes as she patted their daft heads. 'Horrid me, did I shut you away?'

Rosie's soft nose went into her hand to give her a lick, while Elvis nudged her with his snout. After he'd done it for the fourth time, while jerking himself towards the bar, they all managed a laugh as, taking the hint, Jasmine went to fetch an apple from the fruit bowl and a chew for Rosie from the cupboard.

Still watching the odds munching away, Livvy said, 'I called Dave on the way here to let him know I'd be staying the night, if you want me to.'

Eva smiled. 'Thanks, but you don't have to.'

'I know, but I thought . . . Actually, Don rang me as I got here. He asked me to stay. He doesn't want you to be on your own tonight.'

Wanting to run from the words, or scream at him that he should be here himself, not asking her niece to fill his place, Eva's eyes went to Jasmine. 'You can stay too, if you like,' she said, 'but I can't promise you're going to like what I have to say about your father.'

'It's OK, I don't feel as though I like him very much myself at the moment,' Jasmine replied.

Hating the reason for Jasmine's words, Eva looked down at her hands and saw how badly they were shaking. The horror of it, the dread, the pain were coming over her again. He'd gone. He wasn't coming back. Patty could no longer be in her life. She felt so alone, and afraid – so foolish, angry and filled with vengeance. She wanted to do something terrible to both of them, or to herself to punish them . . .

'If you don't feel up to going into the shop tomorrow,' Livvy said softly, 'I mean, I know you work here on Saturday mornings anyway, but if you don't want to come in later, we can easily manage.'

Unable to think that far ahead, Eva picked up her wine again, but as she took a sip another rush of panic swept through her as she wondered what

Don and Patty would be doing tomorrow. 'I'm sorry,' she gasped. 'I'm not dealing with this very well . . .'

'Nobody could,' Livvy told her forcefully. 'It's just the worst.'

Eva put her head back in an effort to stem the tears, but it didn't work because they just kept coming. 'So he went straight there,' she said raggedly.

'If it's any consolation,' Livvy said tenderly, 'Mum's in a terrible state too. I mean, OK, she deserves to be, but it's not like she doesn't care, because she really does.'

'Knowing that just confirms how serious it is,' Eva pointed out, and almost immediately wished she hadn't, not only because of how much it hurt her, but because of the regret that shot to Livvy's eyes. Then with a wry, shaky laugh, she said, 'It's odd, isn't it, that they should be together down there, while I'm up here with you, their children. Can you make any sense of that?'

Livvy and Jasmine exchanged glances as they shook their heads.

'But we're here for you all the way,' Jasmine told her.

'Jake will be too,' Livvy assured her.

Reaching for their hands, Eva held them tightly as she thanked them. There was no point in telling them that she'd rather be alone, because this wasn't easy for them either. And actually, with so many demons already starting to rise up from her past, maybe it wasn't a good idea for her to be on her own.

Chapter Eleven

Eva was surfacing from the depths of a dream, slowly becoming aware of early morning sunrays slanting through chinks in the curtains. She could hear a dog barking – was it Rosie? – and the seagulls crying. With her eyes still closed she rolled over to snuggle into Don, and gave a murmur of complaint when she found he wasn't there.

Then she remembered – and as her heart flooded with panic she sat bolt upright, almost crying out in denial. It couldn't be true, it just couldn't – but images of him and Patty waking up together were already taunting her with their cruel reality. She could see them moving into each other's arms, their bodies joining, their limbs entwining. She knew how it was to feel him holding her, his thighs locked to hers. He was tender and rough, rocking with a gentle, sleepy rhythm. Patty's eyes would close, her back would arch . . . Throwing aside the covers, she stumbled to the bathroom, already retching as the betrayal stifled and choked her. She had to get rid of the images, the torment, the jealousy, the fury . . .

When there seemed no more left inside she sank to the floor, her heart thudding a punishing tattoo, her eyes wet with tears and strain. Her breath was ragged, shallow and fearful. She wrapped her arms round her head and pressed her knees to her chest. She couldn't stand it, she just couldn't, yet she knew from before that this was how it was going to be from now on, the pain, the longing and despair that would churn her up inside, ravage and destroy her and never go away. Already trying to get through the next minutes was causing her to panic, but what about the days, weeks, months, even years to come?

Squeezing herself into an even tighter ball, as though to escape time and keep out the world, she fought back more nausea along with the pointless, pathetic hope of what else this early morning sickness could mean. She knew already it wasn't possible, and anyway, it would be the wrong way to try and make Don stay with her.

The longing for her son was suddenly so intense it was eclipsing everything else. She needed to know if he was all right, if the day was drawing close when she'd finally be able to look at him, speak to him, maybe even hold him. If she could do this, she'd have a reason to go on.

Hearing a knock on the bedroom door reminded her that Livvy and Jasmine were there and would probably be worried about how she'd slept, and how she might be this morning. Even if she could put it into words she wouldn't tell them, not only because of how self-pitying it would sound, but because she didn't want to make them feel any worse about what their parents had done than they already did. What an irony that they should be here, looking out for her, Jasmine especially, when not much more than a week ago they'd had virtually no relationship at all. With a horrible twist in her heart she realised why Don and Patty hadn't been keen for Jasmine to work at the shop: if she and Jasmine became close it would make it so much harder for them to be together.

'Eva, are you awake?' Livvy called out. 'I've brought you some tea.'

Not wanting Livvy to see her in such a state, Eva started to drag herself up, calling back, 'Could you take it downstairs? I'll come and join you in a minute.'

After Livvy had gone Eva stood over the wash-basin, splashing cold water on her face. As she looked at herself in the mirror she felt the terrible reality of what was happening starting to submerge her again. Her scars seemed so livid this morning, as though the pain inside was inflaming them, bringing them back to life as cruelly as the day they'd been inflicted. What she couldn't see, but was able to feel far more deeply, were the scars across her heart, the ones that had been left by her mother, Nick, herself – and the fresh, terrible wounds from last night, so deep and raw that the pain was almost impossible to bear. She tried to take a breath, but her chest was too tight. She drenched her face again. Her eyes were puffy and red, reminding her of how she'd paced the room in the night, picking up the phone and putting it down again, all the time longing, hating, fearing, willing, plotting, and doing as she already had this morning, tormenting herself with devastatingly erotic images of them together.

An hour later, after Livvy and Jasmine had left to go and open the shop, Eva was back in the bedroom staring down at the remnants of a white gauzy mist that was drifting like a whisper across the fields, and the playful sparkles of sunlight on the dew. She and Don had loved to take Elvis and Rosie for a walk on a morning like this, wrapped up warmly to keep out the wind, holding hands as they talked, or with arms around one another as they simply strolled and soaked up the splendour of their stretch of the Jurassic coast. She didn't have it in her to take her beloved beasts on her own today, and she wouldn't force herself, because of how it might end. But she would take them, when she was ready to deal with how alone she would feel without Don at her side, and was able to answer their neighbours' queries as to where he was. Her eyes closed as the thought of admitting he'd left her brought more devastation to her heart. It wasn't something she could ever imagine facing up to, she'd do anything to avoid it, but sooner or later she wouldn't have a choice.

Her eyes were stinging with more tears as they moved on around the garden, seeing many more happy memories than flowers and trees. They'd worked so hard on turning it into their own piece of paradise, laying out the lawns and pathways, planting vegetables, trees and flowers, and creating Elvis's private little paddock. She recalled the endless discussions on where to put the summer house and how large to make the pond. They'd known straight away where to set up their private enclave – a place to dine by candlelight on balmy evenings, just the two of them under the stars. If it was warm enough they didn't bother to come inside to be intimate, and now she could only wonder if they'd ever make love again.

How was she going to carry on living here without him? Though in reality it was her house, he was everywhere; there was nothing that didn't remind her of him, and make her want him so much that it was already eating her up. If only he was the kind of man who womanised and cheated, who had a history of leaving and coming back, maybe there would be a chance this wasn't the end – but he wasn't that kind of man. He was honest, decent, and scrupulous in every way. But how could she think that now? He was as capable as anyone of lying, cheating and betraying the woman who'd always trusted him without question and who loved him with all her heart – and knowing that was, maybe, the worst part of all. It allowed her no hope, gave her nothing to hang on to . . .

Feeling a jolt go through her as the telephone rang, she quickly reached for it, hoping, praying it would be him, even though she had no idea what she'd say.

'Eva? Are you there?'

Hearing Patty's voice, she slammed the receiver down and covered her face with her hands. She couldn't, wouldn't speak to Patty, ever again. This was the end for them and knowing it, feeling it, was tearing through her with such force that it was shaking her from head to foot. Her sister was the woman who'd done this to her; who'd been sleeping with her husband, going behind her back and quietly, selfishly destroying her life. How could she have done that? What had happened to turn her into someone so deceitful and cruel? She could never have been in any doubt of how devastating her betrayal would be, how completely and utterly it would shatter her sister's world, yet she'd done it anyway. Why? What had driven her? Where had her decency gone; her love and loyalty? How was she feeling now? Wretched? Triumphant? Happy to be with the man she loved?

How could she love him when she had no right to?

Recalling how afraid she and Livvy had been that Patty's cancer had returned, she suddenly found herself wishing it had. Anything rather than this – except she surely couldn't mean that? Or maybe she did. It was impossible to think straight when she was so torn apart with shock and fury and miserable confusion.

Knowing she had to do something, anything, to try and stop things going any further, she picked up the phone again and pressed in Don's mobile number. She'd want to die if he didn't answer – it would mean he was avoiding her, letting her know in another way that it was over.

When the ringing stopped she said, 'Hello. It's me.'

'I know,' he said softly. 'Are you OK?'

Pain and love mingled in her heart. She could barely speak. 'No, not really,' she admitted shakily. 'I – I can't . . .' She tried again. 'I want you to tell me that you didn't mean . . . That you've changed your mind.'

When he didn't respond she imagined the sorrow in his eyes and sank to her knees, her mouth open in a silent, terrible scream.

'What are you doing today?' he asked gently.

'I don't know. I . . . Where are you?'

'At the boat.'

She clung to it like a lifeline. He wasn't at Patty's. Maybe they hadn't spent the night together. 'Is Patty with you?' she asked cautiously.

'No.'

She almost came apart with relief, but what did it really mean? Nothing, because he could be lying, or maybe he'd only just got there. She wanted to ask if he'd made love to Patty since he'd left, but somehow she managed not to. 'I want to see you,' she said hoarsely. 'I think we should talk.'

'OK.'

No hesitancy or reluctance, it was almost as though he wanted to see her too. Should she take heart from that? 'I can come now if it's convenient.'

'I'm at the mooring in West Bay.'

Half an hour later they were walking along the shingly stretch of East Beach with the warmth of the sun beating down on them, and a fresh, sporadic breeze wafting the scents of seaweed and wet sand. In the far distance the sweeping curve of Chesil Beach glittered in the sunlight, and the sea, gently swelling and soughing, was like a blue bed of brilliant floating stars. It felt strange to be without Rosie and Elvis, but it was good not to have the distraction when they needed this time for themselves.

She'd realised, on arriving, that Don must have been watching out for her, because by the time she'd parked, in front of the Bridport Arms, he was there, opening the car door for her to get out. She hadn't expected him to take her in his arms, so when he had a rush of confused emotions had stolen her words. She suspected the same had happened to him, because his voice was gruff and scratchy when he finally asked if she'd like to go for a walk. She'd wondered if it was because he didn't want to be alone with her on the boat where they'd shared so many happy and intimate times, or maybe Patty was there, waiting for him to come back. She hadn't asked, because she hadn't wanted to know the answer.

As they walked on and still neither of them spoke,

she started to feel afraid that she'd acted too soon. Was it too early for them to be meeting like this? Maybe she should have allowed him some time to realise the full impact of what he'd done, to find out what it was like going home to Patty every evening, to discover, perhaps, that he was missing her far more than he'd expected. On the other hand, she'd felt so panicked and afraid of it all that standing there in her bedroom, certain they were together, she'd been unable to tolerate another hour, even another minute going by without doing something to try and save her marriage.

'Did you manage to sleep last night?' he asked finally, keeping his head down as they pressed their feet into the wet, shiny flats of the sand.

'A little,' she replied. 'How about you?'

'I guess the same.'

She looked up at the golden cliffs soaring skywards beside them, and tried to count the seagulls perched on tiny ledges like ornaments in an old lady's front room. As a distraction it didn't work, but at least it bought her a moment or two. 'You need to talk to Jasmine,' she told him.

His awkwardness was audible as he said, 'I'm sorry, I'd forgotten she was coming. Did she . . .? Did you tell her?'

'Yes, because I had to, but she needs to hear from you what's going on.'

'Of course.' Then, 'I'm sorry. It shouldn't have fallen to you to tell her.'

'No, it shouldn't, but then it shouldn't be happening at all.'

When he didn't respond she clenched her fists tightly in her pockets, willing herself to stay calm, but she couldn't. He had to say something, show some sort of remorse, or guilt, anything at all. What she really wanted was something to hold on to, a few poignant words that would allow her to hope. 'We don't have to go through with this,' she told him forcefully. 'I'm willing to . . . I can forgive . . .'

'Please don't do this,' he broke in gently.

'For God's sake, I have to try something,' she cried. 'I can't just let you go because you've decided . . . Because you don't . . .' She caught her breath. 'It doesn't change anything for me. You're still my husband and I still want to spend the rest of my life with you. Please tell me that's going to happen. Let me hear you say you're not going to leave me, that you still love me as much as I love you.'

Turning her to him, he reached for her hands and held them tightly in his own as he said, 'The last thing I want is to hurt you . . .'

'But you don't have to! I just told you, I can forgive what you've done . . .'

'It's not a question of forgiveness, it's about how wrong it would be for me to go on deceiving you.'

'But it doesn't . . .'

'Ssh, please listen. I really didn't want to have to say this, but . . . I love Patty, I want to be with her and I'm afraid nothing we say here today is going to change that.'

As the sincerity, the quiet force of his words seared through her heart, she felt as though he'd struck her.

Drawing her to him he held her close, trying to comfort her as her heart continued to break, but she pulled away and turned to gaze out to sea. The wind was whipping her hair round her face, the sun was blinding her, but all she could feel was the terrible, shattering reality of her world, her life, falling slowly, inexorably apart.

In the end, grasping practicality as though it were a weapon, she said, 'Do you and Patty intend to stay in the area? If you do, I'll put the house on the market.'

He turned her back to him. 'You don't have to do that,' he told her. 'I admit it's going to be difficult being around one another for a while . . .'

'For a while?' She almost laughed. 'Do you really think this is going to be over in a few weeks, or months? That given the right amount of time I'll be happy to know you're making love to my sister . . .'

'No, of course not,' he answered quietly. 'I just don't want you to do anything hasty, or unnecessary, like selling the house when I know how much it means to you.'

'I thought it did to you too.'

'It does.'

'However, it's mine, not yours, so what do you really care? And anyway, whatever the situation, I suppose you're going to say that Patty means more.'

He fell silent, and she wanted to slap away the closed expression on his face. It was how he always looked when something was hurting him, and the fact that he was finding this so hard was making it a thousand times harder for her.

She turned to walk on, taking long, determined strides as though they might somehow move her away from the sickening madness of it all.

When he caught up with her he tried to take her hand, but she wouldn't allow it.

'I want you to know that I'll be there for you whenever I can,' he told her. 'I'm not just walking away . . .'

'But that's *exactly* what you're doing,' she yelled, her eyes blazing with fury as she spun round to him. 'You've told me it's over, that you want to be with my sister and whatever that might do to me apparently doesn't matter, just as long as you two get what you want.'

'Of course it matters,' he said sharply. 'It's why I'm here now, and why Patty wants to talk to you . . .'

'Forget it.'

'She's your sister, you have to give her the chance . . .'

'I don't have to give her anything,' she cut in savagely. 'What she's done . . . What you're both doing . . .' The words were being sucked away by rage and jealousy. She had to get them back, keep her anger going, because without it she'd collapse inside. 'I have nothing to say to her,' she spat furiously.

'Yet you'll talk to me.'

'Because I want to save our marriage,' she shouted. 'How else am I going to do that if we don't talk?'

He didn't try to answer, merely turned to walk on, his hands buried in his pockets, and his shoulders hunched against a wind that was barely there.

Feeling suddenly light-headed, she stopped to put her hands on her knees. There was such a sense of unreality about everything that it was as though it was happening in another dimension, or to someone else entirely. This time yesterday she was happily married, and now, out of nowhere, her entire life was being torn apart.

'Are you all right?' he said worriedly.

Realising he'd asked this several times, she kept her head down as she replied, 'I don't know.' She didn't think she was about to faint, but nothing around her felt steady, or right.

'Have you eaten today?'

246

She didn't answer. Food was the last thing she wanted.

'Why don't we sit down?' he suggested, and steering her towards the rocks where the sand was drier, he drew her down next to him and tried to pull her head on to his shoulder. At first she resisted, but then she found herself giving in and closing her eyes.

She wasn't sure how much time passed, whether she might even have fallen asleep for a moment, tucked into the safety of his arms and the warmth of the sun, before she finally heard herself saying, 'These last few months . . . ? Did you find it a chore making love to me? Something you had to do to stop me being suspicious . . .'

'Eva, don't do this.'

'I want an answer,' she demanded, sitting up to look at him. 'Was it a chore making love to me?'

'No, of course not.'

'But you don't ever want to again?'

'For God's sake, why are you trying to put words in my mouth?'

'Because I know what you're thinking,' she told him, 'and while you might be too cowardly to voice what's going on in your head, I'm happy to tell you what's going on in mine. When we make love, it's the best thing that's happened to me since the last time we made love. There's nothing that means more to me than when we're together . . .' Her breath was catching, her words were failing. 'And I always thought it was the same for you. No, don't!' she gasped, as he tried to pull her back into his arms. 'I want to hear you say that you're coming home with me now.'

He only looked at her.

'*Tell me.*'

'If I did, it wouldn't be true.'

Her eyes flashed with fury and pain. 'And you never lie, do you?' she spat. 'Every word that comes out of your mouth is the gospel truth, because you don't know how to cheat on your wife, or pretend to be happy when you're not, or say you love someone when you don't. It's not in you to tell those sorts of lies. It's why I trust you and respect you and feel proud that you're my husband, because you're *not someone who cheats or lies.*'

Dropping his head in his hands, he said, 'I'm not sure we're going to achieve anything today. It's too soon. We all need . . .'

Eva sprang to her feet. 'You're right, we're wasting our time. I'll get a lawyer. I take it you want a divorce, then let's have one, but don't think it's going to be easy, because I'm warning you now that it'll be anything but,' and leaving him sitting on the rocks with the sky darkening overhead, she turned to run and stumble across the dunes back to her car.

Patty was already opening the kitchen door as Don got out of his car. When he'd called to let her know he was on his way, she hadn't asked how his meeting had gone with Eva, and now she didn't need to. The taut lines and shadows around his eyes, and then the way he came to wrap her tightly in his arms, left her in no doubt at all of how difficult it had been. Even more difficult than for her, sitting here waiting.

In the end he was the first to pull away, but his eyes remained on hers as he said, 'Are you OK?'

'Of course,' she lied, but she hardly felt she mattered. 'It's you I'm worried about, and Eva. How was she?'

Sighing, he turned to drop his keys on the table. 'Not good,' he answered wearily. Then, 'I have to talk to Jasmine. Apparently she turned up last night.'

'Yes, Livvy told me.'

'You've spoken to Livvy this morning?'

Patty's heart burned with the memory of the call. 'She rang to let me know that she wants no more to do with me until I come to my senses.'

His eyes closed as he gave a groan of despair. 'I'm sorry. That must have been hard to hear.'

'It was,' she admitted, 'but at least she's there for Eva. That's what really counts right now.'

'So do you,' he said, tilting her face so he could look at her.

'Did you tell her I want to see her?'

'Yes, but I think you'll have to leave it for now. She's going to need some time to come to terms with it all and decide what she wants to do. She talked about selling the house.'

Patty's eyes widened in protest. 'But she can't. Her heart and soul is in that place, and anyway it's far too soon to be making decisions like that.'

'I know, and I doubt she was serious. She's very emotional, as you'd expect. I think she threatened it to try and hit out at me.'

Understanding that, and wishing there was a way to take away her sister's pain, not for her own sake, only for Eva's, she said, 'So how have you left it with her?'

Looking more strained than ever, he replied, 'She says she's going to get a lawyer, but I'm not sure she's serious about that either.'

'Oh God,' she murmured, as the awfulness of it all rose through her again in wave after wave of merciless guilt. 'How can we let her go on suffering like this?'

His eyes were as troubled as hers as he said, 'But how can we change anything now we've told her?'

She shook her head, helplessly.

'Are you regretting it?' he asked, seeming suddenly unsure of himself. 'You know, it's not too late for me to sell the business and get out of your life . . .'

'Please don't say that,' she cried, clasping her hands to his face. 'Through the night it was awful . . . I kept wishing we'd tried harder to stop what we feel, but now you're here . . . Now it's happening . . . It's worse than I thought, but I love you so much.'

'I love you too,' he said gruffly. 'More than I know how to put into words.'

'You don't have to.'

He pushed his fingers through her hair, and she knew what he was thinking, because she was starting to think, to feel it too.

'I want to be close to you,' he told her softly.

Feeling desire rush through her like flames, she pressed herself to him and gasped at the power of his need. She needed him too, desperately, madly, and what point was there in denying themselves now? None at all – and as his mouth came hungrily to hers she knew that neither her love for Eva, nor the wretchedness in her heart was strong enough to make her tear herself away.

Chapter Twelve

Time had started to lose all meaning as one day merged into another, and each hour brought a new hope, or despair, or the kind of pain that pushed Eva right to the edge – or into a tempestuous rage like the one that had driven her to shred Don's clothes the day she'd left him on the beach. By the time Livvy had found her at lunchtime, sitting in the middle of the bedroom, with the scissors still in her hand and the debris all around her, she'd been sobbing with shame and regret. What on earth was such a stupid, senseless act going to prove? It might have provided a few moments of savage satisfaction while she was doing it, but it was hardly going to make him change his mind. If anything, she'd robbed him of a reason to come to the house, even though she'd told him never to come back, but she wanted him here so desperately that even if it meant watching him pack she might be able to suffer it. At least he'd be here and maybe then, by some miracle, she'd be able to persuade him to stay.

It was now Wednesday, and though she'd spoken to him several times on the phone, she hadn't seen him since Saturday and had no idea when she might do so again. She felt sure if she asked him to come that he would, but so far her pride, combined with a dread of how it would be if – when – he left, wouldn't allow it. He knew about his clothes because she'd told him. He hadn't expressed any anger, or exasperation; all he'd said was, 'I'm sorry you felt the need to do that.'

The calmness of his reaction had made her want to go and smash up the rest of his belongings, but somehow she'd managed not to, mainly because Jasmine had been there. Though Jasmine had spent most of Saturday evening with her father, doing her best, she'd said, to persuade him to see sense, he'd remained immovable. So, taking a leaf out of Livvy's book, she'd informed him that she wanted no more to do with him until he got a grip on himself, as she'd put it. That her stepdaughter had swayed so readily to Eva's side was mystifying, but nonetheless welcome, even though she really didn't want to cause a rift between the girls and their parents. Or maybe she did. She was in too much turmoil to know anything for certain, though she was thankful for their support because she felt that if she were left in the house on her own for too long she'd probably do something a whole lot crazier than destroying a wardrobe full of clothes. As it was, when she walked Rosie and Elvis in the mornings, she spent far too long staring at the cliff edge, and in the depths of night, when sleep was her enemy and paranoia her only companion, she'd lie in the darkness trying to summon enough courage to make the only possible escape from it all.

Now, after spending a morning at the shop where she'd managed to catch up with some paperwork and had even found the heart to deal with a few customers, she was back at home staring blankly, unblinkingly, at her computer screen. A call from

Coral was what had triggered her downward spiral today, but at least she hadn't ended up falling out with Patty's best friend, which was an achievement considering how disastrously the call had begun.

She'd been at the front of the shop redressing one of the mannequins when the phone had rung, and because Livvy was upstairs in the workroom she'd answered it herself, praying it would be Don, yet dreading it too.

'Eva, it's Coral. I just want to say . . .'

'I'm not interested, Coral.'

'Eva, please listen. I'm calling to find out if there's anything I can do.'

'Are you serious?' Eva cried. 'You obviously knew about the affair, so would you please tell me how you can *do* anything now that . . .'

'I'm offering to help with the shop,' Coral cut in, 'or with organising the show, if you or Livvy can tell me what to do.'

'I'll tell you what to do,' Eva raged, 'you can go back to my sister and inform her that neither her friends nor their bloody charity are ever going to make up for what she's done.'

'Eva! Stop! Please don't hang up. Patty doesn't know I'm calling. I haven't told her for this very reason. OK, she's my friend, and you're probably thinking I should stay loyal to her, and I will, but if I can, I want to be there for you too, because what you're going through . . . Well, let's just say, I know that keeping going at times like this isn't easy, so I want you to know that if there are days when you feel you can't face it all, I'll do whatever I can to help. I'm not sure how good I'll be at sales, or organising, but if I'm there it might at least help to take the pressure off you both for a while.'

Realising then what a huge burden she was turning into for Livvy, who'd practically moved into the house now so they were together most of the time, Eva had ended up accepting Coral's offer and had apologised for being so snappy at first. 'I just don't want Patty trying to use you to get to me,' she explained.

'I understand that, and I promise it isn't happening. However, I do know she's worried about you and is desperate to talk to you . . .'

'I'm sorry, Coral, I don't want to discuss it. Thanks very much again for your offer, and I'm sure we'll take you up on it.'

After ringing off she'd felt her fragile defences starting to crumble, and not wanting Livvy to know she was about to fall apart again, she'd mustered as cheery a smile as she could while telling her she was popping home for a while.

And now here she was sitting at her computer and wishing she'd never turned it on. She hadn't intended to check her incoming emails, she'd only meant to write yet another message to Don to add to the dozens she'd already composed, some of which she'd sent, but most she hadn't. They were all still there, saved in a file she'd labelled *Perdita2* – the outpouring of her shattered emotions, along with reminders of the times they'd been happy, and in others, those written in anger and frustration, she'd made some unforgivable threats. It was a form of communication with him that was both easier and more difficult than seeing him, but in the end it meant nothing, because no matter how hard she tried to fool herself that he would come back, she knew deep down that he'd never have done this if his mind wasn't completely made up.

I've broken your trust, he'd written in an email only yesterday, *so even if I were willing to try again, and I'm afraid I'm not, what we had together can never be recaptured. I'm sorry for how hurtful it must be for you to read those words, but after all the lies of the last few years I want to return to being as honest as I can.*

The message had devastated her all over again, to the point that she hadn't been able to send one back for several hours, finally writing, *Perhaps you could let me know whether to forward your mail to the boat or the office.*

His reply had come a few minutes ago. *Eva, I want to tell you this before anyone else does. I have moved into the barn with Patty, so please could you redirect my mail there. I'll contact the Post Office today to make it official.*

It was because of this email that the one she was actually looking at now hadn't managed to provoke her into the kind of response she would have made a month, even a week ago. She simply couldn't get past the pain of knowing that they were living together now, openly, *brazenly*, for all to see and never mind the hurt and humiliation it was going to cause her. It was making her feel violent inside, defeated – and lost for where to turn or what to do next.

In the end she forced herself to refocus on Johnny Johnson's email, trying harder this time to make herself take it in. *It was a great pleasure meeting you last Friday. I am sorry that I was unable to help you with the matter that you latterly mentioned, but in the former – the letter to the magazine – I can tell you that the name of your champion is Nick Jensen.*

At any other time Eva knew she'd have been straight on the phone to Bobbie, then Patty, perhaps the other way round. Not Don, because he'd always seen Nick as something of a rival, in spite of there having been no contact between her and Nick for over sixteen years. As it was, now she was registering it, she felt a towering fury building inside her, a sense of pure outrage that he'd dared to involve himself in her life in any way shape or form after all these years. Who the hell did he think he was? He had absolutely no right even to consider writing such a letter on her behalf.

Snatching up the phone as it rang, she dashed away the tears as she snapped, 'Hello.'

'Oh dear, is this a bad time?'

Hearing Elaine's gentle voice at the other end, Eva quickly forced her temper down. 'No, no, of course not,' she assured her. 'I was just . . . It doesn't matter. How are you?'

'Very well, thank you. I thought I'd call to let you know I'm back, so if you'd like to get together? I can come to you, or you can come here . . . Whichever suits you best.'

Feeling a horrible struggle starting up inside as she realised how desperately she wanted to lean on Elaine, while knowing how hard it was going to be for her stepmother's tender heart to be torn between her and Patty, Eva said, 'Why don't I come to you? Are you very busy at the moment?'

'Not terribly. Just a few residents and the usual classes, but Maizie and Paul are here for the rest of the month, you know, the owners, and they have things pretty much under control. So I can be free more or less when you like, and I've been mulling over what I could say to the editor about the letter he received.'

'Actually, that's not an issue any more,' Eva said

shakily. *Damn Nick, damn him to hell. None of this would be happening if it weren't for him; she'd have her son with her, she wouldn't be married to Don – in fact, she probably wouldn't even be alive, which might be the best place of all.* 'Other things have happened since we last spoke,' she continued. 'Have you – have you been in touch with Patty at all?'

'No, not yet. I was going to call after I'd spoken to you.'

Eva took a breath. 'Would you mind terribly not doing that until I've spoken to you first?'

There was a moment of surprised silence before Elaine said, 'Is everything all right between you two?'

Forcing herself not to break down, Eva said, 'Let's talk tomorrow. I'll come about eleven if that's OK.'

'Are you sure you want to do this?' Don was saying as he walked to the door with Patty. 'You know it could backfire badly.'

'That's a chance I'm prepared to take,' she told him, flicking a switch to light up the barn's outside courtyard. 'I know she'll lock all the doors before I can reach the house if she sees my car coming, so I have to do it this way.'

She was glad he didn't point out that she could always go to the shop, but he'd know that it was far too public a venue for her to try and talk to her sister there. They needed privacy and no interruptions, and this was the only way she could think of to make it happen when her every attempt to contact Eva in the past few days had been met with a slamming down of the phone, or a complete refusal to answer her emails and texts.

Coming to the Mercedes with her, Don opened

the door and as she slipped into the driver's seat he said, 'I could call to tell her I'm coming, but I think that kind of subterfuge would be taking it too far.'

'It would,' she agreed, already feeling bad enough about the trick she was preparing to play. Gazing up at him in the lamplight, she put a hand out for his and brought it to her cheek. 'Wish me luck,' she whispered.

Leaning in through the window, he pressed his mouth tenderly to hers. 'Try not to let her hurt you,' he said softly.

Knowing it was inevitable, and thinking that it would be no more than she deserved, Patty started the engine and put the car into reverse.

'Hang on,' he said, before she could pull away, 'I'm going to follow in your car and wait in the layby across the road.'

'Why?'

'I don't know. I'll just feel better if I'm close by.'

Loving him for his concern, while aching for her sister, Patty watched him go to lock up the house then turned the Mercedes round as he got into her Audi.

As she drove out of the courtyard to head down the stony lane towards the village, she was once again starting to question the wisdom of turning up on Eva like this.

'To be frank,' Coral had said when Patty had spoken to her earlier, 'I think you're probably the last person she wants to see right now, but it's your decision. Just try to remember she's your sister, not your daughter, which is how you sometimes come across, and I get the impression she really won't appreciate that with the way things are.'

Patty knew it was good advice, since it was true, she did sometimes forget that Eva was capable of standing on her own two feet. However, Patty was in no doubt of how hard Eva would be finding it to cope right now, since no one knew better than Patty how damaging her younger sister's past tragedies had been, and how likely they were to start causing chaos for her now. Losing their mother when she was so young had been a terrible blow for her, and left her with a sense of abandonment that Patty wasn't sure she'd ever really overcome. Even into her teens she'd still been trying to persuade herself that her mother wasn't actually dead as a way of allowing herself to believe that one day she would come back. Then had come the trauma of losing Nick, her first big love, followed by the tragic and terrifying way her career and looks had been taken from her. Then there was the baby, of course – oh God, the baby. That dear, precious little soul whose loss continued to break Eva's heart and haunt them all. Now she was faced with the ordeal of losing Don too – and not to just anyone, but to the sister who'd always been at the centre of her world. It was too much for her to cope with alone, and Patty needed desperately to let her know that she could still be there for her if she'd allow it, especially through the long dark nights of the soul that Patty feared might already have begun.

It was a little after seven thirty by the time she used the remote in Don's car to open the gates. She wasn't entirely certain that Eva was at home, or whether Livvy was with her, but since Livvy generally went to a Pilates class on Wednesdays, Patty had gambled on now being the right time.

Far more nervous than she wanted to admit, she

brought the Mercedes to a stop alongside Eva's Smart car while noting with relief that there was no sign of Livvy's jeep. She still had no way of knowing if Eva had seen her coming in, but there was a chance she hadn't, since the outside door to the conservatory wasn't deadlocked when she tried it, and on going through to the inner door she found her key opened that one too. There was no sign of Eva in the kitchen, or the odd couple, but the lights were on so someone was around somewhere. Then she heard a door opening and closing nearby, and a moment later Eva appeared from the direction of the odd couple's den.

Eva's eyes rounded with shock and fury. 'What the hell . . .!' she exclaimed, her tone making it clear that she'd expected to see Don. 'How dare you sneak your way into my house? Get out! Get out now!'

'Eva, please listen to me . . .'

'Get out!' Eva raged, starting towards her.

'I need to talk to you . . .'

'Didn't you hear me?' Eva yelled. 'I'm not interested in anything you have to say. You're nothing to me now. All your lies and deceit, pretending to be loyal and that you put everyone first . . . It's all just bullshit. A front you've been putting on while you've been *sleeping with my husband.*'

Patty blanched. 'It wasn't . . .'

'I can't believe you've got the nerve to come here,' Eva raged on. 'Have you got no shame? What kind of woman are you? How low can you sink? No, don't answer,' she snarled when Patty tried to interrupt, 'I want your keys, and your remote control, then get the hell out of my house and never come back.'

Patty's heart was thudding painfully as she said,

'Eva, this isn't the way to deal with what's happening . . . What are you doing?'

'I'm showing you the door,' Eva told her, shoving her towards it. 'It's right behind you . . .'

'For heaven's sake! Can't we try to be reasonable?'

'There's nothing reasonable about breaking up my marriage,' Eva seethed in her face, 'or about ruining my life. I *love* him, Patty and you know it, so why the hell did you do it?'

'I tried not to,' Patty cried. 'I swear, I did everything I could to make myself stop . . .'

'Then you didn't do enough. Now, get away from me and don't bother trying to trick your way in again because you'll find all the locks have been changed.'

As she stumbled back into the conservatory, Patty tried to grab Eva's hands, but she wasn't fast enough. The slap to her face sent her reeling, and a moment later the door slammed so hard it was a miracle the glass didn't break. She watched Eva turning the key, saw the tears pouring down her cheeks and knew, even before Eva sank to the floor, that everything was overwhelming her in a way that she, Patty, needed to do something about.

'Eva, let me in,' Patty cried, banging on the door. 'Please, don't stay here on your own like this. You have to let me in.'

Eva didn't answer, she simply staggered back to her feet and went to the panel of buttons below the TV. A moment later every security shutter in the place started to descend.

Only just managing to make it through the outer conservatory door, Patty gave a sob of frustration and despair as she realised that all she'd achieved by coming here was what she'd most feared – she'd made things even worse than they already were.

'I'm terrified she might try to harm herself,' she said to Don when she went across to the layby to join him.

His eyes were fixed on the gates; the grimness of his expression showing that he shared the fear. 'I should go over there,' he said.

'Can you get the shutters open?'

'No, but I can try talking to her on the entryphone.'

'If you go now she'll know you've been out here all along. Why don't you try your mobile instead?'

Taking it from his pocket, he pressed in the number of the house. Eva answered on the third ring.

'That was a disgusting stunt you just pulled,' she told him before he could speak. 'Letting Patty drive your car so I'd think it was you.'

'It was the only way we could think of . . .'

'I told you, I don't want to see her. As far as I'm concerned, she's *dead*.'

'Eva, please . . .'

'That's all I have to say,' and she slammed the phone down.

Turning as Patty tugged his arm, he looked to where she was pointing and saw Livvy's car pulling in through the gates. Presumably she hadn't seen them or she'd surely have stopped.

Clicking off at his end, Don continued to watch Livvy's tail lights until they disappeared around a curve in the drive. 'At least she won't be on her own now,' he said bleakly.

Relieved too, though worried for Livvy, Patty said, 'Actually, there's something we were both forgetting.'

Turning to look at her, his eyes searched her face as he said, 'Maybe I can guess what you're going to say. She hasn't given up hope of finding her son, and if anything will keep her going we know that will.'

Patty nodded and let her head fall back as she closed her eyes. 'We just have to pray that's the only hope she's holding on to,' she murmured, 'because I can't think of a worse time for her to start trying to convince herself that our mother's still alive.'

Surprised, and doubtful, Don said, 'Do you really think she would?'

'I don't know. She's never wanted to believe in her death, and no one's ever told her how Mummy died. That really isn't something she needs to start dealing with now.'

After waiting for the shutters to open, Livvy dropped her mobile back in her bag and went through the conservatory into the kitchen, surprised not to see Rosie and Elvis and worried about why the house had been so securely locked up this early in the evening. 'Is everything all right?' she said to Eva, whose back was turned as she stared up at the CCTV. 'Why were the shutters down?'

'I – uh, I just got a bit anxious,' Eva answered, keeping her eyes on the screen. 'I heard a noise outside and I didn't know what it was.'

'What kind of noise?'

'Oh, it was probably just a squirrel or a fox, nothing to worry about, I'm sure.'

Dropping her things on the bar, Livvy went to give her a hug. 'I can tell you've been crying,' she said against Eva's hair, 'so are you sure that's all it was?'

With a sigh, Eva drew a crumpled tissue from her sleeve and blew her nose. 'Actually, your mother came,' she confessed. 'She used Don's car so I didn't know it was her until she was already in.'

'Oh God, why did she do that?' Livvy cried angrily. 'What happened? She's upset you, obviously . . . Come and sit down,' and drawing her to a chair she sat down with her.

'I completely lost it,' Eva sighed, 'but they shouldn't have tricked me like that.'

'Dead right they shouldn't.'

'And what does she think she's going to gain from forcing me to talk?'

Livvy shook her head in bewilderment.

'I can't forgive her, if that's what she's after, and I sure as hell don't want to listen to the sordid details of how it all came about. All I want is my husband back and for everything to be the way it was before.' As though registering her own words, she turned to stare dismally out at the darkness. 'That can't ever happen now, can it?' she said quietly.

Wishing with all her heart that she could say it would, Livvy reached for her hands and squeezed them hard. 'I'll tell her to leave you alone,' she said decisively.

Taking a breath, Eva shook her head. 'I don't want there to be a problem between you two because of me,' she said. 'She's your mother. She loves you and she hasn't done anything to hurt you.'

'Wrong. Doing what she has to you has hurt me a lot. I really mean that, Eva. I hate seeing you like this and knowing she's the cause. It makes me ashamed of her. It's like she's let everyone down, including herself. I spoke to Dad earlier and he's disgusted with her too – not that he's got much to shout about, but at least he didn't have an affair with you, or go off with one of his other sisters-in-law. Apparently he's been on Mum's case for ages to pack it in, but she wouldn't listen.'

Eva swallowed hard as her eyes went down.

'Oh God, I'm saying all the wrong things, aren't I?' Livvy groaned. 'Sorry.'

'No, no,' Eva assured her. 'It's me who should be sorry. I meant to have some dinner waiting when you got back. I thought Dave was coming with you?'

'He should be here soon. Why don't I fix something for you?'

'No, I'm fine. I've already eaten. There's some fresh salmon in the fridge and plenty of salad. I expect Dave will want some potatoes or rice.'

Keeping hold of her hands, Livvy said, 'What did you eat?'

Eva's smile was faint as she looked at her. 'I hope you're not about to start bossing me around,' she tried to quip.

'You haven't had anything, have you?'

Sighing, Eva said, 'I'm just not hungry.'

'Well, maybe you'll change your mind once it's in front of you,' and going to the fridge Livvy started to take things out.

'I'll go and freshen up before Dave gets here,' Eva said, standing up. 'There's some beer in the cooler if he'd prefer that to wine.' At the door she turned back. 'Did I mention earlier that I'm going to see Elaine tomorrow?'

Livvy smiled. 'Yes, you did, and Coral's coming in for a couple of hours to cover.'

Eva nodded, and after meeting Livvy's eyes for a moment she continued on her way, leaving Livvy feeling secretly relieved that she wasn't going to be

265

on her own in the shop the next day. It wasn't that she couldn't cope, because most of the time she could, but when she'd left the gym just now she'd spotted the girls Jasmine had thrown out of the shop hanging around the bus stop. There had been some boys with them this time, and the way they'd watched her go by had been horribly unnerving. Luckily nothing had been said, nor had anyone tried to block her way, nevertheless the relief she'd felt when she reached her car in safety had been almost overwhelming.

She wouldn't mention anything to Eva about it, after all nothing had actually happened, so there was no big deal. Besides which, Eva already had enough problems on her plate without having to worry about a bunch of idiots who might, or might not, be trying to make mischief at the shop.

Thinking of which, she needed to let her mother know that she was only making things worse than they already were by forcing her way in here the way she had.

Patty was half sitting, half lying in Don's arms, snug in front of the fire with the lights low and Nat King Cole crooning 'Unforgettable' in the background, when her mobile bleeped with a text. Handing her wine glass to Don she reached over to pick up the phone from a side table and her heart tightened painfully when she saw who the text was from. As she read it she felt a hundred times worse.

Please don't keep trying to talk to Eva, she doesn't need it.

Passing the phone to Don, she sat forward to bury her face in her hands.

After reading the text, he shut the screen down and ran a hand over her back.

For the past hour, since returning home, they'd been talking about whether they should carry on living together, indeed even seeing one another, considering how difficult it was proving for everyone, including them. Though they hadn't come to a decision, the very thought of parting seemed to be making them hold on even tighter, as it always had, and Don's last words before Patty's phone had interrupted were, 'It hasn't even been a week yet, so let's at least give it more time.'

Though Patty had always known the early days were going to be the hardest, after her encounter with Eva this evening she was no longer sure what to do for the best. Certainly she couldn't allow Eva to go on the way she was with only Livvy – as kind and loyal as Livvy was – to support her. Apart from anything else it was too much for Livvy, especially when she had so little experience of life herself.

Taking the phone back from Don she pressed in a number, and turned to look at him as he asked, 'Who are you calling?'

She waited a moment, then making the connection she said, 'Elaine, it's me, Patty.'

'Oh, what a nice surprise,' Elaine said warmly. 'How are you, dear?'

'I'm – uh, yes fine. Are you still in Cornwall?'

'No, I got back this afternoon. I was just unpacking.'

Even though the lightness in Elaine's voice made it clear that she didn't know what had happened, Patty still said, 'Have you . . . Have you spoken to Eva recently?'

There was a moment before Elaine replied, warily, 'Only briefly, earlier. Is everything all right? I got the impression something might be . . . Well, you tell me.'

Giving the only answer she could for the moment, Patty said, 'It's a long story. I've had too much wine to get in the car now, but maybe I could come over tomorrow.'

'Actually, Eva's coming at eleven. Have you two had a falling out?'

Patty's insides wrenched with guilt as she said, 'It goes deeper than that, I'm afraid.'

'Then perhaps, dear, you'd better tell me now what it is.'

Patty took a breath as she looked at Don.

'Whatever it is,' Elaine said kindly, 'I'm sure it's nothing we can't sort out. So come along now, I'm listening.'

In spite of it being one of the feistiest days of autumn so far, with driving rain and wind lashing the countryside, Eva was still finding something calming about the grounds of the rambling old house and spiritual retreat where Elaine was the resident minister. Everything had been designed to maximise the benefits of the five elements, creating a gentle harmony between each of the gardens and the various temples and teahouses which in themselves exuded yet more tranquillity. Undoubtedly because of the weather, there was no sign of any residents or coaches, who were often to be seen sitting cross-legged in the meditation garden with its softly running waterfalls and willowy grasses, or in the sensory garden absorbing the natural stimulation of lavender, sunflowers, bamboo and nasturtiums. The most beautiful and uplifting space, to Eva's mind, was the sacred garden which was where, in good weather, Elaine conducted her ceremonies and spiritual communications. With its seven-circuit labyrinth, exquisite koi ponds and orchids, exotic succulents and shrines it would always hold a special place in Eva's heart, because it was where, just over ten years ago, Elaine had blessed her marriage to Don.

Unable to allow herself to think about that now, she drove on past a sign directing visitors to the residents' quarters and yoga hall, then another announcing that today's t'ai chi was being held in the glasshouse. By the time she pulled her car to a stop outside the welcoming arch of a double-front door, Elaine was already waiting on the front steps. She was plump and rosy-cheeked, with wispy, silvering hair, liquid brown eyes and a disarming smile that occasionally broke into a surprisingly raucous laugh. Indeed, for someone of her dignified calling she was given to some rather risqué humour, and when daring exploits managed to find their way on to the agenda, she was often first to sign up. However, today was not one for hang-gliding or parachuting or chasing the hunt, it was one she'd generously set aside for her late husband's younger daughter, and seeing the concern in her eyes Eva felt a sudden horrible urge to run. She didn't want to go through with this, she didn't want to tell Elaine what had happened, because as soon as she did it would make it real in a way that she just couldn't bear.

'Come in, come in, my dear,' Elaine said, pulling Eva into a fulsome embrace. 'I've made some fresh mint tea, which I know is your favourite, and please don't groan, but I actually have some angel cake.'

Having to smile, Eva followed her into the grand

old entrance hall which doubled as a reception for the paying guests, though no one was around at the moment, apart from a cleaner who was dusting the desk. Helping herself to a rune from the basket by the door as she passed, Eva glanced at it then placed it into Elaine's open hand.

After casting a quick glance at the symbol, Elaine stood aside for Eva to lead the way along a dark, narrow hall to Elaine's private quarters.

'You've chosen Kauno,' Elaine told her, 'which some might say denotes mental anguish.'

Feeling her heart churn, Eva said, 'And what would you say?'

'Me? I'd be more inclined to go for the more positive aspect, which suggests that you are coming into a new understanding of life and its meaning.'

Eva almost laughed. 'Well, I guess that's one way of putting what's going on in my world,' she remarked, and pushing open the door to Elaine's cosy, cluttered sitting room she felt the warmth of the fire embracing her. 'You've changed it around in here,' she commented admiringly.

'Oh, I've just got rid of a few things, that's all,' Elaine responded, with a dismissive wave of a hand. Eva knew that just about everything in the place, from the amulets and crystals to the candlesticks, dream-catchers, exotically patterned rugs and hand-painted incense burners, had some kind of history or meaning, all of which Elaine could recite on asking. She often enjoyed listening to her step-mother's stories, but it wasn't why she was here today. 'I was hoarding far too much,' Elaine went on, going over to the large stone fireplace where a fancy-handled teapot was keeping warm on a burner, 'which is no good for the head, you know.

You can hang your coat on the stand there, next to the radiator, so it'll be nice and snug for when you go out again.'

After doing as she was told, Eva went to sink into one of the deep purple sofas that dominated the room and as the heat from the fire reached her again, or maybe it was the scent of a specially chosen incense, she felt her tension starting to unravel for the first time since the dreadful scene with Patty last night. She wasn't entirely sure now whether or not she regretted exploding the way she had, except there was nothing in her at all, not a single, rogue shred of curiosity, that wanted to hear what Patty had to say.

'Now, I know you don't want sugar,' Elaine was mumbling as she filled a Moroccan tea glass with a vivid green brew, 'but I do hope you'll have some of this delicious cake that I made myself.'

Eva looked askance at the cake, all plump and airy and set out on a bone-china serving plate complete with silver slice and lace doily. Then, eyeing Elaine suspiciously, she said, 'Did your nose just grow an inch?'

Elaine gasped in surprise. 'Oh my goodness, did it?' she cried, giving it a prod. 'You know, I do believe you're right.' Her eyes were starting to twinkle. 'I suppose I must have got it at the farm shop, which means it'll be one of Mrs Egerton's.'

Used to the way her stepmother often treated her like a child, Eva accepted an enormous slice of her least favourite cake, and took a bite before setting it down next to her tea glass.

'So,' Elaine said, holding her cup and saucer in both hands as she turned her full attention to Eva. Then in the direct, but gentle way she had of coming to the point, she said, 'I believe rather a lot's happened since I went off to Cornwall.'

Feeling her heart turn over, and an absurd urge to ask her to make it right again, Eva said, 'I guess that means you've spoken to Patty?'

There was only sadness in Elaine's eyes, and more compassion than Eva could bring herself to see. 'She called me last night,' Elaine told her. 'I have to admit, I'm still feeling horribly shocked, but my feelings are hardly relevant, are they? It's the effect it's having on you that counts.'

Eva started to speak, but found she couldn't.

'I want you to know that I'm going to do everything I can to bring you and Patty back together,' Elaine continued.

'It's not Patty I want,' Eva protested. 'It's my husband.'

Realising her mistake, Elaine blinked as she said, 'Yes, of course, but you two have always been so close . . . All right, all right, we'll leave that for the moment,' she added when Eva started to protest again.

Sorry she was being so uptight when Elaine was only trying to be kind, Eva said, 'Actually, I didn't come here to talk about that. I mean, I was going to tell you, obviously, but I don't think anything we say here today is going to change it, do you?'

As Elaine only looked at her, Eva felt a new panic flare in her heart. Why didn't Elaine contradict her, give her something to hold on to instead of just sitting there looking helpless and sad?

Eva took a breath. Though she wanted to rant and rave and swear all kinds of revenge on her sister and husband, she wasn't going to allow herself to upset Elaine that way. Instead she was going to force them out of her mind, eject them, banish them straight to hell and focus only on what really mattered. Her heart was starting to thud erratically. She knew what she wanted to say, but it was hard to make the words come. Even if she could, she was already asking herself what was the point, when Elaine had no more power to help her find her son than anyone else had. There was nothing anyone could do, and since it would only distress Elaine further to be asked, which wouldn't be fair, in the end she said nothing.

'Eva?' Elaine prompted gently. 'If you didn't come here to talk about that, then what . . .'

'I was wondering,' Eva broke in, in a rush, 'I mean, I realise you never knew her, but it would be . . . Can I ask you to tell me what you know about my mother? Patty always finds it difficult to talk about her, but I was thinking, maybe Daddy told you things . . .'

As Elaine's surprise disappeared into a deep crimson glow, she reached for a copy of *The Kindred Spirit* and used it to fan herself. 'I'm sorry, it's my age,' she explained.

Familiar with the frequency of Elaine's hot flushes, Eva waited for the moment to pass, feeling anxious and foolish and as though something inside her was slipping slowly away.

In the end, after putting the magazine down again, Elaine said, 'Before I answer that, I can't help wondering why you're asking now.'

Being so immersed in a turmoil of loss and grief, it was a moment before Eva realised that Elaine could be stalling. Her heart tightened as she looked at her stepmother, and tightened again as she sensed a discomfort, or was it caution, in Elaine that she hadn't expected at all. 'I guess,' she began tentatively, 'because I've been thinking about her a lot since this happened. I keep wishing she was still here, or that I'd known her better.'

Elaine gave a smile of understanding.

'I expect you know,' Eva continued, looking down at her hands, 'that for a long time I wouldn't allow myself to believe she was dead.'

'Yes, I did know that,' Elaine confessed, 'but you do now?'

Eva tried to nod. Then her eyes were stinging painfully as they came back to Elaine's. 'I know it's a stupid, pointless thing to say, but I wish it wasn't true,' she told her.

'That's perfectly understandable.'

'I still even try to persuade myself sometimes that it isn't, but deep down I know Daddy would never have lied to me like that.'

Elaine's smile was tender. 'No, he certainly wouldn't have,' she agreed.

Eva lowered her eyes. She hated feeling so pathetic, so desperate for a mother she'd hardly even known, but it had started to come over her so powerfully that it was almost impossible to hold back her tears.

'I think I should call Patty,' Elaine said, reaching for her phone.

Eva's head came up. 'No. Why? I don't want to speak to her . . . Elaine, please stop dialling.'

Putting the phone down again, Elaine took an unsteady breath.

'Patty and I have nothing to say to each other,' Eva snapped.

Elaine's eyes held gently to hers. 'But if you want to know about your mother . . .'

Eva's heart gave a jolt of confusion. 'Know what about my mother?' she demanded. 'You're making it sound as though . . . Is there something to know, I mean more than I already . . .? Oh my God, she is dead, isn't she?'

Without any hesitation Elaine said, 'Yes, of course she is. As you just said yourself, your father would never have told you she was if she wasn't.'

'No, but . . .' Her mind was spinning; she didn't seem to have a proper grasp on what was happening. 'Elaine, I think you're hiding something from me. You are, aren't you? What is it? You have to tell me.'

'Oh dear,' Elaine murmured, putting a hand to her head. 'I had no idea you were going to bring this up today, that we'd find ourselves . . . I'm sorry, dear, but you really should talk to Patty.'

'For God's sake, why?' Eva cried, leaping to her feet. 'What can be so awful that you can't tell me yourself?'

'Nothing's awful, nothing, it's just that . . . Oh Eva . . . Patty would never forgive me . . . If you'll just let me call her. She'll come right away, I know she will, because she's waiting, hoping to hear from me.'

Enraged and confounded, Eva clasped her hands to her head as she shouted, 'I just told you, I don't want to see her.'

'Eva, please calm down . . .'

'How can I, when I know you're keeping something from me?'

'Not by choice. It's simply not my place . . .'

'No! Don't say I have to talk to Patty, because it's not going to happen.'

'Then I'm afraid,' Elaine said, looking as regretful as she sounded, 'your questions will have to remain unanswered.'

Boiling with frustration, Eva stormed towards her coat and might have grabbed it if she'd had the courage to leave. Instead she started to pace, feeling so torn and disoriented that she hardly knew what she was thinking. If it was true that Patty was keeping some sort of secret about their mother, and had been for over thirty years, then it was almost as unforgivable as her treachery with Don. In fact, her sister clearly wasn't to be trusted about anything, which made Eva wonder what else she might know and was keeping to herself. Where did the lies begin and end? How was she, Eva, ever going to get to the truth?

Suddenly rounding on Elaine, she said, 'My mother died in a car crash, right? That's what I was told, and that's what happened.'

Elaine's eyes were dark with feeling as she said, 'I'm going to call Patty,' and picking up the phone she pressed in the number again.

Though Eva wanted to shout at her to stop, to push it home to her that she could hardly bear the thought of even looking at her sister, never mind listening to what she had to say, she forced herself to hold back. If she wanted answers, then it seemed this was the only way she was going to get them without bullying Elaine.

When Elaine clicked off the line again, Eva said, almost breathlessly, 'Is she coming?'

Elaine nodded.

'Then I want you to stay in the room with us, and if she tries to start talking about Don, you must promise to make her stop.'

'You have my word,' Elaine assured her, 'now please come and sit down and try to finish your tea.'

* * *

'I'm almost there,' Patty was saying to Don on the phone.

'So she's agreed to see you?'

'I'm presuming so. Elaine didn't say much, only to come.'

There was a moment before he asked, 'What do you want me to do?'

Checking her mirror as she turned into Elaine's drive, she said, 'I don't think there is anything, unless . . . Maybe you should be nearby in case she wants to talk to you too.'

'Do you think she will?'

'I've no idea, but if she does . . .'

'I'll get in the car now and go to the Lamb. From there I can be at the retreat in a couple of minutes.'

After ringing off, Patty pulled up next to Eva's Smart car, and stepping out of her own she inhaled deeply, hoping to absorb some of the soothing energies that flowed around the estate. She was trying to collect herself, to recapture what she could say to Eva that might in some way help her, but unlike last night when she'd felt ready to face her, this morning she was struggling to hold herself together. There was nothing right about what she'd done, no way of excusing it, or reasoning it through, she'd betrayed her sister in the worst imaginable way and no amount of apologising or pathetic self-justification was ever going to change it. So why had she ever imagined there was anything she could do? She'd never be able to forgive this kind of betrayal herself, so why on earth did she think Eva could?

As she started towards the house she realised she was losing sight now of why she was here. What good was it going to do, forcing a confrontation on Eva that Eva really didn't need, and that she, Patty, had no way of controlling? Maybe it would be best if she just got back in the car and drove away. Yes, that was what she would do. Except Eva must have agreed to see her or Elaine wouldn't have rung, and if Eva was willing, brave enough, to see this through, then she had to make herself go through it too.

Forcing herself up the steps she rapped twice on the heavy front door, then turned her tired, frightened eyes to the stormy sky above, as though somewhere up there she might find at least a trace of the strength and courage she needed to get her through the next hour.

Chapter Thirteen

Eva could feel her own hostility filling the room as she watched Patty coming in through the door. The scars on her cheek felt raw and angry, her heart was as tightly closed as her fists. She was sitting on one of the sofas and didn't move when Elaine got up from her chair to greet her elder stepdaughter.

'Come in, dear,' Elaine said, discreetly thanking the receptionist who'd brought Patty through. After closing the door, she said, 'I've made some fresh tea for us all.'

Patty's eyes were on Eva, and only briefly left her as Elaine took her coat. Going to sit on the other sofa, Patty flinched at the hatred she could sense streaming her way.

Eva's voice was cutting as she said, 'You think you're here to talk about what you've done to my marriage, don't you?'

Patty glanced awkwardly at Elaine.

'Well you're wrong,' Eva told her. 'What you've done is for you and your conscience to live with. I don't need the detail, and I certainly don't need to watch you squirming and snivelling around trying to explain yourself . . .'

'Eva, dear,' Elaine broke in.

'It's OK, Elaine,' Patty said. 'She needs to tell me what she thinks . . .'

'Don't you *dare* patronise me!' Eva cried.

'That's not what I'm doing.'

'It's what you always do.'

'Only in your head . . .'

'No, in yours, Patty, in *yours*. You've told yourself for so long that you're in charge, that you always know what's best, that you've actually come to believe it. Have you never noticed that time's moved on, that I'm a grown woman now, that I feel the same way other women feel, especially when my own sister lies to me and *steals my husband*.'

Visibly flinching, Patty glanced at the tea Elaine was offering and shook her head. 'I don't expect you to forgive me, or to try to understand,' she said to Eva, 'I hardly know myself how it happened . . .'

'Oh for God's sake,' Eva cut in scathingly. 'You're not stupid, you knew exactly what you were doing. You were *lying*, Patty. In fact, so many lies, so much deceit has come out of you that I doubt you even know what the truth is any more.'

Patty's face was ashen. She had no words to defend herself, nowhere to turn for excuses or some kind of comfort that would help her sister.

'Don't you have anything at all to say?' Eva demanded scornfully.

'I'm sorry,' Patty whispered. 'Sorrier than I'll ever be able to put into words.'

Eva's eyes flashed. 'But not so sorry that it stopped you doing it. You knew what it would do to me, how it would devastate my world, but you went ahead with it anyway. Well, please don't ever delude yourself that there's one ounce of forgiveness or understanding in me because there isn't, and nor will there ever be.'

Patty swallowed and lowered her eyes.

Eva watched her with contempt, her breath shallow, her hands clenched tightly together.

In the end Patty said, 'I'd like to . . .'

Eva broke straight in. 'I'm not interested in what you'd like,' she spat. 'Nothing about you matters one iota to me now. All I want from you is the truth, Patty, if you're able to tell it – if you even know what it is any more.'

Patty's eyes were confused as she looked up. 'I thought . . . Isn't . . . ?'

'I'm not talking about what you've done with my husband, I'm talking about our mother and what you've been keeping from me.'

Shocked, Patty turned to Elaine.

'Don't worry,' Eva shouted, 'she hasn't broken your confidence, but I know there's something and now *you* are going to tell me what it is.'

Patty seemed to shrink into herself as she started to shake her head. 'No, not like this,' she protested.

Sitting forward, almost as though to strike her, Eva cried, 'Yes, like this. Here, now, today, you're going to tell me what else you've been keeping from me . . .'

'Eva, please don't . . .'

'*Just tell me,*' Eva seethed. 'What happened to her? What's the big secret?'

Stricken, Patty turned to Elaine.

'What *happened* to her?' Eva raged. 'Is she even dead?'

'Oh Eva, yes, of course she's dead,' Patty gasped. 'We'd never have told you . . .'

'Then for God's sake, what is it?'

Patty's eyes were full of dread.

'What did you do to her?' Eva demanded.

Patty flinched again. 'I didn't do anything . . . No one did . . .'

'Then what are you hiding? What despicable lies have you been telling all these years . . .'

'Eva, stop, please . . .'

'No, you stop. I want to know the truth and if you don't tell me right now, then so help me God . . .'

'All right, all right,' Patty shouted. 'She killed herself. We didn't want you to know, because the reason she did it . . . the reason . . .' Her voice was shredding, she couldn't go on.

Eva's face had turned white. She could dimly feel herself starting to shake, and when she tried to speak she found she couldn't. Elaine came to sit beside her and took her hand, but Eva's eyes remained fixed on Patty. Their mother had committed suicide. She was saying the words to herself, but couldn't quite grasp them. Her head was spinning, everything was blurring and fading. For a moment she thought she might be starting to pass out.

'Why?' she finally managed. 'What made her . . .?'

Patty's face was ravaged as she lifted it from her hands. 'What does it matter now?' she said brokenly. 'It happened such a long time ago.'

'Tell me why she did it.'

Shuddering with more sobs as she tried to catch her breath, Patty said, 'She was depressed . . . After she had you she just couldn't seem to get back on top. She'd try and for a while she was fine, but then the blackness would come over her again and there was nothing Daddy or I could do. She wouldn't let us near her during those times, she wouldn't look at you either; she just wanted to be on her own. The doctor gave her pills and sent her for counselling, but nothing ever seemed to work.'

Eva had become very still. The words were conjuring pictures she'd never seen before, of her mother in torment, turning her back on her children, withdrawing from the man she loved. They were nothing like the woman whose photos she had in her album. It wasn't the same woman at all.

'Sometimes she'd stand next to your bed watching you,' Patty went on. 'She didn't speak, or move. We had no idea what was going through her mind, but we were terrified she'd do something to harm you.'

Eva's heart turned over.

'She never did,' Patty said hastily, 'but with the way she was we could never be sure what she might do. She hit me once, around the face, so we knew she was capable of lashing out. She used to hit Daddy a lot too, and throw things, then she'd go out and not come back for hours, sometimes even days. Usually she went to Granny's, her own mother, and sometimes she'd take you with her. We knew you were safe when Granny was there, so we didn't try to make her bring you back.'

Unable to imagine how traumatising it must have been for Patty, Eva could only look at her sister and wonder why she'd kept this locked up inside for so long.

'We knew she was suffering from a severe postnatal depression,' Patty continued, 'she knew it too, but a diagnosis isn't a cure and nothing, just nothing, ever seemed to get her over it. Then Granny died and it was . . . She just . . . couldn't take any more.'

As she started to break down again Elaine went to hold her close, while Eva tried to move past the shock to a place where she could breathe again.

They couldn't be talking about the mother she'd known, because that woman had been beautiful and happy and used to swing her around and pretend she could fly. She baked birthday cakes and lit candles, read stories at bedtime and snuggled in with her after she'd had a bad dream. She was trying to picture that woman, to reassure herself that she had existed, but all she could see was the woman Patty had described.

Getting up from the sofa, she went to stand at the window. The rain was all but horizontal now, and the wind so fierce that the willows were bending almost to the ground. There seemed such a strange, other-worldly sense to everything, the way she was feeling, where she was, what she was hearing . . . In the end she turned around and heard her own voice like a ghostly echo saying, 'How – how did she do it?'

Bringing her head up, Patty pushed away more tears as she said, 'She took the car . . . No one knew because she was at home on her own that day. I was at school, you were . . . you were at nursery and . . . and . . .'

'Here,' Elaine said softly, handing her a tissue.

Taking it, Patty dabbed at her eyes. 'Daddy went home at lunchtime,' she continued, 'and that was . . .' She tried to catch her breath. 'That was when he found the note. He called the police straight away.' Putting a hand to her mouth as though to stifle a scream, she forced herself to go on. 'It was already too late . . . She'd already . . . she was already . . .'

'Sssh, ssh,' Elaine soothed, patting her hands. 'It's all right.'

Tears were shining in Eva's eyes as she watched them, and tried not to feel for what her sister had been through at such a tender age. She didn't want to soften towards her – it had happened a long time ago and wasn't going to change, or justify in any way what was happening now.

'Daddy didn't know,' Patty pressed on, 'until he got to the hospital, that you had been in the car too.'

Eva's heart jolted.

'You were thrown clear as the car went over,' Patty whispered brokenly, 'and you were hardly injured at all. Just cuts and bruises and concussion.'

Eva's head started to spin. It was as though the world was dipping and swaying away from her. She'd caused the depression that had killed her mother, so was that why her mother had tried to kill her? Because she blamed her for ruining her life?

'It turned out that she'd gone to pick you up from the nursery,' Patty continued, 'and we think, because of the timing, that she must have taken you home. We don't know if she took you out of the car, then put you back in again, or if she left you there while she went inside to write the note. Maybe the note was already written . . . We have no way of knowing. The only thing we could be certain of was where and how she died, and that she had intended to do it. Why she took you with her we'll never know, because there was nothing in the note to say that she meant to. The doctor said it was possible, if you were sleeping, that in her state of mind she'd even forgotten you were there.'

Eva could picture the cliff road where it had happened, the blind bend, the deep ravine . . . Her father had taken her there once, when she was in her teens, to show her where her mother had died. It was his way of trying to make her accept that her mother wouldn't be coming back, and she guessed it was from that day that she had finally ceased to believe otherwise. It must have been so hard for him to be there, to watch her throw the flowers they'd brought down on to the rocks below. Had he imagined his wife breaking apart the way the stems had? Had he felt the shock and grief all over again? Patty hadn't been there that day. It had been just the two of them, and Eva was remembering now how tightly her father had held her when they'd returned to the car. So tightly it had hurt, and she'd pushed him away. It wasn't hard to imagine what had been going through his mind then; he'd even said, very softly, 'I'm so lucky to have you.'

'And Patty,' she'd said.

'Of course,' he'd smiled, holding her face between his hands, 'and Patty too.'

Looking at Patty now, she felt her heart expanding with so much emotion that it was hard to make herself speak. 'I don't understand,' she managed in the end, 'why you've never told me this before.'

Regarding her with swollen, bloodshot eyes, Patty said, 'I know I probably should have, but at the time . . . You were so young, and Daddy felt you wouldn't be able to understand.'

'But what about later?'

'We talked about it sometimes, Daddy and I, but he always ended up deciding that there was no need for you to know the truth. It wouldn't bring Mummy back, he used to say, and so he didn't see the point of telling you something that would only upset you and maybe make you resent Mummy, or feel afraid of her in some way.'

'So instead I'm lied to and treated like a child long after . . .'

'Eva, we held it back because we love you, you must understand that. It wasn't . . . Eva, please don't walk away.'

'I'm sorry, but I don't want to hear any more,' Eva told her, reaching for her coat.

'What about the note? Don't you want to know what was in it?'

Eva stopped dead. Patty still had a note, her mother's final words that she'd kept to herself all these years, as though she, Eva, had no right to it. 'What does it say?' she demanded. 'Is she blaming me? Does she say I ruined her life?'

'Of course not!' Patty cried. 'There was nothing like that in it at all. She doesn't blame you, no one does.'

Eva looked at Elaine.

'Your mother's illness wasn't anyone's fault,' Elaine said gently. 'These things just happen sometimes.'

'But if she'd never had me . . .'

'You can't think that way . . .'

'It was what Daddy was always afraid of,' Patty broke in, 'that you'd feel responsible in some way, and you're not. How could you be, when you were just a child?'

Eva's eyes returned to Elaine.

'Please don't leave yet,' Elaine implored. 'I know this has come as a shock, so you should allow yourself some time to assimilate. Let me get you more tea, or perhaps something a little stronger?'

Eva shook her head. 'I don't want anything, thank you,' she answered. 'I just . . .' She looked at Patty, then away again. 'If you don't mind,' she said to Elaine, 'I'd like to be on my own for a while.'

As she went to put her coat on, Elaine said, 'If that's what you want, then why don't you stay here, by the fire? Patty and I can always go somewhere else, but we'll be close by if there's anything you want to ask. It's a horrible day out there and you probably ought not to be driving with all this so fresh in your mind.'

Flinching inwardly at the words, Eva took a breath and finally ended up letting go of her coat.

Avoiding Patty's eyes as she and Elaine left the room, Eva waited for the door to close before going to curl into a corner of the largest sofa. For a long, almost mesmeric time she sat staring into the fire, inhaling the perfumed air around her and trying to come to terms with the last few minutes. Having no memory of that time was making it seem unreal, as though it had happened in a film; or as if it were an item on the news about another family, another little girl. She tried to capture a sense of speed or terror; the feeling of being thrown, of falling against rocks, but nothing inside her stirred. Should she be glad of that? Would it help in some way to have a small flicker of recognition? Whether it would or not, there was none.

Closing her eyes, she let her head fall back against the cushions. She was thinking of the three photos in her album that showed her mother looking happy and carefree. Because her memories had been formed around those pictures, she was finding it hard now to see her mother any other way. Was it possible Patty had lied again? Had she made it all up in order to distract Eva from the terrible truth they were living through? It hardly seemed likely, but even so, if Elaine hadn't been in the room maybe she would be prepared to think the worst.

Aware of a growing tightness in her chest that was making it hard to breathe, she sat forward and put her head in her hands. She wished she could understand why she, Patty and her father hadn't been enough for her mother; why her love for them hadn't made living seem worthwhile, but she guessed depression didn't allow its victim to see things rationally. It only stole into them like a silent, baleful shadow, moving slowly, inexorably all the way through them, gradually closing down all their hopes and dreams, until finally there was no light left. She recognised the feeling of futility and despair, the dread of going on, because it was how she felt in the dead of night when she lay awake thinking of Don and longing for him with all her heart.

There were so many questions that still needed to be answered, but for the moment she only wanted to stay quietly where she was, allowing the strange feeling of connection that had begun stirring inside her to do what it would. She'd never be able to see her mother, or hear, or touch her, yet the few happy memories she had of her seemed to be wrapping themselves around her like gentle, loving arms.

Was she here in the shadows of this room? Did she know what was happening at this moment, in the lives of her daughters? What would she say, or do, if it was in her power to speak or act? Though Eva would never have any answers to that, she felt, in spite of the empty room she was in, that she wasn't alone. At least not for these moments, which was why she couldn't, wouldn't, move for fear of what would be lost if she did.

*   *   *

In the small kitchen next door Elaine was gazing out of the window, while Patty spoke quietly to Livvy on the phone.

'I understand Coral hasn't taken care of the shop on her own before,' she was saying, 'but I need you to be able to come home to the barn . . .'

'But why?'

'I'll explain when I see you. Is Coral with you now?'

'She's just popped out.'

'OK, well if she's not happy about holding the fort you'll have to lock up for the rest of the day.'

'Mu-um! I'm right in the middle . . .'

'I need to talk to you about Eva and the chat I've had with her this morning.'

'You've seen her?' Livvy said, sounding shocked. 'I thought she was going to Elaine's.'

'That's where I'm calling from. Now, please do as I ask and be ready to come to the house when I call again.'

'OK, if you say so, but before you go I think you should know that I've told Jake about you and Don and he's on his way home.'

Somehow Patty managed not to groan.

'He's not happy,' Livvy went on. 'He's definitely with Eva on this, so I don't think he'll be staying at the barn.'

Not allowing herself a moment to feel jealous of her children's loyalty to Eva, Patty said, 'Call him back and tell him he has to go home.'

'I can try, but like I said . . .'

'I heard what you said, now, please just do as you're told.'

As she rang off Elaine went to open the outside

door. A moment later Don came in, looking worried and uneasy.

Patty kept her distance as she said, 'I hope I've done the right thing. I just thought it would be best if you were here.'

'Where is she?' he asked, seeming to understand that any physical contact with Patty in front of Elaine would be wrong.

'In there,' Patty answered, pointing to the other door.

'Maybe I should go and check on her,' Elaine suggested. 'I can't see that it would do any harm.'

However, before she could get to her feet the door opened and Eva came into the room.

The instant she saw Don her face tightened, and whatever she'd been about to say seemed to die on her lips.

'Are you OK?' Patty asked awkwardly.

Turning to her, Eva said, 'I'd like to see the note.'

Patty's eyes went down. 'I – I don't have it any more,' she said.

Eva stared at her harshly. 'More lies, Patty?' she challenged.

'No!' Patty cried. 'It . . . I don't know what happened to it, but I can remember everything it said. I can tell you . . .'

Eva's tone was scathing as she said, 'You're the last person I want to hear speaking my mother's words,' and turning away she went to reach for her coat.

'Are you sure you want to go now?' Elaine protested. 'There's so much . . .'

'I'm sorry,' Eva interrupted, 'maybe we can talk another time, just the two of us.'

Stepping forward, Don said, 'Why don't you let me drive you?'

Eva's eyes turned cold. 'I'm quite capable,' she responded.

With a quick glance at Patty and Don, Elaine said, 'I'll come to the door with you.'

Left alone in the kitchen, Patty closed her eyes as she took an unsteady breath. 'I thought . . . I don't know what sort of reaction I expected. She seemed so . . . I don't know . . . Just not like the Eva we know.'

'She's been through a lot,' he reminded her. 'It's bound to be taking its toll.'

Patty nodded and sighed, then suddenly froze as Elaine shouted, 'Patty! Patty! Come quick.'

Don was first through the door with Patty close behind, already terrified of what they were about to find.

'So where's Eva now?' Livvy demanded, confused and anxious.

'At home,' Patty replied. 'She was insistent that she'd just tripped and fallen on the step . . .'

'I should go to her,' Livvy interrupted, reaching for her bag.

'No, wait . . .'

'You can't just leave her on her own!'

'She's not on her own. Don's with her. Elaine was sure she'd blacked out for a moment so we refused to allow her to drive herself. Do you know when she last ate?'

Livvy shook her head. Her agitation was almost infectious as she tried to cope with a worsening situation. 'I keep making her meals,' she said, 'but all she seems to manage is one or two mouthfuls, which is hardly surprising when you think of what she's going through. And now this, about her mother, Granny . . . I don't understand why you had to tell her now.'

Feeling the rebuke like a slap, Patty said, 'I didn't mean to. When I went over there I thought she was ready to talk about what's happened. It turned out she was asking Elaine . . . Oh God, Livvy, I wish I'd *never* had to tell her, because I still believe the same as Grandpa did, that it's not something she needed to know.'

'So instead you lied to her?'

'It wasn't so much a lie as trying to spare her the truth.'

'Whatever spin you put on it, as far as she's concerned you lied about that and you lied about Don.'

Patty's head went down. Her conscience was already beyond guilty, and this was making it so much worse. 'I've told you before . . .'

'I know what you told me, that you fought it and fought it, but you couldn't give him up. The trouble is, Mum, he wasn't yours *to* give up. He was hers and now she's ended up losing both of you. Why are you shaking your head? You know she has . . .'

'No, she hasn't,' Patty came in quietly. 'Don's going to stay with her. He's not coming back here.'

Livvy became very still. 'You mean, not tonight?'

'Not at all,' Patty replied, and turning away she willed herself not to break down. It wasn't only Don, though God knew in the days to come that would be the worst of it, it was all the talk of her mother, the reliving of the past, that was making everything so difficult now.

'Are you crying?' Livvy said worriedly.

'No,' Patty sniffed, shaking her head.

'Yes you are. Oh Mum, I wish I knew what to do . . .' Livvy put her arms round her.

'It's OK, I'm fine,' Patty insisted, hugging her back. 'It's just been an emotional day, and . . . You're right, he was never mine anyway, and now I've ruined everything . . .'

'You don't know that for sure, and anyway, like we've said before, you don't get to choose who you fall in love with. It was just mean of fate, or whatever, to have made you fall for him. So I guess it's not your fault really.'

Patty couldn't help but smile. 'You've always been a sucker for tears,' she teased softly.

Livvy rolled her eyes. 'I suppose that makes me a bit like you then.'

'I suppose it does,' Patty responded, folding her in her arms again. It felt so good to be close to Livvy like this, so right and vital, the way it used to feel when her mother held her. It had been so long since she'd allowed herself to think of that. 'What time are we expecting Jake?' she finally managed to ask.

'His train gets in at half four. I said I'd pick him up from the station. Actually, I probably ought to go in a minute. Will you be all right?'

'I'll be fine. Shall we eat at home tonight? Will Dave join us?'

'I guess yes to both. What are you going to do till I come back?'

'I might go and lie down for an hour. I've got a bit of a headache and I didn't sleep too well last night.'

Gazing deeply into her eyes, Livvy said, 'You're doing the right thing letting him go back to Eva, you know.'

Forcing the words from the tightness in her heart, Patty said, 'Yes, of course.'

'I know you won't want to hear this now,' Livvy went on, 'but you will get over him.'

Unable to say any more, Patty brushed a hand over Livvy's cheek, and after watching her go out to her car she turned away from the door, so racked with grief that there was simply no way she could hold it in now. How, after so many years, could her mother's suicide still devastate her this much? No one, not even Elaine, had any idea how difficult she found it to talk about that time. Whenever she did it brought everything back in a way that she simply couldn't endure. There were times when she even hated her mother for what she'd done. It had been selfish and cruel to a point that could never be forgiven. She should have thought about all the hurt she was going to cause, how she would destroy their lives and how much she, Patty, would miss her. But she hadn't. The only one she'd thought about, or even seemed to care about at the end, was Eva. It was there in the note she'd left, the note that was even now in Patty's bedside drawer. Yes, she'd lied to Eva, and she was already regretting it, but it was a part of their mother that was hers, that she'd never wanted to share with anyone. Only she and her father – and the police – had ever read it, so only they knew that Eva had mattered to their mother more than she had.

How could that be true? What kind of a mother had favourites?

What kind of a mother committed suicide?

No real mother would ever abandon her children.

Her eyes closed as she was suddenly swamped

by the memory of a nurse walking away with a baby. She could hear the squeal of her shoes on the polished floor, see the gentle sway of her hips. Her breath caught harshly on a sob. Eva had abandoned her son as cruelly as their mother had abandoned them, and she, Patty, had done nothing to stop it. She'd simply sat there, watching, listening and saying nothing as Eva rejected her own child. How could she have done nothing to save her nephew? The fact that she'd just been diagnosed with cancer, and had no way of knowing how well, or not, she would respond to her treatment, was surely reason enough. No one had ever condemned her, not even Eva. They'd all understood that she'd been so scared at the time, traumatised even, by her own news and by what had happened to her sister that she really hadn't had a choice. She'd had to put her own children first, and Eva, in case Livvy and Jake ended up needing their aunt to be their mother.

It had seemed to make sense then, and in a way it still did now, but she could no longer deny that she could have – *should have* – taken Eva's son into her home. And the terrible, unforgivable truth of why she hadn't was something she still, even now, couldn't bring herself to face.

'Eva, you're not listening.'

Eva was standing at the window, watching the changing colours and shapes of a stormy sunset shadowing and lighting the bay. 'I think it's you who's not listening,' she told him calmly. 'I've just said I'd rather be left on my own.'

Dashing a hand through his hair, Don forced himself not to sigh. 'I'm not talking about staying with you until you feel more able . . .'

'I know what you're saying,' she interrupted, 'and I don't need your pity.'

'It's not pity . . .'

She turned to face him. 'You've made it clear that you want to be with Patty, so go. I'm sure she'll be waiting.'

He didn't move, only looked at her.

'Didn't you hear what I said?'

'Patty isn't expecting me. She knows I'm staying here.'

'Then I'm sure she'll be relieved when she finds out that you're not.'

As she turned back to the window, seeming so remote that she could have been at the other side of the horizon, he could only watch her helplessly. 'Eva, I'm worried about you,' he said. 'After what . . .'

'You're afraid I'm going to follow in my mother's footsteps, is that it?' she cut in bluntly. 'If it is, then you don't need to be.'

Having had his fear voiced and denied was, he found, reassuring. Nevertheless, he said, 'You shouldn't be here on your own.'

Her eyebrows went up. 'You were happy to leave me alone before,' she reminded him.

'There was nothing about it that made me happy.'

'Surely there must have been. You were going to be with Patty, remember? There wouldn't have been much point to that if she didn't make you happy.'

Shifting uncomfortably, he said, 'You know what I'm saying, and . . .'

'Anyway, Livvy'll be here soon. She texted earlier to say Jake's coming too, so you see, I won't be on my own. And Jasmine's arriving early tomorrow, she said.'

'Livvy's with her mother now. Patty thought she

should know that you and I are getting back together.'

At that, Eva's eyes flashed with anger, but though she looked as if she might say something, in the end she merely turned to stare out to sea again. 'Go to Patty,' she told him coldly. 'I don't want you here.'

Not sure what to do, he gazed down at Elvis and Rosie as though they might be able to tell him. Eva's mobile rang, and picking it up she checked who it was and clicked on.

'Livvy, hi. Is Jake here yet?'

'I'm just on my way to get him,' Livvy answered. 'Mum told me about Don and that you're . . . you're back together?'

'No, Don and I aren't back together. In fact, he's just about to leave.'

Livvy sounded despairing as she said, 'I really don't get what's going on here.'

'I'm sorry . . .'

'Are you all right? Mum told me about Granny and everything . . .'

'I'm OK. A bit shocked, obviously, but I guess that's only to be expected.'

'So *did* you pass out at Elaine's? Mum thought you did.'

'No, I tripped, but no one would believe me, which is how come Don is here and my car is still at the retreat. I'll have to go back tomorrow to pick it up.'

'I can take you,' Don put in.

'You won't be here,' she reminded him.

'What do you want me to do?' Livvy asked. 'Shall I come there with Jake, or go back to Mum's? Actually, if Don's going to be with Mum I guess I should come to you.'

'As you like. Will Jake be staying too?'

'I expect so, if it's all right.'

'Of course it is. I'll see you when you get here.'

After ringing off Eva went through to the laundry room to collect some clean towels. When she returned to find Don still standing where she'd left him, looking confounded and lost, she felt herself falter for a moment. 'I'm going to get a room ready for Jake now,' she told him. 'Perhaps you wouldn't mind feeding Rosie and Elvis before you leave.'

'Eva, this isn't . . .'

'I don't want to argue any more,' she interrupted. 'Our marriage is over, we both know that, and frankly, having you in the house is making it a lot harder to deal with. So please be gone by the time I come back down again.'

It was almost eight o'clock by now, and after watching her niece and nephew wolf down a giant bowl of spaghetti carbonara Eva was still sitting with them, drinking wine and managing to laugh at Jake's stories of Sicily. She kept thinking of how proud her mother would have been of them, and wondering how often Patty had thought the same. She was filled with admiration for the way Jake could make her and Livvy feel as though they were a part of his adventure with his vivid and often outrageous descriptions, particularly of what he and the others had got up to while there. It was reminding her of how high she used to get on visiting new places and meeting other models, stylists, photographers, advertising clients. The parties they used to have. The wild and reckless adventures with not a single care in the world. She'd never been to Sicily, or Cartagena, where Jake was apparently heading next, but there was no rule to say she had to visit everywhere before she died. Besides, she belonged here now, in Dorset, and though she had no idea yet of how she was going to bear it with neither her sister nor Don as a part of her life, she'd already made up her mind that she wasn't going to run away from the home she'd created and loved.

'Shall I open another bottle?' Livvy suggested, emptying the first one into Jake's glass.

'Definitely,' Jake cried. Then, remembering his manners, 'I mean, as long as it's OK.'

Smiling, Eva got up to go to the cooler. 'What's mine's yours,' she told him. 'Mum and I always used to say that to each other. I think she's taken it a bit far with Don though, don't you?'

The joke misfired, but the moment passed as she handed a bottle to Jake to open and sat down again. Having them here was wonderfully soothing, she was finding, and distracting in a way that didn't take her so far away from the heartache that it hit her like a blow when she came back again. She thought of Don down at the barn with Patty and felt herself folding inside, but then she quickly switched her thoughts to her mother and provided she didn't think of the final hours, she found herself feeling the calmness she'd experienced for those few precious minutes earlier. It had disappeared as soon as she'd walked into Elaine's kitchen and seen Don, leaving her shaken and almost panicky, which was why she'd missed a step on leaving. But it had come back later, like a lifeline, and she was holding on to it as if it were part of her.

'Would you like to talk about what's happened today?' Livvy said gently. 'I mean, we don't have to if you don't want to, I just don't want you to think that you've got to keep it all bottled up . . .'

'I'm fine, honestly,' Eva assured her, 'but it's sweet of you to ask.' Her eyes started to twinkle. 'I'm enjoying listening to this reprobate,' she said, ruffling Jake's hair. 'Tell us more about Bobbie. Did she stay in Sicily for the whole time you were there?'

Finishing up the slice of cheese he'd just helped himself to, Jake said, 'Actually, she flew back a few days ago, and to be honest it all went a bit flat for a while, because she's so out there, isn't she? It's like we didn't really know what to do with ourselves, because she was the focus of everything.'

'She was always like that,' Eva told him. 'People just gravitate to her.'

'And she is so hilarious with Manuela. They could give Elvis and Rosie a run for their money, those two. Talk about an odd couple.'

'They're pretty legendary,' Eva agreed.

'I'd love to see her again,' Livvy sighed. 'It seems ages since she was last here.'

'We'll have to invite her,' Eva decided. 'She's always so busy that we'll probably have to book months in advance, but I'll give her a call. Is she going to Cartagena with you?' she asked Jake.

He shook his head. 'No, I don't think so. The last time I saw her, which was yesterday when she only took me . . . Wait for this . . . To *the Ivy* for lunch. Oh my God, that reminds me, a friend of hers came over to our table to say hello, and asked me to say hi when I saw you.'

Not surprised, since she'd known a lot of Bobbie's friends way back when, Eva was intrigued as she said, 'Who was it?'

Jake was looking apologetic to show he'd already forgotten the name.

'It doesn't matter,' Eva told him. 'Just as long as you were having a good time.'

'Oh, no, that's right,' he exclaimed, suddenly remembering. 'He's called Nick ... Nick ... something-or-other.'

Feeling a strangeness inside that was more unsettling than pleasant, Eva said, 'Nick Jensen?'

'That's him!' Jake cried, with a clap of his hands. 'Jensen. That's his name.'

Careful not to let her feelings show, Eva smiled and lifted her glass. There was no need for Livvy and Jake to know anything about Nick Jensen, who he was, how he fitted into her life, or how furious she was that he'd dare to send a message through her nephew. In fact, how dared he even admit that he knew her? After the way he'd shut her, and their son, out of his life sixteen years ago he had no right to behave as though she might actually be pleased to hear from him, any more than he had a right to protest to a newspaper on her behalf. What had happened between them was in the past, over, done with, and as far as she was concerned that was exactly how it would stay.

Chapter Fourteen

It was hard to believe that over six weeks had passed since the day Eva had learned the truth about her mother – the very same day that she'd told Don to go. She'd never imagined herself doing that, and still felt surprised, even regretful about it, but knowing she could never trust – or respect – him again, she'd felt she'd had little choice.

If only love and hope could be so easily banished.

Time often felt somehow surreal now, much like her existence, making what she'd managed to achieve in these bizarrely short, yet eternal, weeks seem almost incredible. She knew that Don and Patty had been expecting her to fall apart, and God knew how often, in her private moments, she had, but somehow she was managing to keep going. Exactly where her inner strength was coming from was difficult to say, and there were definitely times when it deserted her completely. However, after reaching the bottom, when it simply wasn't possible to get any lower, she'd find herself calling on those few precious minutes at Elaine's when she'd felt close to her mother. It was as though, she sometimes thought, her mother was willing her not to take the same way out that she had. Suicide wasn't an answer; it wouldn't give her the release or the end to her pain she was seeking.

Though it worried Eva very much to think that her mother's soul, even now, might be in torment somewhere, Elaine could never be convinced.

'It's in your mind,' she'd tell her, 'everything is, which gives you the power to change it.'

Eva was sure that it was spending so much time with Elaine over these past weeks that had enabled her slowly, but steadily, to come to terms with the way her mother had died, and to find the strength to start turning her life around. Though, in spite of everything, it might be breaking her heart to be estranged from her sister, she kept telling herself that one day it would stop hurting as much, and eventually at some point in the future they would become used to no longer being a part of one another's lives. As devastating as the thought was, she'd come to understand – and was sure Patty had too – that this was the price of betrayal, and no one, not even the innocent, escaped how bitter and unforgiving it could be.

Lately, especially over these last few days, she'd even started to see some light. In fact, where she was now, today, and what she was doing, was proof in itself of how far she'd come in such a short space of time.

'This is so cool, isn't it?' Livvy whispered excitedly. 'I never imagined it would be anything like this.'

Loving how thrilled Livvy was, especially as she was making this happen mainly for her, Eva said, 'We have our wonderful Bobbie to thank for it.'

'And you,' Livvy reminded her loyally. 'I mean, you're the one who decided to pull out all the big guns. If you hadn't, no one would be here.'

'Well, a few would,' Eva responded wryly, 'but it's true, this is a very different fashion show to the one we sent out invitations for.'

Which was why they'd had to relocate from the Summer Lodge at Evershot to a much larger, but equally luxurious venue near Bournemouth, where there was a ballroom big enough to provide seating for two hundred guests with a division down the middle to accommodate a ten-metre catwalk. There was also a spacious adjacent room where the three models Bobbie had sent could make their quick changes – and most importantly of all, at least as far as some were concerned, a free bar was linking the event room to the reception. This was where Eva and Livvy were now, greeting their guests as they flowed in, gorgeously and even outlandishly clad in everything from Jackson to Conran to Christian Dior. The hotel staff were handing out glasses of champagne, while the photographer that Eva's new PR agent had hired for the day jostled with his colleagues from various glossies and tabloids to capture the most saleable shots of the event.

The really big news for the editors was that Eva – Angelina – had agreed to be photographed after the show with the models who'd come to help promote Perdita's exclusive designs. However, she was insisting that each of the designers whose creations she sold at her shop should also be photographed, and that Livvy, whose amazing flamenco dress was the highlight of the show, must be given as much credit and coverage as her own small collection, if not more.

'Are you sure you're ready to be famous?' Eva had teased her on their way here.

'Bring it on,' Livvy had declared. 'Do I have to give interviews as well?'

'For the trade press, certainly.'

'What about the tabloids and *OK!* and all that?'

'If you want to, I'm sure they'll be delighted to have you.'

'Because I'm your niece?'

'For now. Later, you'll have your very own spotlight. In fact, if it's what you want, I'm going to make sure of it.'

'OMG, this is soooo cool,' Livvy cried in rapture. 'And we're definitely working on opening more shops?'

'In time, if things work out. Bobbie's already on my case to start one in London, but that might be a tad ambitious for now. I thought we should start looking somewhere more like Brighton, or Bath – big, but not too big, and definitely glam.'

'I am so with you on this,' Livvy told her earnestly. 'And now we've got Coral pretty well trained up, we can think about hiring another part-timer to help out while we're busy taking over the world.'

Only wishing she was able to make it happen as fast as Livvy would like, Eva started to thread her way through the crowd to go and check on proceedings backstage. Her journey was constantly interrupted by friends and strangers, all wanting to wish her luck on what many assumed was her very first show as a designer. In comparison to the more intimate affairs she'd held up to now in local hotels, or the arts centre, she guessed it probably could be seen that way, so she accepted their enthusiasm graciously and promised to catch up again later.

'Aha, here she is!' a familiar voice cried as Eva

squeezed her way between two clothes racks into the changing room.

Seeing her gorgeous friend Carrie-Anne, Eva's face instantly lit up. 'You're here!' she cried, holding out her arms. 'How did you get in without me seeing you?'

'I saw that you were busy out front so I came round the back,' Carrie-Anne told her, hugging her hard. 'I haven't seen Bobbie yet. I take it she's here?'

'Oh, she's definitely around somewhere. Carrie, I'm so thrilled you could make it.'

'So am I, sweetie,' Carrie-Anne assured her, her smoky blue eyes melting with affection, 'but it was touch and go thanks to those flaming air-traffic controllers in France. You know, this show is going to be sensational, I can feel it in my bones.'

'It will be now you're here,' Eva informed her, standing back to get a good look at her. With her flawless caramel complexion, wicked sloe eyes and shamelessly pouty red lips – not to mention the stunning figure that had graced every high-end catwalk, magazine cover and specialised TV advertisement – she could have been put on the earth for the sole purpose of selling, and now designing, her own range of supremely classy and wildly exotic lingerie.

'I've always said we should do a show together,' Carrie-Anne reminded her, 'and now you're getting into the game we'll make sure it happens. God, I'm going to enjoy this one, I just know it. I'm assuming I have a front-row seat.'

'Where else?'

'Next to you?'

'Actually, next to Bobbie, because I'll be back here bossing everyone around.'

Carrie-Anne hit her forehead. 'Of course, you're the designer – and I've got to tell you, some of this stuff, Angie – Evie – is simply to die for. You've got some serious talent going on here, girl.'

'Not just me,' Eva reminded her, stepping aside to make room for someone who was struggling to open up an ironing board.

There were so many bodies in here – models at mirrors, stylists primping dummies, hairdressers coiffing wigs, make-up artists creating high-concept art – that there was hardly any room to move. However, the atmosphere was electric, and the gales of girlish laughter, yells from the wings, and sudden bursts of music prepping for the show, were making it feel so like the old days that Eva was starting to sink into a wonderfully strange warp of time. It seemed everyone was thrilled to be here, as much for her as for Bobbie, and the fact that she'd never previously met any of her models, or the technical team, didn't seem to be mattering one bit. They'd already established a wonderful rapport during last night's rehearsal, and if the way that had gone was any indication then Carrie-Anne was right, the guests who'd journeyed here from all over really could be in for a sensational show.

'Well, everything seems to be nice and chaotic in here,' Eva remarked, glancing at the clock and feeling her stomach churn with nerves. 'Just how we like it,' she quipped, knowing it was time for the guests to begin taking their seats.

'What can I do?' Carrie-Anne offered. 'Put me to use any way that helps.'

Loving her more than ever, Eva said, 'Actually, you could go and start rounding everyone up. The press are going to be thrilled that you're here, but please don't let them hold things up. We have to be out of the place by five so they can set for another function at eight.'

'Leave it to me,' Carrie-Anne told her.

'Before you go,' Eva said as she started to leave, 'can you stay over tonight?'

Carrie-Anne pulled an apologetic face. 'I really, really wanted to, you know that, but I just can't get out of the dinner I told you about. The clients are too big.'

Crushed, but managing to hide it, Eva said, 'Not to worry. We'll just have to make sure we get together next time I'm in London.'

'You bet.' Then tilting Eva's face to look into her eyes, she said, 'I know Bobbie has to rush back too, so please don't tell me you have no one to celebrate with.'

'Of course I do,' Eva tried to laugh. 'There's Livvy, and Coral who's been helping out at the shop. Actually, Livvy designed the flamenco dress for her, but she's recut, lengthened, straightened, flounced, you name it, for one of the girls.'

Carrie-Anne's eyebrows were raised. 'Off the subject,' she told her.

'OK, I was about to say I'm sure Coral will be free – actually, you'll probably meet her out front. She was going to model today, before we grew to where we are now. It's really floating her boat to know that the star creation was originally designed for her.'

'We don't say floating the boat any more,' Carrie-Anne told her gently, 'and we're still off the subject.'

'And the subject was? Oh, yes, tonight. There's Livvy, probably Coral, and Jasmine, Don's daughter, who's also around here somewhere.'

Carrie-Anne's eyes became more intense. 'And the man himself?' she prompted.

Eva shook her head. 'Please don't let's go there. I'll catch up with you before you leave, OK?'

Still regarding her closely as she backed away, Carrie-Anne said, 'Count on it.'

A quarter of an hour later, as the last-minute arrivals were taking their seats, and Bobbie prepared to go onstage to deliver the welcoming speech, Eva met her old agent's eyes across the dressing room and felt her heart flood with affection. There was no way in the world an event this size could be happening without her, and when she considered how kind, yet unobtrusive Bobbie had been over these last few weeks, not to mention what a pivotal and supportive part she'd played in her life, it made her feel quite emotional. Sometimes things could be said without words, and garrulous and loud as Bobbie often was, today she was being her much more subtle and sensitive self. She hadn't even mentioned the fact that Jake had met Nick at the Ivy, proving that she was as committed to their pact of never mentioning Nick as Eva was.

Feeling Livvy and Jasmine come up either side of her to link her arms, Eva continued to gaze into Bobbie's eyes as she mouthed the words, 'Time to sing.'

Bobbie gave a choke of laughter, since it was what she always said to her girls before a show, reminding them that there were more difficult things to do in life than parade up and down showing off clothes. Or, in her case today, make a welcoming speech.

'Are you OK?' Jasmine whispered, as Eva hugged the girls' arms.

'Great,' Eva whispered back.

'I feel sick,' Livvy muttered, staring glassy-eyed at the vista of an incredible future.

'Don't worry, she's not serious,' Jasmine assured Eva.

'I'm glad you're here,' Eva told her.

With an embarrassed laugh, Jasmine said, 'Where else was I going to be today? We're in this together, us three, all the way to the stars, so no way was I going to miss blast-off.'

Immediately feeling guilty for thinking that this evening was going to be an anti-climax with only Livvy and Jasmine to celebrate with – and possibly Coral – Eva pressed a hearty kiss to Jasmine's forehead as she said, 'I have a lot to thank you for.'

Colouring, Jasmine said, 'Not really.'

'Yes I have, but we'll save it for later.' She wanted desperately to ask if Jasmine had told her father about today, and what, if anything, he'd said, but she restrained herself. Nor had she given in to the urge to ask Livvy about Patty, though she knew they must have discussed the show, probably endlessly, as it was such a big deal for Livvy. She imagined both girls – or certainly Livvy – had received a text by now wishing them luck, but her own phone had stayed silent from both quarters. She'd never admit how desperately she wanted it to ring, nor would she dwell on how much she was missing Patty today, who'd always been there for every major event in her life. She was simply going to carry on smiling and applauding as Bobbie, looking disgracefully scrumptious in a fruity-patterned kaftan with matching bandanna, strutted grandly on to the stage.

It was as Bobbie started to speak that Eva felt her mobile starting to vibrate, and if she could have been sure it wouldn't break into a ring, as it sometimes did, she'd have left it. As she couldn't, she quickly pulled it out of her pocket and was fumbling for the off switch when she realised it was simply a text.

Thinking of you today. I know it'll be great. Miss you Px

Hastily shutting the phone down, Eva forced herself to go on listening to Bobbie, who was telling everyone how thrilled and honoured she was to be introducing Perdita's first major show.

'Of course you all know who's behind the name,' she was saying with her best mischievous smile, 'it's one of the most courageous and beautiful young women I know. Many of you will remember her as Angelina, and you'll no doubt also remember just how brightly she used to light up the world. From the moment I first set eyes on her when she was only seventeen years old I've always found there to be a very special quality about her, one that defies words – or at least my ability to capture them – but anyone who knows her will understand what I'm saying. Every time you meet her you seem to come away feeling that something good has just happened to you. It might not have been anything she said, or did, in fact it might very well have been nothing more, or less, than the way she looks at you. I'm sure you all know the look. It's the one that seems to touch you with a kind of magic and makes you feel a little more important than you actually are. It's the look that made her famous, and in its way it transcends even *her* extraordinary beauty.'

As everyone started to applaud she turned a page, and the wattage of her smile decreased as she said, 'We all know what Eva went through, sixteen years ago . . .'

Eva stopped listening. She had no desire to be reminded of that time when all it meant to her now was the terrible reality of losing her son – a son most people in the room had no idea even existed. His sixteenth birthday had come and gone several weeks ago, with no word from his adoptive parents to say that they'd received the card she'd sent. Patty had contacted her that day, with much the same sort of message as the one she'd just sent, in spite of the fact that she'd told Patty over and over that she wanted no more contact with her. She wasn't sure what Patty was expecting by trying to stay in touch, but if it was to keep a link going, maybe even soften her enough to send a message back, then she should prepare herself for a big disappointment. Eva had no intention of acknowledging this text any more than she had the last one. Nor was she going to allow her lying, cheating sister to ruin this special day that Bobbie had made possible, with reminders of how those who were supposed to be closest to her had so bitterly betrayed her.

'Any word from Livvy?' Don asked, passing his coat to a waiter as he sat down at the corner table, opposite Patty.

'Not yet,' she replied, fighting the urge to touch his hand as he laid it on the table between them. They still never indulged in any public displays of affection, indeed it was rare for them even to be seen out together, but they'd decided to chance coming to the Riverside tonight since Eva and their daughters were all the way over in Bournemouth. 'Have you heard from Jasmine?' she asked.

'No.' His eyes locked with hers, and seeming to

sense what she was thinking, he said, 'It's all right. Let everyone stare, to hell with them.'

'Someone is sure to tell Eva.'

'It's not as if she doesn't already know.'

Accepting the truth of that, Patty looked down at the papers she'd been reading before he came in, and scooping them up slipped them into her bag.

'Did you send her a text?' he asked.

Patty nodded. 'I haven't heard back.'

He was still watching her closely. 'We've still got a long way to go,' he reminded her gently.

She knew that, but it never helped much to hear it. And the fact that she'd attempted to put Eva first when she'd tried to give him up – the day she'd told Eva about their mother – hadn't achieved any kind of reconciliation. How could it, when Eva had rejected him and refused to have anything to do with either of them ever since?

Patty couldn't explain why Don meant so much to her, he just did. She only had to think about him to want him, to look at him to love him. He made her feel to a depth she hadn't even known was possible before, both physically and emotionally. He said it was the same for him, and she had no reason to doubt him considering what he'd given up for her, and how powerfully he always responded to her. There was something special between them, something holding them together so tightly that neither their consciences nor their judges could tear them apart. Yet the terrible price she was paying might eventually do that, because losing Eva was starting to feel like losing a vital part of herself.

'You're the only person I can say this to,' she'd told Elaine when they'd met for lunch at the weekend, 'but she feels like the only link to our mother – well, of course she does, because she is. I don't understand why, after all these years, that should matter the way it seems to.'

'It always matters,' Elaine had responded kindly. 'And between you I think you've created something more powerful than the bond sisters normally share, perhaps even more special than the one we have with our mothers.'

Patty had often wondered about that herself, but this was the first time she'd ever spoken of it. 'I'd never admit this to Eva,' she'd said, after a while, 'but there are times when I've felt so jealous of her. We've all loved her so much, Daddy, me, Don . . . She's always mattered so much to everyone, more than the rest of us, and sometimes it's as though . . . Well, sometimes I've been left feeling as though I hardly matter at all. How self-pitying is that?'

Elaine's tone was exceptionally gentle as she said, 'The way you feel is perfectly understandable, my dear. In fact, I'm sure there are some who wouldn't blame you at all if you hated your mother, or Eva, for the way you were left to cope with everything. It seemed to be assumed that you'd take it all on, your father's devastation, your baby sister's upbringing, never mind her sense of abandonment, and you were only twelve when you lost your mother. Very young indeed, but old enough for it to have shattered your world. So it's all credit to you that you aren't burdened with resentment or anger, or any of those horrible, negative emotions that accompany a sense of lack.'

Patty's eyes went down as she said, 'Sometimes I feel full of them.'

'Of course you do, we all do at times, but the point is you don't act on them.'

'Don't I? Wouldn't you say what I've done with Don was acting on them?'

'If you didn't love him, I might think so.'

Swallowing drily, Patty said, 'I lied to Eva about the letter Mummy left. I still have it.'

At that Elaine had seemed flustered, and extremely dismayed. 'Are you going to do something about that?' she'd asked, making it clear by her tone that Patty must.

Patty shook her head. 'I know I should, but if I do she'll know . . . Everyone will . . .'

'Know what?' Elaine prompted.

Patty took a breath. 'Like I said, Eva's always meant so much . . . I just can't help wondering if my mother thought about me at all when she took her own life.'

'Whatever she thought about, you have to remember the state of mind she was in – and then you must tell yourself that the past is the past, and in spite of how difficult and lonely it must have been for you at times, trying to fill your mother's shoes while you missed her so much, you only have to look at how you've turned out to feel proud of who you are and what you've achieved.'

Patty's smile was weak as she tried to accept the praise; her heart was heavy with guilt.

'I have a question for you,' Elaine had continued. 'It won't be an easy one to answer, so don't feel you have to do so straight away. Do you think there's a chance that what's happening between you and Don could be you trying to prove to yourself that for once you can matter more?'

The bluntness of the question had taken Patty's breath away, and several minutes had passed while she'd tried to face it honestly and bravely. In the end all she could say was, 'I understand why you might think that, and I've even thought it myself at times, but in spite of the jealousy I've felt towards Eva, and the frustration, and, yes, loneliness, of always knowing that I have to take care of myself while everyone takes care of her, I love her far too much to consciously or unconsciously hurt her like that.'

Elaine showed no expression as she said, 'So you have no doubts about your feelings for Don?'

'None at all.'

In the days since their chat Patty had wondered if she'd answered that question too quickly, too defensively, but even if she had it was only because she truly didn't have any doubts. She loved Don in a way that went beyond words, because it went beyond her level of understanding. What she couldn't be clear about, however, was how much longer they could continue to live under this sort of strain. It was easier when they were at home, just the two of them, but even then whenever Jake rang from his latest modelling assignment, or Reece was in touch for one reason or another, she was left feeling beaten and shamed by their condemnation. Going out could be nothing short of hell, with old friends cold-shouldering them, or even making a point of expressing their disgust. Of course there were always those who'd rather not get involved, particularly colleagues and clients, but even they weren't quite managing to disguise their surprise or disapproval. Don's answer was almost always the same as the one he'd given just now, 'To hell with them,' but she knew he wasn't finding this any easier than she was. What made it worse, for her at least, was the way everyone was siding with Eva.

Not that she blamed them, she was sure if she was in their shoes she would too, but once again it was as if her feelings, her dreams, her life, mattered less than her sister's.

'Are you going to answer that?' Don prompted gently.

Looking down at her phone and seeing it was Livvy, she quickly picked it up. 'Hi, how did it go?' she asked, driving some excitement into her voice. 'I was expecting to hear from you ages ago.'

'Sorry, it's been completely manic,' Livvy cried, 'but it was fantastic. Everyone loved the flamenco dress. The model had to keep coming back on because they wouldn't stop applauding. OK, Bobbie and Carrie-Anne were making them clap, but honestly, Mum, it was amazing. And then I only had to go on and take a bow. I felt like a full-on celebrity with all the flashes going off and everyone trying to get to me. Jasmine even came up and asked for my autograph! She said she wanted to be the first to get it, because it might be worth something one day.'

Laughing shakily, Patty said, 'I'm sure it will. Is she still with you?'

'Yeah, she's right here sending a text to her dad. It's been totally wicked, Mum. I wish we could do this every week, except I'd never be able . . . Oh God, I almost forgot. Everyone was really mad about Livvy's loons, you know the trousers I make with the zips that go from the bum right down the back of the legs? Carrie-Anne's even ordered a pair. She reckons they're going to be the next big thing.'

'They will be if she wears them,' Patty told her. 'I'm so proud of you, darling. You were obviously a huge hit.'

'I have to admit, it was pretty cool, and Eva's like totally blown away, because everyone was really nice to her and kept saying how fantastic it was to see her, and great that she's making a comeback. I don't think she quite sees it like that, but she went along with it anyway. I'll text you in a minute with a list of the papers you have to get tomorrow, and we definitely have to buy a copy of *OK!* this week, because they were there too. And *Elle* and *Closer* and . . . Oh God, I'll send the list when the PR girl sends it to Eva.'

'Be sure you don't forget. Where are you now?'

'We're on our way back. Eva's in the taxi behind with the publicity people, and once she's finished with them she's taking us to the Riverside for a celebration dinner. Yay! Bring it on!'

Putting out a hand to stop Don from ordering any drinks, Patty said, 'How far away are you?'

'I don't know, about ten, fifteen minutes, I guess. Why?'

'Because Don and I are at the Riverside.'

'Oh no, Mum! It'll spoil everything if she sees you.'

'I know, I know. Don't worry, we'll leave before you get here. Just thank goodness you rang.'

'Dead right. Oh God, I'm sorry, I guess that sounds mean, but you've got him and she hasn't and I don't think she needs reminding of that tonight.'

Knowing it was unlikely Eva forgot it for a moment, Patty said, 'We're on our way out now, so the coast should be clear by the time you get here.'

'What on earth's going on?' Don demanded as she rang off.

Getting to her feet, Patty said, 'Eva's on her way here with the girls. If Arthur had been in tonight

I'm sure he'd have warned us, but he isn't so we have to count ourselves lucky that Livvy rang when she did.'

'We can't keep running away like this,' Don protested as he signalled a waiter to bring their coats.

'I know, but do you really want to sit here when she walks in with our daughters and have the whole place come to a standstill?'

'No, I guess not, but to be frank I'm starting to care a lot less about Eva than I am about you. She's clearly not going to pieces the way we thought she would . . .'

'Grief, loss, high emotion has an energy all of its own,' she interrupted, 'and what's worrying me is what might happen to her when the high of this show finally runs out.'

'Whatever does happen,' he said, as they got to her car, 'you need to start coming to terms with the fact that you can't always be there to save her, and nor can you go on refusing to accept that she's capable of standing on her own two feet.'

'So you think she can?'

'As far as I can see she's proving it.'

'Which means you're refusing to take any more responsibility for her?'

'No, it means that I'm backing off treating her like a child, which is something we've both done for far too long. Now, we'd better get out of here before they turn up. I'll see you back at the barn. Would you like me to pick up some Chinese on the way?'

'OK.' After sitting in the driver's seat, she lowered the window and looked up at him. 'I can't see a time when we'll ever be able to run into her without it being utterly horrible for us all.'

Reaching for her hand, he said, 'Time moves on, things change and before you know it she'll probably meet someone else.'

Unable to imagine that, Patty said, 'Even if she does, I know in my heart that she's never going to forgive me.'

'You might be surprised,' he said softly, and after squeezing her hand he stood back for her to start reversing out of her space.

The following morning Eva came downstairs just before eight to find, to her amazement, that Livvy and Jasmine hadn't only already been out for the papers and conjured up a feast of a breakfast, but they'd also fed and walked Rosie and Elvis and filled the ducks' trough with pellets.

'Good morning,' Jasmine cried cheerily as she pulled out a chair for Eva to sit down. 'We have scrambled eggs, sausages, bacon and grilled tomatoes, and/or muesli with fresh fruit, and/or porridge with skimmed milk and Greek yoghurt.'

'Here's your coffee,' Livvy declared, setting a mug down next to her. 'White, no sugar, and your orange juice is right there, already poured.'

With a bewildered but delighted laugh, Eva said, 'Is it my birthday?'

Livvy frowned. 'I don't think so,' she answered, looking at Jasmine. Then, brightening again, 'No, it's definitely not your birthday, so I'm guessing it must be our way of trying to say thank you for yesterday, which was absolutely fantastically brilliant.'

'And for dinner last night,' Jasmine added, 'which was also absolutely fantastically brilliant, but we noticed that you didn't eat very much, so we decided you must be starving by now.'

Eva could only wish that she was, for their sakes much more than her own, but she knew already that she was going to have as big a struggle as she'd had last night to manage more than a few mouthfuls. It was seeing Patty, then Don driving out of West Bay that had stolen her appetite, and the memory of it this morning was having the same effect all over again. However, she had to make an effort to get past it or she was going to end up spoiling this extended celebration for Livvy and Jasmine, which was the last thing she wanted. Today was almost as exciting for them – Livvy in particular – as yesterday had been, and already Livvy was tearing open the papers to show her how much coverage they'd received.

It was impressive, there was no doubt about that, and Eva had to admit the energy that seemed to be coming off the pages, as well as from Livvy and Jasmine, was actually starting to give her a buzz. She wasn't particularly surprised to see so many library photos of herself from the early days, and a precis of what had happened to end her career was only to be expected. So she skipped past all that and found, to her great satisfaction, that not only had the show itself been given a full double-page spread in three of the tabloids, but Livvy's flamenco dress had actually made the front cover of the *Daily Mail*. Almost equally pleasing was the fact that none of the contributing designers seemed to have been forgotten, and there was even a shot in one of the papers of Carrie-Anne holding up a pair of Livvy's loons and declaring them the next big thing.

'I can't believe it! It's so fab, fab, fab,' Livvy shrieked, jumping up and down with joy. 'I wonder if Dave's seen it yet?'

'I thought you weren't going out with him any more,' Jasmine piped up.

'No, but we're still good mates and I know he'll want to see this. Oh, look! It's us three. Oh my God, it's a horrible one of me, but you look fantastic, Jas. And you, of course,' she added to Eva.

Glowing with pride, and colouring to the roots of her hair, Jasmine looked at the picture, then at Eva. 'I guess it's lucky my mother doesn't get this paper,' she commented. 'She'd go mental if she saw this.'

With a quick glance at Eva, Livvy said, 'Someone's bound to show her though. And anyway, what's her problem? You're enjoying yourself, which any mother ought to feel pleased about, and it's not as if Eva's even with your dad any more.'

Flinching inside, Eva said, 'I take it she knew you were coming yesterday.'

Jasmine shrugged. 'I told her, but whether or not she remembered is anyone's guess.'

Eva and Livvy exchanged looks.

'Actually,' Jasmine went on, blushing again, 'she's never really very interested in anything I'm doing. I mean, she gets on my case about stuff all the time, you know like am I doing my homework, is my room tidy, where am I going every time I go out, but the next thing she's on the phone to one of her friends, or she goes out somewhere and it's like she's forgotten I'm there.'

'Is she cool about you coming here now?' Livvy asked. 'I guess not, if she'd go mental about seeing your picture in the paper.'

Jasmine's colour deepened as she said, 'I won't tell you the kind of things she says now, because actually they're almost worse than before, and I feel ashamed of how spiteful she can be. I mean, she knows what it's like to be left so you'd think she'd be a bit more sympathetic.'

Swallowing drily, Eva reached for Jasmine's hand and gave it a squeeze.

'Has she never met anyone else?' Livvy ventured.

'Yeah, she goes out with different blokes now and again, I think she does Internet dating, actually, but nothing ever seems to work out.'

Feeling for how lost she seemed, apparently hardly able to connect with her mother, and now finding it difficult with her father too, Eva said, 'If you found it easier to stop coming here . . .'

'No way am I going to give up my job and stay at home with her every weekend,' Jasmine cried hotly. 'Especially when she's out half the time anyway.'

'When's she expecting you back?' Livvy asked.

Jasmine's eyes were still on Eva. 'I told her I'll be here till Sunday, if that's OK. I'm on study leave today and tomorrow, so I thought I might as well do my homework here and then I can go into the shop as usual on Saturday. I mean, I can go home again and come back on Friday, as usual, if you'd prefer . . .'

'You're always welcome here,' Eva told her warmly, 'you know that.'

Clearly moved, Jasmine tried to hide it by looking at the picture of the three of them again. 'It's actually quite good of you, Livvy,' she insisted. Then, 'I wonder if Dad's seen it yet.'

Getting to her feet, Eva went to help herself to more coffee. She'd have liked to be alone for a moment, free from having to put on a front, but knowing it would leave the girls feeling flat she pushed past the images of Patty and Don sharing breakfast together, and returned to the table.

'I reckon we're going to be rushed off our feet today,' Livvy declared, flicking on the TV. 'I wonder if there's anything on *Daybreak* or Sky about our show.'

'We only had the PR camera there,' Eva reminded her, 'but I guess they could have streamed their video over to a couple of the channels by now.'

'I bet Livvy's right,' Jasmine commented, 'you'll get loads of people turning up today, so maybe I ought to come in with you.'

Smiling, Eva said, 'Tell you what, why don't you stay here and concentrate on your studies, and if things start getting out of hand at Perdita's I'll give you a call.'

'OK, cool. Can I come in at lunchtime? I could bring sandwiches and stuff.'

'Great idea,' Eva agreed. 'Is Coral in today?' she asked Livvy.

'This afternoon, if she's recovered from her hangover by then. Jeez, did she put it away yesterday, and last night. Did you see her?'

'She was on a real high.' Eva smiled. 'I think she's very proud of her connection to the flamenco dress.'

Livvy grinned. 'It was good that she joined us at the Riverside, wasn't it? I was afraid it might seem a bit, you know, boring for you after all your mates had gone. Not that me and Jas are boring, you understand . . .'

'I'm definitely not,' Jasmine informed her.

'No, me neither. In fact, I think we're just about the most interesting people on the planet.'

'Definitely,' Jasmine agreed.

'Absolutely,' Eva chimed in, reaching for the phone. 'Hello?' she said, before checking the ID.

'Hi, it's me,' Patty said softly.

Eva immediately stiffened.

'I just wanted to congratulate you on the show's success. I take it you've seen the papers this morning?'

'Yes, we have, thank you.'

'It's great that it went so well. Livvy must be over the moon.'

'She is.'

There was a long pause before Patty said, 'Did you get my text?'

'I did, thank you. I have to go now,' and putting the phone down Eva felt herself starting to shake. Excusing herself she ran upstairs to finish dressing for the busy day ahead. She was going to push that phone call out of her mind right now and make sure not to let it back in again.

'What are we going to do with all this food?' Jasmine said, looking at the table in dismay. A beat later her eyes came up to Livvy's, and as they realised they were thinking the same thing, they looked down to find two willing takers gazing innocently up at them.

Chapter Fifteen

For several weeks now Sadie Larch had been trying to pluck up the courage to speak to one of the girls who worked at Perdita's on Saturdays, but so far it hadn't worked out. She'd started off wanting to speak to the owner, Eva Montgomery, but she never seemed to be there at weekends, and Sadie couldn't get over to Bridport on weekdays, thanks to school. She popped across in the evenings sometimes though, because her nan lived in West Bay, and she'd actually seen the girl called Livvy coming out of the gym one night. (She'd only found out her name a couple of days ago, from the papers.) Sadie had nearly nerved herself to go up to her that night, but when she'd realised Livvy was scared, she'd ended up backing off.

If it weren't for the uppity new Saturday girl with serious attitude who'd thrown Sadie and her best mate, Tara, out of the shop a couple of months ago like they were shoplifters – *shoplifters, the girl could die for that* – then Sadie was sure she'd have made more progress by now. As it was, she and Tara had resorted to driving up and down the main road both sides of Bridport trying to find a big white house that overlooked the sea, which was about all they knew of it from the *Where Are They Now?* piece. In the end, though they hadn't been able to see a house from the road, they'd decided it must be the one with the huge gates and massive white walls that had security cameras on the top. They'd been up there twice trying to find out if they were right, but still hadn't found the nerve to ring the bell.

The trouble was, this could all turn out to be hugely embarrassing and even get Sadie into a shed-load of trouble if she had it all wrong, which was why she'd decided, now that she knew this Livvy person was Eva's niece, that it was best to speak to her first. Her cousin, Richie, still didn't think she should speak to either of them, but she wasn't going to listen to him, because she knew that deep down inside he actually really wanted her to.

Wasn't it just typical, though? Having made up her mind that she was going to approach Livvy this weekend, come what may – and let the uppity little ginger nut dare try and throw her out again – the whole bloody world was going to the shop, after the fashion show they'd had last Wednesday.

'We're never going to get in there,' Sadie grumbled, as Tara came back down the lane shaking her head, indicating that the coast still wasn't clear. Sadie wished her friend would lose weight, but she'd never say so, because Tara was really sensitive about being obese. A few less burgers might do the trick, but hey, maybe she, Sadie, should keep her opinions to herself.

'There's only a couple of people in there now,' Tara reported, scooting forward to avoid a speeding roller-skater thundering past the market stalls of Bucky Doo Square. 'Trouble is, by the time they leave someone else is bound to have turned up.'

'What about the girl with spots and freckles?' Sadie asked. 'Is she there?'

'You mean *Jasmine*?' Tara said derisively. They'd learned Jasmine's name the same way they had Livvy's, from the papers. 'Bet she's a right cup of tea.'

Rolling her eyes at the lame joke, Sadie said, 'Let's give it till half past and if it still looks like a no-go then, we'll give it up for the day.'

'I got to tell you,' Livvy trilled ecstatically as she closed the door behind her, 'I am so loving being famous.'

Laughing as she threw a cushion at her, Jasmine said, 'And it's not going to your head or anything.'

'Not a bit,' Livvy assured her. 'OK, they might mainly be coming to get a look at Eva, but I've had no less than *three* orders for my loons in the last two hours, which makes six in total since the show, and we've got four, no five, consultations booked in for next week.'

'It is pretty cool,' Jasmine agreed, 'and don't forget you've had quite a bit of interest in your flamenco dress.'

'But no orders.'

'*Yet!* It's pricey, so not everyone's going to be able to afford it. Anyway, I don't know about you, but I'm famished, so I'm going to run up to the deli for sandwiches.'

'Go for it! What time did Coral say she'd be here?'

'Around about now, but you know Coral, an hour or two here or there . . .'

Livvy waved her out of the shop, and seizing the moment's respite to call Eva to report on what an active morning they'd had, she was about to pick up the phone when it rang.

'Hey! It's me! I just got the English papers,' Jake

shouted down the line. 'This is amazing. You are like such big time all of a sudden.'

'Yeah, really,' Livvy laughed. 'Where are you, for God's sake?'

'Still in Thailand and loving it. You should come.'

'I'll be on the next plane. Have you spoken to Mum? She's worried about not hearing from you.'

'Hello! I'm texting her all the time! Doesn't she get them, or something?'

'I think she does, but she's in a weird headspace at the moment. You need to be here. When are you coming back?'

'Def in time for Christmas. I so love that Eva's back on top. Is she OK?'

Deciding to give the short answers, Livvy said, 'She seems fine. Coming down a bit after the show, but business is really picking up, which is great.' Should she say again that she was worried about their mother? Maybe not, since there was nothing he could do from Thailand, except worry, and she could do that for both of them. 'I need you to bring some silk back for me,' she told him.

No response.

'Jake?'

Still nothing.

Realising they'd lost the connection, she put the phone down and was on the point of trying Eva when the door opened. She looked up, all smiles for the new customer, until she saw who it was and her heart turned over.

'Oh God, please don't look scared again,' the petite girl with a scruffy ponytail and a really cool fake-leopard coat cried. 'I just want to talk to you. We're not here to cause any trouble, honest.'

Livvy's eyes flickered uneasily to the large,

scowling girl who'd come in behind her, with inch-long eyelashes and uneven pink streaks in her hair. 'What do you want?' she asked cagily.

Coming forward, the smaller girl said, 'My name's Sadie and this is Tara. I know you're Livvy because we read about you in the papers.'

Slightly less nervous now, but still wary, Livvy waited for her to go on.

Starting to colour up, Sadie said, 'Eva, she's your auntie, right?'

Livvy nodded cautiously. They presumably knew that from the papers too.

'Well, I was wondering,' Sadie went on, going even redder, 'was her name . . .? I mean, before she got married, was her name Eva Winters by any chance?'

Livvy went very still. She was trying desperately to think where this could be going, but was coming up blank. 'Why do you want to know?' she asked carefully.

Sadie flicked a glance at her friend. 'It's not really me who wants to know,' she answered awkwardly. 'I mean, I do, but it's my cousin, you see . . . He thinks, or I suppose it's more me who thinks that . . .' Taking a quick breath, she blurted out in a rush, 'Do you know if your aunt had a baby, quite a long time ago, who she had adopted?'

Livvy's heart jarred with shock. Who was this girl? What the heck was she talking about? From an echoey distance she heard herself say, 'No, she . . . I mean, why are you asking?'

Sadie's brilliant blue eyes were full of misgiving as she said, 'I know this is going to sound a bit crazy, and you can tell me to go if you like, but it's just that my cousin was adopted when he was a baby and a couple of months ago, just before his birthday, we found this envelope with loads of papers in it and one of them turned out to be his birth certificate – I don't mean the one he's always had, with my auntie and uncle's names and everything, but the one they must have given him when he was born and it says that his mother's name was Eva Winters.'

Livvy's throat had turned totally dry. OK, that was definitely Eva's maiden name, but all the same, they still must have the wrong person. 'I'm not sure . . .' she began hoarsely, with no idea what she was going to say next. 'I mean, as far as I know,' she stumbled on, 'my aunt's never had any children so I don't think it can be the same Eva Winters.'

Sadie looked so defeated that Livvy added, 'What makes you think it might be?'

Sadie's cornflower eyes came back to her. 'OK, you're going to think this sounds really dumb now,' she said, 'but he kind of looks like her.'

Livvy definitely thought that sounded dumb – or made up, anyway.

'He's absolutely drop-dead,' Tara chipped in.

Livvy glanced at Tara, then back to Sadie. 'Listen, I'd know if my aunt had had a baby,' she told her, while realising that she actually might not. 'So is there some other reason why you think she . . .'

'The timing works out,' Sadie said hastily. 'When she was in hospital, after the time she was attacked? She was in there for ages, right, and I know no one ever said anything about her having a baby then, but we've been looking on the Internet, and we found a story in one of the papers that said she'd given birth to a little boy. Her agent was interviewed after that and said it was nonsense, but if it *was* true . . .'

She trailed off, looking as though she was no longer sure she believed it herself.

Livvy's heart was thudding hard. *If it was true*, she was thinking. But it couldn't be, because her mother, or Eva, would have told her about something like that. Wouldn't they?

'I was wondering,' Sadie went on, sounding as though she already knew she was on to a lost cause, 'if you thought it would be all right for me to speak to your auntie. I promise I don't want to make any trouble, and if you think . . .' She broke off and turned around as the door opened.

'Livvy, darling, I'm so sorry I'm late,' Coral gushed as she came to drop her bag and coat on the sofa. 'The hairdresser took forever to finish my highlights, then I bumped into Susie in the high street who's dying to have a look at your designs.'

Livvy smiled vaguely at the other woman who'd come in, and was already sifting through the rails.

'I'll come back another time,' Sadie murmured.

'No! No, wait,' Livvy cried as Sadie and Tara headed for the door. 'Please don't go yet.'

As the door closed behind them Livvy turned back to Coral.

Blinking, Coral said, 'Friends of yours?'

Livvy looked at her blankly. 'No, they just . . . Can you hold the fort for a while?' she asked. 'Jasmine'll be back any minute.'

'Of course, but what . . .?'

'I can't explain now,' Livvy interrupted, going to get her coat. 'Do you happen to know where Mum is?'

Nonplussed, Coral said, 'She was at home when we spoke about an hour ago.'

Grabbing her car keys and mobile, Livvy left the

shop. She pressed in her mother's number as she started down the lane. 'Good, you're still there,' she said when Patty answered. 'Please don't go anywhere, I'm on my way over.'

'Why? What's the urgency?' Patty demanded. 'Has something happened?'

'No! Yes! Actually, I'm not sure. I'll explain when I get there. Just don't go out, OK? There's something I need to ask you.'

Half an hour later Patty was staring at Livvy in amazement. She wanted to believe what she'd just heard, but wasn't sure she dared to. 'Tell me again what this girl said,' she demanded.

Looking both bemused and impatient, Livvy repeated it. Then added, 'Mum, for God's sake, is it true? Did Eva have a baby?'

Patty swallowed hard and nodded. 'Yes, she did,' she said faintly. Then, 'Oh my God, Livvy. You can't imagine what this could mean . . .'

'Well no, how would I?'

'Why on earth didn't you go after them when they left?'

'I didn't know what to do,' Livvy cried. 'This came at me out of nowhere, remember?'

'Of course, of course. What did you say to them?'

'Hello! What was I supposed to say? I can't know the family secrets if no one ever tells me.'

'OK, sorry. Let's try to think rationally. She said the boy is her cousin . . . Did she tell you how old he is?'

'No, but apparently he had a birthday recently, and . . . *Mum!*'

Peeling her hands from her face, Patty said, 'It's all right, go on.'

'Right, well, she said the timing worked out from when Eva was in hospital after the attack. Is that when she had a baby?'

Patty nodded.

Livvy threw out her hands. 'So why didn't anyone ever tell me?' she demanded angrily.

'Maybe we should have,' Patty conceded, 'but we did our best to keep it secret at the time, and over the years . . . It's something we hardly ever talked about. It's been very difficult for Eva. She bitterly regrets what she did . . . Oh, Livvy, we have to find him. What was the girl's name again?'

'Sadie, but that's all she told me. I've got no idea what her surname is, or where she lives.'

Groaning with frustration, Patty said, 'What about the other girl?'

'I can't even remember her name. I'm not even sure they told me.'

'Have you ever seen either of them before?'

Grasping at that as though it might help, Livvy said, 'Actually, yeah, they've been in a couple of times, but they were acting so weird that I thought they were shoplifters.'

'So what happened?'

'Nothing. They just hung around for a bit then left. Apart from one time when Jasmine threw them out.'

Patty's eyes widened.

'We thought they were shoplifters,' Livvy insisted.

Shaking her head in despair, Patty said, 'So how are we going to find them?'

'How do I know?' Livvy's mind was reeling, trying to deal with how she'd screwed up even though it wasn't her fault. And then there was the fact that Eva had *a son* . . . 'I'm sorry,' she said miserably, 'if I'd known . . .'

'It's OK,' Patty interrupted, picking up the phone. 'You're not to blame. Hi, it's me,' she said to Don when he answered. 'Can you talk?'

'Sure, what is it?'

'Livvy's here,' she told him. 'Apparently some girls came into the shop earlier asking if Eva had a son.'

There was a moment of stunned silence before he said, 'Who are they?'

'I've no idea, but whoever they are, we have to find them. Livvy and I are at the barn. Is there any chance you can come?'

'It'll take me about an hour from where I am,' he replied. 'Doesn't Livvy have any way of contacting them?'

Patty's eyes went to Livvy as she shook her head. 'Apparently they left when Coral came into the shop . . .'

'She said she'd come back,' Livvy interrupted.

Patty regarded her eagerly.

'Just not when,' Livvy added lamely.

'Well, it's going to be damned difficult trying to track someone down with no name, phone number or photograph,' Don sighed, 'but I'll get there as soon as I can.'

As she rang off Patty said to Livvy, 'Whatever happens now, please don't breathe a word of this to anyone, especially not Eva, because if it turns out to be some sick hoax, or something else we haven't even thought of, and we don't manage to find him . . .'

'It's OK, I get it,' Livvy assured her. 'But remember, if you guys didn't have so many secrets we wouldn't be in this position, because if those girls are on the level we wouldn't be looking for him now, chances are we'd already have found him.'

Bitterly regretting not having told Livvy before, over the days that followed Patty became so angry with herself, and so frustrated, that she could hardly speak to anyone without biting their head off.

'You have to calm down,' Don told her as gently as he could one evening. 'Getting yourself worked up like this isn't helping anyone, least of all you.'

'I know, but when I think of the difference it would make to Eva if we could find him . . .'

'We will, it's just going to take time, and it's not as if she knows anything about it, so we can't feel that we're letting her down.'

'But I do, and it's really eating me up.'

'Then maybe you should keep reminding yourself that the girl told Livvy she'd be back, and if she's come this far trying to find her cousin's real mother, is it likely she'd give up now?'

Sighing, Patty said, 'I guess not, it's just the not knowing.'

Taking her hands, he waited for her eyes to come to his. 'I don't want to put a downer on this,' he said softly, 'but please keep in mind that even if we do find her cousin, we have no idea what's happened over the last sixteen years, what kind of family he's been with, or what kind of boy he's grown into.'

Patty's eyes were tormented as she looked back at him. 'But he's her son,' she reminded him.

'Yes, if that really is who he is, but we don't know for certain. In fact all we really know is what this girl, Sadie, told Livvy, and as we have no idea who Sadie is, or where she came from . . . Well, what I'm trying to say is that anyone could be behind this. Even Sadie herself might not know why she's doing this.'

Patty blanched. 'You were with the police for too long,' she told him.

Not arguing with that, he said, 'I'm just giving you the benefit of my experience, but that doesn't mean I'm not keeping an open mind. I'm just trying to persuade you to keep one too and not to get your hopes too high. That's all.'

Chapter Sixteen

'Livvy, what on earth's going on?' Eva demanded, trying not to sound rattled. 'That's the fourth time in nearly as many minutes you've been to look out of the door, are you expecting someone?'

'No, no,' Livvy assured her. 'I uh – I just want to make sure the wind hasn't blown over our new sign. I think it was a great idea of Jasmine's to put one out on the square so everyone knows where to find us now. Don't you?'

Appearing highly sceptical, Eva let the matter drop and returned to the office, while Livvy, as soon as the coast was clear, went back to the door and peered down the lane again. It was Thursday now, and there hadn't been sight or sign of Sadie or Tara. To make matters worse, no one in the square seemed to recognise them from the descriptions Livvy had given.

'They're about seventeen or eighteen,' she'd said. 'One's quite small and blonde, really pretty actually, with a little ponytail and amazing blue eyes, and the other's about twice her size with shoulder-length black hair and electric pink highlights. If you'd seen them you're sure to have noticed them.'

In fact, a few of the traders had, but unfortunately it didn't mean they were able to tell Livvy who the girls were. However, they were intrigued to find out why Livvy wanted to know, and should they send the girls her way if they happened to turn up again? Livvy had assured them they must, because one of them had left something quite valuable in the shop that she needed to return.

'I'm going up to London next Tuesday,' Eva announced, as Livvy wandered into the office. 'I've just checked with Coral and luckily she can come in that day, and the next if I decide to stay over.'

'What are you doing there?' Livvy asked, leaning against the door.

Though Eva's eyes were ringed with dark shadows, a playful light emerged as she said, 'Our new PR people want to go over the plans they've drawn up for next spring, and I'll have to talk to the accountant about what kind of budget we should allow ourselves.'

'Things are going pretty well now,' Livvy reminded her. 'I mean, I know we haven't had many people in today, but yesterday we were inundated, and it was *Wednesday*.'

'Indeed, but don't let's get too carried away, because we've got no idea how long our new-found fame is going to last. Hello, is that someone coming in I just heard?'

Returning to the shop to find a couple of tourists browsing the front rails, Livvy settled herself behind the till ready to be of assistance, while Eva went back to the invoice that she'd slipped out of sight when Livvy had come into the office.

It was from Johnny Johnson, the private investigator, who'd included a hard copy of the email he'd sent almost two months ago apologising for not being able to help with her search and informing her that Nick Jensen had written the letter to *Saturday Siesta*. Clearly Mr Johnson was much quicker off the mark with his investigations than he was with his accounts, Eva reflected.

After writing Mr Johnson a cheque and slotting it into an envelope she sat thinking about Nick for a while, feeling, to her surprise, less anger towards him than usual, as she wondered where he might be now and what he was doing. Of course it would be the easiest thing in the world to find out, she only had to pick up the phone to Bobbie, but she wouldn't, because all she actually wanted from Nick Jensen was to know where their son might be. And if he knew that, so would Bobbie, and since Bobbie would never have kept that information from her, she was being ludicrous all over again even to think this way.

So what should she think about? Patty and Don? Christmas looming on the horizon? She'd considered inviting Elaine to keep her, Rosie and Elvis company on the big day, but maybe Patty had already beaten her to it. Even if she hadn't, their stepmother would be bound to feel horribly torn between them, so maybe she, Eva, ought not to put her through it. Livvy would probably feel torn too, and Jake. And then there were Don's brothers and their wives, who always came to Dorset for the celebrations. She wondered if they'd already arranged to go and stay with Don and Patty at the barn. The very thought of everyone celebrating together around Patty's table, the turkey in the Aga, the wine flowing, a roaring fire, silly hats, gaily wrapped presents, was tearing her apart inside. Both her sisters-in-law had been in touch after the break-up to say how sorry they were, and to insist that if there was anything they could do she must let them know. She hadn't heard from either of them since, but there again she hadn't contacted them either.

'Do you reckon we ought to chase up our Christmas cards?' Livvy said, coming back into the office. 'We put the order in ages ago, so they should have been here by now.'

'I'll do it,' Eva told her. 'We probably ought to start thinking about what we're going to put in the window too.'

Livvy tilted her head to one side, as though trying to get a better look at Eva's face.

'What?' Eva asked.

'Nothing. Except, I guess . . . Well, I don't suppose you're looking forward to Christmas much, are you?'

Eva's eyes went down. 'Not really,' she confessed, 'but there are a lot of people out there who are a lot worse off than I am, so I'm going to try my best not to feel too sorry for myself.'

Livvy stood looking at her for a while.

Eva threw out her hands. 'Wasn't that a good enough answer?'

'It was great,' Livvy assured her, 'I'm just like, you never know, it might not turn out to be as bad as you think.'

As Eva's heart turned over she tried to smile.

'Honestly, it might not,' Livvy insisted. 'I mean, anything could happen between now and then.'

Getting to her feet, Eva said, 'If you've found a way of turning back time, then that would probably do it, but since I guess you probably haven't I'll love you anyway for your optimism and make sure Santa sees you're properly rewarded.'

'Actually, I reckon you're the one he's got his eye

on,' Livvy told her mischievously, 'but then, show me a bloke who hasn't?'

Laughing, Eva said, 'I know you don't expect me to answer that, so tell you what, I won't.'

'And you haven't told Eva any of this?' Elaine was saying the next morning, as she took the cup of tea Patty was passing her.

'I dare not,' Patty replied, sitting down at the table where she'd been going through the household accounts when Elaine turned up. 'At least, not until we know if the girl is genuine.'

Elaine nodded agreement. 'It would be awful to get her hopes up, only to find out it's all some ghastly scam on the part of some tabloid hack trying to make a name for themselves.'

'That's what Don's afraid of, and given the timing of this girl's sudden appearance on the scene, straight after all the coverage for the show . . . Except Livvy says the girl has been in the shop before.'

Elaine looked interested.

'They thought she was a shoplifter,' Patty said wryly. 'Apparently Jasmine even threw her out once, which I suppose ought to make us wary in itself, in case the girl's after some sort of revenge.'

Elaine looked doubtful about that.

'So do you think there's a chance she does know where he is?' Patty asked hopefully.

'Of course it's possible,' Elaine replied, 'but you already know that. The big question for me, if it is genuine, is what role are his adoptive parents playing in it all?'

Having asked herself the same question a hundred times, Patty sighed as she stared down at her tea. 'I've no idea,' she answered. 'The girl says she's his cousin so I guess she must know them – I wonder if she realised that Livvy's his cousin too?'

Elaine watched her walk to the sink and waited until she seemed to reconnect with the fact that she wasn't alone. 'I mean if it is him,' Patty finally added.

'Come and sit down,' Elaine said gently.

Looking surprised, Patty said, 'I'm fine.'

Elaine smiled. 'And I didn't even ask.'

Patty seemed confused.

'If you don't mind me saying, you look awful,' Elaine told her bluntly. 'How much weight have you lost since all this happened?'

'I've no idea. It doesn't matter . . .'

'Yes it does, and I happen to know Don is worried about you too, which is mainly why I'm here.'

'Why? What did he say?'

'Just that, that he's worried, and seeing you now, so am I. You're not yourself, Patty, that much is clear, and I have a feeling you've been avoiding me lately, so let's put an end to that, shall we, and try to get to the bottom of . . .'

'There's nothing to get to the bottom of,' Patty interrupted. 'Honestly, everything's fine. We just need to get this sorted out for Eva . . .'

'Which will happen in its own time. Meanwhile, you've got something bottled up there that . . .'

'Guilt!' Patty broke in with an unsteady laugh. 'That's what it is, pure guilt. I've stolen my sister's husband and now I'm trying to live with it. Or him – and I don't know if I can do either.'

'Oh dear,' Elaine murmured. 'This is very much what I was afraid of.' Her eyes didn't let go of Patty's for a moment. 'But that's not everything, is it?' she challenged quietly.

'What do you mean?' Patty countered.

Elaine waited for her to answer the question herself.

'I don't know what you're talking about,' Patty insisted.

Folding her hands together, Elaine kept her tone gentle as she said, 'You must show Eva the note your mother left.'

As Patty's eyes closed her fists clenched at her sides. 'Why does everyone always care so much about Eva?' she seethed. 'What about me, and the way I feel? Don't I count for anything? Am I so . . . so . . . Oh for God's sake . . .' As she started to break down, Elaine went to take her in her arms.

'I'm OK, I'm fine,' Patty told her.

'No you're not,' Elaine argued, 'far from it, in fact, which is what happens when your conscience is eating away at you.'

'I told you . . .'

'Please, listen. I'd like you to come and stay with me at the retreat for a few days.'

Patty shook her head. 'I can't. I have to work, and I need to be here for Don. No, Elaine. I really appreciate the way you're trying to help me, but I'm fine, honestly.'

'Then your definition of fine is very different to mine. However, I won't try to force you, I just want you to think over what I've said, about the note, and about coming to stay, and if you change your mind you know where I am.'

'Thanks, Dad,' Jasmine said, opening the car door to get out.

'Don't I get a kiss?' he protested.

Leaning back towards him, she planted a dutiful peck on his cheek and picked up her bag.

'You know, if there's anything you want . . .' he began.

'I'm cool.'

'How are things with your mother?'

With an exasperated sigh, she said, 'You could have asked me that when we were at the cafe having breakfast, so why are you bringing it up now? You're going to make me late.'

'I'm sorry. I guess I should have. Are you – are you OK about staying at Eva's? You know you'd be very welcome at the barn.'

'Oh what, and just dump Eva the way you did? That would be really nice of me, wouldn't it? But then you're used to doing things like that.'

Smarting, he said, 'Jas, I swear, leaving my wife isn't something I make a habit of.'

Jasmine's face was strained as she replied, 'Funny, that's not how it looks from where I am.'

Sighing, he tried to reach for her hands but she snatched them away. 'You might not believe this,' he said softly, 'but no one means more to me than you.'

Her voice was choked with tears as she snapped, 'Then how come Eva's the only one who ever makes me feel like I matter?' and springing out of the car she slammed the door shut and hurried off out of the car park, knowing she'd be long gone before he could turn his enormous Merc around, or even park it to come after her.

With bitter tears stinging her eyes, she marched up South Street, wishing with all her heart that she could leave home altogether and come to live here, with Eva and Livvy, and never have to see either of her parents again. Except her father was in Dorset, of course, so there was no getting away from him, and for him to have said that she meant more to him than anyone was total, utter rubbish, because he never showed it and anyway she didn't want him to care about her. She had her job now, and she was going to do well in her A levels, and at uni, and when the time came she was going to ask Eva if she could become her business manager, or something like that, because more than anything she wanted to carry on being a part of Perdita's. Livvy might even let her share the flat upstairs, or maybe Livvy would have moved into a bigger place by then, because she was obviously going to be rich and famous.

She didn't see two girls coming out of the Electric Cinema cafe until one of them jostled into her and stepping aside she was about to treat them to a filthy look when she recognised them as the girls she'd practically thrown out of the shop.

Quickly putting her head down, she hurried on.

'Hey, wait!' one of them shouted. 'Are you the girl who works at Perdita's?'

Terrified, Jasmine swerved round a market stall, darted in past the next one, then dashed down the lane to the shop.

'Blimey, what's up with you?' Livvy cried, as Jasmine practically threw herself in through the door and shut it behind her. 'Are you OK?'

Jasmine tried to nod. She was looking back down the lane, praying she hadn't been followed. 'I think so,' she panted. 'Oh God, they scared the hell out of me.'

'Who?' Livvy asked, coming to peer down the lane with her.

'Those girls. You remember, the ones I threw out, they were only . . .'

'Oh my God, you've seen them?' Livvy clasped hold of her. 'Where are they? What did they say? No, don't worry about that, just stay here,' and tearing open the door she took off down the lane into South Street, searching frantically for a little blonde fountain of a ponytail and a dyed-black shaggy thatch with luminous pink streaks. Spotting them outside the Electric Cinema, she ran breathlessly up to them. 'Sadie? I'm Livvy, remember? You came in . . .'

'Of course I remember,' Sadie interrupted. 'I was just coming to see you.'

'Oh thank God, thank God,' Livvy gasped with a laugh. 'What you asked me about my aunt . . . ?'

Sadie regarded her warily.

Suddenly overcome, Livvy choked, 'Oh God, look at me,' trying to wave her tears away. 'It's . . . I think you could . . . What I'm trying to say is my mother would like to talk to you. I'll call her right now. She'll come straight away.'

Patty was turning into Duck Lane on her way to Seatown when Livvy rang. Using the steering-wheel controls to click on, she said, 'Hi darling, did you get my message earlier . . .'

'Mum, listen!' Livvy cut in excitedly. 'Sadie came back. She's here with me now, at the shop with her friend Tara. And Mum, wait for this . . . Oh my God . . . his name's Richie and he only lives in *Chard*!'

Unable to continue driving Patty pulled in to the side of the road, struggling to hold back her emotions. His name was Richie. And Chard was just over the county border in south Somerset, no more than twenty miles away.

'Are you still there?' Livvy cried. 'Oh please don't say we've been cut off.'

Making herself speak, Patty said, 'I'm still here.'

'Mum, you have to come. They said they'll wait. Where are you?'

Having lost a sense of her surroundings, Patty tried to think. 'Uh, not far, I can be there in ten minutes. Where's Eva?'

'At home doing her charity stuff, the way she always does on Saturdays.'

'OK, but take the girls for a coffee just in case she decides to come into the shop. We need to be absolutely sure about this before we break anything to her. Can Jasmine manage on her own for an hour?'

'I guess so. I don't see why not. Actually, it's down to her that we found them, only she ran away from them because she didn't realise we were looking for them.'

Breaking into a tearful laugh, Patty said, 'But you've got them now. This is great news, Livvy. Do you really think they're telling the truth?'

'Yeah, actually, I do, but you need to speak to them yourself.'

Still dazed by it all, and afraid in case it didn't work out, Patty replied, 'OK, just don't let them go.'

After ringing off and turning the car round, she connected to Don. 'The girl Sadie has turned up,' she told him, her voice thick with tears. 'She and her friend are with Livvy at the shop. I'm on my way there now. Apparently his name . . . His name's Richie. Oh God,' she sobbed as she laughed. 'Do you think it's going to be all right? They're not tricking us, are they?'

'I'm going to dare to hope not,' he said. 'Do you want me to come with you? I can be there in ten.'

'No, both of us might be too much. I think it should be just me and Livvy for now. Apparently Jasmine found them.'

'Does Jasmine know?'

'I presume she must by now. She's going to be at the shop on her own while Livvy's with me, so it might be a good opportunity to go and have a chat with her, if there aren't too many people around, you know, explain things a little.'

'OK, will do. Now listen, I want you to go into this carefully, because we still don't know what motive they might have for tracking Eva down, or, more to the point, how they've managed it.'

'I hear you,' Patty replied, 'but let's try to stay optimistic.'

'Of course,' he said softly, clearly wanting to offer the right encouragement.

Twenty minutes later Patty walked into the Electric Cinema cafe to find Livvy tucked into a far corner, with two teenage girls. As she threaded her way through the tables to join them she couldn't help being aware of how apprehensive she was feeling – and relieved to see no one she knew.

'Sadie, Tara,' Livvy said, as Patty reached them, 'this is my mum, Patty. Like I already told you, she's Eva's sister.'

Smiling at the girls, Patty shook hands with the blonde one. She guessed she was Sadie, given the silver S dangling from a chain round her neck. She was as petite and clear-complexioned as a doll, and indeed looked like one with her wide blue eyes and rosebud lips. The other girl was heavier and wearing far too much make-up, Patty thought, but most kids did these days, including Livvy, so she wasn't going to hold that against her.

'We've ordered some coffees,' Livvy told her as she sat down, 'and then we thought we probably ought to wait for Sadie's mum to get here. She's on her way and she wants to talk to you, if that's OK?'

Surprised, but pleased by this unexpected news, Patty looked at Sadie as she said, 'Of course. Is she in Bridport, or does she . . .'

'She's at my nan's down in West Bay,' Sadie informed her, 'so she should be here any minute.'

Patty glanced at the other girl, then back again. 'And – and Richie?' she dared to ask, the unreality of it making her emotional all over again.

Sadie shrugged. 'He's at home, I think, or he might have gone to watch his mates play rugger. He's the team captain, but he got an injury a couple of weeks ago so they're not letting him back in the side until he's properly fit.'

Feeling an instinctive surge of concern, Patty said, 'I hope it wasn't anything serious?'

'Something to do with his shoulder, but he says he's fine.'

Sitting back as their coffees were delivered, Patty waited for the server to leave before saying, 'So you're his cousin?'

Sadie nodded as she took a sip of her cappuccino. 'His dad is my dad's brother, only his dad died about four years ago.'

Patty wasn't entirely sure how to react to that, but was saved from saying anything as Sadie suddenly called out, 'Mum! Over here.'

Turning around, Patty saw a petite, harried-looking

woman with neat fair hair and large anxious eyes coming towards them. Her parka coat had seen better days, as had her bag, but since she hadn't expected to be meeting anyone new today, least of all Richie's natural aunt, Patty could only wish that she wasn't dressed quite so smartly herself. 'Hi, I'm Patty Preston,' she said, getting to her feet and holding out a hand to shake.

The woman's face relaxed a little as she smiled. 'Isabelle Larch,' she said, taking Patty's hand. 'Everyone calls me Izzie.'

'I'm Livvy, Patty's daughter,' Livvy told her, vacating her own chair so Izzie could sit down. 'Can I order you a coffee?'

'That would be nice, thank you. A latte, no sugar,' and sinking into the chair she placed her bag on her lap and unbuttoned the collar of her coat. 'Well, I don't know about you,' she said, unravelling her scarf, 'but I'm still a bit blown away by all this, because madam here only told me on Wednesday of this week what she's been up to. Has she told you, I didn't even know they'd found the birth certificate, let alone that they'd managed to work out as much as they have.'

Though Patty smiled, she was watching the woman closely, and so far she was having no problems with what she saw. However, she must keep reminding herself that they had a long way to go. 'So do you think Eva . . . my sister is Richie's mother?' she asked, cautiously but directly.

Izzie nodded. 'I don't have any doubts,' she assured her. 'Not since I spoke to Linda, my sister-in-law – his adoptive mother. I called her as soon as this one told me what she'd been up to, and it turns out Linda's known for quite some time.

Apparently, a social worker told her when there was some stuff going on about a letter-box scheme – something else I never knew anything about until this week.'

Feeling her throat starting to tighten, Patty said, 'So how come he isn't with his adoptive mother any more? Or is he? I'm sorry, I don't think I'm quite . . .'

'It's OK, I know I need to explain,' Izzie acknowledged, nodding a thank-you to the waitress who delivered her latte. 'I'm not sure how much time you have . . .'

'As much as you need,' Patty told her.

Izzie's eyes softened gratefully, and after taking a sip of her coffee she said, 'I don't suppose Eva's coming to join us?'

Feeling her guard going up, Patty replied, 'Actually, this is going to mean a great deal to her, so we thought . . . We haven't told her yet.'

Though Izzie seemed slightly flustered by that, her words were reassuring as she said, 'I understand. You want to check us out for yourself first, make sure we're above board and everything. I don't blame you. You never know who you're dealing with these days, and after what your sister's been through . . . You can't ever be too careful, can you?'

Patty smiled her appreciation.

Izzie looked down at her coffee and took a moment to gather her thoughts. 'Am I right in thinking you don't have any idea who Richie's adoptive parents are?' she asked, glancing up again.

Patty shook her head. 'Eva's tried to find out, she's even been through the courts . . .'

'Mm, I knew about that. It was a long time ago,

353

wasn't it? I don't suppose Richie could have been much more than four . . .'

Deciding not to mention Eva's more recent attempt, Patty waited for her to go on.

'I don't think Linda, my sister-in-law, knew who his birth mother was way back then,' Izzie said, 'but I suppose only she can say for sure. I know she didn't go to the court, though. Neither of them did, her or Tim. They let the social workers deal with it all, which we all thought was for the best. It got her into a right state though, I can tell you that much. She could never make up her mind what to do. I kept saying to her, "You can't promise one thing and end up doing another, it's just cruel. So either let his birth mother be in touch and send her some letters back from time to time, or don't agree to do anything at all." To be honest, I presumed she'd opted for no contact, because once the ruling came through that they didn't have to provide any details if they didn't want to, she hardly mentioned it again.'

'So you didn't know that she had agreed to take part in a letter-box scheme?'

Izzie shook her head. 'Of course, I do now,' she said, 'but like I said, I only found out this week when Linda herself decided to tell me. There's been another court ruling recently as well, I hear.'

Patty nodded.

Izzie tutted in dismay. 'Yeah, she told me about that too, and all the birthday cards and letters over the years that your sister sent. Linda still has them, she says, much good that's doing Richie. I don't mind telling you, I was shocked when she told me and pretty angry, so I had to hang up the phone. I called her back after though, and she's promised me now that she'll send them to him. They haven't turned up yet, but it's still early days, so I'm prepared to carry on giving her the benefit of the doubt for now.'

'So where is she?' Patty asked. 'And why isn't Richie still with her?'

Izzie sighed and looked down at her coffee as she tried to decide the best way to answer that.

'I've already told her Uncle Tim died,' Sadie piped up.

Izzie glanced at her daughter, then back to Patty. 'That was quite a shock, when he went,' she said. 'Mervyn, my husband, took it quite hard. I'm sorry to say they hadn't spoken for a few years by then, but I suppose blood and water and all that . . . You couldn't wish to meet a lovelier man than our Tim, good as gold he was, but then the drink got hold of him, and I guess you could say it was what ended up killing him. He was on his way home from the pub one night, drunk as can be, and he probably didn't even see the lorry coming.'

'Oh no,' Patty murmured. 'How old was he?'

'He'd just turned forty-six. It was a crying shame, because, like I said, he was a good bloke at heart. It was losing his job that triggered it all. OK, he always did like his whisky, but hardly ever to excess, it just all started going downhill for him after he was laid off, and he couldn't ever seem to turn it around again. I wish I could tell you that his wife was of some help, but if you met her . . . Well, what can I say? Another kindly soul, I'll give her that, but honest to God she's got to be one of the most insecure people I've ever met. Don't ask me what made her like it, I don't go digging round in people's private affairs, but I can tell you this, she doesn't have an ounce of confidence in herself, which is tragic in its way. She hardly has any friends, never goes out anywhere, I mean apart from the usual stuff, you know, shopping, taking the kids to school, dentist, doctor and all that. It'll be why she never wrote back to your sister, I'm sure of it. She'd have wanted to do the right thing, but then she'd have been terrified of saying something wrong, making your sister think the worst of her . . . Heaven only knows what goes through her mind, because I swear she doesn't think like the rest of us, nothing like, in fact. Poor love, you can't help but feel sorry for her, but you don't half want to shake her at times, I can tell you.'

Realising she'd never really allowed herself to imagine what her nephew's adoptive parents might be like, Patty was feeling quietly stunned to be faced with such a sad and, it had to be said, inadequate picture of them. 'So where is she now?' she asked.

Izzie put her coffee down and dabbed the foam from her top lip. 'Living up north with her brother,' she replied. 'She went about nine, ten months ago. She'd been talking about it for a while, ever since Tim went, in fact . . .' She turned to Sadie, 'Have you told her about Una?'

Sadie shook her head.

With a sigh, Izzy said, 'Una. Dear thing. She came along just after Richie turned five. A big surprise to everyone she was, because Linda was sure she couldn't have any of her own. It was why they went for adoption. Then suddenly, out of the blue, it turns out she's pregnant. She had to spend the whole time flat on her back, and it's sad, but true, that dear little Una has never been a healthy child. Sweet, but all skin and bone she is, and talk about sickly. From what I've already told you about Linda, you can probably imagine she's scared out of her wits of something happening to her. Ever since the poor mite was born her mother was forever dropping Richie round to me in case he'd picked up something from school that he might pass on to his sister. It got so that Richie was spending more time at our house than he was at his own, which is how come he and our Sadie are so close, he's more like a brother to her than a cousin.'

Patty glanced at Sadie and smiled.

'Don't get me wrong, Linda adored Richie,' Izzie went on. 'Still does, I'm sure about that – when you meet him you'll realise it's hard not to – but that wretched woman was always so torn about the right thing to do. It was only when her brother's wife ran off with some other bloke, last winter, that she finally decided to move up there and live with him after talking about it for years. The trouble was, Richie didn't want to leave his school or his friends, nor us, it has to be said. He was adamant he wasn't going to go, so in the end Merv and I told her we'd be happy to have him with us at least until he'd done his GCSEs and then we could sort out what to do from there.'

'He sits them next year,' Sadie informed Patty.

'He's a bright boy,' Izzie added proudly. 'Does well in most of his lessons and he's sport mad, isn't he, Sade? Especially when it comes to rugger.'

'Everyone likes him,' Tara announced.

'Apart from Dudley,' Sadie reminded her, 'but like I keep saying, Dudley needs to get a life.'

Izzie rolled her eyes. 'Dudley's real name is Russ,' she explained. 'He's my eldest boy – I've got two, Russ fifteen, Jack thirteen and then there's Sadie

357

here who's about to turn eighteen. They call Russ Dudley – and don't ever let him hear you,' she warned Sadie, 'after the cousin in *Harry Potter*, because I'm afraid my lad's got a bit of a jealous streak where Richie's concerned. He's got a slight weight problem too, and he's not comfortable around girls . . .'

'He's a right muppet,' Sadie broke in.

'That's enough,' Izzie chided. 'And we're not here to talk about Russ, he'll grow out of his silly nonsense soon enough. We're here to discuss Richie and my meddling daughter's . . .'

'And what harm has it done?' Sadie challenged. 'Linda obviously wanted Richie to find his real birth certificate, or she'd never have put it in the envelope, would she?'

'It's true,' Izzie conceded with a sigh, 'and that's my sister-in-law all over for you. She never goes about things in a straightforward fashion. When I spoke to her, a couple of days ago, after madam here decided to tell *me* what she was up to, Linda surprised the life out of me when she said she'd actually been waiting for my call. I said to her, "So why didn't you just tell him, rather than go about it in such a roundabout way?" and her answer was, "I didn't want to upset him."' She threw out her hands. 'If you'd know what to say to that you'd be doing a lot better than I did, I can tell you, and if it weren't for the fact that Miss Nosy here went poking through all the stuff Linda sent down, months ago now, we'd probably still be none the wiser, because Richie, God bless him, had barely even got round to opening it.'

'I take it Richie knows about what you found, and everything?' Livvy thought to ask Sadie.

'Oh yeah,' Sadie assured her. 'I mean, he always knew he was adopted, ever since he was little, so it didn't come as a surprise. We used to make up all these stories about who his real mum and dad might be, so it was like, totally amazing when we realised that his real mum was actually famous. He was like, oh my God. We were dead excited. Well, I was. He did his usual Mr Cool – if you knew him you'd know what I mean – but I reckon, underneath it all, he's dead nervous. He keeps saying that if she wanted to get in touch with him she would, so we should just ignore it. Well, we know now that she tried. Oh my God, I can't wait to tell him. He'll be like, no way.'

Unable to stop herself smiling, Patty said to Izzie, 'Has he spoken to his . . . to Linda since all this came to light?'

Izzie nodded. 'They were on the phone for quite a long time last night, but I didn't ask him too much about it after. Anyway, he says he doesn't want to go up there, particularly. Don't get me wrong, he's very attached to her in his way, but between us, it's not the kind of bond most parents have with their kids.'

'He's closer to you, really,' Sadie told her.

'Maybe,' Izzie conceded. 'But love him as I do, I have to say it would be lovely to reunite him with his real mother. To see him with someone who he really belongs to and who can give him everything he deserves. Oh look at me,' she laughed as she grabbed a napkin to dab away her tears.

Having the very same problem, Patty said, 'So where do we go from here? I want to do what's best for him, but obviously I have to think of Eva too.'

Izzie nodded as she blew her nose. 'Of course. I

suppose you'd better let me have a chat with him first. You know, prepare him a bit and make sure he's ready for it. We don't want to be getting your sister's hopes up, do we, if he suddenly starts getting cold feet on us.'

'He won't,' Sadie insisted.

Patty smiled at her. 'I'll wait to hear from you,' she said, 'but when you talk to him, please tell him, from his aunt, that his mother and the rest of his family can't wait to meet him.'

Chapter Seventeen

Much later that day Izzie's heart was melting all over the place as she watched her young nephew trying to take in all that she and Sadie had just told him. His head was bowed, his fingers buried in his thick, tousled hair, as his elbows rested on the drop-leaf table that Izzie had pulled out from under the window for them to sit round. Her husband had taken their sons off to the indoor ski slope, mainly to get them out of the way for a while, but it was an outing they all enjoyed – and the closest they were going to get to the real thing, that was for sure. So, for once, the house wasn't vibrating with teenage music, blaring televisions and a cacophony of rowdy voices and thundering feet. In fact it was quiet enough to hear the clock on the mantelpiece ticking, and the hum of the fridge in the kitchen.

'They seem like really nice people,' Sadie earnestly assured him. 'Tell you what, I'd love to have a family like that.'

Izzie turned to look at her. 'And exactly what would be wrong with this one, young lady?'

'Oh, now let me think about that,' Sadie responded cheekily.

Richie's head came up and Izzie's heart melted all over again to see his grin. He was a looker, that was for sure, always had been, but there again, now she knew who his mother was, it was hardly surprising. He was an absolute ringer for her, apart from his hair, which was as dark as it came, and his nose was a bit crooked thanks to his chosen sport. He had her height too, in fact Izzie suspected he might be taller than Eva already, and since he'd started shaving – only a couple of months ago, and probably not more than once or twice a week yet – Izzie had begun to get a real sense of the man he was growing into. How fast it happened, she reflected nostalgically to herself, and how sad for his mother that she'd missed so much of him already.

'This family's cool,' he stated. 'I don't really need another.'

'Oh, get out of here,' Sadie scoffed. 'You know you're dying to meet them all really.'

His grin started to fade. 'I was,' he admitted, 'but now it's like supposed to happen . . .' He shrugged. 'I can't really see the point. I mean, how's it going to work?'

'No one can answer that yet,' Izzie said gently. 'We just have to take it one day at a time, and see how well you get on together.'

'Do I have to go and live there?'

'No, not yet anyway. You might find that you want to after a while, but until then you'll still be here, with us, going to the same school, getting under my feet . . .'

'OK, got it! That's what this is really about . . . You're trying to get rid of me.'

Not as taken in by the teasing light in his eyes as he'd probably have liked her to be, Izzie said, 'My love, that's not something you ever need to worry about, because no matter what happens, now or any time in the future, you'll always have a home here with us.'

'Definitely,' Sadie added.

His eyes went down and Izzie heard him swallow.

'Duh!' Sadie exclaimed.

He looked up again.

'You're supposed to say the same to us now,' she informed him, 'because I'm telling you, if those gates and the walls outside are anything to go by . . .'

'Sadie, that's enough,' Izzie cut in firmly. 'This isn't about houses, or money, or who's living where, it's about Richie meeting his real mother for the first time, and whether or not he's ready to do it.'

Sitting back in his chair, Richie inhaled deeply and blew out his cheeks.

'Not a good look,' Sadie told him.

'Sadie,' Izzie warned.

'It's not like I don't want to meet her,' he admitted, 'I mean I do, but what if . . . Well . . .' he started to colour, 'what if she doesn't like me?'

'Oh, give me a break,' Sadie cried. 'Who could *not* like you?'

Richie grinned. 'I guess you've got a point,' he conceded.

Laughing, Izzie said, 'I was thinking that it might be a bit easier for you if you met her sister first.'

He frowned. 'You mean the one you saw today? Patty?'

'That's right. I'm sure she'd agree to it if we asked.'

'I bet she would.' Sadie nodded. 'Actually, I think that's a really good idea, Mum.'

'Would you like us to be there too?' Izzie offered. 'I'll drive you over there, of course, but we can come in with you, if you like.'

'You mean when I see the sister, or when I see . . .'

He looked at his aunt helplessly. 'What am I supposed to call her?'

Curious to know the answer to that, Sadie looked at her mother.

'Well, I guess you should call her Eva,' Izzie replied uncertainly.

'Not Mrs Montgomery?'

Izzie wrinkled her nose. 'That definitely sounds too formal. Tell you what, we'll check with Patty, who we're already calling Patty, so I'm sure Eva will be fine.'

Putting his hands behind his head, he took another deep breath. 'OK, so what am I going to talk to her about?' he asked. 'I mean, if I do go and see her.'

Again Sadie looked at her mother.

'Well, I'm sure she'll be keen to hear all about what you're up to at school, and what sports you like,' Izzie answered. 'You can tell her about the holidays we've been on . . .'

'I can't sit there talking about myself the whole time,' he protested.

'You don't normally have a problem,' Sadie informed him.

Pulling a playful punch, he said, 'Wouldn't it be better if I asked her about her?'

'It would certainly be polite,' Izzie agreed.

'What, you mean like how she got into modelling?' Sadie suggested.

'Yeah, I suppose so, but we know that already, don't we?'

'You haven't heard it from her, though.'

'True.'

'You could ask if she has any other children. I don't think she does, do you, Mum?'

Izzie shook her head. 'I'm sure Patty would have mentioned it, if she did.'

'I could always ask why she didn't want me when I was born,' Richie said edgily, his cheeks suffusing with an even deeper colour.

Feeling for the turmoil inside him, Izzie's eyes narrowed. 'I don't think that would be a good idea on a first meeting,' she responded carefully.

'I wasn't being serious,' he said, still looking moody. 'Well, I was, because I'd like to know, but OK, I can see it probably wouldn't get us off to a great start.'

'And you'd better not ask who your father is straight off, either,' Sadie warned.

Richie's face tightened. 'I don't get why his name's not on my birth certificate,' he said, almost angrily.

Sadie glanced at her mother. 'The thing is, Rich,' she said gently, 'there's a chance you'll have to get your head round the fact that she might not actually know who it is. If you think about the kind of life she was living back then, probably partying every night, I expect they were all on drugs . . .'

'You don't know that for certain,' Izzie interrupted, 'so don't let's paint too bleak a picture, but Sadie's right, you probably shouldn't ask about him straight away. Just take some time to get to know her, and for all you know, she'll end up telling you anyway. So don't let's worry about that. What we have to decide now is if you're feeling ready to go through with it.'

Richie's eyes went to Sadie, then back to his aunt.

'No one's forcing you,' Izzie reminded him, knowing that for his sake she had to hide her own feelings about the possibility of eventually having to let him go. At the same time, she mustn't allow him to think he wasn't wanted. It was a very fine line to tread, and considering the way her heart was aching already, and how her protective instincts were closing in around him, she doubted she was ever going to find it easy.

Lowering his head, he dashed both hands through his hair, and left it standing on end as he looked up again. 'When are we supposed to do it?' he asked.

'We haven't set a time. I told Patty I'd call her once I'd spoken to you. Apparently she isn't going to say anything to Eva until she's heard from us, so you don't have to worry about feeling as though you're letting anyone down.'

Richie looked at Sadie again. 'I've got to do this, haven't I?' he said.

'We've talked about it a lot,' she reminded him, 'and it's what you want really. And it'll be dead cool, you'll see.'

Turning back to his aunt, he shrugged and said, 'OK, I guess I'm up for it if she is.'

Smiling as she swallowed a lump in her throat, Izzie said, 'How could she not want to meet you?'

Eva was strolling through the wild-flower meadow with Rosie and Elvis, admiring the dewy cobwebs that stretched over hedgerows like crystal nets, and catching little showers of raindrops from leaves overhead. She was thinking of the Sunday mornings she and Don used to go down to the Hive Cafe for breakfast. He'd usually have a full English, while she went for smoked haddock and scrambled eggs, and all the time Rosie and Elvis would be waiting impatiently in the Range Rover – or on the terrace with them if the weather was good – for their leisurely walk along the cliff path, sometimes as far as West Bay and back. They'd almost always run into someone they knew, stopping for a chat and to gaze out at the spectacular view, which, on a clear day, rolled and sparkled across the waves all the way to the blurred mound of headland at Lyme Regis. If it was cold and stormy they'd sometimes huddle together on a memorial bench, snug in their embrace as they watched the marauding army of white horses bucking and diving to the shore and crashing up over the rocks. She couldn't help wondering if he was doing those things with Patty, even now, as she was recalling them, and if he was, were either of them sparing a thought for her?

As the sky darkened a fine, gauzy mizzle began sweeping over the fields, though she barely noticed it as she watched Rosie and Elvis prodding about in ditches and puddles, occasionally romping on ahead before bounding back with glee and mud plastered all over their daft little faces. It made her smile, in spite of the ache in her heart.

The loneliness wasn't getting any easier, nor was the longing showing any signs of abating. Weekends were always the worst, when she struggled to fill her time; but so were the mornings when she woke up alone; and the evenings when he didn't come home; and all day long when she wanted to call and couldn't. Then there were the times the pain reached out like a hand to snatch away her laughter, and the emptiness opened like a cavern to swallow her heart. If she'd allow it, she knew every minute of every day would be weighted by grief, for her marriage, her sister, her mother . . .

After opening the gate to let Rosie and Elvis into the orchard, she closed it behind her and scooped up the sodden tennis ball that Rosie had dropped at her feet. Elvis was already beetling off to forage for fallen apples, so for the next few minutes Rosie could have a game of fetch all to herself. As Eva sent the ball sailing through the air and watched her beloved retriever go tearing after it, she laughed as she sobbed and turned her face to the sky.

It sometimes helped, she found, to talk to her mother in her mind, to feel her close and tell herself that no matter how desperate or afraid she was, her mother, wherever she was now, would be willing her to stay strong and go forward. More than anything, she felt certain, she would want her to try to mend things with Patty, but she would surely understand why that couldn't be possible. Perhaps her mother, like Elaine, would accept that during this time, when emotions were at their most intense and most terrible, it was best not to interfere. Elaine listened and consoled, and occasionally advised, but only on how Eva should search within herself for resources that would help get her past the worst of the pain. Deep breathing and visual-isations of letting go; cleansing after tears to remove the toxicity that her heart had just shed; and encour-agement to express everything she was feeling, particularly the anger and resentment, treating it as though it was an exorcism of worthless demons, or, as Elaine also called it, a spring-clean of the soul.

Hearing someone calling her name, Eva turned around to see Livvy standing on the footbridge over the pond and waving. Waving back, she might have carried on through the orchard if she hadn't noticed that Livvy was beckoning to her. Did she want to go home yet? Not really, but the rain was getting worse, so perhaps it was time to hook Elvis on to his lead, since he'd never be coaxed from his fruit feast otherwise.

'You're back earlier than I expected,' she remarked, as Livvy came to open the gate into the garden. She didn't ask where Livvy and Jasmine had taken off to before she was even up this morning. They'd almost certainly gone to have breakfast with their mother and father, and it would be easier not to hear it.

'Hang on, hang on,' Livvy was saying into her mobile, 'I heard but . . . Yes, I'm here now. What's happening your end?' There was a pause as she listened to the reply, then with a squeal of excitement, 'You're kidding me! Oh I can't wait to see him.'

Presuming she was talking to a friend about some boy who'd caught her eye, Eva pressed on ahead through the vegetable garden, scolding Elvis as he made a quick grab for a potato plant, and hustling Rosie around the summer house to go in through the next gate on to the lawn. Once Livvy had locked up behind them, Eva freed Elvis from his lead and ushered both animals round to the side of the house where she tied them up, and hosed them down, before going inside to fetch towels.

When she came out again she saw, to her surprise, that Livvy was standing in the porch of the summer house, still on the phone. Whoever she was speaking to, it wasn't Jasmine, since Jasmine's mobile was on the kitchen table where she'd left it earlier. As soon as Jasmine got back the three of them would be on their way out again, since Eva had promised to go and help decorate the shop for Christmas. It might still only be the first week of December, but the entire town was already lit up, with the only gloomy spot lurking in their alley. Left to her it might have stayed that way, but it wouldn't have been fair to deprive the girls of the joy of creating their seasonal magic, and she knew if she tried to get out of going herself they'd either start bullying her into it, or declaring that they wouldn't go either.

She'd decide later what to do about decorating the house, though feeling as she did now she strongly doubted she'd find the heart. Besides, what would be the point if she wasn't going to be here? She hadn't actually committed to Barbados with Carrie-Anne yet, or to London to stay with Bobbie, but she guessed she'd opt for one or the other, since it would be easier all round if she wasn't here. Elaine wouldn't feel torn between her and Patty, Livvy could go to her mother with an easy conscience, Jasmine was presumably staying with her mother anyway, and Patty and Don wouldn't have to feel terrible about her being up on the hill all alone. Not that she particularly cared how they felt, but she did care how she felt, so it would definitely be wiser to go away. Mrs H would no doubt be happy to throw her own family Christmas here, taking care of Rosie and Elvis the way she usually did when her employers went away.

'OK, right,' Livvy declared, coming on to the terrace and grabbing a towel. 'Let's get these two inside and then I've got something to tell you.'

Casting her a teasing smile, Eva said, 'So what's his name?'

Livvy did a double take. 'What do you . . .?' Then, catching Eva's meaning, 'Oh, right, you think I've met someone. Wrong. Well, I might have, or at least I'm going to, but that's not what this is about. I mean it is, but I think I should just shut up now and . . . Great, here's Jas. I'm just going to talk to her,' and dropping Rosie's towel she all but leapt in through the door and quickly closed it again.

A few minutes later, with a marginally less wet odd couple, Eva ushered them into their den for a drink and a more thorough drying out, before returning to the kitchen to find out what all the whispering was about.

'Coffee, chair,' Livvy announced, putting the former in front of her as Jasmine pulled out the latter.

Smiling in bewilderment, Eva did as she was told, and looked from one to the other as Livvy checked her watch and Jasmine bunched a hand to her mouth, clearly trying to stifle some excitement. 'What on earth is going on?' Eva demanded.

'OK,' Livvy said, sitting down next to her, 'Mum is going to ring any minute . . . No, no, don't look like that, you have to speak to her, Eva. I promise, everything's all right, and you're going to really want to hear what she has to say.'

Eva was already shaking her head.

'You have to,' Livvy insisted. 'I swear it's absolutely brilliant news and there's no way in the world I'd try to make you do this if . . . Oh God, that's her,' she gasped as her mobile started to ring. Checking, she gazed fiercely into Eva's eyes as she clicked on. 'Hi, Mum, yes, she's here,' she said. 'I'll hand you over.'

Eva drew back.

'Eva, please, just hear what she has to say,' Jasmine begged.

'You don't have to speak if you don't want to,' Livvy told her, 'all you have to do is listen. I'll even hold the phone, if you like.'

Realising she wasn't going to get out of this, Eva

took the mobile, while knowing already that even if Patty gave her the best news of all, that she'd broken up with Don, there was still no turning back for them. The betrayal was absolute, the forgiveness impossible.

'OK, Mum, she's listening,' Livvy shouted.

'Eva, my darling,' Patty said, her voice turbulent with emotion, 'I'm just about to arrive at your gates . . .'

As Eva started to protest, Livvy put a hand over her mouth.

Pushing it away, Eva said, 'I don't want to see you, Patty.'

'I understand that,' Patty replied, 'but I have someone with me who I *know* you'll want to see.'

'Patty, I've just . . .'

'Eva, listen to me please. Are you listening?'

'Go on,' Eva said stiffly.

'Eva, his name is Richie.'

Eva frowned, then her heart gave a tremendous jolt as Patty's meaning . . . Suddenly terrified she might be misunderstanding, she looked at Livvy, and seeing the euphoria in Livvy's eyes she felt herself starting to shake.

'He's your son,' Patty whispered, 'and he's with me, so please let us in.'

Chapter Eighteen

Dropping the phone, Eva clasped her hands to her face, trying to catch her breath. 'I don't understand,' she gasped as Livvy wrapped her in her arms. 'How did she find him? Oh God, *please* tell me I'm not dreaming.'

'You're not dreaming,' Livvy laughed. 'I swear, it's really him.'

'But how? I mean . . . Oh God, I can't believe this. Have you met him? Oh Livvy, have you *seen* him?'

'Not yet, no,' Livvy cried, tears flooding her own eyes. 'It's all happened really fast, since yesterday, actually . . .'

'Here they are,' Jasmine announced from where she was watching the screen, and rushing to push the button to open the gates she let out a 'Yes!' of triumph.

With her heart in her mouth Eva watched the monitor, still hardly able to make sense of this as Patty's Audi came into the drive with another, smaller car close behind. 'Who's that?' she asked Livvy.

'It's his auntie,' Livvy explained. 'She's really sweet. You wait till you meet her, you'll see what I mean.'

His auntie . . .? What about the woman who'd adopted him?

As both cars left the screen she turned to Livvy again, suddenly afraid though she couldn't think why.

'It's all right,' Livvy said, putting calming hands on her shoulders. 'Everything's going to be fine.'

'But look at me! My face is terrible and . . .'

'You're gorgeous,' Livvy told her gently.

'Stunning,' Jasmine added with feeling.

Eva had lost all colour.

'Take a deep breath,' Livvy advised.

Eva tried to do as she was told, but it barely happened. She'd waited so long for this, had almost given up hope, and now he was here. *He was here.* 'Are you sure . . .?' She dashed a trembling hand through her hair. 'What am I trying to say? How long has Patty known where he is?'

'Just since yesterday,' Livvy reminded her. 'His cousin is one of the girls who kept coming into the shop, you know, the ones we thought were shoplifters.'

Eva looked blank.

'Never mind,' Livvy said. 'Mum and Izzie – that's his aunt – will tell you everything . . . Oh Eva, don't cry.'

'I'm sorry,' Eva choked, trying to pull herself together, but it was hardly possible. 'What am I going to say?' she gasped. 'Does he know why I let him go? Is he angry? Oh God, Livvy, what if . . .'

'Sssh, ssh,' Livvy interrupted. 'From everything his aunt told us he sounds really cool. You know, like Jake, but younger. Well, maybe not like Jake, but you know what I mean.'

'I'll put more coffee on,' Jasmine decided. 'Or should I get out some champagne?'

Eva couldn't think how to answer. It was all too

374

sudden, so totally unexpected that she still couldn't get a grip on it. Then she was afraid she might not be up to it, that she was so shattered and disoriented after all that had happened that she'd end up letting him down again . . .

'Come here,' Livvy said, grabbing her into a hug. 'You're going to be fine, OK? You're his mother, he wants to meet you and Mum says this is what you've always wanted.'

'It is,' Eva sobbed. 'Oh God, it really is, but landing it on me like this . . .'

'She knew you wouldn't want to wait. As soon as she found out, which was like, completely out of the blue yesterday morning . . . We didn't tell you then because she had to make sure everything was kosher, you know, that there wasn't anything fraudulent or dodgy going on, and then she arranged for him to come over to the barn today so she could meet him and make absolutely sure . . . Oh, Evie, look at you,' she wailed, hugging Eva again. 'I know it's a shock, but it's wonderful, isn't it?'

'Of course,' Eva spluttered through her tears. 'But I'm going to look a wreck. I have to pull myself together.'

'Here, dry your eyes,' Jasmine urged, grabbing the kitchen roll.

'Where's your bag?' Livvy demanded. 'Let me brush your hair. Not that it matters what you look like, you're beautiful anyway and he's going to absolutely love you. How could he not?'

'He couldn't,' Jasmine assured her, starting to bounce up and down in excitement. 'This is like so amazing.' Then, frowning worriedly, she said to Livvy, 'Do you think we should be here? Maybe we ought to make ourselves scarce?'

'No way!' Livvy cried. 'I mean, maybe later, but it would be really awkward if it was just the two of them at first. Wouldn't it?' she said to Eva, suddenly uncertain herself.

Hardly knowing how to answer, Eva simply blew her nose and tried again to believe this was happening.

'Crikey, I'd better go and unlock the door,' Livvy suddenly remembered, and shoving the rest of the kitchen roll at Eva she scooted across to the conservatory where she flipped the lock on the outer door and ran back again.

'Champagne,' Jasmine declared, and dived towards the cooler. 'Shall I open some? It's still early, maybe it ought to be coffee?'

Eva still didn't answer. Her eyes were fixed on the conservatory now, where Patty had just come in and was holding the door open for someone else to follow. First came a small, neat-looking woman in a red felt coat and black frilled scarf. Next was a pretty teenage girl with silky blonde hair, enormous eyes and a complexion that was almost like porcelain.

Then came a young man who was still a boy, and Eva's heart started quietly breaking apart.

'Oh my God,' she murmured, pressing her hands to her mouth. He was here. Her son, her very own boy whom she'd given birth to and longed for all these years and was terrified she might never meet ... Was this really him, coming towards her? She couldn't even begin to doubt it when the chaotic mass of dark brown hair, strangely arresting yet sleepy eyes, put together with his height that must surely be six foot already, and the sheer magnetism of him, made him so incredibly like his father that it was taking her breath away.

As though they had a life of their own her hands reached out to him, then she pulled them back. She didn't know what to do or say and she could see he was awkward too.

Finally, holding out her hand to shake, she said, 'Hello, I'm – I'm Eva.'

Taking her hand, but keeping his eyes down, he said, 'I'm Richie. It's good to meet you.' Then his eyes came to hers and suddenly she didn't care any more, she had to hold him, and wrapping him tightly in her arms she hugged him as though she'd never let go.

'Thank God,' she tried to whisper, but it barely came out. Realising how tightly he was holding her too, she squeezed him harder still. This was a miracle, a dream coming true. She was so happy that her heart was overflowing with more tears and love than she'd ever known was possible. Holding him transcended everything. His man's body – still a boy's – was the body of *her son*, and even if this moment was all life ever allowed them she'd be grateful for it, just to know that he was alive and healthy and so *incredibly* handsome . . . Feeling him turning away she tentatively let him go, and kept a hand on his shoulder as he struggled to pull himself together.

'It's all right, my love,' she heard someone say behind her. Eva didn't look round, she just kept her eyes on her son who was crying and trying so very hard to stop.

'I'm sorry,' Eva whispered brokenly. 'I'm so, so sorry.'

He turned back, and her heart contracted to see his reddened eyes and lopsided smile.

'That really wasn't cool, was it?' he said, trying

to laugh at himself, but his emotions were clearly still very close to the surface. 'What a wuss.'

Eva longed to hug him again, but was afraid it might be too much. 'You don't look much like one to me,' she told him, teasingly.

He was looking past her now, and starting to laugh. Turning around to find Rosie and Elvis barrelling towards them, she gave a sob of pure pride.

'Who's this?' he demanded, immediately going down to their level.

'I thought they should join in,' Livvy explained, her cheeks as wet as everyone else's.

'Of course,' Eva said, and stooping to fuss her adorable beasts too, she made the introductions.

'You're so cool,' Richie told them, delightedly. 'Elvis, huh?' he laughed, ruffling Elvis's coarse black hide. 'Can you sing? And you're Rosie. What a doll.'

Stepping forward with a hand out ready to shake, Livvy said, 'Hi, I'm Olivia, your cousin. Everyone calls me Livvy.'

Standing up and shyly taking her hand, he said, 'I'm Richard, but everyone calls me Richie.'

Melting with joy, Livvy followed his eyes to Eva's as he turned to look at her again.

Eva's heart was in her throat. Was this boy, *this man*, really hers? It hardly seemed possible. He was like a miracle, a dream coming true. She wanted to believe that some sort of special bond was already forming between them, but she guessed it was too soon for that. All that mattered was the fact that he was here.

'I'm Jasmine,' Jasmine declared, coming forward. 'I'm kind of your stepsister.'

'Good to meet you,' he told her, shaking hands.

Coming in gently, Patty said, 'Evie, this is Izzie Larch, Richie's aunt.'

'Oh gosh, I'm so sorry,' Eva apologised, finally remembering her manners. 'Hello, I'm Eva, it's a great pleasure to meet you. Thank you so much . . . I . . . I hardly know what to say.'

Izzie was smiling through her own tears as she took Eva's hand between both of hers. 'We've read so much about you,' she told her, 'and we've seen you in all our magazines and things, but you're even lovelier than I thought.'

Aware of how visible her scars were without any make-up, Eva smiled at the kindness and turned to the wide-eyed young girl beside her, who was looking nothing short of awestruck as she gazed around the kitchen and down at the animals. 'And you are?' she said gently.

Shyly taking Eva's hand, the girl said, 'Sadie. I'm Richie's cousin.'

Eva smiled. 'Welcome to Rosie and Elvis's pad, Sadie,' she said. 'As you can see, you're rather in demand.'

Glancing down as Elvis nudged in for some attention, Sadie touched him gingerly until Richie took hold of him more boisterously and found himself assaulted from behind by Rosie. As he laughed and tried to fuss them both Eva caught Patty's eye. She felt her heart contract as the moment resonated so deeply between them that for a moment it was as though there was no rift, no betrayal, nothing at all keeping them apart.

As tearful as everyone else, Patty said, 'It's Sadie we have to thank for this.'

Glancing at the girl, who seemed to be gaining a little more confidence with Elvis, Eva was about to speak when Jasmine said, 'Would anyone like champagne?'

To Richie, Eva said, 'Would you?' She could hardly believe how handsome he was, and grown up, and yet so teenagerish in his loose-fitting rugby shirt and typically slouched jeans. She felt ready to burst with pride.

'Great, if everyone else does,' he replied, the sparkle in his eyes showing how thrilled and blown away he was by all that was happening.

As Livvy bounced off to do the honours, Eva said to Richie, 'If you only knew . . . Do you know? Did you get my letters and cards? I sent them all the time.'

His eyes lost some of their shine as he said, awkwardly, 'Yeah, I heard that you did, but I haven't seen them yet.'

'My sister-in-law's sending them,' Izzie told her.

That he had been cheated out of what was rightfully his, even though she had long feared, and even suspected it, was only possible to bear because he was here. Eva looked at Izzie as she said, 'What's happened to the people who adopted him?'

Glancing at Richie, Izzie said, 'His dad died about five years ago and when his mother went up north to be with her brother, back at the beginning of the year, Richie decided to stay with us.'

His mother had let him go, just like that? How could she?

Knowing she was in danger of asking too much too soon, Eva somehow managed to hold back her feelings and glanced briefly at Patty again before saying to Richie, 'I'm sorry about your dad.' Receiving a nod from Patty to confirm it was the right thing to say, she looked at Richie again. It was hard to imagine him with parents who were strangers, even though she was far more of one in reality. And devastating to think of his adoptive mother abandoning him, especially after she'd done the same herself. It was unthinkable, unforgivable and utterly shaming. How could she, or anyone, ever do anything to hurt this wonderful young man who was already lighting up her world?

'Why don't you all sit down?' Livvy suggested from behind the bar.

Obediently going to the table where Jasmine was setting out glasses, Eva sat Izzie one side of her and Richie the other as she said, 'I have to apologise for not being better prepared. Livvy only sprang this on me a few minutes ago, so I know almost nothing about anyone yet – except the most important thing, of course.' She paused, smiling at Richie. 'I know that you're probably the best-looking sixteen-year-old I've ever seen, but I guess I could be biased.'

'Oh, don't worry about embarrassing him, will you?' Livvy chided as Richie blushed to the roots of his hair.

'I'm sorry,' Eva laughed, 'it just slipped out. I'll try not to do it again.'

'I'm cool.' Richie shrugged, still red, and poking his tongue out at Sadie.

'Of course once we found out who his mother was,' Sadie piped up, 'we all realised straight away why he's so fit.'

As Eva glanced at Patty again she knew what Patty was thinking – that he was just as much like his father, if not more. However, now wasn't the time to be mentioning Nick – in fact, Eva didn't want to think about Nick at all, because he didn't deserve to be a part of this.

After the champagne was poured and everyone was sitting around the table with a glass in front of them, Eva raised hers and said, 'I hope I'm not going to embarrass you again, Richie, well, I'm sure I am, but hopefully you'll forgive me if I propose a toast to you and say you've just made this far and away the very happiest day of my life.'

Though he did colour up again, he said, 'Actually, it's pretty cool for me too. I just hope I'm not going to turn out to be a disappointment.'

Eva's eyes widened in shock and protest. 'You could never be that,' she told him earnestly.

'Just wait,' Sadie warned.

'No, he couldn't.' Izzie laughed with everyone else. 'We're very proud of him, and with good reason.'

'His head is getting so swollen here,' Sadie complained.

After treating her to a smug grin that made her pretend to gag, Richie raised his glass with everyone else as Livvy proposed a toast to Sadie for the efforts she'd made in bringing Eva and Richie together. Then they were all laughing again as Sadie told how she and her friend had come into the shop a couple of times, not really knowing what they were hoping to achieve, it had just seemed like the right place to start – and had ended up being thrown out by Jasmine.

'We thought you were shoplifters.' Livvy grimaced. 'I'm really sorry, we just had no idea.'

Richie gave a choke of laughter, earning himself a smiley kick from Sadie.

'No worries,' Sadie assured Livvy. 'I can kind of get why you'd think that. Anyway, we didn't only come into the shop, we drove up here to the house a couple of times too. We sat outside for ages hoping you might come out. We never rang the bell because we didn't know how to explain who we were over the entryphone.'

Remembering the little car parked at the gates and how it had unnerved her, Eva could only apologise for being such a faint heart. If only she'd known. To think he'd been so close while she'd been trying to come to terms with that terrible ruling . . .

'Then I didn't help matters,' Jasmine picked up, 'by running away from them yesterday morning.'

'That's the kind of effect they usually have on people,' Richie assured her.

'You are so funny,' Sadie told him.

As everyone laughed again, Livvy said curiously, 'The night I saw you, when I came out of the gym, you didn't know I was going to be there?'

'No way,' Sadie replied. 'We were just hanging out round there, because we were staying at my nan's that night. I was going to come up to you then, but . . .'

'You scared her off,' Richie interjected. 'See, I told you, she can't help it.'

'I'm going to whack you in a minute,' Sadie warned.

'I was there that night,' Richie told Livvy, 'so I saw you too.'

Livvy beamed at him. 'That is so cool,' she told him.

Apparently not quite knowing why, Richie shrugged as though pleased, and looked down at his drink.

'Of course Richie never did anything to help us get in touch with you,' Sadie went on, looking at Eva again. 'He kept saying you wouldn't have had him adopted if you wanted him, so we shouldn't be bothering you, but I kept saying that we should at least try.'

'I'm so glad you did,' Eva told her with feeling. When she looked at Richie she wasn't sure whether she wanted to laugh or cry. He appeared embarrassed, yet oddly roguish, as though on the brink of teasing someone if only he could think of the right thing to say.

From where she was leaning against the bar, the only one who hadn't sat down, Patty said, 'I'm so happy to welcome you to our family, Richie. I can tell already that you're going to make a big difference around here, and I hope your aunt Izzie and your cousins know that they'll always be every bit as welcome as you are.'

'Thank you.' Izzie smiled gratefully, raising her glass.

Eva was smiling at Izzie as Patty said, 'We already talked a little bit about my sister on our way here, Richie, so you know how special she is to us, and I have no doubt that you'll soon find out how special she is too, and come to feel the same way . . .'

'OK,' Eva interrupted, trying not to be annoyed that Patty had been discussing her with Richie, 'shall we not make this too deep? It's only our first meeting, for heaven's sake.'

Though she hadn't meant to sound so curt, even cutting, she'd clearly managed it, because the next instant Patty was saying, 'I'm sorry, I didn't mean . . . I was only . . . Actually, I should probably be going now. Richie, Izzie, you have my number if you need it . . .'

'I'll walk out with you,' Eva said, getting to her feet. 'Help yourselves to anything,' she told the others. 'I'll be right back,' and somehow resisting dropping a kiss on Richie's head she followed Patty out through the conservatory.

Moments later they were standing next to Patty's car, and Patty's face was ashen as she listened to Eva saying, 'Don't think I'm not aware of what's going on with you. You're telling yourself that now I have my son I'll be so focused on him I'll forget what you've done, and you're right, I will be focused on him, but be sure of this, Patty, nothing, not even Richie, will ever make up for the way you've betrayed me.'

'Eva, that's not . . .'

'You're probably even persuading yourself that I'll have someone to take care of me now, to make sure I don't do anything stupid like follow in our mother's footsteps because my husband and sister are sleeping together . . .'

'For heaven's sake . . .'

'You have *no* idea how damaged he might be by his past,' Eva raged, 'what issues he might have going on inside as a result of his upbringing which we don't yet know anything about, so to think you can start burdening him with mine just so *you* can get on with your life . . .'

'Eva stop! You've got it wrong . . .'

'No! All I got wrong was trusting you the way I did, and now you can't even find the time to stay and make him feel welcome, no doubt because you have to rush home to Don. Well, go, Patty! Get out of here and don't bother coming back, because you're not wanted.'

As she turned away, Patty grabbed her and spun her back. 'I'm leaving because the last thing I want is that boy to sense the atmosphere between us,' she cried furiously.

'Then you're right to go, because that's never going to change.'

Though Patty continued to glare at her sister, she could see that there really wasn't anything to be gained from pursuing this now, so turning around she got into her car and started the engine.

As she drove away, Eva stood watching her, knowing that she should never have allowed herself to get so worked up, that if anyone was going to ruin this day it would be her if she didn't get herself under better control. Her emotions were running too high, were too fragile and explosive, so she must give herself a moment now to calm down and remember that hurting Patty and feeling jealous about Don had no place in her life today. All that mattered was her son.

Hearing the sound of laughter as she went back inside, Eva felt what remained of her tension melting away, and when she saw how well Richie was already bonding with Rosie and Elvis, who, shameless pair, were crowding him for more fussing, she had to force herself not to throw her arms around him again. It was going to be so easy to overwhelm him with her feelings, to keep on telling him how happy he'd made her, but she must try to take it slowly, allow him time to feel as relaxed with her as he already seemed to be with Livvy and Jasmine.

'Ah, there you are,' Livvy declared, 'we were just saying that you and Richie must have thousands of things you want to ask each other, so it might be a good idea if the rest of us took off for a while to give you a chance to talk. He's terrified, he said, but . . .'

'I so did not,' Richie protested, blushing again.

'. . . he's up for it if you are.'

386

Eva's eyes were shining. 'Sounds like a great idea to me.'

'It's OK, she won't morph into Cruella de Vil or Countess Bathory the minute we've gone,' Livvy assured him.

'She only does that on Tuesdays,' Jasmine added.

'Countess who?' Eva demanded.

'They reckon she's the serial killer who inspired Dracula,' Richie told her, 'but I think she only went for girls, so I'm feeling pretty safe.'

As everyone laughed at Eva's expression, Izzie got to her feet, saying, 'They're all into vampires these days, so be warned.'

Remembering that was indeed true, Eva's tone was wry as she said, 'And I thought I was pretty out there with Elvis.'

Apparently loving being talked about, Elvis launched into one of his livelier snort-and-jig routines, while Rosie did Richie the great honour of presenting him with her ball.

'I thought I'd take the girls down to the Bridport Arms,' Izzie was saying as she and Eva led the way out to the drive. 'Shall we say about an hour? Is that long enough, too long? You tell me.'

Though Izzie was sounding bright and friendly, Eva felt sure she must be riddled with misgivings and anxieties over what was happening, and wished she could find a way to reassure her. However, she knew that only time, and a successful building of a relationship with Richie, could do that.

'I'm sure an hour will be plenty enough for him,' she said jokily, 'so let's go for that. And maybe we can get together sometime soon to have a chat about things?'

Izzie seemed to like that. 'Of course, you just let

me know when and where and I'll be happy to. He's no trouble, I can promise you that, which isn't to say he doesn't have his moments . . .'

'I heard that,' Richie told her.

'You were supposed to,' she chuckled, reaching up to tousle his hair.

'I don't mind driving if everyone wants to get into my car,' Jasmine offered.

Moments later they'd all piled in and were shouting out good luck as they took off towards the gates.

Standing beside Richie, Eva tried to think of a way to break the awkwardness developing between them.

'Are you hungry?' she ventured. 'Would you like something to eat?'

Following her inside, he said, 'I guess a bit, if you are?'

Doubting she'd be able to eat a thing, she sat him down at the table and went to raid the fridge. 'I seem to have plenty of cheese and ham,' she announced, 'so take your pick, omelette, baguette, croque monsieur . . .'

'Croque what?' he interrupted.

Grimacing, she said, 'Monsieur. It's basically cheese and ham on toast.'

He shrugged. 'Sounds cool. If it's OK, I'll have that.'

As she started to prepare the snack she noticed him gazing out across the garden to the sea.

'This place is totally awesome,' he commented, almost under his breath. 'Sadie said it was – not that she'd ever been inside before today, but you know, when she drove up here with Tara . . .'

'It's a pity she didn't ring the bell,' Eva responded,

388

'but I can understand why she didn't. Anyway, the important thing is that you're here now, and we have so much catching up to do I hardly know where to begin.'

Turning to look at her, he seemed uneasy, in a way that turned her heart inside out. *Please let him want to know me,* she was panicking behind her smile. She wouldn't be able to bear it if he didn't.

As she started to speak he did too, and they both stopped awkwardly.

'You first,' she said quickly.

'No, you,' he insisted.

'I was only going to say I'm so glad you came.'

He nodded and looked down at his hands.

'How about you?' she prompted, fearing that he wasn't so glad. 'What were you going to say?'

Shrugging he said, 'I was just going to ask how long you've lived here?' He looked around the kitchen and told her simply by his expression that he'd probably never seen anything like it.

Trying not to think of how he should have grown up here, she said, 'Well, I've owned it for about seventeen years, but it had to be completely renovated before we could move in, so we've – I've actually lived here for fourteen.'

'Awesome,' he murmured. 'It's like something out of a magazine.' Then, not quite meeting her eyes, he said, 'So you don't have any other children?'

Guessing Patty must have told him that, or perhaps he'd read it somewhere, she felt a wave of gladness sweeping over her that she had remained exclusively his, provided, of course, it was what he wanted. 'I'll tell you one day why you're my only child,' she responded, feeling instantly embarrassed by the intimacy of the words she'd chosen, 'but it's probably a bit heavy going for today.'

He was looking into her face now, and she felt acutely aware of her scars. 'Was it something to do with the attack?' he asked quietly.

She swallowed as she smiled. 'Not exactly,' she replied. 'I mean, it didn't leave me incapable of having any more, if that's what you're thinking.'

He went on looking at her, but after a moment she realised he'd lost focus as he tried once again to take everything in.

'I still don't know very much about you,' she reminded him, 'apart from the fact that you live with your aunt and apparently have a very good relationship with your cousin.'

'Oh, Sadie, yeah, she's cool. We've been like best mates for as long as I can remember. I mean, she gets on my case about stuff every now and then, but I guess I probably do the same to her.' He stopped, seeming to think he'd said enough. Then to her surprise, and relief, he continued. 'I keep telling her if she could play rugger she'd be the perfect person, and she says if she could play rugger she'd be weird or a hooker because she's small, so she won't be taking it up any time soon.'

Not surprised to hear about the rugby, considering his shirt, Eva laughed as she said, 'I take it you play the game.'

'Oh, just about every chance I get.'

'What position do you play?' she asked, glancing up.

'Number eight,' he replied, making it sound as ordinary as any other position.

Her eyebrows arched. 'Now why aren't I surprised?' she said teasingly.

'Are you a fan?' he asked.

She pulled a face. 'That might be overstating it, but if there's an important game on I usually watch. Which team do you follow?'

'Exeter Chiefs,' he answered, as if there were no other. 'And you?'

'I'm not dedicated enough to have a team, but I can always be talked around.'

Grinning, he took some nuts from the dish she put in front of him, and spotting four hungry eyes gazing up at him he said, 'Is it OK to share?'

'Of course, it's just important to remember that Elvis should never have any meat, or any kind of animal product.'

Eyeing Elvis closely he said, 'Mm, I guess that could be a bit cannibalistic, so that means none of my thingy monsieur, Elvis baby. You'll just have to make do with a peanut.'

As Elvis scoffed down a handful and Rosie chomped more delicately on her allocation, he remarked, 'I've never known anyone have a pig as a pet before. It's really cool.'

'I'm glad you think so.' She smiled. 'I'm pretty mad about him myself.'

Hoping that Elvis would be his pet too one of these days, she carried their food to the table and marvelled yet again at the miracle of his size and obvious athleticism. It was almost impossible to stop looking at him. Could this gorgeous, humorous, seemingly intelligent hunk of a boy really be hers? Were all those awful, endless years of not knowing where or even who he was really and truly at an end? She wanted to pinch herself to make sure it wasn't a dream and that he was actually sitting right here at her table, eating food she'd prepared and telling her about himself in a way that seemed slowly but surely to be growing in confidence.

'So your husband,' he said, biting into his sandwich, 'the one we read about, the ex-policeman? I guess he's not here today?'

Putting her sandwich down as her mouth turned dry, Eva took only a moment to decide that she must answer with the truth. 'Actually, we're not together any more,' she told him quietly.

A painful colour rushed to his cheeks. 'Oh, sorry,' he responded. 'I didn't mean . . . It was just . . .'

'It's OK,' she assured him. 'You were right to ask, and I don't want to start off with secrets between us, so I should probably tell you now that he left me about two months ago.'

His eyes widened in disbelief. 'He left *you*?' he queried, as though unable to imagine anything so bizarre.

She almost smiled at the loyalty as she nodded. 'He's living with my sister now, Patty, who you've already met.'

More colour rushed to his cheeks as apparently feeling right out of his depth now he looked down at his food.

'It's really not something for you to worry about,' she assured him hastily. 'I'm surviving, and you turning up like this . . . Well, it's giving me a whole lot more to think about than what they might be doing together.'

His eyes came back to hers.

Trying to swallow her anxiety, Eva said, 'I really think we're going to get along, don't you?'

For a moment he appeared uncertain, then breaking into an impish smile, he replied, 'Yeah, I

392

reckon we might, as long as you come and watch me play rugger.'

Laughing delightedly, she said, 'Starting today, I promise never to miss a game, home or away.'

Had she overstated it, made it sound as though she was going to overwhelm him? If she had, he didn't seem to mind, because he was biting into his sandwich again and giving a playful wink to Elvis.

A few days later Patty was walking down through her campsite, passing the caravans, some luxurious, others more modest, that would soon start filling up for Christmas. A couple had coloured lights in the windows already; one even had a tree, but most were still in darkness waiting for their owners or renters to arrive.

At the end of the park she climbed over a grassy verge packed with seaweed and flotsam and descended on to the beach where a handful of anglers were casting into the waves, and a speedboat was skimming like a rocket across the bay. The sun seemed lacklustre behind its veil of cloud, but the wind, though cold, wasn't bitter or driving.

Taking out her phone, she scrolled to Elaine's number and pressed to connect. 'Hi, it's me, Patty,' she said when Elaine answered. 'Are you OK?'

'Yes, I'm fine dear, thank you,' came the reply. 'How are you?'

The sun seemed to burn her eyes for a moment, and then was gone. 'Yes, I'm good,' she said, staring down at the smashed shells at her feet. Why was she so nervous about speaking to Elaine? What was she expecting Elaine to say? 'I was – I was wondering if you might have seen or spoken to Eva since Sunday?' she asked, feeling the silence between her and Eva opening like a physical gulf in her heart.

'As a matter of fact I've just returned from taking her to the station,' Elaine said cheerily, 'so I know all about Richie and how the Universe has brought them together at last. A wonderful story. I don't mind admitting it brought tears to my eyes, and gladdened my heart so much that I'm arranging a ceremony of thanksgiving for later today. Eva won't be here, unfortunately, because she's not back from London until Thursday, but you're very welcome to join us if you have time.'

'I'll try to make it,' Patty promised. Then, 'So you haven't met him yet?'

'No, but she's bringing him over next weekend, on Saturday I believe, because he's playing rugby on Sunday so he won't be free. He sounds a lovely boy, from everything she told me.'

Swallowing drily, Patty said, 'Yes, I think he is. Certainly what I saw of him. It's fantastic news, isn't it?'

'The very best – and it could hardly have come at a better time.'

Unsure whether her stepmother was thinking of an antidote to betrayal, or the approach of Christmas, Patty felt a painful twist in her conscience anyway. 'No, it probably couldn't,' she agreed shakily. 'So how did she seem to you? Do you think she's coping with it all right?'

'I most certainly do, and now I have to wonder why you're asking.'

Taking a breath, Patty said, 'I'm just concerned, that's all. She's been through such a lot lately, and I keep wondering if I should have delayed all this until she'd had more time . . .'

'Patty, my dear, you would never have had my blessing if you'd tried to keep her son from her a minute longer than necessary. She deserves this more than anyone I know, and from what I've heard so far he deserves her too.'

'Of course,' Patty said quietly. Her head was bowed again and the sound of seagulls was like an audible tearing in her heart. 'I just . . . I needed to be sure she was OK. I've talked to Livvy, obviously, and she says she's fine, over the moon is how she puts it, and it sounds as though they all had a fabulous day on Sunday.'

'They did. And now we've dealt with that, I imagine we're soon going to get around to the real point of your call.'

Tensing as more nerves clenched her insides, Patty turned her back to the sea as in a voice strangled by tears she replied, 'I'm trying to.'

'Patty,' Elaine said gently, 'I know this is breaking your heart almost as much as it is Eva's, but I'm sorry to say that when you started your relationship with Don it was never going to end any other way.'

'So are you saying he should have stayed with her even though he was no longer in love with her? Is that the kind of marriage you'd have wanted for her?'

'Are you absolutely sure he was no longer in love with her?'

Shaken, even shocked, Patty turned very still. 'I know what he told me, and I can't see why he would lie.'

'No, nor can I, but I know he has always cared very deeply for you both and it's possible he became confused . . .'

'He's not a child, Elaine. He's a grown man who knows his own mind.'

'Then perhaps what we should really be discussing is your mind, and the issues you have regarding Eva and your mother.'

Patty's eyes closed as every muscle in her body tried to reject the words. This was why she'd been afraid to speak to Elaine, why she wanted to ring off now before Elaine could say any more, because Elaine knew the truth and was no longer flinching from speaking it.

'I understand what a painful subject this is for you,' her stepmother continued, 'but you know in your heart that sooner or later you will have to face it. So, as I told you once before, when you're ready to do that, my door will be open.'

As the call ended Patty sank to her knees in the sand and buried her head in her hands. Why had she rung Elaine when she'd known it would end like this? It was as though Elaine was already in touch with the demons she kept buried, locked, squashed into a small dark part of herself, where they should stay, because they had no use or worth, no meaning or purpose. They were just jealous, possessive, iniquitous little thoughts that belonged to a child, not a grown woman – a child whose mother had taken her own life when she was twelve years old, not four, like Eva, so she'd been old enough to understand her mother's reasons for doing what she did. Except she never had understood, not really, nor did she understand why Eva had seemed to matter more, when Patty was the eldest and if Eva hadn't come along their mother might still be here.

Why hadn't she mattered? Why had everything always been about somebody else? Apart from Don no one had ever seemed to realise how lonely she felt inside, nor had they gone out of their way to make her feel special or prized. She was the one they all leaned on, and only he seemed to understand that sometimes she needed to lean too. He'd always been there for her, ever since he'd come into their lives, giving her the kind of moral and physical support that she'd lost when her mother had left, support that Reece had never known how to provide. Was it any wonder she'd fallen in love with Don when he'd gone to such lengths to help her put her life back together after Reece walked out, and to make her feel that she still mattered when she'd all but lost sight of her sense of worth? She hadn't meant anything to happen between them, she truly hadn't, but by the time she'd realised how wretched it made her feel every time he went home to Eva, how desperately she wanted him for herself, it was already too late.

'Are you absolutely sure he was no longer in love with her?' Elaine had asked, and as the words crushed their doubt into her heart she could feel herself buckling under the dread of what she knew she must do.

Chapter Nineteen

'Oh, another text,' Eva cried happily, and opening up her BlackBerry she practically sparkled to see who it was from. In the next instant her heart was aching with guilt and dismay. It couldn't have been more different in tone to the other messages Richie had sent over the past couple of days, updating her on what he was doing, asking about Rosie and Elvis, or giving her the change of venue for his match next Sunday. This time with no warning, no preamble at all, he'd said, *So why did you give me up when I was born?*

Swallowing hard, she passed the phone over for Bobbie to read. 'I guess he finds it easier to ask this way,' she said shakily.

Bobbie nodded agreement, and handed the phone back. Her eyes went to Eva's as she said, 'So what are you going to tell him?'

'The truth, of course,' Eva replied, 'but not like this,' and opening up a reply screen she wrote, *It's a long story and I promise I will tell you, but not in a text. For now, please don't ever doubt that I regret it with all my heart and I couldn't be happier that you're back in my life. Xx*

After sending it, she sat staring down at her wine. 'Don't look so worried, it was bound to happen,'

Bobbie reminded her, 'and you'll handle it, when the time is right.'

Eva sighed and picked up her glass. 'Of course,' she said. 'I just hate to think of him being upset, which he obviously is, probably angry too, and hiding behind his phone.'

Bobbie's expression turned droll. 'From everything I know about children you should think yourself lucky, because the face-to-face can be pretty bloody with teenagers, and I'm sure it'll come.'

Grimacing and laughing, Eva glowed once more as a renewed surge of incredulity and happiness washed over her. 'Can you believe, I'm actually getting texts from *my son*?' she cried.

'Sure I can believe it,' Bobbie responded drily as she took a sip of her drink, 'that's the third one since you got here and you only turned up half an hour ago.'

Eva gave a girlish laugh that got lost in a bolt of unease. 'I know we've got a long way to go,' she said soberly, 'and a heck of a lot of ground to make up, but the important thing is, I think he's willing to give me a chance.'

Bobbie chuckled throatily. 'He'd have me to deal with if he didn't,' she responded playfully.

Eva laughed again, and gave a cry of delight as her phone bleeped once more. '*Just heard i got 57/60 geog*,' she read aloud. '*R u sure u want 2 no all ths stuff*? Look,' she said, proudly showing it to Bobbie.

After reading it, Bobbie commented, 'So he's got brains as well as beauty – and was obviously satisfied by your last answer.'

Smiling all over her face, Eva texted back again. *You're brilliant. Def want to know. Where's your friend's band playing tonight? R U still going? Don't worry not*

planning to turn up and embarrass you. Still in London.
After pressing send, she went back to his text to
read it again.

Bobbie was shaking her head fondly as she helped
herself to a small feast of Manuela's succulent cheese
puffs. The fact that Manuela had, only minutes ago,
informed her they were laced with a drug designed
to induce a slow, painful death seemed, if anything,
to be making them tastier than ever. 'You don't know
how glad I am that you waited till you got here to
break this news,' Bobbie told her, as Eva put her
phone down. 'I'd never have forgiven you if you'd
rung or sent an email.'

'I expect she wishes she had now,' Manuela
commented as she came to refill the cheese-puff
bowl.

Eva gave a choke of laughter, since her old agent
had practically crushed her bones she'd hugged her
so hard.

'Are you here again?' Bobbie yawned. 'Didn't I
fire you last week?'

'Actually, was me who fire you, but out of goodness of my heart I take you back again.'

'I humour her in letting her think she has a heart,'
Bobbie murmured in an aside to Eva as Manuela
headed towards the door.

'Don't think I didn't hear that,' Manuela called
out. 'Is you who is deaf with Alzheimer's, not me.'

'I can't wait for Richie to meet you two.' Eva
laughed delightedly. 'He is so going to love you.'

With a mock scowl Bobbie said, 'You're already
sounding like a teenager,' but the light in her eyes
was giving her away. 'So he's a rugby player, is he,
and he's saying he wants to study politics when he
goes to uni – where did that come from?'

Eva shrugged. 'No idea, except it tells us he's his own person, doesn't it, which is fantastic. I'm meeting up with his aunt on Friday for a general chat about things, so I should be better informed after that.'

Bobbie's eyes narrowed. 'And what are you going to tell her – or him – about his father when they ask, which you know they're bound to sooner or later?'

Eva's smile faded as her insides tensed. 'Actually, I've been thinking about it quite a lot since the weekend, and it's not that I don't intend to tell him, because obviously I do, again when the time's right, it's just . . . Oh, another text,' she cried chirpily, and opening up her BlackBerry again she read out, '*Its a rehrsl so in marc's grge. U r not embarrassing. Evry1 wnts 2 meet u.* Oh, Bobbie, this is so amazing, isn't it?' she cried ecstatically.

'It certainly is,' Bobbie agreed.

'I've just got to be careful not to overdo it, or get things out of perspective, which I could very easily, considering everything else that's going on.'

Bobbie's eyebrows rose.

'Not that I want to get into that,' Eva warned hastily. 'Though I have to admit I thought Don might have been in touch by now to say he's pleased about Richie, or to wish us luck, but he hasn't. Which, as far as I'm concerned, shows us that he's really not the man we thought he was.'

'Mm, I must say it surprises me too,' Bobbie sighed, 'but, as we all know, men are peculiar creatures who tell themselves all sorts of rubbish when it comes to dealing with emotions, especially their own. How's Patty?'

'I've no idea. Actually, can we change the subject?

I really don't want to talk about them. I spoke to Shelley earlier. It was very brief – you know how busy she always is – but you can probably imagine how thrilled she was to hear the news. I've made an appointment to see her in January to talk things through.'

Bobbie nodded approval and for the next few minutes she patiently allowed Eva to run on about the meeting she'd had with her new PR people that day; how business was improving at the shop; what she might buy Richie for Christmas, until finally Bobbie raised a hand to stop her.

'We can go on avoiding the subject of Nick for as long as you like,' she said, bluntly, 'at least you can, but I'm not going to. He's Richie's father, and as such he has a right to know . . .'

Eva's eyes flashed. 'How can you say that?'

'Wait!' Bobbie chided. 'I know you'd like Richie to be all yours, but he isn't, so you need to make up your mind pretty swiftly what you're going to do if the boy asks to meet his father, because it's highly likely he will.'

Feeling almost as though she'd been slapped, Eva was still bristling as she said, 'You can't have forgotten that Nick wanted nothing to do with us when Richie was born, so I don't see . . .'

'Eva, it was sixteen years ago, and Nick's circumstances at that time were a lot more complicated than you realised . . .'

'He was married, they had a child and he didn't want to leave them. What more did I need to know?'

'Actually, quite a lot, but as we know other things happened that night, and now, after all this time, rather than tell you myself what he was facing, I'm more inclined to let him do the talking.'

Eva wasn't going to back down. 'I'm sorry, Bobbie, but I really don't want to see him.'

'And I really don't see that you have a choice.'

Since she didn't, she couldn't argue, but her eyes were still glittering with resentment as she said, 'Has he ever told you why he contacted the magazine about me?'

'No, but you're aware of what his letter said, so I think it speaks for itself.'

'But he had no right taking issue with *anyone* on my behalf.'

Bobbie merely shrugged. 'Well, he did, and it's hardly relevant to what we're discussing now, is it?'

'I don't know, because I've no idea what's going on in his head, or where he is . . . Is he still in Italy?'

'No, as a matter of fact he's been back in London for several years. At least this is his base, he travels around quite a lot. In fact I'm due to have dinner with him tomorrow night in New York, if I can stay awake that long.'

Starting to feel horribly wrong-footed, even outmanoeuvred, Eva got to her feet and began to pace. All that really mattered, she kept reminding herself, was Richie, and that she did what was right for him, and if that meant putting her own feelings to one side, then so be it. It might not be easy, but for his sake, she realised, she could do anything. 'I suppose,' she said in the end, 'I ought to find out whether or not he wants to meet Richie, just in case he doesn't. I'd have to prepare Richie for that, because if he doesn't . . .'

'Enough,' Bobbie pronounced, turning off her mobile as it started to ring. 'You're creating your own scenarios when, until you speak to him, you've no idea what he's going to say.'

'If he is going to reject his son again then he can damned well look me in the eye when he does it.'

Appearing faintly amused by that, Bobbie said, 'I don't imagine he'll have a problem looking you in the eye. Now, we should be going off to dinner, my love. I have to be up at five in the morning to get my flight.'

Patty was sitting at the table in her kitchen, barely hearing the rain that was hammering down outside, or feeling the warmth from the Aga that was steaming the windows and thickening the air. In the hearth, the fire she'd just lit – out of habit, or to kill time, she couldn't be sure – was starting to throw up a lively flame, while the old grandfather clock Reece had left behind was about to chime the hour. Six o'clock on a Thursday evening, three weeks before Christmas – it would be the first without Eva, the first that she and Don would spend together as a couple.

Except it wasn't going to happen that way.

She'd made up her mind what had to be done; all she needed now was the courage to see it through.

Picking up her mobile as it rang, she saw it was Livvy and clicked on.

'Hey, Mum, did I leave my red and black scarf there earlier? I can't find it anywhere.'

Looking at it, draped over the back of a chair, Patty said, 'Yes, it's here.'

'Great! I was afraid I'd dropped it somewhere. Can you pop it into the shop if you're passing? Eva's back from London now, but she'll be out between two and four tomorrow if you can make it then.'

Hating that they were having to work out how she could avoid running into Eva, Patty said, 'If I'm passing I will.'

'Cool. If not, I'll try to get over at the weekend. Are you going anywhere?'

'Nowhere in particular. How about you?'

'I'm working all day Saturday, as usual, then on Sunday Jas and I are going with Eva to watch Richie play rugby. His aunt's invited us for tea after. Isn't that sweet?'

Patty's heart contracted so painfully that it was a moment before she could say, 'Lovely.' She was recalling the times Eva had joined her for Livvy and Jake's sporting occasions. Now, at last, she was able to watch and cheer on a son of her own, and Patty would have loved nothing more than to be able to go along with her.

'Are you OK?' Livvy asked. 'You sound a bit down.'

'No, I'm fine,' Patty lied. 'Just trying to decide what to make for supper. I guess you'll be eating with Eva.'

'Actually, we've got so much work on that if we eat anything tonight it'll be a takeout. Did I tell you, we're interviewing for another part-time assistant tomorrow and Coral's decided to take her job on permanently, so if it all works out I should be able to go with Eva when she's checking out possible new shops in the new year.'

Feeling as though everything was running away from her, Patty said, 'Does she have anywhere in mind yet?'

'There are a couple of options in the pipeline. I think she's quite keen on one we have the details for in Bath . . . Did you get Jake's text?'

'I did. He'll be home next Monday and staying until the fourth of January.'

'When he's off to Hong Kong, jammy thing. If he

carries on like this he'll have all his uni fees covered and some. Bet that pleases you.'

Patty tried to smile. Though she knew Reece, or even Don, would make sure Jake's fees weren't an issue, she dearly wished she was in a position to take care of them herself. If she'd had a full education or a modelling career, maybe she'd have been able to.

Hearing a car pulling up outside, she felt her insides starting to contract with nerves. 'I should go now,' she said to Livvy. 'I'll do my best to drop the scarf in tomorrow afternoon,' and ringing off she shut down the phone before slipping it into her pocket.

'This is a nice surprise,' Don said, stomping his feet on the mat as he came in from the rain, 'I thought you weren't back till seven.'

'My last meeting was cancelled,' she told him, staying where she was instead of going to greet him the way she usually did.

She watched him hang his coat on the back of the door and looked up at him as he came to embrace her. Before he reached her she put up a hand to stop him. 'Please don't,' she said quietly. 'I . . . There's something I have to tell you.'

Surprised, then immediately concerned, he asked, 'What's happened? Are you OK?'

She tried to nod, but shook her head.

'Is it Eva? The kids?'

Noting how high on the list her sister remained, she lowered her eyes as she said, 'They're fine. Everyone is. It's just . . . It's what's happening between us . . .' She clenched her hands tightly, trying to make herself go on. 'I want you to leave,' she told him quickly. She hadn't meant it to come out quite like that – she'd been unsure she'd be able to say it at all – but it was there now, an invisible force charging the air with a terrible truth that was also a lie.

When there was only silence, she lifted her eyes to his and felt herself breaking apart inside.

'You don't mean that,' he said roughly.

It was true, she didn't, but for all their sakes it was what she had to do.

'Patty, for God's sake . . .'

'Don, please. You know what we're doing isn't right. It never has been, and nor will it ever be, so we have to start being honest with ourselves. I think you still love Eva, and that you never stopped . . .'

'Patty, listen to me,' he cut in forcefully. 'Whatever you're telling yourself, you're wrong . . .'

'I know I'm right . . .'

'. . . yes, I do have strong feelings for Eva, I've never denied that, but it's not the same as the way I feel about you. For Christ's sake, you have to know how much I love you . . .'

'I know you think you do, but maybe we got carried away . . . Everything became confused, or misunderstood . . .'

'No, no, no. I'm completely clear on the way I feel about you. So maybe this is you trying to tell me you're having doubts about me?'

'No!' Her eyes were wild. 'Yes. Oh God, I don't know, but look at the way things are. My family's split in two, we hardly ever hear from any of our friends, we're afraid to go out in case we bump into Eva, and what's going to happen at Christmas? I have a nephew now, and you have a stepson, are we just going to ignore that? Think how hurtful it'll be to Eva if we do.'

407

'So what are you suggesting? We can't invite them here, and she's obviously not going to invite us there . . .'

'She wouldn't have to if you were already there.'

His eyes widened with shock. 'Patty, I don't know what's got into you . . .'

'I think you should go back to her, Don. It's the right thing to do. The only thing.'

Grabbing her hands, he held them tightly in his own as he forced her to look at him. 'I went back to her once, remember, at your insistence, and it wasn't what any of us wanted. Patty, please, just tell me what's happened.'

Pulling her hands free, she turned away from him and went to stand over the fire.

'Is it Livvy? Jake? Has one of them said something?'

'No, it's me,' she cried. 'I can't bear what I've done to my sister, or the reasons behind why I did it . . .'

'What are you talking about?'

'I should have tried harder to end our relationship . . .'

'You did everything you could, we both did.'

'We couldn't have, or it would never have come to this.'

Going to her, he made her turn and face him. 'For once in your life, Patty,' he said, gazing fiercely into her eyes, 'you have to start putting yourself first. Ever since I've known you she's seemed to matter more to you than anyone, sometimes even more than your children . . .'

'Don't say that,' she cried, pressing her hands to her face. 'She was a child when our mother died. I had to take care of her . . .'

'But she's a grown woman now, and you have to start letting go sometime . . .'

'Maybe, but not like this. No, Don, please don't say any more. I want you to leave . . .'

'I'm not letting you do this. For Christ's sake, you're not the first sisters this has happened to.'

'She's more than a sister, you know that . . .'

'You're *not* her mother.'

'But I'm the nearest thing she had to one, and I can't just ignore that because it suits me to now.'

'Patty, you have to get a better grip on this . . .'

'No, it's you who has to try and understand that I don't want it to be this way, I'd give anything for it not to be, but the truth is our mother did what she did because of Eva, and a part of me hates Eva for that, even though I know it's not her fault. She couldn't help what was going on in our mother's head, she didn't even know, for God's sake, but that doesn't change the fact that having Eva . . . having Eva . . . She used to love me, we were so close, and then she didn't think about me any more, even when she died, and now I have to ask myself if I've taken you from Eva to try to prove that I matter too?'

Blinking in total bewilderment, he simply stared at her as he struggled for a response.

'I'm sorry,' she mumbled. 'I know it's . . .'

'Patty, listen to me,' he broke in urgently, 'you've got to know how much you matter to me, to all of us, and you can't seriously believe that breaking us up is going to alter the past, or repair things for you and Eva . . .'

'You might not think so, but over time, if we're no longer together . . . If I put her first then I'll know I haven't acted out of some awful, selfish sense of injustice, or need for revenge, and if she realises she's still that important to me then maybe we can start to repair things.'

His face was taut with incomprehension as he looked back at her. 'I can't believe you're thinking this way,' he told her. 'It's crazy. It's just not making any sense.'

Her only answer was to close her eyes and put her head in her hands.

'And what about me?' he asked bluntly. 'Am I just supposed to carry on as though we don't mean anything to one another any more? As though I don't have any feelings?'

'You're stronger than we are,' she insisted. 'You'll be able to cope in a way that Eva and I can't.'

'No! It's *you* who can't cope, Patty, not her . . .'

'That's not true.'

'Yes it is, you only have to look at how well she's holding herself together, turning her life around, while you, my darling, are starting to fall apart – which is why I have to be here, so that someone who loves you and is prepared to put you first, even if you won't, is taking proper care of you.'

Knowing she'd never felt more desperate to hold on to him, to cling to him and never let go, she forced herself to move past him and over to the door. 'If you really want to put me first,' she said shakily, 'then please do as I ask and . . .'

'Patty . . .'

'Even if it's only for a few weeks,' she cried. 'We have to have some space, some time to think . . . Oh God, I'm sorry to do this to you now, but you can go to one of your brothers . . .'

'And what will you do?'

'I'll be OK. I just . . .' Unable to say any more, she unhooked her coat and started to put it on.

410

'Where are you going?' he demanded.

'I'll stay at one of the cottages tonight to give you the chance to gather up your things.'

Furious and riddled with frustration, he said, 'And if I don't?'

'Then I'll carry on staying at the cottage,' and pocketing her keys she let herself out into the rain, unable to bear the pain and confusion in his eyes a moment longer.

Eva was sitting with Izzie at a window table of the Bridport Arms, gazing out across the rain-spattered harbour towards the boats that would remain beached in mud until the tide turned. Along the jetty the fish and chip stalls were gaily decorated with Christmas lights, and the Riverside restaurant beyond was aglow with its own seasonal cheer. 'It's bizarre,' Eva was saying, 'to think of how often I've been here in West Bay, in this very pub even, and all the time Richie might have been here too.'

Izzie was smiling gently. 'We saw you a few times,' she admitted, 'you even spoke to him once, when he was about five. I remember we were all dead chuffed that someone famous had been nice to him.'

Stunned by the fact that she'd actually spoken to her own son without realising it, Eva quickly made herself push it away. Now wasn't the time to try and deal with it. To distract herself, she wondered where Don's boat might be moored now. There had been no sign of it when she'd arrived, and since the night she'd spotted him driving out of West Bay, with Patty just ahead, she hadn't seen him at all.

Realising she must let that go too, she turned to Izzie and said, 'So where does your mother live?'

'Just up over the back,' Izzie replied, 'in one of

the old terraced houses. Most of them are still council-owned, but she managed to buy hers a few years ago.'

Realising how proud she was to say that, Eva's heart warmed with affection. 'It's a lovely spot,' she told her, 'virtually right on the beach.'

'The kids certainly enjoyed it while they were growing up. They still do in the summer.'

Eva wondered if she was trying to remind her that Richie had a shared history with her family, and whatever happened in the future that would never change? There was no edge to her voice or suspicion in her eyes, but she must surely be worried about how everything was going to play out.

Before Eva could think of a way to reassure her, Izzie said, 'Did you grow up anywhere around here?'

'No, we weren't near the sea at all. I sometimes wonder if that's why we can't seem to get enough of it now.'

'You mean you and your sister?'

Eva nodded, then moving straight past Patty, she said, 'I like to think of Richie playing with his cousins in the sand, jumping about in the waves, climbing the cliffs, thinking he was king of the world the way children do.'

'That pretty much sums him up,' Izzie admitted with a smile. 'He's a good boy,' she went on quietly. 'Not perfect, but show me one who is. The important thing is, his heart's in the right place and a more generous spirit you could hardly wish to meet, but he's sensitive too, and I should hate to see him hurt.'

Loading her tone with feeling, Eva said, 'I promise, I'm going to do everything in my power to make sure I never let him down again. You probably have no idea how much I regret giving him up but I swear I do.'

Izzie's eyes were intently on hers and seeming reassured, if only for the moment, her expression softened. 'He's a mischievous one too,' she added with a twinkle. 'Too blinking clever for his own good at times, so be warned.'

Finding herself able to laugh now, Eva said, 'It's wonderful to hear you talk about him like that. It makes me feel very proud. Not that I can take any of the credit, of course . . .'

'He has your genes,' Izzie reminded her generously.

Still smiling, Eva said, 'Would you mind if I asked about his adoptive mother?'

'Feel free,' Izzie replied. 'I just wish . . . Well, I'm sorry she's not here to see you herself, but if you knew her, you'd understand how hard she finds it to meet new people – and, obviously, you're not just new, you're . . . Well, you're *you*.'

'Why didn't she ever write to me about Richie?'

With a sigh, Izzie said, 'I'm not sure if this is going to make any sense to you, but I know she wanted to, she just didn't have the courage. She feels terrible about it now, and even worse about not giving Richie the cards and letters you sent . . .'

'Have they turned up yet?'

'Actually, they came yesterday. I didn't hand them over straight away, instead I asked him if he'd rather be with you when he reads them, and he's decided to think about it. I don't suppose you've heard from him today?'

'Yes, I had a text while I was on my way here.'

Izzie looked relieved. 'That's good. It'll mean he's

got over the funny five minutes he had before school this morning.'

Eva's eyes widened. 'What happened?'

'Don't look so worried. Just keep in mind that all that's happening is a pretty big deal for a boy his age, enormous, in fact. Obviously it is for you too, but with him being so young, and a bit confused . . .'

'What happened?' Eva repeated.

Izzie flipped a hand, making light of it. 'Oh, he was just going on with some nonsense about not wanting to see you at the weekend . . .'

Eva's heart contracted. 'But why?'

'Frankly, I don't think even he knows why. Chances are he was testing us in some way, or maybe he wanted you to persuade him to change his mind so he'd know you care.'

'But he surely can't be in any doubt about that now?'

Izzie's eyes were gentle as she said, 'I'm afraid it'll probably be a while before he can make himself totally believe it.'

'Of course,' Eva whispered. 'It would be wonderful if it could happen overnight, but . . .' She took a breath. 'I'll just have to make sure I do everything I can to let him know that he's the most important person in the world to me.'

Izzie smiled. 'And you will be to him soon enough, I've no doubt of it.'

Eva regarded her gratefully. This woman wasn't her enemy, she was simply looking out for the boy she loved, probably as one of her own. 'So I should still come to collect him at ten tomorrow morning?' she asked.

'Absolutely. He might well kick up again between now and then, but if he does, it'll be no more than

414

a bit of a show for us, so we don't think he's a pushover, dying to get away from us, which I don't think he is. But obviously he's pretty fascinated by you, and as nervous as he is, I really don't think he's going to miss out on seeing you again.'

Understanding his complexity, while still fearing that he might change his mind, Eva said, 'Do you think I should invite Sadie to come along too? Or one of his friends?'

Izzie gave it some thought. 'No, I think you need more time on your own,' she decided, 'the two of you, because before you know it you're going to have rugby, school, mates, girlfriends and all sorts of other stuff to be dealing with.'

Both daunted and thrilled, Eva asked, 'Is there a special girlfriend?'

Izzie shook her head. 'Sadie says not, and she'd know. If you ask him he'll tell you he doesn't want to be tied down so he's playing the field.'

Eva bubbled with laughter at the irony in her eyes, and taking heart from how well they were getting along, she said, 'Going back to his mother. Does he have very much contact with her?'

Izzie nodded as she took a sip of her drink. 'She rings every week, on a Sunday morning,' she answered. 'They have a catch-up with everything then, though I think he spends most of the time chatting to his little sister, Una. You know about her, I take it?'

'Yes, Livvy told me.'

'He's very fond of her in spite of them being like chalk and cheese and five years apart. She's just like her mother, shy as a little mouse and not much bigger. You only have to look at her to think she's going to break.'

Wondering when – if – she'd ever get to meet Una herself, and hoping she would if she meant so much to Richie, Eva asked, 'So how attached would you say he is to Linda – his mother?'

Izzie tilted her head as she thought. 'I'd say probably more than he lets on, but he definitely always seemed closer to Tim. He took it pretty hard when Tim went, well, they all did, but I think it was worse for Richie, losing his dad.'

Eva's heart tightened as she thought of Nick, but she wasn't ready to mention him yet, at least not unless Izzie asked.

'That Linda,' Izzie went on, 'she always used to worry herself sick about the way people were drawn to Richie. She'd even tell him to stop pushing himself forward and getting on people's nerves, when the poor little mite was just being a normal boy who got a bit above himself at times, the way they all do, but I never saw him going out of his way to get himself noticed when he shouldn't. Even if I say so myself, he always seemed more comfortable when he was home with us, especially after Tim went. He's close to our Sadie, you saw that for yourself. It's always been her he talked to about his "real mother" and whether or not he should try to meet you. Sadie was all for it, of course, which is how come we're sitting here now. Left to his own devices I'm sure he'd have been too nervous and shy.'

Loving Sadie for her assertiveness, Eva said, 'And what about your other children? How close is he to them?'

Sadie rolled her eyes.

'Jack, my youngest, practically hero-worships him,' Izzie answered. 'He always got on well with our Russ too, the eldest, until the last few months, but Russ'll grow out of his nonsense soon enough.'

'Nonsense?'

'Oh, it's the old jealousy thing again. Richie's more popular, better at rugger, does well at his lessons, whereas it's all a bit of a struggle for poor old Russ. He's hoping to join the police when he's old enough, so he's got his mind set on that at the moment, which'll hopefully help sort him out a bit.' She waved out to someone passing the window. 'My mum's next-door neighbour,' she explained. 'So, anyway, you're going to pick Richie up after training tomorrow morning, and take him to meet your stepmother, I hear? Apart from his blip earlier, he's been talking about nothing else all week. That and the animals, and how cool you are, and the fact you're coming to watch him play on Sunday with his cousin Livvy and stepsister Jasmine. Blinking full of it he's been and I have to tell you it's doing my heart good, because he deserves to feel like he's the centre of someone's world, and who better than his own mother?'

Deeply moved by Izzie's generosity of spirit and feeling her heart swelling with joy, Eva said, 'Believe it or not, he was always the centre of my world, even when I didn't know where, or even who he was, and this past week has been just incredible. It's like the future really means something now, because he's a part of it – the main part of it, in fact. I just worry about how angry he is with me . . . Not that I blame him, I just need to find the right way to deal with it.'

Izzie nodded her understanding. 'The only sensible answer I can give to that,' she said, 'is that we shouldn't try to rush anything, either of us. Take it at his pace, and do our best to answer his questions when they come up.' She fixed Eva's eyes with hers. 'I expect you realise what the big one's going to be for him, don't you?'

Admiring her candour, Eva nodded. 'I do. And I promise you, I have every intention of telling him about his father, I just want to speak to Nick first to make sure . . . Well, I just think it would be wiser. Nick and I haven't been in touch for a very long time and the last thing I want is something to be said, or done, that might end up making Richie feel anything less than the wonderful young man he is.'

Smiling appreciatively, Izzie said, 'I think that sounds a good decision.'

'I have to go back to London next week,' Eva continued, 'so I'm hoping to see Nick then.'

Izzie's eyes stayed on hers. 'If you do, then I wish you good luck and please let me know what happens.'

'Mum! Are you here?' Livvy shouted as she let herself into the barn. She knew her mother was at home because the Audi was outside, but finding no sign of her in the kitchen, or her study, she went through to the hall where a light was shining under the furthest door.

'Can I come in?' she said, giving a knock.

Receiving no reply she opened the door anyway, and finding the bedroom empty she called out again.

'Mum! Where are you?'

'In here,' Patty responded from the bathroom.

Hearing the swish of water and clink of a glass Livvy came to an abrupt stop, appalled by the prospect of walking in on her mother and Don. 'Are you alone?' she asked tentatively.

'Yes, I am. What are you doing here?'

'I came to pick up my scarf.'

Finding her mother submerged in a steaming, milky bath, with scented candles casting a soft, romantic glow around the walls and a bottle of Merlot next to a glass on the side, she said, 'Well, you obviously weren't expecting *me*.'

Patty's mouth twisted as she tried to smile. 'I thought you were going out tonight,' she said. 'Isn't that what you said in your text, that you and Jasmine are taking Richie to meet Dave and some of his friends in Bournemouth?'

'That's right, but I was passing and they've already gone on ahead, so I thought . . . Are you OK? Your eyes look all puffy. You've been crying.'

'No. I've just taken my make-up off, and it's been a long day, so I thought I'd come and have a nice long soak.'

Knowing that was what her mother did when stressed, Livvy came to sit on the edge of the bath and helped herself to a sip of wine. 'So where's Don?' she asked. Then, 'Please don't tell me he's about to come cavorting naked through the door . . . It will so do my head in. I'll go . . . Just tell me where the scarf is.'

'In my car, I forgot about it yesterday. And there's no rush, I'm not expecting Don. Tell me how things are with Eva and Richie.'

Livvy shrugged. 'All I know is that they spent the afternoon with Elaine, and then he was up for coming over to Bournemouth with us tonight. Sadie's driven over from Chard to come too, and Jasmine's gone in Sadie's car with them while I popped in here.'

Thinking of how remiss she'd been in not trying

419

to get closer to Jasmine, while remembering it was probably for the best that she hadn't, Patty said, 'So Eva's not going with you tonight?'

'No. We asked her, but she keeps saying Richie doesn't want his mother hanging around in bars with him, and he says he does, and she says he's only saying that . . . You should hear them. Anyway, Sadie brought a couple of his mates with her too, so there's a load of us getting together. It should be really cool.'

Unable to stop herself, Patty said, 'I hope no one's drinking and driving.'

'Duh! That's your generation.'

'The statistics still show . . .'

'OK, OK, no one is, all right?'

Feeling absurdly as though her role as a mother was vanishing along with everything else, Patty sank beneath the water to wash away the tears of self-pity as they stung her eyes.

'Hello! That was a bit long,' Livvy protested, as Patty came up again. 'You don't have anyone hiding under there, do you? No, don't answer that.' When her mother didn't laugh, or even seem to connect with what she was saying, Livvy's eyes narrowed with concern. 'What's up?' she asked. 'And please don't say you're fine, because I can tell you're not.'

'I'm fine,' Patty said. Livvy wasn't as quick at reading her as Eva, she was thinking, but she was getting there.

'Hello. This is me,' Livvy said, waving. 'You know you can tell me anything.' She gave a playful gasp. 'Oh my God, I'm starting to sound like you.'

This time Patty did manage a smile.

'So where *is* Don?' Livvy asked.

Taking a breath to stifle the wrench in her heart,

Patty said, 'Actually, I'm not sure . . . Have you been to Eva's this evening?'

'No, I came straight here from the shop, and I probably won't see her because we're all crashing at mine later before we go to watch Richie play rugger tomorrow. Why?'

'No reason, just being chatty.'

'Mu-um!'

It took Patty a while to decide what to tell her, and even when she began speaking she still wasn't sure what she was going to say. 'I think that's where Don is,' she finally answered. 'It's probably why Eva couldn't come with you this evening, because they're having . . . a talk.'

Livvy went very still.

In a voice that she couldn't quite make steady, Patty said, 'It's probably best if I tell you now that we've broken up. Don and I . . . We . . .' She couldn't go on, her throat was too tight.

'Oh no,' Livvy groaned, burying her head in her hands. 'I don't believe this. I'm the one who's supposed to have all the relationship problems, not you two.'

Patty might have laughed, but found she couldn't.

'What happened?' Livvy asked gently.

Overcome by her daughter's empathy, Patty had to submerge again for a moment. 'It doesn't really matter,' she said. 'We came to an agreement . . . I think . . . He'll probably go back to Eva.'

Livvy sat staring at her, her eyes full of misgiving. 'Why isn't this feeling right?' she finally demanded.

'It will, because it is,' Patty told her. 'And if it turns out that he's not with Eva tonight, please don't say anything to her, because I'm sure it'll only mean he's choosing the right moment to ask to go back.'

Livvy was still looking decidedly troubled. 'So where does that leave you?' she asked, starting to detest Don for all the heartache he was causing.

Desperately close to breaking down, Patty picked up her wine. 'Here, in the bath pampering myself,' she replied.

Finding herself at a total loss as to how to handle this, Livvy very nearly got into the bath, fully clothed, to give her mother a hug.

'You should go now,' Patty told her. 'They'll be wondering where you are.'

'But I can't leave you like this.'

'I'm fine, honestly. Doing the right thing always makes you feel better.'

'Except you don't.'

No, she didn't. In fact she could hardly have felt worse. 'You're putting words in my mouth,' she chided. 'Now, please don't take this the wrong way, but I'd rather be on my own for a while. We can talk later, on the phone, if you like, and don't forget to call tomorrow to let me know how Richie's rugby match goes.'

'Tell you what, why don't I ring Jas and tell her I can't make tonight . . .'

'No, don't do that. It'll be important to Richie that you're there, and I'm perfectly all right, really.'

'Then I'll let Eva and Jasmine go with him to the rugby tomorrow, and come here. We can hang out together, just the two of us, go for a walk, chat, watch a movie in front of the fire . . .'

'Actually, I'm thinking of driving up to Heathrow tomorrow to collect Jake from the airport. It'll save him hanging about for buses, or having to go into London to catch a train. Livvy, please,' she pressed as Livvy looked like she might object again, 'just carry on with your arrangements and we'll get together on Monday or Tuesday, after Jake's slept off his jet lag.'

Still seeming very reluctant to leave, Livvy said, 'You'll call, won't you, if you need to chat, or if you want me to come over?'

'Of course. Now go. And don't forget the scarf.'

'Can I get you anything before I go?'

'I have everything, thank you. Go on, shoo, I want to get out now and I'd rather do that unobserved.'

'Why?'

'Livvy!'

'All right, all right, I'll go, but I'm taking this bottle of wine out to the kitchen, because I don't want you falling asleep in the bath.'

A few minutes later, after hearing Livvy's car going out of the drive, Patty pulled herself up from the water and reached for a towel. She hardly knew what she was going to do next, apart from dry herself – perhaps get ready for bed, or maybe she'd pull on some jeans and a sweater and go into her study to do some work. Knowing she barely had the heart to walk there, never mind turn on her computer, she wrapped the towel around her and went to lie down on the bed.

It felt cold in the room after the heat of the water, and cheerless with the curtains still open and no moonlight filtering through the clouds. Reminding herself that this was how Eva would have felt over the last few weeks, but worse, thanks to the double betrayal, made her so wretched that she had to banish the thought before it tore her apart. This suffering was no more than she deserved, she reminded herself, and if it could in some way make Eva's suffering less then it would be worthwhile.

Was he with Eva now? She knew he'd stayed here last night and left first thing this morning, because he'd called to let her know that the coast was clear for her to return. Remembering the bemused anger in his voice intensified her longing, and made it almost impossible not to reach for the phone. If she could be sure he wasn't with Eva she knew she wouldn't be able to stop herself, but if he was with Eva she had to give them the chance to try and work things out.

She thought of her mother and felt so much anger and pain that she knew if it weren't for Jake and Livvy, she'd end it all now. It was what she wanted, more than anything, if only to serve her mother right. She'd follow in her footsteps, drive herself over a cliff, slit her wrists, take an overdose, then no one would be left to take care of Eva. How would everything work out then?

Closing her eyes as her mobile started to ring she tried not to will it to be Don, but it simply wasn't possible. Just in case, she went to retrieve the phone from her bag, and seeing his name she choked on a sob.

'Hi, it's me,' he said when she clicked on.

'I know. How – how are you?'

There was a trace of irony in his voice as he replied, 'I've been better. How about you?'

'The same, I guess. Where are you?'

'If I said outside wondering if I can come in, would you let me?'

Feeling her entire body yearning for it to be true, she said, 'Are you?'

'No, but I could be.'

She tried to take a breath, but it was hard. 'Have you spoken to Eva?' she asked.

'No, because I don't have anything to say to her. It's you I love, you I want to be with. Please, Patty, let me come back.'

Wanting nothing more than to tell him to come right now, she said, 'I have to go.'

'Patty! Don't ring off.'

'I have to.'

'No, all you have to do is stop hurting us both as if it's in some way going to make up for what we've done to Eva.'

Swallowing hard, Patty said, 'Eva told me herself that nothing will ever do that.'

He fell silent, and she could almost feel his frustration and confusion. 'What the hell is this about?' he asked in the end.

'I've already told you, I need to sort out why I've done this . . .'

'We fell in love, Patty, that's why we did it.'

'But I think it goes deeper than that and . . .'

'For God's sake, how can anything possibly be deeper?'

At any other time Patty might have smiled and teased him with something along the lines of 'Spoken like a man,' but tonight all she managed was, 'It just can,' and forcing herself to do what she had to, she ended the call.

Chapter Twenty

Eva's throat was hoarse from shouting so much, and neither Livvy nor Jasmine's were much better, though Jasmine had left now to drive back to her mother's. Richie's team-mates had all dived on him after the match, as thrilled by the new support he'd brought along as they were to have him back on side. They'd still lost, but at 17–15 it had hardly been a humiliating defeat, and Richie's captaincy as well as his two tries had made Eva practically levitate with pride.

After the game they'd motored off to the Christmas fair at Richie's school, where they'd bought an enormous star for the top of the twelve-foot tree Eva and Richie had bought at the farm shop yesterday (to be delivered before next weekend, when he was coming to help decorate it); some jazzy tights for Livvy, a purple bouclé scarf for Sadie and a scrumptious-looking home-made chocolate sponge to take home for the tea Izzie had stayed behind to prepare.

'I feel like I'm eating you out of house and home,' Eva was protesting, as Sadie came round for a second time with her mother's delicious cupcakes. 'But they're so good, I can't resist.'

'The rule in this house is to go for it while you

can,' Sadie told her. 'If you don't Richie'll scoff the lot and still come back for more. And look at him, he never puts on an ounce. It's just not fair.'

Since his mouth was full Richie could only give her a wink, and though Eva laughed she felt suddenly fearful for the hearts he was surely destined to break. Just please God don't let one of them be hers.

'So how's your shoulder after the match?' Izzie asked him.

'Yeah, cool,' he replied, giving it a flex. 'Flaming hooker booted me in the shin though. He was lucky I didn't get him back.'

'Oh, we've got to tell Eva about that time he got the prop,' Sadie cried excitedly. 'Remember, the one who nutted him . . .'

'Oh God, not that again,' her brother Russ grumbled. (He actually was quite like the cousin in *Harry Potter*, Eva was thinking, though not as fat and marginally better-looking.) 'I'm out of here,' and snatching another slice of sponge from the plate, he was about to leave when his mother said, 'Russ, where are your manners?'

His shoulders sank. 'Mum. How many times are we going to have to hear that story? And it's so not funny.'

'It's brilliant,' young Jack informed Eva and Livvy, his bright blue eyes and freckles making him utterly adorable, Eva thought.

'Sit down, Russ,' his father barked.

'Dad!'

'Don't argue, and anyway you know food's not allowed in the bedrooms.'

In fact, Eva found that easy to believe, since everything in this snug little semi-detached at the heart of a seventies housing estate, from the velveteen indigo carpet, to the sky-blue taffeta drapes, to the beige corduroy three-piece suite, was utterly pristine. At the same time it was still managing to feel wholly welcoming (if she discounted the way Mervyn was regarding her warily), with its faux-brick chimney breast and gas log fire. There were numerous family photos, trophies and prized ornaments hanging on the walls or placed decorously on shelves and a forty-two-inch high-definition TV screen that was currently obscured by a brightly coloured authentic-looking Christmas tree.

'Go on, Sadie,' Mervyn encouraged, his Somerset burr more pronounced than the others, and the gleam on his balding head changing from red to gold in time with the fairy lights around the window. 'Let's hear it again, because it is a bit of a cracker.'

Loving the way Richie's eyes were shining as he tried to look bored, Eva slapped Livvy's hand away from her cupcake as she attempted to steal it.

'So, what happened,' Sadie began, clearly the chief teller of this story, 'was that him and some of his team-mates got into this ruck with the other side . . . Who were they again?' she asked Richie.

'Fairford Grammar.'

'That's right. Well, one of the Fairford props, Alfie Curtis, he's always had it in for Richie ever since Richie won player of the year back when they were twelve and Alfie thought he should have got it. Anyway they go into this ruck and Alfie only nuts Richie really hard in the face. It was definitely deliberate, everyone saw it – except the ref, of course. So Richie gets up with blood pouring out of his nose and starts going after Alfie who's walking off thinking he's got away with it. Next thing he knows Richie's got hold of his shoulder and spun him round. You should have seen the look on his face. Honest to God, we all thought he was about to do it in his pants, actually I reckon he might have. Anyway, everyone was cheering Richie on and Alfie the muppet definitely thought he was in for a good slapping, especially when Richie goes like he's going to nut him back. Everyone's yelling, "Let him have it!" or "Kill him!" and stuff like that, but you'll never guess what Richie did. He only grabs Alfie's collar in both his fists, pulls him right up so Alfie's toes are nearly off the ground, then he goes and plonks this great big kiss on Alfie's cheek. Oh my God you should have seen Alfie's face. "You're gay, you're gay," he starts shouting. "I'm not gay. You don't do that to me." Everyone was in fits, even the ref. And now the really big joke is, no one ever says anything to Richie about it, but whenever they see Alfie they go, "Are you gay?" or "Give us a kiss," and Alfie goes totally mental, which just makes it funnier.'

Trying not to choke on her cake as she laughed, Eva wished she could tell Richie how like his father he was, because that sort of stunt had been quite typical of Nick.

'Oh, excuse me, I'd better take this,' Livvy said, jumping up with her mobile. 'Is it OK to go in the kitchen?'

'Of course,' Izzie responded, waving her through.

Feeling fit to burst, she'd eaten so much cake, Eva said, 'How long have you lived around here?'

'Oh, most of our married lives,' Izzie answered, glancing at Mervyn as he cleared his throat, 'and all the time in this house. It only had three bedrooms when we first bought it, but we remortgaged about ten years ago to put on the extension so we've got four now, and a much bigger kitchen. It's still a bit of a squash with all of us, but we're managing and we wouldn't really want to be anywhere else, would we, love?'

'No, this is good enough for us,' Mervyn commented gruffly.

'All our friends are round here,' Izzie continued, 'and it's not a bad neighbourhood, I can say that for it. No crime to speak of, and you feel like the kids are safe when they're out playing in the street. We're even getting carol singers of an evening, and I've been hearing on the news how lots of places haven't seen any for years. It's a real shame that, because it's a lovely way for the kids to earn a few bob at this time of year.'

'Providing they can sing,' Sadie piped up. 'You should hear some of them. Honest to God, you have to pay 'em to shut up and get lost or something drastic would happen to your ears.'

'It's true, I'm afraid,' Izzie lamented. 'Christmas doesn't always bring out the best in people, does it?'

Laughing, while realising she still had a way to go to win Mervyn over, Eva said, 'It must be lovely to feel part of a community.'

'More cake?'

Eva almost groaned. 'I swear I've eaten too much already.'

'If you like cake I've got a couple in the larder that just need icing for Christmas,' Izzie told her generously.

'Oh, Mum's Christmas cakes are to die for,' Sadie gushed. 'And her puddings. Actually, we like the puddings the best, don't we, Jack?'

'Definitely,' he agreed.

'With brandy butter,' Richie put in.

'Bring it on,' Russ drooled.

Trying to make it sound nothing more than chatty, Eva asked, 'So what are you all doing for Christmas?'

Colouring slightly Izzie glanced at Mervyn, then Richie, as she said, 'I'm not really sure yet. We thought . . . Well . . .'

'I wanted to say,' Eva came in quickly, 'I mean, I don't want you to feel under any obligation or anything, but if you'd all like to come to me you'd be very welcome. Obviously I understand if you'd rather be in your home . . .'

'Oh, no, no, them days is long gone,' Izzie told her hurriedly. 'The kids is all grown up now and we went out last year, didn't we, Merv? Was a bit of a disaster, I have to admit, but that was the hotel's fault. It wouldn't be anything like that at yours. Are you sure, though, because there's a lot of us, and you probably only want Richie really.'

'No, I'd love it if you all came,' Eva insisted, looking at Mervyn.

'She's got an amazing tree,' Richie told Izzie and Mervyn. 'It's vast and we can't leave Elvis and Rosie on their own, can we?'

As Eva flooded with joy at the way he seemed to be seeing them – him, her, Rosie and Elvis – as a family, Livvy came bouncing back into the room saying, 'Sorry about that. It was my mum letting me know she's at the airport waiting for my brother. Anyway, what were you saying about Rosie and Elvis?'

'That we can't leave them on their own for Christmas,' Richie explained. 'So we're all going to Mum's. Isn't that cool?'

Eva somehow stopped herself from gasping as Livvy turned to her, and from the look in Livvy's eyes she hadn't missed it either. Nor, she could tell, had Izzie. Richie had just referred to her as Mum, and if she could get any happier she truly didn't know how it was possible.

'I expect you'll be there too, won't you?' Sadie said to Livvy, tactfully covering the moment before Richie felt embarrassed.

'Um, uh, I guess so,' Livvy answered awkwardly. 'We usually all get together. We'll see, anyway, but it's fantastic that you'll all be there.'

Later, as they walked outside into the misty darkness where Christmas lights were twinkling in most windows and a few reindeer had taken up glittering residence on a few rooftops, Eva leaned into Richie as he slipped an arm around her.

'Thanks for coming today,' he whispered.

'I wouldn't have missed it for the world,' she assured him, transported by how relaxed and affectionate he was being with her. It shouldn't be long, she was thinking, before she could broach the subject of him coming to live with her, and she was daring to believe he would want to.

'How could he not?' Livvy laughed when Eva confessed her thoughts on the way home in the car. 'The house we were just in versus your house? No mother versus mother? Where's the contest?'

'Actually, I think theirs is a pretty special house,' Eva informed her, 'and he's obviously very happy with Izzie and her family, so I don't think we should take anything for granted.'

'Maybe not,' Livvy agreed, stifling a yawn. 'But wasn't that amazing when he called you Mum? I was like, oh my God, did he really say that? He's so cool, isn't he? I wish I'd known him for ever.'

Wishing exactly the same, Eva said, 'I already love him beyond anything, but the next thing I know he's going to be eighteen and gone again.'

'What?' Livvy cried in astonishment. 'Oh no, don't tell me, you're already panicking about him going off to uni?'

Eva couldn't deny it.

With a cry of despair, Livvy said, 'He will go, because he has to, and when the time comes it'll be totally cool, and he'll be back for weekends all the time . . . But hey, don't let's try dealing with that until we have to. For now, what's brilliant is that they're all coming to you for Christmas.'

Though Eva was still thrilled at having her invitation accepted, she wasn't unaware of the split loyalties Livvy could be facing. 'Don't worry, I understand that your mum has to come first for you,' she said softly.

Glancing down at her hands, Livvy replied, 'Actually, I'll have to be with her, or she'll be on her own apart from Jake, and I couldn't bear that.'

Frowning, Eva said, 'But she'll have Don.'

Livvy's head came up as she looked at Eva in the passing streetlights. 'So you and Don . . . ? I mean, Mum said . . . Well, she thinks you're back together, or that he's going to try to get back with you if he hasn't already.'

Eva's heart skipped a beat. 'But I made it clear when he tried before . . . It's not what he wants. It's not what I want either.'

Livvy's face was pale with confusion. 'Are you sure?' she asked.

Eva's head was spinning. Was she? It was impossible to say, when it was coming at her out of the blue like this, except it would never – *could* never

– work between them again. It was true, love and dreams didn't just die because you wanted them to, and the torment of rejection was still very much with her, but since her respect for Don and her trust had gone she knew that they'd never be able to rebuild what they'd once had. He surely had to know that too, so why on earth would he tell Patty he was coming back to her? Then, realising that Patty, or her conscience, must be trying to make it happen, Eva felt her heart churn with painful emotions. 'Don and I won't be getting back together,' she said quietly. 'You should probably tell Mum that.'

Livvy was still looking at her. 'OK, I will,' she said.

Eva turned to her with a smile that covered the ache in her heart. In spite of discovering an inner strength during these past couple of months that she'd barely even known she had, the loss of her sister and her husband was something she knew she'd never really get over. Not even having Richie back in her life was going to make up for what had happened. However, he was already filling up her world with another kind of happiness and a love that was so different, and so special, that she couldn't imagine anyone or anything ever mattering as much as him.

'So Jake's plane has landed?' she said, understanding for the first time how much it would mean to Patty to have her son home for Christmas.

'Apparently,' Livvy replied. 'I'm dying to hear how he got on in Cartagena. He hardly sent any texts and now Mum's decided to take him on into London for a couple of days' Christmas shopping before they come back here. I just hope he hasn't got himself involved with a Colombian, because that will just about do her head in.'

'Why? Do you think he has?' Eva gasped, thinking drug cartels, kidnapping, torture . . .

'No, not really,' Livvy responded, clearly wondering what had happened to everyone's sense of humour. 'Anyway, when exactly are you going to London this week?'

'Wednesday and Thursday, so back in plenty of time for the weekend. Do you think you'll come and watch Richie play again next Sunday?'

'Yeah, I'd definitely like to. I expect Jas will want to come too. And Jake, knowing him. Remind me what you're doing in London?'

'Meeting with the publicity people again, and a couple of German agents. And actually' – her heartbeat was starting to slow – 'between us, I'm hoping I might meet up with Richie's father.'

Livvy's jaw dropped. 'No way,' she murmured. 'Oh my God. That is major. Does Richie know?'

'No, I don't want to say anything until I've had a chance to find out how Nick wants to play it.'

Livvy nodded agreement. 'I guess that makes sense. So how are you feeling about it? Oh my God, this must be totally blowing your mind.'

Since it was starting to, Eva said, 'I admit I am feeling a bit nervous, but more for Richie's sake than my own. If it turns out that he doesn't want to be part of Richie's life, and I have to break that to Richie . . . Well, I'm not sure what I'll do, but I can tell you this much, I won't be letting him get away with it as easily this time around as I did the last.'

Livvy was frowning. 'Do you reckon it's likely he'll want nothing to do with him?'

Forcing herself to relax a little, Eva replied,

'Actually, not from what Bobbie said, but who knows what will happen. I guess we just have to wait and find out.'

Nick Jensen was sitting at his desk staring thoughtfully from the window of his fourth-storey office, with one hand still on the telephone he'd just put down, the other folded into a fist that he was tapping against his chin. To say that Bobbie's call had come as a bolt out of the blue wouldn't have been entirely true, since she'd told him when they'd met up in New York last week that she had some news for him. It hadn't been appropriate to go into any detail at the time, she'd said, since there were others at the table whose discretion couldn't be relied upon. And another opportunity hadn't arisen for them to get together again before he was due to fly back to London.

After returning he'd spent so much time in meetings, or in editing suites, or on the sets of various projects he had in production, that he'd had little time to wonder what Bobbie's news might be. If it had crossed his mind at all it had been only fleetingly, and had left him feeling hopeful that she might be about to put a new client his way. What hadn't occurred to him was that she was about to turn his entire life upside down.

'I'm sorry to do this on the phone,' she'd said, 'but I'm flying out again tomorrow and I promised Eva I'd speak to you this week.'

Simply hearing Eva's name had brought him to a standstill. What Bobbie had told him next had caused his head to spin.

'She wants you to know that she's in touch with your son. In fact she's starting to build a relationship with him, and there's a chance, she tells me, that he'll go to live with her when everyone feels the time is right.'

That was when Nick's heart rate had gone up.

'She wants to see you,' Bobbie continued. 'She'll be in London tomorrow and Thursday, and she's willing to rearrange her meetings to suit you.'

For a moment he'd felt himself spiralling back to the time of the attack, the screams, the blood – so much blood – but then he'd regrounded himself and was able to breathe again. 'What does she know about me now?' he asked, trying to keep his tone neutral.

'I thought I'd leave that to you,' Bobbie replied. 'What she probably won't tell *you* is that her marriage has recently broken up. It's been a particularly difficult time, because he's gone off with Patty.'

Nick couldn't believe it. The shock was so great that even he had felt the whip of betrayal. 'Patty, her sister?' he said, needing to be sure.

'Indeed. Please don't say I mentioned it, because I'm sure she won't want you to know. The only reason I'm telling you is so that you don't make the mistake of thinking Don will be bringing any influence to bear on whatever relationship you might choose to have with your son. I'm presuming you'll want one, but of course I could be wrong.'

Though he'd opened his mouth to speak, no words had emerged.

'His adoptive father is dead and the mother's somewhere up north. He's been living with an aunt and uncle for the past year or so. Now, if you've got a pen handy I'll give you Eva's mobile number.'

After jotting it down he'd managed at least one sensible question before Bobbie rang off. 'Does Eva want me to have a relationship with him?'

There was a moment before Bobbie said, 'I think I'll let her answer that. You know how to get hold of me if you need to.'

'Bobbie!'

'Yes?'

He hadn't been ready to let her go, but had no idea what he wanted to say. Then, realising for the moment there was only one thing, he said, 'Thank you.'

Now, minutes were ticking by and he still wasn't picking up the phone to call Eva. Nor would he until he had himself under full control, and considering the emotions Bobbie's call had aroused, he was aware that could take some time.

Getting to his feet he went to stand at the window. At six foot two with short, silvering hair and deep-set brown eyes he was still a striking-looking man, with the kind of smile, it had been remarked, that should have been in front of the camera rather than behind. Since it was not a place he'd ever wanted to find himself, either as a photographer or as an exec producer as he was now, the comments always slid past him like strangers in a crowd.

Fifty feet below his suite of offices the river appeared dull and lifeless in the afternoon gloom, with only a couple of booze cruisers offering the odd glimmer of seasonal cheer. On the far embankment a stream of headlights inched and stopped, then inched and stopped again. He watched the progress through his ghostly reflection, feeling as though he, not it, was the metaphor. He was aware that at any moment someone could come bursting through the door behind him demanding an answer, or a decision, or needing to pass on information he'd requested. He'd react on cue, give them what they wanted and they'd go away again. It would happen several times, he felt sure, before he'd feel ready to pick up the phone and make the call to Eva.

It was pitch-black outside and most of his staff had gone home by the time he poured himself a stiff drink and punched in the number Bobbie had given him.

Her voice was slightly hesitant, but breathtakingly familiar as she said, 'Hello?'

'It's Nick,' he told her.

Long seconds ticked by and he couldn't even imagine what must be going through her mind. Was she experiencing anything of his apprehension and anticipation? Such shallow and immediate emotions were only scratching the surface for him, but right now he could go no deeper. It would be delusional to think they were anything like the same people who'd once loved each other, yet they were still connected and always would be through their son.

'How are you?' she asked.

Answering truthfully, he said, 'I'm not sure. Shocked, I guess. Bobbie only called me today.'

'Yes, she rang me a while ago. I was beginning to think I wouldn't hear from you.'

'I'm sorry. Where are you?'

'At Carrie-Anne's apartment in Chelsea. Where are you?'

'At my office – in Chelsea Harbour.'

A silence followed as their proximity seemed to speak its own words, yet he had no idea whether to suggest they get together now or later. 'Is Carrie-Anne with you?' he asked in the end.

'No, she's in Rio. I'm staying here because Bobbie's flat is full up tonight. She told you, of course, why I want to see you?'

'Yes, she did.'

'And are you OK about it?'

How could she even begin to think he wasn't, except she had no reason to think otherwise? 'She said you were willing to rearrange your meetings. I'm prepared to do the same.'

To his surprise there was a catch in her voice as she said, 'Thank you. Yes, I'll do that.'

'If you give me the address I can come now,' he told her.

'Actually I . . .' She broke off, as though rethinking her objection. 'If you're sure.'

'I'm sure.' And after writing down the address he said, 'Can I ask one thing before we hang up?'

Sounding uncertain, she said, 'I guess so.'

'What's his name?'

As Eva put the phone down she stood gazing at her reflection in the huge picture windows that formed an entire wall of Carrie-Anne's penthouse apartment. The night beyond was as black as infinity, with no sign of a star nor hint of the moon. A few raindrops were meandering down the glass like tiny lost souls and the sound of the wind was reminding her, oddly, of when she was a child and her mother used to tuck her in tightly. How strange that her memory should produce that long-forgotten feeling now. Did it mean that her mother was close by, ready to offer protection, strength, moral support? Perhaps she was trying to deliver a warning. *Eva, take care of your heart. This man broke it once, don't let him do the same to your son.*

There was no risk of that. At least she hoped not, and her own heart was safe, because the love that had all but consumed her when she and Nick were together had faded and died many years ago, proving that time really was the great healer. Would it be like that with Don? she wondered. Feeling a sudden need to speak to him, to hold on to him before she lost him for ever, she took a deep breath and waited for the moment to pass. She had to believe that these surges of panic would cease one day, or there would seem no point to going on. Except Richie was the point. Richie, her son. Even to think of him made her heart want to sing. He'd texted a while ago to wish her good luck with her meeting tomorrow. He had no idea that a far more crucial meeting had come up tonight, and it was best that way, at least until she had some idea of the role, if any, that Nick might want to play in his life.

Though she'd had days to prepare herself for this, rehearsing what she was going to say, and how she should respond to whatever he might reply, she was finding, as she started to pace, that almost everything was deserting her. Remembering that Bobbie had given her reason to feel optimistic was only managing to buoy her for a moment, because the fear that Nick might want to enfold Richie into the heart of his family was like an undertow continually trying to submerge her. If he did, and Richie wanted to go, she knew she'd have to let him, but the mere thought of it was making it hard not to flee this apartment before Nick arrived. Yet seeing Richie at weekends, perhaps for holidays and during visits to London, would be so much better than not knowing him at all.

'You're wasting energy on a fear that has no substance,' Elaine had told her calmly when she'd rung earlier. 'It's all in your mind. At this point in time you have no idea what's going to happen, so the best way you can help yourself is to stay focused on the now.'

'Except I need to prepare myself . . .'

'Eva, my dear, if we counted up the hours we spend worrying about things that never happen, we'd probably find we've wasted half of our lives.'

Speaking to Elaine was always soothing, not only because of her common sense, but because the tone of her voice always managed to convey the quiet force of her own inner calm. However, without recourse to Elaine now she was starting to work herself into a state again, so taking several deep breaths she made herself recall the mantra Elaine had given her to recite in moments of stress. *I am trusting and patient; I am calm; I understand everything is happening perfectly; I have faith.*

It was amazing how effective those four short lines could be, she was thinking after the fourth time of repeating them. It was stunning, in fact, because she was already starting to breathe more easily. *All you have to fear is fear itself* – another of Elaine's favourite little homilies that she often floated into a storm like a life raft on its way to the rescue.

'For what it's worth,' Elaine had said at the end of their earlier call, 'I really don't think Nick will try to take him away from you – and even if he did, I don't believe Richie would go.'

Clinging to that, as though Elaine had some kind

of privileged connection to the future, Eva went to check her appearance in the bedroom mirror. She couldn't think why she was bothering about her scars now, except they would remind Nick of the night of the attack. It was when he'd told her their relationship was over, that he couldn't stay with her and be a father to their child. Only minutes after leaving he'd returned with Bobbie and become caught up in a violent struggle to save her life. How desperately during the months, even years, that had followed she'd wished he hadn't succeeded.

How shocking it was to know that she had once thought that way, to realise that she had allowed a broken heart to push her into an obsession so selfish and consuming that not even giving birth to her own child had brought her to her senses. Was it because she was older now that she was able, she hoped, to be more rational, or was it because she didn't love Don as much as she had loved Nick?

As the buzzer sounded, letting her know he'd arrived, she felt herself turn weak inside. Then, with a wry glance in the mirror, she reminded herself that though this wasn't going to be easy, for all sorts of reasons, she was in no way going to allow her fears to get the better of her.

By the time the private lift rose to the apartment she was standing at the door waiting for him to come through. When he did her head started to swim a little, as though the swing back in time was making her dizzy. He was exactly as she remembered, just as tall and good-looking with the same intense, even penetrating eyes, and the uncanny magnetism that she'd almost forgotten and had always found so irresistible. She could feel it now, like an invisible hand drawing her to him, but it had either lost some of its potency, or she was no longer as susceptible, because after the briefest moment it seemed to have gone.

'Hi,' he said softly. 'It's been a long time.'

She found herself smiling. She knew he'd noticed her scars, how could he not, but all she could see in his eyes was a kind of tenderness, and she was surprised by the rush of warmth she felt towards him. What had happened to all the anger and resentment she'd harboured over the years, the barrier she'd deliberately erected before he'd arrived to keep him at a safe distance? She didn't imagine any of it was far away, but for the moment at least she seemed to have no need of them, so turning aside, she said, 'Come in. Can I get you a drink?'

'Only if you're having one.'

Going through to the kitchen where hidden lights were funnelling shadows around the glossy crimson cabinets and three discus lamps were like small halos over the breakfast bar, she said, 'I thought I'd have wine, but there's everything here.'

'Wine's good for me,' he told her, looking around at their impressive surroundings. 'So this is where Carrie-Anne lives now,' he remarked, with no little irony.

Taking two glasses from a touch/slide cabinet, she said, 'The lingerie's been a great success.'

Sounding amused, he said, 'Yeah, I guess I knew that,' and unbuttoning his coat he went to perch on the edge of a tall stool.

'You can take it off if you like,' she told him. 'Your coat,' she added, when he cocked an eyebrow in the way she remembered too well.

As he got up again he held out a hand to take the bottle she was starting to open.

In spite of wanting to tell him she could manage she passed it to him, and stood watching his hands as he pulled the cork. She'd always loved his hands, she remembered, but it wasn't their masculine elegance that was causing her heart to quicken now. It was the scars that ravaged them.

Her eyes shot to his, but he wasn't looking at her. Why on earth had no one ever told her about this? She looked at him again, and remembering the tenderness in his eyes when he'd seen her scars, and how he hadn't mentioned them, she realised he'd probably want her to do the same for him. So forcing herself past the shock, she asked, because she was interested, and in a voice she hoped sounded no more than chatty, 'Where are you living these days? What happened to Italy?'

His grimace was tinged with more irony as he passed the bottle back. 'It's a long story which I'm sure we'll get round to,' he replied, 'but these days I live just across the river during the week, in Battersea. At weekends I'm generally in Hampshire. And you're in Dorset?'

She nodded, and might have reminded him that he knew the house because he'd found it with her, some seventeen years ago, but somehow it didn't seem appropriate. So she simply poured the wine while he finally took off his coat and hung it over the back of a chair.

'Shall we take our drinks through?' she suggested.

Standing back for her to lead the way, he followed her into the sumptuous sitting room with its curved leather sofas, original oriental artworks

445

and a plush silk carpet that had cost, according to Carrie-Anne, almost as much as the apartment.

'Your friend always did have style,' he commented drily, as he waited for Eva to sit down before deciding where to sit himself.

Choosing one of the sofas and waving him towards the other so he was close, but not too close, she told him, 'She's only recently redone it. Apparently it has a ten-page spread in *Interiors* next month.'

Nodding to show he was impressed, he raised his glass and said, 'Here's to seeing you again.'

She smiled and wondered why she'd been so nervous when, if she'd stopped to think, she'd have remembered that he'd always had a gift for putting people at their ease. And the years, apparently, had done nothing to change that. 'And to you,' she responded. 'It's a Gavi, by the way. I hope you like it.'

'One of my favourites,' he assured her, and after taking a sip he raised his eyebrows to indicate approval.

'So you live in Battersea and Hampshire,' she said, settling in more comfortably, 'but I don't know what you're doing these days. Am I allowed to ask?'

'Sure you are. I have part ownership of a production company that specialises mainly in corporate training videos, but we make the odd pop video too, usually low budget, and we've had a few documentary series broadcast on the non-terrestrial networks. It's pretty hectic, or it was until the recession hit. We haven't particularly noticed the downturn yet, because we're still editing one series and shooting another, but once they're complete we don't have a whole lot of things rushing our way. So, it's down to yours truly to pull something out of the bag before next spring.'

'That's your role, getting the commissions?' she asked, trying to stop wondering what sort of partner he was referring to, while still struggling to grasp the reality of them sitting here in this room together. It felt so bizarre, almost surreal. This man, who was virtually a stranger, had once meant everything to her, and though he no longer did, on some level she was neither ashamed nor surprised that he had.

'Primarily,' he replied, 'but I act as exec producer once the projects are under way. My partner is more hands-on with it all, going on shoots, sitting in editing rooms, organising crews, that sort of thing. I tend to travel more, mainly in search of co-finance. And your shop is doing fantastically well, I hear?'

Almost laughing at the way he'd managed to turn the subject so effortlessly and swiftly to her, her expression was wry as she said, 'How typical of Bobbie to overstate it, but it's true things do seem to be on the up.'

'I saw the papers after your recent show. It's quite a unique idea you've got going there, pooling local talent to offer something exclusive at an affordable price. I can see why they're so interested.'

Taking a sip of her wine, she regarded him carefully as she said, 'Speaking of papers, I've been informed by a very reliable source that it was you who wrote to *Saturday Siesta* about their feature on me.'

Though his eyes sparked with humour, he looked curious as he replied, 'I never told Bobbie, so I'm intrigued to know how you found out.'

Giving it some thought, and realising it wasn't a route she wanted to go down yet, she playfully repeated his words as she said, 'It's a long story, but I'm sure we'll get round to it. So what made you do it?'

He seemed incredulous. 'I was incensed, of course. Or I was once I found out they'd gone ahead without consulting you. Considering everything you'd been through, and how rarely you've ventured into the public eye since, any jackass should have been able to work out why you wouldn't want to be featured. With the amount of nutters there are around, those responsible for that article were causing you an untenable amount of stress at best, and at worst they were putting you at risk. So I told them what I thought and threatened legal action if they didn't at least send you an apology.'

Eva's eyes were dancing. 'Did you mean it about the legal action?' she asked.

'Yes!' Then with a sheepish twinkle, 'I don't know if I had a case, but it sounded good and from what Bobbie tells me it got a result.'

'It did,' she confirmed, amused and touched by how concerned he'd obviously been. 'So what else are you doing these days when you're not exec producing or being Mr Angry with the papers?'

He tilted his head to one side. 'I guess that about sums it up,' he decided. 'All work and little time for play.'

She wondered how long they were going to continue hedging around the subject of his wife – or, more importantly, their son and the reason she'd given him up for adoption. Considering what a terrible, dark time that had been, and how light-hearted they were managing to be with one another now, she'd have preferred not to go there at all. But then he was saying, 'There's something I have to tell you, something I should have told you the night we broke up, or at least when you rang from the hospital to find out why I hadn't been to see you.'

As his eyes went down she felt her heartbeat starting to slow.

'It seems crazy now that we didn't want anyone to know,' he continued, staring into his glass, 'but perspective always seems different with hindsight. When you're in the heat of it all, feeling terrified out of your mind, not knowing which way to turn . . .' His eyes came to hers as he said, 'The reason I broke up with you, the reason everything happened the way it did after that, was because Maddy, my daughter, had just been diagnosed with acute meningitis. It sent us into a total panic. We thought we were going to lose her, and we nearly did. I was beside myself. I hardly knew what I was doing from one minute to the next. I wanted to come to you, but I couldn't bring myself to leave her side – and I knew what it would do to my wife if she found out I'd been. She was going through so much already. She didn't need to be dealing with that too. So I stayed with her, alternating shifts through endless days and nights, willing Maddy to stay with us, not to let go.'

Appalled that she hadn't known any of this, though accepting it had happened during a time when she was barely conscious, Eva whispered, 'And did she? Stay with you?'

He nodded, and even now, all these years later, he seemed to experience the same rush of relief. 'In the end, yes, she did, but it was a hell of a long haul and for weeks, months, we had to live with the fear that even if she did survive her brain would be damaged beyond repair.'

Aware of what a difference this might have made to her, if she'd known, Eva said, 'Why on earth didn't you tell anyone?'

'I guess we thought, in that bizarre way you do when you're in the thick of it, that if it got out it would make it real, or worse . . . I don't know. All kinds of crazy things go through your head at a time like that. And Sally – my wife – didn't want the press getting hold of it and tying it in some way to what was happening to you, or camping out at the hospital like ghouls waiting to find out who was going to die first, Nick Jensen's girlfriend or his daughter.'

'I didn't . . .' Eva cleared her throat, 'realise that she knew about me.'

He shook his head. 'Nor did I till then, but it turned out she'd known practically the whole time we were seeing one another. She told me after – we were in Italy by then – that she'd lived in constant dread of the day I came home to tell her I was leaving. It never occurred to her, she said, to dread something happening to Maddy.'

Thinking of Elaine's warning about how much time people spent worrying about things that never happened, Eva said, 'I take it Maddy's all right now?'

Looking relieved all over again, he said, 'She's fine, thank you. A typical twenty-year-old if ever there was one, and with no memory whatsoever of what happened to her when she was four.'

Eva smiled. 'That's good. Is she still at home with you, or has some far-flung university claimed her?'

'Actually, she's reading English and French at UCL, and because it's cheaper to live with Dad, that's where she is. I tell her it's why I have to get out at weekends, to escape her terrible music and dreadful friends, and the answer I usually get is something along the lines of "Yeah, yeah, yeah, you can't live without me and you know it, so let's stop pretending."'

Finding herself laughing, Eva asked, 'So how long have you been back from Italy? Quite a while, by the sound of it.'

'It'll be eight – no nine – years in February. I don't know if it was a mistake to go in the first place, or not. I guess it worked out for Sally – she was the one who wanted to start afresh after Maddy was given the all clear, and I suppose I went along with it because I knew if I didn't she'd go anyway and take Maddy with her. So we sold the house, ploughed the proceeds into a run-down farmhouse just outside Forte dei Marmi, on the Tuscan coast, and not much more than eighteen months later she had the restaurant-cum-pensione she'd always dreamed of.'

'And what about you? Did you give up photography altogether?'

'More or less. We got so busy with the business and then Matilda, our youngest, was born, and Sally started talking about expanding the restaurant and building more rooms . . . We went for it, it wasn't a huge success, but it wasn't an out-and-out failure either. The trouble was it just wasn't what I wanted to do. I didn't want to live in Italy either. Don't get me wrong, I love the place, but it's not my language, my culture, and I kept getting this feeling that real life was passing me by. Knowing this from our occasional chats on the phone, or from when she came to stay, Bobbie took it upon herself to put me in touch with Ted Gray, who's now my partner. And the rest, as they say, is history.'

Eva blinked. 'So where's Sally now, and Matilda?'

'Still in Italy, and still loving every minute of it. Sally got married again a couple of years ago to the owner of the stables where Matilda keeps her pony, and Matilda's threatening to come and live with me too, when it's time for her to go to uni. That's if she goes, at the moment she's saying she probably won't bother.'

Feeling strangely unsteadied by the fact that he was no longer married, Eva tried to steer her mind from it as she said, 'How old is she now?'

'She was fourteen a week ago, so Maddy and I went over for her birthday. Fortunately, Sally and I have managed to stay reasonably good friends, much helped, I have to say, by the arrival on the scene of the dashing Diego, so our get-togethers tend to be fairly civilised.'

'And what about you?' Eva dared to ask. 'Have you married again, or met anyone else?'

'No, but every now and again I find myself being talked into blind dates, the way we single chaps of *un certain âge* often are by well-meaning female friends. So far I've been a bit of a let-down, I'm afraid, because I haven't managed to gel with anyone, and I'm told supplies are running low.'

Choking on a laugh, Eva said, 'Well, I can't imagine they're having much of a problem falling for you, but I guess it has to be a two-way thing or there's just no point.'

'Exactly.' He held up his glass. 'Any chance of a top-up?'

'Gosh, yes,' she cried, springing to her feet. 'Sorry, I'm being a very bad hostess.'

As she went to fetch the bottle she was trying to make up her mind whether to tell him about Don, but in the end she decided not to for fear of how it might be construed. Besides, tonight definitely couldn't be about her, it could only be about Richie and what kind of relationship, if any, Nick might

452

want to have with him. So far she was daring to feel as optimistic on that front as Bobbie had indicated she should be, and aware of a new lightness coming over her, she refilled their glasses and settled back into her corner of the sofa.

'So, are you going to tell me about our son?' he asked softly.

Feeling her heart contract with pride and love, she said, 'Of course. I just . . . I wondered . . .' Her eyes went down as the shame of what she'd done to Richie crept in from the past, reminding her that it couldn't be ignored. 'Did Bobbie ever tell you why I gave him up?' she made herself ask.

He nodded. 'Yes, she did, and I don't have enough words to express how deeply I hated myself for pushing you to it. If I'd known at the time I like to think I'd have stopped you, but with the way things were with Maddy I can't honestly say that I would have.'

'Did you . . . Did you ever see him at that time?'

He shook his head. 'And that makes me feel even worse, that our child, a tiny defenceless creature, came into the world needing his parents every bit as much as any child could, and I didn't even go to see him, much less hold him, or offer him a home.'

Knowing the reason why now, Eva was able to say, 'You weren't to blame. I was the one who gave him away as if he didn't matter at all, and believe me, I have never forgiven myself for that, and I never will.'

'Then you should, because the circumstances you were in back then – that we were both in – meant that no one was in the right place to think straight, let alone make a sensible decision about anything. I believe even Patty, who was always such a rock, had her own problems going on, so the timing of his birth couldn't have been worse, poor little chap.'

Hearing the tremor in his voice caused her throat to tighten as she thought of her tiny baby being passed around by strangers, because his parents hadn't been able to accept him. 'Did Sally ever know?' she asked hoarsely. 'Does she know now?'

'Yes, she knows. It was what terrified her the most, that I would leave her and Maddy, while Maddy was fighting for her life, to be with you and our son.' He pressed his thumb and forefinger hard into his brows. 'Maddie was still in hospital when you gave birth,' he said. 'It's a dreadful thing having to choose between your children. I hope to God I never have to go there again.'

Understanding the wretchedness of his dilemma, Eva sat forward to reach for his hand. 'I guess the important thing now is that we've found him,' she said.

Keeping his head down, he nodded – and realising he needed a moment to get himself together, she let go of his hand and sat back again.

'I have photographs,' she told him, when he looked up again. 'They're only on my BlackBerry, but they're still pretty good. Would you like to see them?'

With a roll of his eyes, he said, 'Now what do you think the answer would be to that?'

Laughing, she hurried over to her bag, and pulling up the shots she'd taken on Sunday, she handed him the phone with directions of how to scroll through.

'Thank you for sounding like my daughter,' he said drily. 'I happen to have one of these myself.'

Feeling absurdly excited to be sharing her pride,

454

she sat down next to him, but before he could get started she said, 'You might need to prepare yourself for how much he looks like you.'

'OK,' he responded, drawing it out.

A moment later he was studying a close-up of Richie in his rugby kit, grinning and looking straight into the lens. Turning to her incredulously, he said, 'You're kidding me, right? Apart from my colouring, he's exactly like you.'

Astonished, but nonetheless thrilled, she looked at Richie's face and decided that Nick might have a point. 'His legs are like yours,' she insisted, and almost blushed as she realised how intimate that might sound.

'Well, I'm glad they're not like yours,' he commented wryly, and moving on to the next shot he whispered a triumphant *yes* to see the number on Richie's back.

'And he's captain,' Eva told him, wanting to make sure he understood just how important their son was.

Next Richie was pushing in the back of the scrum; after that he was diving recklessly at another player's feet; then there were a few blurry shots that she hoped depicted his speed rather than her ineptitude, and *then* he was poised ready to score a try. Even Nick cheered when he caught the euphoria of the next one, which was Richie three feet off the ground with three other players reaching for him. Then the same adorable young man was slouched in an armchair next to a Christmas tree, either smiling, poking out his tongue, or putting up a hand saying 'no pap', which she had to explain to Nick, until she realised that actually she didn't because of course that was something he'd understand.

No one, she was thinking to herself, as they went through the shots again, would know that this boy, who appeared so full of health, confidence and mischief, had ever lacked for anything, and yet he had, because the most important people of all hadn't been there for him.

Until now.

Chapter Twenty-One

'Jas, is anyone in the shop with you?' Livvy asked via the intercom in the workroom.

'Two people,' came the reply. 'Why? Do you need something?'

'No, I just want to have a quick chat. Let me know when you're on your own, OK?'

'Will do.'

Clicking off again, Livvy continued to pin the Anna Sui-inspired jacket she was creating for a woman who'd come all the way from Oxford to discuss her requirements – and ultimately place an order. Having two more exclusives on the go, her own design of a frock coat, and a Balenciaga-style pant suit, meant she was pretty full-on in the studio these days, but their new part-timer was due to start on Monday, so with Coral increasing her hours after Christmas they were pretty well covered.

What was concerning her more than the workload at the moment was her mother, again. Ever since she'd got back from London, having left Jake there for a few more days, Patty had either been too busy to chat on the phone, or was calling at really odd hours to make sure Livvy was OK.

'Of course I am,' Livvy had grumbled at two fifteen that morning. 'What are you doing up at this time?'

'I was having a bit of a problem sleeping,' Patty confessed, 'and then I realised I hadn't spoken to you all day . . .'

'So you call me in the middle of the night? Mum! I'm working tomorrow.'

'I know, I'm sorry. It was thoughtless of me. I just wanted to make sure you're all right.'

'Well I won't be if I can't get back to sleep. Why don't you make yourself some cocoa, see if that works?'

'Good idea.' Then, 'I'll ring off now then.'

'OK.' Livvy waited, but her mother didn't hang up. 'You're still there,' she groaned.

'Sorry. I was waiting for you to go first.'

'I'm putting the phone down now.'

'Actually, before you do, are you at the flat or at Eva's?'

'The flat, if you must know. Why?'

'I was just wondering. So, Eva's at home on her own?'

'No, Jasmine's there tonight.'

'And Don, I expect. Jasmine will be pleased about that.'

'I've told you already, Mum, Don's not with Eva and she doesn't want him back.'

'I don't think she means that.'

'She does, so why don't you call him?'

'No, I can't do that.'

'Mum, can we please have this conversation at a more civilised hour? I have to be up at six . . .'

'Yes, of course, I'm sorry. Goodnight, darling, sleep well,' and the line went dead.

Half an hour ago, when Livvy had tried calling her mother, she'd had to leave a message because there was no reply. Jake had rung just after that, wanting to know if it was him, or was their mother losing it.

'She only rang at six this morning to ask me if I'd seen Don. I mean, why would I have seen Don?'

'Oh Lor',' Livvy murmured, starting to get really worried now. 'Unless he's in London. Do you know if he is?'

'Funnily enough, he doesn't confide his movements to me.'

'She's being really weird at the moment,' Livvy admitted. 'You know they've broken up, don't you?'

'Of course. Is he going back to Eva, do you know? That's what Mum says.'

'I know, but whatever she thinks a reunion definitely doesn't seem to be featuring in Eva's plans. She's got too much else going on with Richie and everything.'

'Can't wait to meet our new coz. He sounds really cool.'

'He is. You'll get on great with him, I know it.'

'It's going to be an interesting Christmas.'

'Tell me about it. It's really starting to mess with my head just thinking about it. Anyway, I'll give you a call as soon as I hear something from Mum. Oh, and don't forget it's Dad's birthday on Friday so send a card.'

Now, Livvy was just stepping back to inspect her handiwork when Jasmine came over the intercom, saying, 'OK, all clear. I'm on my own for the moment.'

Wasting no time, Livvy dropped the pins on the table and ran downstairs to find Jasmine carrying a couple of dresses from the fitting room back to the rails.

'I was wondering if you saw your dad for

breakfast this morning?' Livvy asked, going to pour them both a coffee.

'Actually, no I didn't,' Jasmine replied. 'I can't seem to get hold of him at the moment. Have you spoken to him, by any chance?'

Livvy shook her head and passed over a mug. 'Has he told you that he and my mum have broken up?'

Jasmine's eyes widened, almost fearfully. 'No, he hasn't. Why . . .? I mean, what . . . ?'

'My mother seems to think he wants to go back to Eva, or that he should, or that . . . Actually I don't know what's going on with her, I only know that he's not with her any more, and given the mess she seems to be in, I thought we ought to call him.'

Looking decidedly worried, Jasmine took out her phone and pressed in Don's number. 'Hey, Dad, it's me,' she said when he answered. 'Where are you? Did you get my message earlier?'

'I did,' he confirmed, 'and I was about to call. Sorry I couldn't make breakfast this morning. Is everything OK with you?'

'Everything's fine, I'm just a bit worried about you. Livvy told me about you and Patty . . .'

'Yes, I'm afraid that's not good news, and I would have told you myself, but frankly I was hoping to get it sorted out before I had to.'

Wrinkling her nose in confusion, Jasmine looked at Livvy as she said, 'So what is happening? And *where* are you?'

'Right now I'm at Uncle Pete's in Tonbridge, and I'll probably stay on for the next couple of days. Patty needs some space, she says, so I'm trying to give it to her.'

Jasmine's eyes were still on Livvy's. 'So you're not thinking of going back to Eva?'

His tone was dark as he said, 'I don't know what Patty's telling you, but I haven't seen or spoken to Eva for weeks. Perhaps you can pass that on, as she won't speak to me.'

'OK, I will, but actually I don't really think that's a good thing, do you, Dad? Just because you don't want to be with Eva any more doesn't mean she's stopped existing, or has got over it already. In fact, she's still your wife, and according to you, you still care about her, but I wouldn't say not being in touch at all is the right way to treat someone you care about.'

Loving what she was hearing, Livvy gave her a big smile of encouragement.

'Of course you're right,' he conceded, 'I'm handling things pretty badly and I . . . I guess I need to do something about it.'

'Good, you do that. I have to go now, but don't forget to let me know where you are in future.'

'Brilliant,' Livvy told her as she rang off. 'He so deserved that. The trouble is, I'm still not sure what to do about Mum.'

Picking up the shop phone as it started to ring, Jasmine said, 'Hello, Perdita's, Jasmine speaking.'

'Hi, it's me,' Eva told her. 'Just checking everything's OK with you girls, and to let you know that Richie and I are about to leave Chard.'

'Hey Richie,' Jasmine called out.

'Hey Richie,' Livvy echoed.

'Hey everyone,' he called back.

'We'll be at the house most of the afternoon,' Eva continued, 'though if the rain keeps off we'll probably pop out for a walk with the odds. I'll have my phone if you need to get hold of me.'

'Great,' Jasmine responded, turning to Livvy with

461

a baffled look. All this usually went without saying, so why was Eva bothering?

'That's it, better ring off now,' Eva told her, 'we're about to go into a dip.'

'Everyone's acting really strangely at the moment,' Livvy grumbled after Jasmine related the call. 'It must be a generational thing, because look at us, we're OK, aren't we?'

'Totally,' Livvy agreed, and with a shrug of bewilderment she turned to greet a couple who'd just come in the door.

Eva was wiping away tears of laughter as Richie stared at her from a face full of tomato soup that had just exploded from a carton as he opened it.

'It's trick soup, isn't it?' he demanded, his deadpan expression making it funnier than ever.

Holding her sides, she managed to say, 'How does it taste?' and then off she went again as he stuck out his tongue to check.

'Pretty good,' he decided, 'but I reckon it'll be better hot. Do you have a saucepan big enough for my head?'

Throwing him a roll of kitchen towel, she said, 'Use the bathroom at the end of the hall. And then,' she added as he took off that way, 'we should sort out a bedroom for when you come to stay.'

'Sounds cool,' he called back, and her heart lit up like a hundred Christmases. No fuss, no big deal, just *sounds cool*, to let her know that he was as chilled about staying here as she was to have him. Amazed and heartened by the way nothing ever seemed to faze him, she set about cleaning off the soup-splattered cabinets, while Elvis and Rosie gazed on, having already taken care of the floor. She could only hope that he was up for what else she had in store today, because it was a whole lot bigger than spending the night here.

Hearing her phone bleeping with a text she quickly dried her hands and dug it out of her bag, half expecting it to be a message from Nick. Her heart did a painful somersault when she saw it was from Don.

Just wanted to say how pleased I am for you about Richie.

Forcing herself not to be angry, since she had no intention of allowing her cheating, lying husband to ruin today, she immediately deleted the message, put the phone away again and carried on with what she was doing. The fact that it had taken him so long to be in touch over something he knew to be so vital to her completely nullified the sentiment as far as she was concerned, but even if he did mean it she had too much else on her mind to care.

Since returning from London a day later than planned, she'd been focusing entirely on today since it could – and probably would – turn out to be one of the most important days of Richie's life. Feeling a shudder of nerves passing through her, she checked her phone again just in case she'd missed a message from Nick, but she hadn't. It wasn't that she was expecting one, particularly, but since they'd seen each other on Wednesday they'd spent hours talking on the phone, mostly about Richie, and had got together for lunch yesterday to finalise their decision on how best to go forward. The fact that he was being so sensitive to their son in the planning of this, and so thoughtful towards her, was making her so happy and yet anxious that she barely knew how she was feeling from one moment to the next.

'What I want to know is how you feel about *him* now,' Carrie-Anne had demanded when she'd called from Brazil to find out how the first meeting in sixteen years had gone between Nick and Eva.

'All I can tell you,' Eva had responded, 'is that it wasn't difficult to see why I fell so hard back then.'

'Oh my God!' Carrie-Anne squealed excitedly. 'It went that well. Of course, I knew it would . . .'

'No you did not, you were as anxious as I was, just a tad better at hiding it. Anyway, please don't get carried away . . .'

'But this is exactly what you need . . .'

'Carrie-Anne, stop! It was all a very long time ago, we're completely different people now, and anyway, this isn't about me and Nick, it's about Richie. He's the only one who matters, to both of us . . .'

'I appreciate that, but if his parents get along, or better still get back together . . .'

'I'm not listening to any more of this. My head's all over the place as it is, and you're making things ten times worse.'

'OK, just make sure you keep me up to speed with everything, won't you? I'm not due back in London until after the New Year, but if you need the flat, you know it's yours. Except he has one of his own, doesn't he?'

Smiling to herself as she emptied a fresh carton of soup into a saucepan, Eva breezed past Carrie-Anne's romantic scenarios to a place where she and Nick were simply good friends – and, more importantly, good parents, because Richie was really all that mattered.

'OK, young man, soup's under way,' she declared,

when he returned from the bathroom all tousled hair and shiny cheeks. 'How many slices of bread?'

'Six, please,' he replied, sinking into a chair.

Eva's jaw dropped.

'Two each for them,' he explained, pointing at the odds, 'and two for me.'

Laughing and rolling her eyes, she said, 'You spoil them and they know it, look how they watch your every move.'

Grinning down at them, he gave them both a quick ruffle before getting up again to go and wash his hands. 'Are you having some?' he asked, noticing only one bowl and spoon on the counter top.

'I had a huge breakfast,' she lied. Food definitely wasn't on the agenda for her today, at least not until the next few hours were behind her – and perhaps not even then.

'So, tree decorating this afternoon,' he said as she followed him to the table with his soup and bread. 'Do you reckon the one we chose is big enough?'

Shooting him a look, since he knew that the gardener had been forced to chop the top off the monster that was now in the sitting room in order to get it in there, she said, 'Actually, before we go and get everything down from the attic, there's something I want to talk to you about.'

His eyes came worriedly to hers. 'I hope I haven't done anything wrong,' he said, seeming to mean it.

'Don't even think it,' she assured him. 'No, what I want to discuss is something that you might have been wanting to ask me about, but haven't quite known how to.'

For a moment he seemed to be searching his mind, then his cheeks reddened as he said, 'Actually, yeah, there is one thing.'

'Go on,' she prompted gently.

He glanced at her uneasily, then back to his soup. 'Sadie said I shouldn't say anything, because you might not want to talk about it, but . . .'

As his words ran out Eva put a hand over his. 'Are you wondering about your real father?' she asked.

His face seemed to tighten as he nodded. 'If you don't know who he was,' he said belligerently, 'or if he was mean to you, or anything . . .'

'His name is Nick Jensen,' she interrupted gently, 'and he was a photographer back in the days when I was modelling.'

His eyes sharpened and his hostility seemed to recede as he said, 'Isn't that who took the iconic shot of you?'

Feeling her heart melt that he knew, she said, 'That's right. We were very close back then and, who knows, we might still be if life hadn't intervened in the way it did.'

He was still watching her closely, his lunch apparently forgotten.

'He was married to somebody else when I fell pregnant with you,' she explained. 'I know we were wrong to be having an affair, but I think it's important for you to know that we loved each other very much and if circumstances had been different . . .' she took a breath, 'we'd never have let you go.'

His eyes were so intense now that she put out a hand to touch his cheek.

'You already know I had you four months after the attack,' she continued, 'and that the reason you were adopted was because I . . . Well, I was in a very bad place at the time, and I've already told you how deeply I regret the decision I made. What I didn't know then, and actually only found out this week, was what was happening in your father's life at the time.'

Richie still didn't speak, simply went on looking at her as she said, 'I could tell you, but if you're willing to meet him he'd like to tell you himself.'

There was a moment before Richie seemed to connect with what she'd just said. 'He wants to meet me?' he asked, almost incredulously.

Smiling as a lump formed in her throat, Eva said, 'Yes, he does. Very much, in fact.'

Richie swallowed and turned to stare out of the window.

Not sure how to read this reaction, Eva decided to continue anyway. 'We got together when I was in London this week,' she said, 'and, surprise, surprise, we hardly talked about anything else but you. He wanted to know everything about you, and I did my best, but you're so special, and so incredibly like him that it would be wonderful if he could meet you to see for himself . . .'

'I thought I looked like you.'

Laughing, she said, 'Funnily enough that's what he said when I showed him the shots I took last weekend, but you definitely have his colouring, and I'm quickly beginning to realise how much of his character you seem to have inherited too.'

Richie half frowned. 'I guess that's good, yeah?'

'Very,' she assured him.

Suddenly his eyes filled with tears, and belatedly realising what an enormous impact all this was having on him, she quickly got up to cradle his head against her. 'I'm sorry, I shouldn't have sprung it on you like that,' she said, holding him tight. 'We've hardly had time to get to know one another, and here I am, rushing things when you need time to get used to it all. But I promise you, nothing has to happen until you feel ready.'

Turning away from her, he said angrily, 'It's really dumb to cry.'

'No it isn't. It's perfectly understandable.'

Wiping his eyes with the heels of his hands, he stared moodily into the garden, more upset, she suspected, about making a spectacle of himself than about anything she'd told him. 'So what's he like?' he asked gruffly. 'I mean, I know what you said, but is he still married? Does he have any children?'

'He split up from his wife quite a while ago, but you have two half sisters.'

He took a moment to digest this. 'How old are they?'

'Maddy's twenty and lives in London. Matilda's fourteen and lives in Italy with her mother.'

A lengthy pause elapsed as he absorbed this new information. He not only had a father, but two half sisters, one older, the other younger than him and apparently living abroad. 'I've got to tell Sadie,' he said. 'She'll be like . . . no way.'

Feeling for the way he was holding on to his familiar connections, Eva said, 'Why don't you call her?'

He turned to look at her. 'Does she know? Did you tell her you were going to talk about my dad today?'

'I told your aunt Izzie on the phone last night, so I imagine Sadie knows by now.'

He sat with that for a moment, but instead of reaching for the phone, he said, 'So where is he? Does he live round here?'

'He has a home in Hampshire, which is where he is now. I told him I'd call if you want to see him.'

Richie nodded and swallowed loudly. 'I do want to meet him,' he said tentatively.

Eva smiled. 'He'll be very pleased to know that.'

Slumping back in his chair, he said, 'This is totally wild. It's completely . . . like awesome.'

Catching hold of his hands, Eva squeezed them hard. 'Like I said, we don't have to do anything until you feel ready to.'

He gave a shrug of one shoulder. 'I'm kind of ready,' he admitted grudgingly.

Her heart tripped. 'Does that mean you'd like me to call him?'

'Yeah, why not? Sure, let's do it.'

Pulling out her mobile, she searched for the number, and after pressing to connect she offered the phone to him. 'Why don't you say hello?' she suggested.

As the blood rushed to his cheeks she felt sure he was going to refuse, but then he said, 'Does he know my name?'

'Of course he does,' she laughed.

He shrugged mischievously, then taking the phone he held it so she could hear too. The ringtone stopped and a moment later Nick's voice was saying hello.

Looking at her, Richie said quietly, 'Hey, it's Richie.'

There was the briefest moment before Nick replied, 'Hello, son,' and Eva clapped her hands over her face to stifle an enormous sob.

An hour later Richie was standing in the kitchen watching his father coming through the conservatory, while Eva stood to one side, watching them both, so full of emotion she hardly even dared to breathe. It was like a dream, a strange and beautiful dream. She could tell that Nick was as nervous and close to the edge as she was, but his eyes were only on Richie – and when, without uttering a word, he pulled his son straight into an embrace, Eva completely lost it.

'I'm sorry,' she wept, as they turned to her and started to laugh. 'It's just . . . Seeing you together . . .'

Nick whispered something to Richie, adding, 'What do you reckon?'

Richie nodded. 'Definitely,' he said, and the next thing she knew she was in an enveloping embrace with them both. It was only when Richie started to break down that Eva pulled away from Nick to wrap her son in her arms. However, embarrassed, Richie turned roughly away.

'It's OK, son,' Nick told him, putting a comforting hand on his shoulder. 'We're all crying.'

It was a while before Richie was able to turn back to them, his eyes still wet with tears, his tender young skin scarlet with confusion.

'Here,' Eva said softly, handing him a square of kitchen roll.

'Thanks,' Nick sobbed, taking it and dabbing his eyes.

Laughing, Richie took the next square and blew his nose. 'Sorry about that,' he said. 'It was just a bit . . . You know.'

'I do,' Nick agreed, his eyes still lit with humour, his damp lashes showing that his emotion was real. 'We've got a lot to talk about, you and me. So much to catch up on.'

'Do you like rugby?' Richie asked him eagerly.

'Mad about it, and I know you play because your mother showed me the pictures. Number eight, huh?'

Richie tried not to beam. 'I guess they had to choose someone,' he said modestly.

'Can I get you anything?' Eva asked Nick. 'Tea, coffee, something stronger?'

'I'm good, thanks,' he answered, still looking at Richie. 'So you are my son,' he declared, sounding both amazed and proud beyond bearing. 'How lucky can a man get?'

Richie's head went down shyly, then glancing at Eva he said, 'Shall I get the odds out again now?'

'The odds?' Nick repeated.

'You wait,' Richie told him, and hurrying over to the den he opened the door so fast that Rosie and Elvis virtually tumbled out on top of him.

'Hey! Who are you?' Nick laughed as Elvis led the charge towards him. 'And you?' he added as Rosie skidded to a halt at his feet. 'What a pair. Aren't you just something else? Eva, I always knew you liked animals, but a *pig*!'

'He's not just any pig, are you, Elvis?' Eva protested.

'Elvis? That is just perfect. And he's a handsome chap, that's for sure. But not nearly as gorgeous, *or* as brazen as you,' he chuckled, as Rosie rolled on to her back for a tummy rub.

'Do you think I might have inherited that effect on women?' Richie wondered innocently.

Eva and Nick blinked, then burst into laughter. 'You are definitely your father's son,' she informed him drily. 'Now, how about I take the even odder couple for a walk and leave you two to get to know one another – though I'm feeling as though that's already happened.'

Nick's eyes were more serious as he looked at Richie again. 'What do you say we take these guys for a walk?' he suggested. 'If you think they'll come with us,' he added to Eva.

Gazing down at them despairingly, she said, 'They'll go with anyone who's got a pair of wellies and a pocketful of treats.'

'Ah, that could be a problem,' Nick responded. 'I'm sure you can provide the treats, but I don't think my feet will fit into your wellies.'

With hardly a moment's hesitation, she asked, 'What size are you?'

'Eleven.'

'Then problem solved.' It was only when she went to dig about in the shed while Richie fetched his walkers from the car that she started to feel odd about the fact that Nick was about to step, quite literally, into Don's boots. She almost wished she could prevent it now, and yet why should she? If anyone belonged here today it was Nick, and if he needed to borrow wellies in order to take his son for a walk then he jolly well could. In fact, as far as she was concerned he could have them.

'OK, boots are on the feet,' Nick stated a few minutes later, 'treats are in the pocket, but already disappearing fast. I guess we're good to go.'

'Right with you,' Richie told him, quickly zipping up his jacket.

'Are you going to be OK?' Nick asked Eva.

Smiling all over her face, she said, 'Some of us have a Christmas tree to decorate.'

'We'll help when we get back,' Richie assured her.

'Great,' Nick said, clapping an arm round Richie's shoulder as they started outside. 'I'm glad we're having this time together, because I need some advice and I reckon you're just the person to give it.

I've been thinking about auditioning for *The X Factor*.'

Richie glanced at him, and hardly missing a beat, he said, 'Cool. What, you mean for the over-twenty-fives? What song are you going to sing?'

Almost helpless with laughter, Eva watched them stroll on down through the garden, completely loving the fact that Nick Jensen had definitely met his match in his son.

'Mum, at last,' Livvy cried into the phone. 'Where have you been all day?'

'I'm at Elaine's,' Patty told her. 'I'm sorry, I should have let you know.'

'It's OK, just as long as you're all right.'

'I'm fine. Was there anything in particular you needed me for?'

'No, I don't suppose so, not really. How long are you going to be there?'

'Probably until tomorrow, or Monday. There are a few things I need to work through in my mind, and you know how good Elaine is for that sort of thing.'

'OK, well at least I know you're in safe hands. You'll call, won't you, if you need me?'

'Of course, but I'll try not to make it the middle of the night again. I'm sorry about that, I just seemed to lose all sense of time. Would you mind letting Jake know that you've spoken to me?'

'Sure. I'll call when we ring off.'

'Thank you.'

'So I'll talk to you on Monday about what you might want for Christmas, shall I?'

'That'll be lovely, and at the same time I expect you'll tell me what you want.'

Cheered by her mother's more familiar irony, Livvy said, 'Better go then. Lots of love to Elaine,' and after ringing off she took a deep breath before looking at Jasmine.

'So at least we know where she is,' Jasmine stated.

Livvy nodded, but before she could say any more the phone rang again. 'Hello, Perdita's, Livvy speaking.'

'Hi, it's me,' Eva told her. 'Just wanted to let you know that Richie's father is offering to take us all out for dinner tonight, so can you two be back here by seven?'

Livvy blinked her eyes hard. 'Who?' she asked.

'Richie's father. His name's Nick, remember? I promise you'll like him,' and the line went dead.

'Well?' Jasmine said when Livvy simply stared at her.

'That was Eva,' Livvy finally managed. 'Apparently Richie's father is taking us out for dinner tonight.'

Jasmine's eyes widened in amazement.

'Is it just me, or are you getting the feeling we're on a different planet to everyone else?' Livvy demanded.

With a sputter of laughter, Jasmine said, 'It's like you said earlier, we're OK, it's the rest of them who are weird.'

'I think I need to speak to Mum again,' Livvy decided. As she waited for the connection her eyes returned to Jasmine. 'You realise this could change everything, don't you?'

Jasmine nodded, then shook her head. 'How?'

'I don't know,' Livvy confessed, then groaning as she was bumped through to voicemail, she said, 'Hi, me again. Call as soon as you get this message. It's urgent – not life-threatening and Jake's OK, just I need to talk to you.'

Since returning from their walk Nick and Richie had brought the Christmas decorations down from the attic, helped drape most of them on the tree and were now slumped companionably in front of a rugby match, yelling and jumping up whenever their team scored (their team today was Wales, apparently), or shaking their fists at the ref every time he made a bad decision, which was every time it went against them, it seemed.

Marvelling at how simple and straightforward things could be at times for men, while feeling she might turn religious just to be able to thank someone for this unbelievable turn her life had taken, Eva carried on with the finishing touches to the tree. Knowing that Richie was going to be with her at Christmas was almost too much to take in, when hardly more than a couple of weeks ago she'd been practically suicidal with the fear of having to spend it alone. Another reminder, she was thinking as she stood back to assess where to put a homeless snow-flake, of how right Elaine was about the time wasted worrying or dreading the future, when anything could happen at any time to alter the course you thought you were on. It could also be a caution, she reflected more dismally, not to feel too happy, because that could vanish just as quickly. However, today she'd rather tell herself to forget how contrary life could be and just enjoy the good times now they were here.

Very philosophical, she smiled to herself, as she filled a few more gaps with crystal moons and glittering stars. Then recalling how she'd stiffened in Nick's arms just now, when he'd only been hugging her to say thank you for letting him spend some time with his son, she began trying to think of a way to make it up to him.

Her first thought was to pay for the dinner he'd so generously invited them to this evening, but that was hardly going to do it when it really wasn't about money. Perhaps she should invite him to stay over so he could come and watch Richie play rugby tomorrow. As good an idea as that sounded, she'd have to be careful about the way she phrased it to avoid giving the wrong impression, and she should do it privately so that Richie wouldn't know if his father had a prior arrangement and couldn't cancel it. Her heart leapt as she considered inviting Nick for Christmas, and maybe she would, even though he'd almost certainly made plans with his daughters by now. However, it wouldn't hurt to let him know he was welcome, and they could probably work out some other time to get together over the holiday anyway.

Putting aside her decorations as the phone started to ring, she laughed and winced as a giant cheer erupted in the next room. 'Hello, Eva speaking,' she said into the receiver.

'Eva, my dear. How lovely to hear you,' Elaine said warmly, as though she, Eva, had made the call.

'Elaine, I have to tell you,' Eva said, 'that you spook me sometimes the way you do things. I was just about to pick up the phone and call you, but you beat me to it.'

'Oh, I do love the way the Universe moves sometimes, don't you?' Elaine chuckled delightedly. 'Or

476

maybe we'll just call it telepathy. Labels really aren't important. Shall you go first, or shall I?'

'You,' Eva invited.

'Actually, I have a feeling it should be you.'

Laughing, Eva said, 'OK, so if I started by telling you that even as I speak Nick and Richie are sitting together in my den, watching rugger, what would you say?'

Elaine gave a gasp of surprise, but her tone was wonderfully droll as she said, 'I guess I'd have to ask, who's winning?'

Loving the response, Eva said, 'I have to admit it feels like me at the moment. Nick's taking us all for dinner tonight and we're hoping you might be able to join us.'

'What a very generous thought,' Elaine replied heartily, 'but I'm afraid it's not possible for me to get away this evening. You will send Nick my best though, won't you, and thank him for offering to include me?'

'Of course I will, and we'll arrange something for another time when you can get away. So now, why don't you tell me what you rang to say?'

'OK,' Elaine responded. 'It's just a quick call really, to ask you to come here tomorrow. I would have said tonight, but now I know Nick and Richie are there . . .'

'What time?' Eva interrupted. 'I have to take Richie to rugby for two.'

'Of course you do,' Elaine sympathised. 'So why don't we say ten?'

'That's fine. I'll be there. Can I bring anything?'

'Just you will be perfect. Now, before you go, I know you have a lot on your mind at present, but will you do a small thing for me tonight?'

'Name it.'

'Please try to spend some time thinking about your sister and – I'm sorry to inject a sad note into proceedings at the moment – what losing your mother might have meant to her. That's all I ask, my dear. God bless,' and she was gone.

Chapter Twenty-Two

The air was still and dank as Eva let herself quietly out of the house just after nine thirty the next morning. In the distance she could hear the musical chime of church bells mingling with the swooping cries of the gulls. As she made her way to the car raindrops dripped down from gutters, while the ground squelched underfoot, still sodden after a torrential downpour during the night. She wondered if it had woken any of her guests. If it had she'd heard no one moving about, nor had there been any signs of anyone so far this morning.

Smiling indulgently to herself as she thought of how much wine they'd managed to consume at the restaurant last night, she got into the car and put the heater on high ready to combat the cold. Even Richie had managed to down a glass or two more than he should have, but it had been such a special occasion she hadn't had the heart to try and stop him. He might wish she had when he finally woke up, but there didn't seem much chance of that happening any time soon. When she'd popped up to the top floor to put an ear to his door before leaving he was still lost to the world in the room that he'd claimed as his, next to Jasmine's.

Eva had suspected, when she'd offered Richie the

choice of whichever room he liked, that his unself-ish nature would never allow him to request either of the ones that Livvy and Jasmine had made theirs, even though both had a sea view and much more space. He could have gone for the enormous guest room with its own dressing room and bathroom, since she'd have been perfectly happy to redecorate it for him. However, he'd opted for the attic studio with its high, sloping ceilings, vast skylights and twin double beds. There was a bathroom next door which Jasmine had sworn she was happy to share – unless, she'd added later in a quiet aside to Eva, Eva felt it was time for her to move out now that her father was no longer there.

Knowing that both the question and tears were vino-induced, Eva had wrapped her in her arms and told her to stop talking nonsense. 'You'll always be welcome here, and don't you forget it,' she'd scolded gently. Then, with a playful narrowing of her eyes, 'However, whether you'll always want to share a bathroom with a teenage boy is a whole other thing, but I guess we won't worry about that tonight.'

The next lot of tears had been Richie's when she'd hugged him goodnight and the enormity of every-thing swamped him again. The way he'd clung to her as he sobbed, as though terrified she might let him go again, had made her break down too, and when Nick had found them in such a sorry state he'd gathered them into his arms and cried loudly along with them, which had ended up making them laugh.

Midnight had long gone by the time Richie had finally fallen asleep and she and Nick had crept quietly back down to the main landing. This was when Nick had decided to take his turn at talking nonsense, saying he'd get a taxi to take him to a hotel, or maybe he should call someone he knew in Dorchester to ask them to come and get him. In the end she'd managed to push him into the guest room along with an assurance that she really didn't think he'd planned this – if he had, she felt sure he'd have at least brought a toothbrush, maybe even a razor. As luck would have it there was a fresh supply of both in the en suite bathroom, and even a brand-new pair of stripy pyjamas in the chest of drawers, she informed him. The look on his face as he'd registered the last generous offer had made her want to howl with laughter.

It was after one by the time she'd finally got into bed herself, exhausted, still a little tipsy, and elated in a way she could never have imagined possible only two short months ago. She wasn't even missing Don, she told herself, though she had to admit it was him she was thinking about as she turned out the light. It still felt strange not having him there, and a night never passed when she didn't lie staring into the darkness wishing there was a way to turn back the clock, or at least to make the pain and longing go away. However, last night, in spite of her inner turmoil, she'd managed to close her eyes and say a silent thank you to whoever might be listening for everything that was happening to her now. She knew it was still early days and everyone was on their best behaviour and that some much more difficult times probably lay ahead, but she wasn't going to allow herself to worry about them now. She was simply going to enjoy the moment and be grateful. She might have drifted off then had Elaine's call not floated to the front of her mind and pulled her awake again.

Why, she'd wondered, did Elaine want her to think about how it had been for Patty when their mother died? Was Patty suffering over it now? Maybe Elaine was hoping by her suggestion to soften Eva's feelings towards her sister, to coax her into understanding how wretchedly full of guilt Patty was feeling and so be able to find it in herself to forgive her. With so much good happening in her life at the moment, it wasn't as easy as usual for Eva to connect with the bitterness she felt towards Patty; however, she knew very well that it was still there, and couldn't foresee a time when it would ever go away.

Gritty-eyed, and slightly spacey after tossing and turning for so much of the night, Eva pressed the remote to open the gates and turned out on to the main road. Though it didn't usually take much more than fifteen minutes to drive to the retreat at this hour on a dull Sunday morning, given the time of year and number of Christmas markets bedazzling the area today there was a chance she might get caught in traffic, and she didn't want to be late. She was looking forward to seeing Elaine, not only to tell her all about Richie and Nick, but to assure her that she had, as requested, thought about Patty through the night. It surely wouldn't surprise Elaine to know that Patty was always on her mind, whether at the front of it, or the back, or seeming to take it over completely. Loving someone as much as she'd always loved her sister meant that Eva could never entirely expel her from her thoughts, or even her heart it would seem, because in spite of everything she couldn't deny that she missed her terribly. However, the hatred she'd felt towards her over the past two months had become every bit as powerful as the love, so powerful that at times it had consumed her to a point that was chilling and disturbing to recall. She'd wanted to hurt Patty more deeply than she'd been hurt herself; to ruin Patty's life, business, everything she held dear; she'd even during one desperate night fantasised about killing her.

That was what love did, she was reflecting now. It took its victims to such extremes that, beautiful and gentle as it could make them, it could also tear their world apart and turn them into cold-blooded monsters. She gave a shudder to think of how far she might have gone, or at least what kind of state she might have been in now, if she were as fragile or unstable as her mother.

Feeling a twist in her heart, she drove on towards the retreat, her mind filling with thoughts of the beautiful, almost angelic-seeming woman who'd given birth to her and who, she'd come to realise, was more of a romantic fantasy to her than a true memory. Yet such was the bond between them that she'd longed for her all her life, and though she might be far from consumed by it now, the need, on some level, was always there. She couldn't imagine it being any different for Patty, indeed it must surely be far worse, because by the age of twelve Patty would have built a very deep and loving relationship with their mother, as well as depending on her, and would have even existed through her the way children did when they were young. It had probably never even crossed her mind that a day would come when her mother wouldn't be there any more. What a terrible, devastating blow it must have been for her when that day dawned. Yet she'd never discussed it, at least not with Eva, because she barely ever mentioned their mother.

Everything had remained bottled up inside her, and the closer Eva got to the retreat now, the more convinced she was becoming that the trauma of what Patty had experienced when she was young was the reason Elaine wanted to see her today.

Eva only wished she could say she didn't care.

To her surprise, when she pulled up outside the front door, it wasn't Elaine who came out to greet her, but Iris, one of the faith healers.

'Come in, come in,' Iris fussed as she bustled her inside. 'It's bitterly cold out there this morning. Enough to freeze the old socks off. Elaine's in her sitting room with a nice big fire going, so pop on through. You know the way.'

Deciding not to take a rune from the bowl at the door, Eva started unravelling her scarf as she headed along the chilly stone passage towards the back of the house. As she passed one of the side chapels, as the staff liked to call the quiet rooms, she could hear the rhythmic murmur of a chant going on inside, and the distant bang and clatter of pots and pans told her that some weekend residents were expecting lunch today. Thinking of food made her tummy rumble. She hadn't had breakfast this morning, but she'd managed two whole courses at the Italian last night, the most she'd eaten at one sitting in weeks.

Tapping lightly on the sitting-room door, she pushed it open and immediately felt the trapped heat along with the heady aromas of woodsmoke and incense, wrapping their welcome around her.

'Ah, here you are,' Elaine said, getting up from the sofa, arms open ready to greet her. 'You're nice and early, that's lovely.'

Eva's eyes were locked on Patty, whose back was

turned as she stacked more logs on the fire. 'Hello,' she said stiffly, as Elaine folded her in an embrace. 'I didn't realise my sister was going to be here.'

Elaine was still smiling. 'No, well, I was afraid you might not come if you did,' she admitted, almost cheerfully.

As Patty turned round Eva's heart jarred with shock to see how haunted, almost wasted she looked. Her face was so gaunt, her eyes so darkly shadowed that she was like a lost, ghostly version of herself. However, her voice was strong as she said, 'Hello, Eva.'

Eva looked at Elaine, and accepting that there was no escaping this without incurring her stepmother's dreaded disappointment, she started to unbutton her coat.

'That's right,' Elaine clucked approvingly. 'Hang it on the radiator ready for when you go out again.'

Ludicrously relieved to know that she was going to be allowed to leave, Eva did as she was told and went to sit next to Elaine on one of the purple sofas. Patty was still standing, until seeming to realise she could sit down, she perched on the edge of the wing-backed chair beside the hearth.

'I think I know what this is about,' Eva began.

Taking her hand and patting it, Elaine said, 'I'm sure you do, but would you mind letting Patty speak first?'

Though Eva's eyes were like flint as she looked at her sister, she was aware of the severe knock her defences had taken from Patty's appearance.

'Don't worry, you'll have plenty of time for your say later,' Elaine assured her, 'but what Patty has to say might affect it, which is why we'd appreciate it if you hung on a little while.'

485

Giving a nod, as though to tell Patty to go ahead, Eva left her hand in Elaine's while reminding herself that no matter what Patty had to say, her betrayal could never, and would never, be forgiven.

'Elaine told me about Nick,' Patty said. 'You must be very happy that . . .'

'He's back in my life?' Eva cut in sharply. 'Yes, I can see that you'd want to think that, it would make it all so much easier for you, wouldn't it, if you could tell yourself . . .'

'Eva, Eva,' Elaine rebuked gently. 'You're putting words in Patty's mouth, and I don't believe that was what she was trying to say.'

Eva's face was tight as she continued to stare at Patty.

'I was going to say,' Patty told her, 'that you must be very happy that Richie is able to get to know his father.'

Though the sentiment was kind, in fact typical of Patty, Eva said nothing. What was going on in her life now had nothing to do with her sister.

Patty swallowed, and after a quick glance down at her hands she said, 'I'm sure you realise, well I think Elaine's just made it plain, that the reason I asked her to invite you today is because I thought I would stand a better chance of being able to speak to you than if I rang or tried to come to the house again.'

Eva's heart remained closed. Yes, she did realise that, and she wasn't especially thrilled to be reminded of how she'd treated her sister the last time she'd been at the house. She guessed Elaine must know all about that by now, and felt almost ashamed to think of the cruel way she'd told Patty to go after Patty had brought Richie to her. Yet why should she feel ashamed? It wasn't as if she'd caused any of this, and after what Patty had done, what the hell did she expect?

Patty cleared her throat and in a voice that wasn't quite steady she said, 'I should probably begin by telling you that Don and I are no longer together.'

Though Eva remained still, her insides were clenching tightly. It was true Livvy had told her, or at least intimated, that there had been some kind of break-up, but Eva had assumed it had far more to do with Patty's conscience than with any kind of lasting intent. In fact, she still thought that. She looked at Elaine and Elaine squeezed her hand, while nodding for her to return her attention to Patty.

'I ended our relationship,' Patty continued, 'because I was afraid that something inside me had made me want to take him from you just because . . . just because he was yours.'

Eva's eyes widened. Surely she hadn't heard that right.

'I thought,' Patty went on, 'I mean I've always known, that I have some very deeply rooted feelings towards you that aren't . . . Well, they aren't particularly good, but I've always done my best to pretend they don't exist.'

Having never sensed anything from Patty besides love and the deepest loyalty – until lately – Eva felt as though she was coming strangely adrift. That she might have bad feelings towards Patty after what had happened was, to her mind, understandable; that Patty might have harboured such feelings towards her for years was so shocking that it seemed to be stripping away all the stability, the beliefs, even the roots she'd always taken for granted.

'It wasn't especially difficult to ignore them,' Patty went on, 'because I know in my heart that the love I have for you is far stronger than the jealousy and resentment I've suppressed since our mother . . . did what she did.'

Eva was barely breathing. *Jealousy and resentment?*

'If you bottle up anything for too long there's a chance it will fester and grow, and then suddenly one day it's making you behave in a way that's usually alien to you. It can even make you think things that don't make sense in the normal way.' She took a breath and as she put a hand to her face Eva could see how badly it was shaking.

'Even though I knew you weren't to blame for what happened,' Patty continued, 'I couldn't help thinking that if Mummy had never had you she'd still be alive, and everything would be the way it was before.'

Eva's heartbeat slowed to a painful thud.

Patty swallowed hard. 'I knew it was pointless to think that way, that there could never be any going back, but I missed her so much and I still remembered the times when she . . . when she wasn't sad and afraid. She used to laugh a lot then and make everything seem easy and right. Daddy used to laugh too. It's not that they were never happy after you came along, because sometimes they were, but it was different. Mummy told me herself once what was wrong with her – I was about ten or eleven at the time, not really old enough to understand what depression meant. I only wanted to know that she'd get better and she promised she would, but she never seemed to. She'd stay in bed for days at a time, refusing to see us or speak to us, and even when she did get up she'd look scared and nothing like she always used to. She hated it when you cried. It made her cry too. She'd tell me to make you stop, because she couldn't stand the noise, so I'd take you into my bedroom and play with you, or I'd give you something to drink to calm you down. Sometimes she'd run out of the house and hours and hours would go by before she came back. When she did she'd scoop you up and hold you tight, saying she was sorry and that she loved you really. She'd dance with you and sing, and I'd watch her and wait for her to pick me up too, and say the same to me, but she didn't. It was like everything had become about you and her, and the way she was, and I didn't matter any more. It sounds silly and self-pitying to say that now, doesn't it, but it was how it felt when I was a child.'

Eva swallowed drily. She could stand almost anything – that Patty might not love her the way she'd always believed; that she could be trying to punish her; even that she really had fallen in love with Don – but that Patty aged twelve, or at any age, should think that she hadn't mattered to their mother was tearing her apart.

'Almost from the time she brought you home,' Patty continued, 'she began teaching me how to change you, to bath you and feed you. Daddy helped, obviously, but on Mummy's bad days when he went to sit with her, I was left alone to take care of you. I remember sometimes wishing that I could take you somewhere and just leave you there so that I could go back and be with Mummy and Daddy. I thought if you weren't there any more everything would return to normal. I even tried leaving you once, when you were about three, but you kept crying and running after me and in the end I just couldn't do it. In spite of everything, I loved you, and we'd become so close. It was as though on some level I already knew how important we were going to be to each other, so I *had* to take care of you. I'd always rush home from school to be with you and be late in the mornings after trying to settle you down, so that Mummy wouldn't have to worry while she waited for the minder to turn up. I didn't realise it at the time, of course, but you started to feel safer, and I suppose more content, with me than you did with Mummy, which meant she felt able to leave you to me more and more. The trouble was, I think it made her feelings of inadequacy and depression even worse to see me coping in a way she couldn't.' As her voice wavered she bit her lips to try and stem a surge of emotion. 'If I hadn't been so capable maybe she'd have tried harder, so maybe it was me who drove her to do what she did.'

Eva gasped. 'No,' she protested, tears starting in her eyes. 'You can't say that. You were just a child doing what you thought was right.'

Patty didn't disagree. 'But I blamed myself for a long time,' she said, 'and I blamed you too, and Daddy . . . I could never talk about her because I hated her for what she'd done, and when Daddy finally let me read the note she'd written . . .' She took a breath to fight back more tears. 'I was eighteen by then, you were still only ten. He didn't want you to see it because he was afraid you'd ask why she'd done what she had and if he told you the truth, you'd end up blaming yourself, or him. He had no idea that I blamed myself, and you, even him sometimes . . . I never told him, I couldn't tell anyone. She was gone, she'd never be coming back so there was no point in talking about her at all, because it wouldn't change what had happened, nothing could ever do that. I remember for years you kept asking me when she'd come back. I'm not sure how much you even remembered her, but you still used to draw her pictures at school and make cards for her birthday and Christmas. It made me so angry that you didn't understand, and angrier still that Daddy would put your cards and pictures up as though she might walk in the door at any minute, because I wanted to make things for her too and be told how much she'd love them. It all sounds so pathetic now, I know, but at the time . . .'

'You were very young,' Elaine reminded her gently.

'It's not pathetic,' Eva argued softly.

Patty seemed to tense, as though unwilling to accept excuses for herself. 'It was all a terrible mess,' she declared sharply. 'We didn't deal with any of it properly. We should have had counselling, you should have been told . . . Instead we just buried our heads in the sand and pretended she'd died in an accident rather than, God forbid, have to deal with the truth. And we went on pretending and lying and secretly blaming one another . . . Or I did. I know you didn't blame me, or anyone really, but I was full of so much frustration and confusion, all kinds of conflicting emotions . . . I got so I couldn't even bear to think of her and I hated it whenever you mentioned her. Then, when Daddy showed me the letter, I hated her more than ever, because what she said . . . In it . . . she only seemed to care about you and Daddy but not about me.'

Eva started to go to her, but Elaine held her back. Eva turned to her stepmother, but Elaine's eyes were on Patty.

491

'I still have the letter,' Patty announced.

Eva froze.

'I'm sorry I lied,' Patty said, 'I just couldn't bring myself . . . I didn't want anyone to know that I hadn't mattered, not even you. Daddy always said I should show it to you when I felt the time was right, and I kept telling myself it would never be right. But lately, since all this happened, I've become terrified of what might be going on inside me. It isn't that I've ever wanted to harm you, not consciously, but I've come to realise that what I'm doing with Don is, in its way, a thousand times worse than anything I could have planned, because I'm breaking your heart.'

As the words buried themselves deeply into her, Eva felt Elaine's hand tighten on hers again. It still wasn't time to go to Patty, but Eva wanted to, so desperately, that it was almost impossible to hold back.

'I'm very jealous of the fact,' Patty pressed on, 'that Mummy loved you more than she loved me. I don't blame her for it, you can't help it if one child means more than another, it just goes that way . . .'

'Wait! Stop!' Eva cried. 'I don't believe that. She couldn't . . .'

'Eva, please let me say this,' Patty interrupted. 'I need to, and though you probably don't feel you owe me anything . . .'

'Don't talk like that.'

'I have to, because this is where we are now, and we've only got here because of me and what's happened in the past.' Patty's eyes were glittering with tears as she put her head back in an effort to stem them. 'I'm going to give you the note now,' she declared raggedly. 'I'm sorry it's taken this long.'

Eva watched her pick up her bag.

'I should probably tell you that you don't have anything to be afraid of,' Patty went on. 'She loved you . . . She couldn't help herself, she just . . .'

Elaine came in gently. 'You don't need to make excuses for her any more,' she said in a whisper, 'or for yourself.'

Seeming to accept that, Patty took a small, crumpled envelope from her bag and Eva felt her senses starting to swim, almost as though she was disconnecting from reality, merely watching and listening to a scenario she had no part in. This note was from her mother, written by her, the last words she'd spoken to her family. It felt so unbelievably important that it was a moment or two before she could make herself take it.

'Would you like us to leave you alone to read it?' Elaine offered as Eva looked down at the envelope. 'If you prefer, you can take it home to read later.'

Eva was staring at her father's name and thinking of the woman who'd written it – and the terror it must have struck to his heart when he'd found it.

Without answering she pulled the note free and unfolded it.

My darling Edward,

Just those three words made her feel oddly dizzy, as though she was in a place she wasn't meant to be and could find no way out.

I am truly sorry to say goodbye this way, but I cannot go on hurting you and our children the way I am. I am so afraid of myself and what I might do, the harm I could cause to your innocent lives without meaning to. I have tried so hard to overcome these terrible, morbid feelings that blight me, to return to the woman I used to be, but the time has come for me to accept that she is never coming back. Please try to remember me as I was before this started, when we were so much in love and happy to be together. I am truly lucky to have known you, Edouardo, my love. It's breaking my heart to see how you're suffering now. You deserve so much more. You should be with someone who can love and care for you in the way I used to, so please think of my departure as a gift of freedom, not as a burden of sadness, or guilt, or blame. I am wholly responsible for what I am about to do, please don't ever forget that.

Please tell Patty to think only of the times when she was sure of me and of herself, and when the sun used to shine on our world. She's a beautiful, gentle girl who I know will always take good care of Eva. As Eva grows up she will have questions: whatever else you tell her, please remember to say, often, that I loved her and that if it is at all possible I will be looking over her and taking care of her from my next life. Perhaps I'll be able to make a better job of it from there. Like Patty, Eva is also a beautiful girl, so adorable and mischievous – a real handful for her sister who copes so well. How am I able to see and say these things and know them to be true, and yet still find myself in the depths of despair? Even knowing that I have so much to be thankful for seems to make no difference. When I say that I love you, Edward, it no longer lights up my soul, it weights me with the guilt of what I am doing to you and the fear of what I have become.

As I leave you, my darling, I shall pray for your

happiness and the chance that one day, somehow,
we shall be together again,
   Your Hannah

Long after she'd stopped reading Eva continued to stare at the letter, feeling the tragedy of her mother's helplessness stealing through her like a pain. She remembered the day she'd sat where she was now and her mother had seemed close by. She found herself wondering if she was with them now, watching and listening, and trying to connect with her daughters on a level that was so profoundly mysterious and powerful that it would never be possible for them to fully understand it. It was simply there, she realised, the bond that joined them together, as invisible, yet as potent, as the aromas filling the air, and as gentle as the light in her step-mother's eyes. They weren't alone, she and Patty, and they could never be apart.

In the end Eva looked at Patty, and seeing how lost and worried her sister seemed, she felt her heart turn over. 'She loved you too,' she whispered.

Patty nodded. 'I know, I just . . . She never said it and she should have.'

'Yes, she should,' Eva agreed.

Patty glanced down at her hands and tried to force a laugh. 'I feel so foolish for minding, for letting it get to me the way it has. I've been so angry, so full of feelings that are terrible and vengeful . . . I think, I hope, I've always managed to hide them, but maybe in suppressing them I've made them worse. I don't know. All I can tell you is that I've never consciously meant to hurt you, not even for a minute, but I know that I have, in the worst imaginable way.'

Eva's voice was hoarse as she said, 'You can't make someone fall in love with you. Don has a mind of his own.'

Patty started to reply, but it took some time for her words to come. 'It's true, but . . . I've gone over and over things so many times in the last few days, in my own mind and with Elaine, and I still don't know . . . All I can tell you is that I truly believed I loved him all the time I was with him, and I still believe it, but if being with him means I have to choose between you, then . . .' Her voice faltered. 'I love you too much, Eva, to let you go.'

Feeling Patty's fear and desperation tightening around her own heart, Eva quickly went to kneel in front of her and wrapped her tightly in her arms. 'I love you too,' she whispered brokenly.

As Patty's slender frame shuddered with sobs, Eva understood that she was crying as much for their mother as she was for the sorrow and regret of what had happened between them. There were so many years of grief locked inside her, so much longing and guilt, a world of misunderstandings and cruelly torn loyalties, that this letting go now could only be the beginning. She had a long and tortuous journey ahead of her, and thank God Elaine was already guiding her. Knowing that she must support her too, Eva pulled back to cup Patty's precious face in her hands. As she looked into her eyes all she was seeing was the sister who was like a mother, the best friend who could never be replaced, the dear, dear person who'd always been there for her no matter what. And to think of how she'd been tearing herself apart for falling in love with a man who so clearly loved her was almost beyond bearing.

'Where's Don now?' Eva asked shakily.

'I don't know . . . I . . .'

'Call him,' Eva said, 'and tell him to come.'

'But . . .'

Putting a finger over her lips, Eva said, 'You put me back together once after my life fell apart, and now I'm going to try to do the same for you. You and Don belong together, and if you can't see that, then all this upheaval and turmoil will have been for nothing.'

Eva was alone in Elaine's sitting room now, absently staring into the fire while Elaine went to brew one of her special mint teas, and Patty spoke to Don in the next room. She couldn't help wondering what they might be saying to one another and a part of her even wanted to run in there and make Patty stop, to tell her that she hadn't meant anything she'd said and that she didn't believe they belonged together at all. However, she knew she wouldn't do it, because she was aware of how different she was now to the woman she'd been just a few short months ago. Something fundamental had changed inside her, and was continuing to change in a way that was making her calmer, stronger and far braver than she'd ever known herself to be before. All her life Patty and her father, then Don, had been there to protect her, sheltering her as best they could from a world where bad things happened – and when something did happen, in the form of the attack, their instincts to shield her had intensified to the point of becoming almost smothering.

It had taken this crisis, this betrayal, to show her just how dependent she had become on Patty and Don, barely moving without consulting one or the other of them, apart from her attempt to make contact with her son. They had even tried to protect her from that, afraid that she would be hurt again and unable to cope. But she had coped, and was continuing to in spite of the heartbreak they had caused her. In fact, she was starting to see just how vital this upheaval had been in their lives in order to start freeing them all from the delicate, needy, child they'd created between them in her. The time for her to grow up was long overdue; it was shaming to know that it hadn't happened before. She must also stop blaming those whom she felt had wronged her – Nick, Don, Patty, Richie's adoptive parents, her own father – for failings that had in fact been her own. She wasn't that helpless, precious child any more, she was a grown woman with spirit and determination and a tenderness of heart that made her strong, not weak. She was no longer staring at the cliff edge, the way she had when Don had first left. In fact, she'd come so far since then that she was already embracing the beginnings of a new life without him or Patty at the centre of it. In truth, it still felt disorienting, even frightening to imagine going into the future without the security and reassurance they'd always provided. However, she wouldn't have it any other way. They all desperately needed to let go of the past, especially Patty whose role in Eva's life had become so confused that neither of them really knew who she was to Eva any more – mother or sister.

Or the woman who'd stolen her husband.

Difficult though it was, and Eva suspected it would never be easy, she must resolve to keep trying to put the betrayal behind her and start recognising Patty as a woman with her own needs and weaknesses, ambitions and fears. As the past hour had proved, she could find it in herself to put Patty first, the way Patty had always put her first before. It wasn't exactly a role reversal, as much as a very necessary evening out of who they were and the parts they played in each other's lives. She understood and was deeply grateful for all the sacrifices Patty had made for her, and realising that Patty had been about to do it again by giving up Don was what had provided Eva with the will and the courage to start forgiving.

It was a time to be feeling grateful too for this second chance she was being offered with her son. She knew for sure that she wasn't about to start getting everything right from now on, any more than she'd be able to banish entirely all the bad feelings towards Patty and Don. What she could do, however, was carry on trying to make gestures of forgiveness, or understanding, or even a light-heartedness that she wasn't necessarily close to feeling in order to make amends to those she loved and to try creating new and lasting bonds. Sooner or later, she felt sure, the gestures would become real, and because she already felt so much better for having tried it, surely it wouldn't be too hard to try again.

A while later, after learning that Don was on his way, Elaine walked Eva to her car, putting an arm around her shoulders and resting her head against hers. 'I'm proud of you,' she told her. 'I know this isn't going to be easy for you, and there'll probably be setbacks along the way . . .'

'The first will be when I see them together,' Eva said, managing to sound wry when she was already dreading it. However, she must stay mindful of what

Patty's presence in her life had always meant to her, and how, over Don, Patty had been prepared to make one of the biggest sacrifices of all.

'It was very courageous of you to invite them for Christmas,' Elaine said.

Since she'd only been able to do it because Nick had already agreed to be there too, with Maddy his eldest, Eva didn't feel courageous at all, only worried that she was already regretting it. 'We don't know yet if they'll accept,' she said. 'I'm sure Don won't want to.'

'Maybe not, but the important thing is that you were brave enough to offer – and that you and Patty are going to find a way to go forward together.'

Knowing that was going to be far harder than Elaine seemed to realise, while accepting that she really didn't want her life without Patty in it, Eva said, 'It seems your Universe has managed to swerve us away from out-and-out disaster, or at least a complete family breakdown.'

'Mm, that happens sometimes, provided you let it.'

'And what about happy endings, does it allow for those too?'

'Oh, now,' Elaine chided, 'you're too old to be believing in fairy tales.'

Laughing, Eva turned to hug her hard. 'Thank you,' she whispered into her jasmine-scented hair. 'Thank you for being you, and thank you for doing what you have today.'

'Believe me, it was all you,' Elaine told her generously. 'Now hadn't you better be running along? I seem to remember you have a date with a boy and a rugby match.'

After turning the car round, Eva pulled up next to Elaine as she waved her over.

'Out of interest,' Elaine said, 'do you think there's a chance Richie's parents might get back together in the fullness of time?'

Though she felt a skip in her heart, Eva knew there was still a lot of healing and a very long way to go before any of them could know anything for certain. However, with a mischievous sparkle in her eyes she delighted her stepmother as she said, 'Didn't I just hear someone say that we're too old to be believing in fairy tales?' and blowing her a kiss she continued on down the drive, smiling happily to herself and suddenly very eager to get home.

Acknowledgements

An enormous thank you to Gill Hall for all the legal guidance regarding adoption. A veritable minefield with many contradictions, misunderstandings and anomalies, so please accept that if your own experience differs to the one portrayed in the book it's likely to be because various councils and social services have their own ways of interpreting and following the law. Having said that, the basic principles are the same all over, so if you feel there are any fundamental errors in the story they will certainly be mine.

Another very big thank you to Scott McGregor of Dorset Police for sharing his insights and knowledge of Bridport. And very many thanks to the charming Arthur Watson, owner of the fabulous Riverside Restaurant at West Bay, Dorset.

And last but not least a huge thank you to Lesley Ann Wood, owner of Lésanne in Chipping Sodbury, for talking me through the running of an exclusive fashion boutique.

Getting to know

Susan Lewis

Read on for exclusive content including an insight into
No Turning Back, all about Susan and an extract from her
new novel *Losing You*

Thank you so much for choosing *No Turning Back* and I hope you found Eva's story as absorbing and touching as I did writing it. Most of us will have struggled with difficulties in our lives and often found ourselves faced with seemingly impossible choices. This book begins with Eva having to make a choice that she is in no position to cope with, much less to fully understand. And once the decision is made there really is no turning back.

I can imagine that most, if not all of us, absolutely dread finding ourselves in a position where we are unable to go back on a decision we come to realize wasn't only wrong, but disastrous. Worse would be when that decision affects a child who is close to us, is possibly even ours. The regret involved would surely thread itself through every minute of every day, whether at the forefront of our minds, or somewhere close by. This is how I saw Eva and her sister Patty as I wrote them, as women who were blessed in so many ways – beautiful homes, loving families, thriving businesses – but who are both constantly tormented by their conscience.

Over the years Eva's love for the son she rejected only grows, as does the need for him, but time after time she is told that her decision to give him up is irreversible. That Patty played a part in the decision has become only one of the crosses Patty has had to bear.

I have tried, in this book, to imagine how it must feel to know that you have let down a child who depended on you, though the real agony of it must surely go beyond the imagination of someone who has never experienced it.

Because it's important to me to end my books on a strong and positive note it was a tremendous joy to write the scenes where Eva and Richie finally come together. And what really got me weeping was Richie's first meeting with his father. So, even though there was no turning back from early mistakes, there eventually came the opportunity for forgiveness and second chances, which I guess we could see as life's balm for disastrous decisions.

I would love to hear what you think. You can write to me through the contact link on my website www.susanlewis.com. Or if you prefer you can share it with others on my Facebook page.

Again, a very big thank you for choosing this book.

I was born in 1956 to a happy, normal family living in a brand new council house on the outskirts of Bristol. My mother, at the age of twenty, and one of thirteen children, persuaded my father to spend his bonus on a ring rather than a motorbike and they never looked back. She was an ambitious woman determined to see her children on the right path: I was signed up for ballet, elocution and piano lessons and my little brother was to succeed in all he set his mind to.

Tragically, at the age of thirty-three, my mother lost the battle against cancer and died. I was nine, my brother was five.

My father was left with two children to bring up on his own. Sending me to boarding school was thought to be 'for the best' but I disagreed. No one listened to my pleas for freedom, so after a while I took it upon myself to get expelled. By the time I was thirteen, I was back in our little council house with my father and brother. The teenage years passed and before I knew it I was eighteen…an adult.

I got a job at HTV in Bristol for a few years before moving to London at the age of twenty-two to work for Thames. I moved up the ranks, from secretary in news and current affairs, to a production assistant in light entertainment and drama. My mother's ambition and a love of drama gave me the courage to knock on the Controller's door to ask what it takes to be a success. I received the reply of 'Oh, go away and write something'. So I did!

Three years into my writing career I left TV and moved to France. At first it was bliss. I was living the dream and even found myself involved in a love affair with one of the FBI's most wanted! Reality soon dawned, however, and I realised that a full time life in France was very different to a two week holiday frolicking around on the sunny Riviera.

So I made the move to California with my beloved dogs Casanova and Floozie. With the rich and famous as my neighbours I was enthralled and inspired by Tinsel Town. The reality, however, was an obstacle course of cowboy agents, big-talking producers and wannabe directors. Hollywood was not waiting for me, but it was a great place to have fun! Romances flourished and faded, dreams were crushed but others came true.

After seven happy years of taking the best of Hollywood and avoiding the rest, I decided it was time for a change. My dogs and I spent a short while in Wiltshire before then settling once again in France. Perched high above the Riviera with glorious views of the sea. It was wonderful to be back amongst old friends, and to make so many new ones. Casanova and Floozie both passed away during our first few years there, but Coco and Lulabelle are doing a valiant job of taking over their places – and my life!

Everything changed again three months after my fiftieth birthday when I met James, my partner, who lives and works in Bristol. For a couple of years we had a very romantic and enjoyable time of flying back and forth to see one another at the weekends, but at the end of 2010 I finally sold my house on the Riviera and am now living in Gloucestershire in a delightful old barn with Coco and Lulabelle. My writing is flourishing and twenty-six books down the line I couldn't be happier. James is still in Bristol, with his boys, Michael and Luke – a great musician and a champion footballer! – so I believe James and I are what's called very happy LATTES (Living Apart Together – don't quite see how that acronym works but I'm told that's what we are!)

It's been exhilarating and educational having two teenage boys in my life! Needless to say they know everything, which is very useful (saves me looking things up) and they're incredibly inspiring in ways they probably have no idea about.

Should you be interested to know a little more about my early life, why not try *Just One More Day*, a memoir about me and my mother? In November, the story continues in *One Day at a Time*, a memoir about me and my father and how we coped with my mother's loss.

1.What made you want to become a writer?

It's something I instinctively felt would happen one day, though I didn't do much about it until I began working in TV drama. Editing scripts, pulling together storylines, dreaming up characters and their backgrounds was something I enjoyed so much that when an agent suggested I turn one of my projects into a book I decided to give it a go. That book was never published, but the bug had bitten and the rest, I guess, is history.

2. Describe your routine for writing and where you like to write, including whether you have any little quirks or funny habits when you are writing.

I have a study at home that overlooks a beautiful spread of lower Cotswold countryside where I aim to be by ten each morning, through until six or seven in the evening. For a long time I wrote seven days a week taking a break only when I was so exhausted I couldn't do any more. Now, I pace myself a little better by doing only five or six days, but even that is pretty gruelling. I don't have any quirks particularly, but I do have a very bad but thoroughly enjoyable habit of drinking a glass or two of wine when I read back over what I've written during the day.

3. What themes are you interested in when you're writing?

I'm always interested in the strange or terrible things fate inflicts on innocent people and how courageously (or not) they strive to overcome it.

4. Where do you get your inspiration from?

The most obvious source of inspiration is life itself. Added to that there are certain authors I find very inspirational in the way they write, such as Lionel Shriver; Jodi Picoult; Anita Shreve; Susan Howatch and Irène Némirovsky whose book, *Suite Française*, played a very big part in my own book, *A French Affair*.

5. How do you manage to get inside the heads of your characters in order to portray them truthfully?

It's all done through imagination, I guess – I can't think that there would be any other way.

6. Do you base your characters on real people? And if not, where does the inspiration come from?

Very occasionally they're based on people I meet, but as a real character is so highly complex it would only ever be one or two aspects of them. I guess you could say that personality traits are perhaps more inspiring than actual characters.

7. What's the most extreme thing you've ever done to research your book?

I once allowed myself to be locked up in a Filipino jail when researching *Last Resort* – that was pretty scary, and it didn't smell too good either!

8. What aspect of writing do you enjoy most?

I enjoy it all, especially when exciting and pivotal things happen that I hadn't seen coming!

9. What's the best thing about being an author?

For me it would definitely be doing the second draft when all the really hard work is done, and the smoothing out is underway. After that comes a lovely freeing time when I hold onto the book before giving it to my editor – this is a period when there is no pressure at all, or anxiety about whether or not she is going to like it. That begins the moment I send it from my computer to hers.

10. What advice would you give aspiring writers?

Probably that you have to be serious about writing to make it work, not simply think 'I'm going to write a bestseller' or 'I'd write a book if I only had time.' It takes a huge amount of dedication and belief in yourself; if you have that then I think the best advice I could give is pay great attention to your characters and who they are, and don't forget to listen to them. It's uncanny how often they'll help out when you find yourself stuck.

11. What is your favourite book of all time and why?

There are many books I could list here, but I'm going to settle for *Suite Française*, because it's the only book I've ever finished reading and then gone straight back to the beginning to read it again.

12. If you could be a character in a book, or live in the world of a book who or where would you be?

I wouldn't mind being one of Georgette Heyer's heroines back in Georgian times, but as they didn't have much in the way of anaesthetic then, perhaps I'd rather be Claudine in my own book, *Darkest Longings*.

I lost my mother Eddress, to breast cancer when she was thirty-three and I was nine. This was back at a time when women, even doctors, spoke in hushed tones about the dreaded Big C. Nothing was discussed, no counselling offered: there was even a kind of shame attached to having fallen victim to this terrible disease. Luckily all that has changed. These days almost two out of every three women diagnosed survive beyond twenty years. Today someone is always there to offer advice and support to those who need it, or simply to lend an ear if all that's required is to talk. Many of these people are doctors, nurses or members of the health-care professions; but just as many are women who selflessly give up their time to be there for those in need. Losing my mother left an irreparable hole in my life, which is why I'm a supporter of Breast Cancer Care and a fantastic Bristol based charity, the Breast Cancer Unit Support Trust. The amazing women behind BUST have raised almost a million pounds in the last 20 years to help provide care and support for the local community, as well as the latest in medical technology for the Bristol based Breast Cancer Unit.

It also means a great deal to me to be a supporter of Winston's Wish, the charity for bereaved children. How I wish this marvellous charity had been around at the time of my family's loss. It's my aim to raise awareness of the vital role Winston's Wish plays in the lives of children who are unfortunate enough to lose a parent.

If you feel you need support, wish to raise money or are interested in learning more about any of these charities you can find them at the following addresses:

www.winstonswish.org.uk Telephone: 01242 515157 Helpline: 08452 03 04 05

www.bustbristol.co.uk Telephone: 0117 9566522 Email: bust@bustbristol.co.uk

www.breastcancercare.org.uk Telephone: 0845 092 0800
Free Helpline: 0808 800 6000

Two lives. Two families. One tragedy.

Lauren Scott is bright, talented and beautiful. At eighteen, she is the most precious gift in the world to her mother, and has a dazzling career ahead of her.

Oliver Lomax is a young man full of promise, despite the shadow his own, deeply troubled, mother casts over him.

Then one fateful night, Oliver makes a decision that tears their worlds apart.

Until then Lauren and Oliver had never met, but now they become so closely bound together that their families are forced to confront truths they hoped they'd never have to face, secrets they'd never even imagined...

Read on for an extract from *Losing You*
Out in hardcover 16th February 2012

Chapter One

'Guess what? I have had *the* most brilliant idea!'

Lauren Scott's exquisite amber eyes were sparkling with mischief as she breezed into the kitchen, where her mother was engrossed on the computer.

'Really?' Emma Scott responded, quickly closing down the email she was reading to reveal a job-search website beneath.

'Yeah, really.' Unwinding a soft brown scarf as she slumped down at the table, all long, booted legs and clouds of icy air brought in from outside, Lauren said, 'So don't you want to know what it is?'

'Mm?' Emma clicked to open another page of the website.

Lauren ogled her patiently, her irrepressible good nature lighting her from inside, as it always did, and lending her fresh young complexion a deliciously warm glow in spite of her wind-rouged cheeks. As she removed her woollen hat the sumptuous waves of her honey-blonde hair tumbled randomly around her shoulders and halfway down her back, and caught the light overhead in a way that made it glint like gold. Her enthusiasm for life was as infectious to others as it was a surprise to her mother, who couldn't claim to have passed on any such sunny

1

gene herself. However, Emma was willing to accept that she'd played a part in the arresting shades of Lauren's eyes, plus the high cheekbones and pixyish chin – and very probably Lauren's inherent compassion for others, since Emma had always considered it important to be as supportive to friends and family as she would wish them to be to her. (Although Emma's consideration hadn't always been returned, particularly where her mother and ex-husband were concerned, she simply breezed on past the defaulters and felt thankful for those who did show up in her times of need.)

In most other ways such as height, hair colour and the dazzling smile that lit up Emma's world, Lauren was just like her father, while Emma's resemblance to her own father was equally striking, if photos were to be believed, and she saw no reason why they shouldn't be. This meant that she was five foot six – a good two inches shorter than Lauren – with an olive complexion, lustrous raven-coloured hair, and could easily be passed by in the street, her attractiveness unnoticed. She had no problem with that, since, unlike her long-dead father who'd been a successful musician in his time, she'd never harboured any desire to stand out in a crowd. However, she couldn't deny loving the little frissons of pleasure she experienced whenever a man she felt drawn to seemed to sense the connection.

She'd definitely chosen the wrong man for that lately, so the least said about him the better, and she certainly wasn't going to answer his email.

'Mu-um! You're not listening to me.'

'I am. I am,' Emma insisted, finally tearing her eyes from the screen. 'Oh God, Lauren, look at you, your lips are blue you're so cold. Where have you been?'

'Only over to Melissa's and I helped some kids build a snowman on the way back. Anyhow, I've got to tell you about my idea because it's totally sick and you are so going to love it.'

Understanding that sick was enjoying a temporary redefinition in teenage-speak as fantastic, or amazing, or totally brilliant, Emma sat back in her chair and folded her arms. 'OK, you have my full attention,' she declared, while reflecting (with fingers tightly crossed) how blessed she was to be able to call this golden child her own. So many of her friends back in London had been driven half out of their minds by the stress of teenage hormones, addictions and even, in two unlucky cases, hush-hush abortions. In fact, before moving away, Emma had reached a point where she'd started to feel almost embarrassed by Lauren's comparatively problem-free journey through what were supposed to be the most turbulent adolescent years. 'Still time for it all to kick in,' she'd often heard herself saying to one mother or another, as if Lauren developing issues would somehow make them feel less singled out as the victims of the dreaded teenage revenge.

'I have decided,' Lauren pronounced, fixing her mother with the kind of look that told her there was to be no argument, 'that *you* should come to India with me in September.'

Emma blinked, blinked again, and stumbled into an incredulous laugh.

'You've always wanted to go,' Lauren reminded her, 'and ever since Donna and I started making our plans I've felt terrible about not including you . . .'

'Lauren, I'm your *mother*! You're not supposed to include me, especially not on your gap year.'

3

'It'll just be for the first couple of weeks, till Donna comes to join me. All right, I could easily delay my flight and go at the same time as her now she's having to be bridesmaid for her sister, but then I thought, why don't *we* – you and me – have a holiday together doing some of the things *you* want to do in India before I take off with Donna?'

Emma was shaking her head in amazement. 'You and your crazy ideas,' she chided, knowing Lauren meant it and wondering how many other girls her age would seriously want their mothers travelling India with them.

'Isn't it brill? I knew you'd love it. So shall we check to see if we can get you on the same flight as me, and then we can work out what we'll do and where we'll stay when we get there. I mean, I know you won't want to do all the backpacking stuff, but I'm cool with five-star . . .'

With a splutter of laughter, Emma said, 'I'm sure you are, but I'm afraid the closest we'll ever get to that is dreaming.'

'That's OK, we can find less expensive places to stay like ashrams or hostels. And we can get trains and rickshaws and go in search of ourselves, or enlightenment, or *love* . . .' Electrified by the theme, she went on, 'Imagine if you found someone like what's-his-name, you know the mega-zillionaire who that actress was married to?'

With dancing eyes, Emma said, 'I suspect you mean Liz Hurley and Arun . . . I'm blanking on his surname . . .'

'It doesn't matter, he might still be free, and if he is, once he knows about you . . . Actually, I'm starting to think the sooner we get out there the better, because we don't want him being snapped up . . .'

4

'Stop it,' Emma protested, getting up and squeezing past Lauren to go and put on the kettle.

'No, come on, Mum, you've got to think out of the box here, not that this house is a box, exactly, well it is, but a lovely box and I'm totally happy in it if you are, but I definitely think we need a holiday and you need a man . . .'

'Lauren . . .'

'OK, Arun what's-his-name might be a bit radical, but you have to admit that us going to India together is seriously cool.'

Emma couldn't deny that if she allowed herself to she might easily become every bit as excited by the idea as Lauren seemed to be, since spending a fortnight living a lifelong dream, especially with her daughter whose company she adored, had even more appeal – in fact way, way more appeal – than becoming the future Mrs Nayar – that was his name – as if there was even a remote chance of that! She was getting as bad as Lauren with her flights of fancy.

'You've got some money now you've sold the business,' Lauren was running on. 'OK, I know you're going to say it isn't much . . .'

'Because it isn't. In fact, I was lucky to come out with anything at all, as you well know, and I need every penny now while I look for a job.'

'Which you'll find no problem, because who wouldn't want you? You're brilliant at everything and everyone likes you and . . . oh Mum, please don't tell me you're going to say no. You can't. It's what you want, I know it is, and think about it this way, if you come with me you won't have to worry about me being in a foreign country all on my own till Donna turns up.'

A very good point – a very good point indeed. Even so . . . 'I'm going to need some time to think about it.'

'What's to think about? Why don't we just go ahead and book?'

'Because we've hardly been in this house a month, we overspent at Christmas and if I do manage to find a job I don't know if I'll be able to get the time off.'

'But it's only January, September's ages away yet, so if you tell them you've already booked something they're sure to be all right about it.'

Dropping a kiss on Lauren's head as she reached over her to take two mugs from a cupboard, Emma said, 'I promise I'll think about it, and if I find a job by, let's say, the end of February and they're willing to let me go, then we'll get straight online to reserve the flight.'

'Yay! I knew you'd go for it,' Lauren cheered, grabbing her mother round the waist. 'I reckon it'll be brilliant for you after all the stress of packing up the business and selling the house . . .'

'Both houses,' Emma reminded her, and immediately wished she hadn't, since it was Lauren's precious father and his crooked – yes, *crooked* – accounting and dubious investments and demanding new wife who'd virtually turned them out on the streets.

Looking dismal, Lauren said, 'It's a real pity Dad couldn't let you hang on to the cottage. He really wanted to, well you know that, but with all the debts that had mounted up . . .'

'We don't need to go over it all again,' Emma interrupted, trying not to sound clipped or bitter and failing on both counts. Her feelings towards

6

Will and Jemima Scott-Robbins (yes, he really had gone double-barrelled since marrying the wretched woman, pretentious, ludicrous, sad bastard that he was) were for her to deal with and not to be laid on Lauren. Not that Emma wasted any time harbouring the bitterness that most said she was totally entitled to after her ex had virtually destroyed the small, and until he got his hands on it, successful catering business she had started *alone* some fifteen years before. She'd never felt right about his insistence that he should resign from his job as an insurance assessor to help expand her company, and she could only wish now that she'd cleaved to her instincts. The debts they'd managed to accrue until he'd abandoned ship – and marriage – to take up with Jemmy, as he called his mistress-now-wife, had turned out to be so staggering that, with a recession upon her and banks fleeing from the rescue, there had been nothing Emma could do to save her dear little empire from crashing. Nor had she been able to hold on to their smart house in Chiswick, unless she'd wanted to declare bankruptcy and turn her back on the debts she owed people she'd known, and who'd trusted her, for years. And the tiny, two-bed cottage his father had left to *both of them* just after they were married, had also been liquidised in order for them to reach a settlement that would help Will to provide a decent home for his new, young family. (The fact that *Jemmy* was absolutely rolling in it hadn't seem to count for anything at all.)

In the end Emma had come out of the ordeal with the grand sum of two hundred and twenty-five thousand pounds, which might sound massive, but almost all of it had gone towards the small, three-bed estate house she and Lauren had recently moved into; the rest – around fifteen thousand – she was counting on to get her through until she was earning again.

The really good part of it all was that she was mortgage-free – at least for now, and if she found a job soon there would be no reason for that to change.

The worst part was that she'd worked so hard to build her business, only to end up back where she'd started.

Nevertheless, she wasn't going to age and enrage herself by focusing on the injustices she had suffered at Will Scott's grabbing little hands; indeed, she did her level best never to think about the TBs (Thieving Bastards as her brother Harry liked to call them) at all. What was the point when they were no longer a part of her life? Nor, mercifully, were they enjoying their marital bliss in either of the homes Emma had created and loved with a passion. Instead, they were luxuriously shacked up in Jemmy-baby's towering town house in Islington along with Ms Scott-Robbins's twelve-year-old twins from a previous marriage and two- and three-year-old Chloe and Dirk (*Dirk*!) the adorable (according to Lauren) fruits of Jemima's union with Will. So with the TBs fully ensconced in London where Jemima practised her sharkery – another of Harry's little witticisms, Jemima being founder and head of some whizzo IT firm – and Emma now settled in only just affordable North Somerset, there was next to no chance of running into them.

Thank God.

In fact, the only contact Emma ever had with Will these days was the occasional text concerning Lauren, usually to ask what she might want for her birthday or Christmas, when he always went preposterously over the top with his gifts. He didn't have to buy his daughter's love, or try to absolve his guilt with five-hundred-pound cheques, or a brand-new car as he had for her eighteenth, because Lauren adored him anyway. Nor did he have to keep making pathetic excuses (another source of his irritating texts) about why it wouldn't be convenient for him and Jemima to have Lauren living with them in London during the week while she finished her last year of school. Lauren was more than happy to stay with Donna and her family, who'd readily thrown open the double front doors of their massive house in Hammersmith, or with Emma's mother, Phyllis, with whom Lauren had a far closer relationship than Emma had managed in her entire life. There was also Emma's wonderfully eccentric and still outrageously flirtatious Granny Berry – her father's mother – who lived some of the time in an airy riverside apartment in Chelsea, and the rest with Alfonso, a dashingly romantic Italian poet, in his rambling Tuscan retreat just outside Siena.

'It's a pity you didn't know your mother before your darling father was so tragically taken from us,' Berry often sighed tipsily to Emma. 'She was a real beauty in her day, you know, and actually not a bad singer in spite of what the critics used to say. They were really quite cruel about her at times, claiming that it was only because of your daddy that she was in the band. That was probably true, I suppose, but none of the other members had a problem with it, and it was always Daddy who did the real vocals, she was only ever part of the backup.' At this point Berry would usually smile mistily and take another sip of Chianti, before going on to say, 'Everyone loved him. I don't mean just his fans, I mean his friends and the people he met on tour, or in the recording studios. You should have seen the turnout for his funeral. Well, you and Harry were there of course, but you don't remember it, do you?'

Emma always felt terrible that she didn't, but since she'd only been three at the time it was hardly surprising. In fact, she had very few memories of her father, and since her mother would never talk about him, she had to rely on Harry's hazy recollections, and the wonderful stories Berry often told about him. And of course there were the two Top Ten hits he'd had with his band, back in the sixties, the royalties from which still provided her mother with a modest income today.

'Your daddy absolutely adored Phyllis,' Berry would insist. 'It was after he died that she changed. Such a terrible tragedy. It broke all our hearts, and I don't think she's ever got over it. It's hard to know though, isn't it, when she won't ever discuss it.'

A part of Emma actually detested her mother for the way she'd so stubbornly and selfishly refused to talk about her father; it made the dozens of silver-framed photographs around her mother's house of a man clearly besotted with his children seem more of a punishment than a kind and loving way of remembering him. She wouldn't even allow Emma to play his records, which was unbelievably mean, Emma always thought, when she never used to tell Harry off if he put them on. Since Harry had been almost eight when the terrible accident had occurred, he had his own memories of their father, which he readily shared with Emma when she was small, though never when their mother was around. What he didn't remember very clearly, however, was their father going out into the garden after an almighty

10

storm to start tidying up, according to Berry. He hadn't realised until it was too late that the broken cables he'd grabbed hold of were live power lines brought down by the wind. Apparently her mother had seen it happen, the frenzied jolting of his body as thousands of volts pumped their lethal energy through him, burning him to death from the inside out.

It was when she considered how horrendous that day must have been for her mother, aged only twenty-eight at the time, that Emma found herself able to feel some sympathy and even tenderness towards her. Not that she ever showed it, she'd learned long ago that her mother wouldn't welcome it if she did – in fact there had even been occasions when her mother had managed to make her feel as though she was in some way to blame for what had happened.

'Ah no,' Berry had assured her, 'it's not just you. In her way she blames everyone, especially God, which makes you wonder, doesn't it, what's going on in her prayers when she rocks up to His place on a Sunday.'

Emma was sure she'd never made Harry feel to blame, in fact she knew that her mother loved Harry much more than she'd ever loved her, mainly because she'd never tried to hide it. Emma would go as far as to say that her mother seemed to like everyone much more than she liked her own daughter, including Will when he'd come into the family. She'd even stayed in touch with Will during and after the divorce, and had gone with Lauren several times to visit the new family in Islington.

How disloyal could a mother get? She'd even seemed to take some pleasure in remarking to

Emma, after one of her visits, how well Will seemed to be doing for himself now, as if up to then she, Emma, had been responsible for holding the lying, swindling, double-crossing swine back. Life was looking blindingly rosy for Will since he'd made a meteoric rise through the ranks of Jemima's company to the position of vice president, whatever that over-blown catch-all of a title was supposed to mean. What it meant to Emma was a) he could afford to provide very generously for Lauren, which indeed he did; and b) the sly-witted, money-grubbing Jemima was stupid enough to be setting herself up for the exact same fall that had left her, Emma, face down in the muck after she'd promoted her husband beyond his capabilities.

What a fool she had been! And what a salutary, and expensive, lesson in love and how never to trust yourself when in it!

'So what are you doing on the computer?' Lauren wanted to know, turning the laptop round so she could see the screen. She read aloud, '"The Rainbow Centre for Children affected by cancer, life-threatening illness and bereavement."' Her eyes were both questioning and knowing as she turned them to her mother.

'It's a local charity,' Emma explained as she set two mugs of coffee on the table and squeezed back into her chair. She was actually becoming quite fond of this new build they'd recently moved into, with its mock Georgian windows and shiny front door, but she had to admit that its bijou interior, after the space they'd had in Chiswick, was taking some getting used to. The kitchen table, not much bigger than a dartboard, was set up against the wall beneath a row of fake-ash cupboards, and had just about enough space in front and to one side of it to accommodate two chairs. The back door, which was at the end of a small hall outside the kitchen, opened out on to a brave little patio (brave for claiming such a lofty status when it consisted of no more than a three-by-three layout of paving stones) and a boxed-in cabinet for the bins was around the corner, next to the side gate. Beyond the patio was a largish dirt patch that constituted the back garden, which Emma intended to turn into a lawn and vegetable patch when the weather improved. At the front of the house were two gravelled areas, four-by-six, fenced in by some fancy black wrought-iron work, and home to a pair of ornate stone pots (currently empty). A jaunty crazy-paved path connected the pavement outside to the front door – no gate yet, but it was due to be fitted by the end of the week.

From the kitchen window, which was above the gleaming new stainless steel sink with single drainer, they could, if so inclined, chart the progress of cars coming and going from their loosely laid-out cul de sac that looped around a central green with Victorian-style lamp posts and a couple of carved wooden benches; or wave hello to a friendly neighbour who might be ambling past with a pushchair, or a dog, or an ageing relative with a Zimmer. (Not much activity going on out there today given the weather, but Emma imagined that would change come spring.)

Since the cottage Will's father had left them was less than a mile away this was an area Emma and Lauren already knew quite well, having spent most summers and school holidays over the past eighteen years enjoying their picture-book country abode and the village nearby. This shining new estate had only been completed in the last year, making many of their neighbours either first-time buyers, or older couples downsizing because their children had left home – or because the recession had done for their larger incomes or businesses. Already Emma had found herself commiserating with a hairdresser who'd been forced to close down the salon he'd opened with a five-hundred-pound loan from his dad almost twenty years ago; a PR executive who'd lost so many clients he'd had to wind up the company that he too had built from scratch; and even a lawyer whose firm had laid off more than half its staff. (She wasn't sure why, but she'd never imagined lawyers being subjected to the devastatingly brutal blow of redundancy.) Finding new positions wasn't proving anywhere near as easy for any of them as this new coalition government had promised when it had started making all the cuts, and as the unemployment lines lengthened it was becoming clear that hope was turning into as rare a commodity as cash.

'So do they have any jobs going at this charity?' Lauren wondered as she sipped her coffee.

'None that pay,' Emma replied, turning the computer back to carry on reading the website, 'but once I've found a job I think I'd like to be involved in some capacity anyway.'

Taking out her mobile as it bleeped with a text, Lauren appeared faintly flustered as she checked to see who it was from.

Amused, Emma said nothing, while guessing it was a new boyfriend, or at least someone she had her eye on.

Seeming to sink with disappointment, Lauren gave a groan of frustration. 'It's Parker Jenkins again. Mum, what am I going to do? How do I get him to accept that it's over between us? It's been nearly three months now and he's still asking if we can get together to talk things through, but there's nothing to talk about. I just don't want to go out with him any more.'

Remembering a time, barely eight months ago, when all Lauren had been able to think about was how to get Parker Jenkins to notice her, Emma said, 'Why don't you tell him you've met someone else? That should get the message across.'

Two vivid spots of colour flew to Lauren's cheeks. 'Because I haven't,' she protested. 'What makes you say that?'

Emma shrugged. 'Just a hunch.' Yes, she definitely had someone in her sights. 'Why not just ask him to stop texting because you've moved on and it's time he did too?'

Lauren looked amazed. 'That sounds a bit mean.'

'Lauren, that halo of yours can be a real pain at times. Tell him to get over it and start looking for somebody else, because that's what you're doing.'

'I so am not. And I'm starting to feel really sorry for the poor blokes you're lining up on that dating website. I bet you haven't said in your profile that you've got a sadistic streak with a penchant for shrivelling egos.'

With a choke of laughter, Emma said, 'I don't even belong to one of those websites . . .'

'Oh come on, don't think I didn't see the way you shut something down when I walked in, because I did.'

With a sigh to try and cover the fluttering of her nerves, Emma said, 'You have a very fanciful imagination, young lady.'

'I don't think so. Anyway, it would be great if you met someone. I wouldn't have to worry about leaving you here on your own all week . . .'

'I'm a grown-up, I can take care of myself and if you're going to worry about me while you're in London, then I'll have to worry about you and frankly I think I'm going to be too busy for that.'

Getting to her feet, Lauren said, 'Just my luck to have a mother who doesn't worry about me.'

'I know, life is so hard for you.'

'You're right, it is. I'm going upstairs to write in my journal.'

Emma's eyes came up. 'Secrets?' she teased.

'Wouldn't you like to know?' Lauren teased back.

'I'm glad you're keeping it up.' She'd given Lauren the journal on her eighteenth in the hope of encouraging her to record some of her memories in her own hand, or, like so much that was done digitally, they would almost certainly end up being lost.

'Actually, I quite love it,' Lauren told her, taking a yoghurt from the fridge. 'Are we still going to the cinema tonight?'

'Is that what we'd planned? Aren't you going clubbing with Melissa and her friends? You usually do on Saturdays.'

Lauren shrugged. 'I don't really feel like it tonight. I know, why don't we get a DVD and curl up with a takeaway in front of the fire?'

Thinking longingly of the log fire they used to build at the cottage, Emma said, 'Sounds good to me, but if we're going out we'll have to take your car because mine is short on petrol and my credit card is currently maxed out.'

'No problem, but remember mine keeps cutting out. Did you book it into the garage, by the way?'

'Yes, it's in for Tuesday, so it should be sorted by next weekend. What time train are you getting tomorrow?'

'Um, I'll probably go about four, I think.'

Emma was about to say she might join Lauren in London for a few days and stay at Berry's when she remembered the cost of the rail fare and quickly reined herself in. There was the expense of getting around to consider too, plus the price of the lunch she'd be sure to have with whichever friends might be free, and the shopping she probably wouldn't be able to resist, plus little extras for Lauren that always seemed to pop up. There was no way she could allow herself to stretch to all that when she hadn't even managed to get an interview yet, never mind a job.

Determined not to feel depressed about her current state of unemployment, or lonely without her friends around her, she returned to her computer, tensing as a plane thundered overhead on its way into Bristol airport. This was a jarring fact of her new life that was taking a while to get used to, the roar of jet engines that seemed to shake the house to its foundations. By way of trying to deal with it she and Lauren had taken to deciding that it must be the ten thirty easyJet from Malaga, or the twelve o'clock KLM from Amsterdam. Occasionally, as a further distraction, Emma would go on to create little stories in her head about the passengers and crew and why they were on board that particular flight.

As the noise of what might have started out as the eleven fifteen from Cyprus faded into the distance it was replaced by the haunting melody of Lauren practising her flute upstairs – a single, hypnotic thread of beauty emerging from the heart of a hellish din. She was preparing for a performance she was giving as part of her A-level course at the end of the month, and though Emma knew she was biased she simply couldn't imagine how Lauren was going to end up with anything less than an A star. She was on target to do just as well in English and humanities so there was every chance she'd find herself reading music at the university of her choice, London's Guildhall School of Music and Drama.

This coming week was going to be the first since moving here that Emma would be in the house alone, as Lauren had already broken up for the Christmas holidays by the time they'd rented a van to transport their belongings from London. Prior to the move they'd been staying at Berry's Chelsea apartment which was a bit of a squash when Berry was there, but fun all the same, simply because Berry usually managed to make everything fun. In fact, Emma had only moved into this house now, months before Lauren was due to sit her A2s, because it simply hadn't been fair to carry on putting upon her grandmother the way she had since the house in Chiswick had been sold. Generous and welcoming as Berry always was, having her open-plan kitchen-cum-sitting room turned into a bedroom for Lauren every night must have been a royal pain in the proverbial.

It was lucky, Emma was musing to herself, as she resisted clicking back through to her email, that she wasn't a complete stranger to these parts, or she and Lauren would have to be putting themselves out there to try and make new friends as well as a new life. At least she would, because Lauren's world wasn't going to change all that much, with her being in London each week, and still at the same school. In fact, it probably wouldn't be long before she started wanting to stay on for weekends, so she, Emma, had better start bracing herself for that.

Just in case any important emails had turned up in the last ten minutes inviting her for a job interview, or requesting more information than she'd provided with her CV, Emma decided she really ought to check her inbox. There was a new message waiting, though not from a potential employer, or from Philip Leesom whose name alone was causing her some disarray – it was from Polly Hunter who lived at the far end of the local village. She'd known Polly for over seventeen years now and was, in a way, possibly even closer to her than she had been to many of her friends in London. Maybe it was not living in each other's pockets that had allowed their friendship to grow the way it had, or perhaps it was simply the natural affinity that had drawn them to each other in the first place. That had happened during a quiz night at the local pub when she and Will had found themselves teamed up with Polly and her adorable, unbelievably handsome husband Jack. Whatever the reasons, it was mainly because of Polly – and her daughter Melissa who Lauren had, in a long-distance fashion, more or less grown up with – that Emma had chosen to move to this part of the world when it had become clear that she could no longer afford to stay in London.

Disaster! Despair! Polly had written. *At father-in-law's in Devon right now. Back Tuesday. Please say we can get together. Does 6 work for you?*

Not sure whether she should be concerned or amused, given Polly's penchant for drama, Emma sent a message back assuring her she'd have a bottle ready and waiting. She and Polly had been through a lot together over the years, traumas and crises that had seen one or other of them dashing up or down the motorway desperate to be there for whichever one was in need. Fortunately there hadn't been anything too disastrous since Emma's divorce, and she could only hope that there would never again be anything like the horrific shock of Jack's sudden death. The illness and suicide that had taken him was a few years behind them now, but nothing could ever be as bad as that, Emma was thinking, simply nothing, unless of course anything happened to one of the girls, but that went without saying and wasn't something any sane parent would ever allow themselves to dwell on.

Since there was still not a single response to her numerous job applications, she decided that perhaps she could allow herself to read Philip's email again, if only to lift her spirits, and then she really must delete it.

Just want to wish you good luck in the new house and if you're ever in London, please be in touch.

That was all, quite simple and straightforward, nothing to get excited about, a polite, brief message that could have been sent by anyone, because he hadn't even signed off. It was only his name in the address box that told her it was from him. What it also told her, if she allowed it to, and she probably ought not, was that he was thinking of her and would like to see her again.

Actually, it probably didn't mean that at all. Why would it, when they didn't even know each other that well, and had certainly never been out on a date, or anything even remotely like it. (Unless the

Saturday afternoon just before the end of last term counted, when they'd run into each other at the library, got chatting and ended up going for a coffee.) Other than that they'd only ever met at the school where Lauren was in Philip's English class and most of the girls, including Lauren, had a mega crush on him. It was hardly surprising when he was a Tom Ford/David Beckham lookalike, and so charming in an intense and interested way that it was impossible not to be drawn to him.

He was also single, which was probably what made him so irresistible as far as the girls were concerned, and Emma had to admit it worked for her too, even though he was a good ten years younger than her. Nevertheless, she wasn't going to allow herself to respond to his email. OK, it might appear rude and unfriendly, but hopefully he'd put it down to how snowed under she was by the move and starting a new life.

Almost laughing to herself as she realised she was behaving more like a teenager than Lauren, she simply hit the delete key and was about to abandon the computer to go and finish off at least some of the unpacking when another message came through from Polly.

Make that two bottles with vodka chasers!